T0366156

Passions
of the Progenitor

James Hendershot

Order this book online at www.trafford.com
or email orders@trafford.com

Most Trafford titles are also available at major online book retailers.

Printed in the United States of America.

ISBN: 978-1-4907-2808-7 (sc)
ISBN: 978-1-4907-2807-0 (e)

Trafford rev. 02/13/2014

www.trafford.com

North America & international
toll-free: 1 888 232 4444 (USA & Canada)
fax: 812 355 4082

Dedicated to my wife Younghee, with thanks, and to my sons, Josh and John and daughters, Nellie and Mia and check-in coordinator Stacy Canon (not pictured), publishing services associate Evan Villadores (not pictured), and book consultant Tanya Mendoza (not pictured).

Contents

vagabond, yet sister of a Supreme High Queen
icy, yet sister to the fire
thirsty, yet sister to the water
wretched, yet sister of an angel
tormented, yet sister of the bears
wearied, yet sister of a sky dancer
burning, yet sister of the air
loved by the winds
drowning, yet loved by the woman from the sea
lost in time, yet loved by a sister from the other cycles

loved by her Master
who gave his seed
she caste him away
imprisoned by an ancient curse
innocent, yet guilty through her blood
daughters of the heavens shared the blood of her seed
honored as Pápain by all the ages
the mother of a Virtuous Empire

nevertheless
scorned and secluded
suffering a death bounty for her crown
from her hermit womb
brought forth the Greatest Queens
from opposite shores of Lamenta they arose.

In separate epochs
they conjugated the Great King
begotten
likewise
of the same progenitor
hence many ages afore
so a Virtuous Empire could drive evil
into the corners of the stars.

Chapter 01

From Baktalórántházai to Bácsalmási

I have loved my wives, and they always loved me. Our love is wonderful and everlasting. Part of this love was with me when I began my life, a life given back to me by Gyöngyösi and will be sevenfold when I die. Nevertheless, that day came when I could say that my road provided me the joy of my wives and our wonderful sons and daughters. We enjoyed filling them with love. Each wife represented a special part of our family. This love is an independent blanket that continues to cover us. In addition, this love continued to grow. Our family realized that this is all of us loving one another. Our family crossed the color of skin lines with our Angel's glowing dark skin. We crossed not only one, but also four types of species' lines. We had one that turns into an Angel, one danced in the sky, another turned into a giant bear, and my special five-inch friend. Our two best friends, a fire woman and a fire horse, would have been married into our family. Except their species, based on a different element, obviously fire and therefore, they were not intra species of the same element. The concept that is running in my mind is that two people can create a love powerful enough to pull in more love. This is true, especially if they rule from their hearts and not their eyes. Love reigned from our hearts, and true love could not see, but can only feel. The important thing is that when we dove into the sea of love, we gave our lives to love and love gave us back our lives. Mighty love kept my wives, and I as its prisoner. We each day we never left from the beginning of our love. Love not at any time freed us. My family remained great neighbors with the Edelényi who aided us during our times of trouble, which increased as our numbers increased. We presented our class to those who were to marry on the power of love as enthusiastic in our last class as we were in our first class. Our special daily three-hour one wife time worked great for us. We changed into using this bonding and fun time.

The wives were creative over the years, especially after their second rounds of delivering their babies, practicing our mating skills faded away. We shared our hearts and worked on feeding our love. The wives also dedicated one hour each day in which we discussed the activities of our children. It was important that we treat each child the same, for even though they had different mothers they all had the same father. In time, the Edelényi influenced our family into new concepts and family practices. The Edelényi did not have the Master rules the family with a stern force. I had never ruled my family, considering that I enjoyed their differences more than a similar behavior system. I constantly enjoyed debating with them, and we celebrated our compromises as if both won, when, in reality, they won usually. Their little hearts would not allow them to gloat so they always reported our debates as settled in compromise. I needed them, and only for the love that remains in their hearts. They needed me. I reasoned that since they have not kicked me off this mountain yet, I was still in business. Addressing our Master / Servant relationship, I had clearly told my wives that we would never have this type of relationship. I could not force a person who wanted to bear my children to give everything they were. No, I wanted more and got more, because I got their true free selves. They skip around our mountaintop and throughout our home with jolly smiles and nonstop singing, humming, or whistling. My wives are extremely happy because they feel as if a part of their lives. They never acted before others as they did within our family. This was because on the other end of our cave, which leads out of this mountain, the people would take them from me and punish them severely. The Edelényi had always practiced the same custom as I do with my wives. I learned this from my Grandpa and father. Still, Grandpa discovered this style during his many visits and saw how it was so much better for the wives. They could concentrate on constructing themselves and not helplessly destroying themselves.

I was a few times throughout the years tempted to take my family back to my hometown village. However, to our fortune reality woke me and opened my eyes to what I had in front of us. I would be taking my family into a dangerous place to survive, flooded with thieves, murderers, and they are telling me now the large Hersonian ships packed with people pirates. They took very little booty when they invaded, mainly concentrating on people. They just about had a free reign throughout our peninsula, except for the Hatvani Mountains in the Dorogi Kingdom demolishes their greedy raiding parties through clever ambushes. The Edelényi received reports that these Hersonian raiders foolishly landed their ships on Sensenites shores. The Sensenites were a dangerous foe in that they used their expert fighting skills to make sure that any enemy they encountered was 100% defeated. They never took captives, but instead burned them as sacrifices to their gods. Afterwards, they would completely sink the invading ships along their shoreline, free the captives and then give the ship unloadable. They left the ships on their shores as a warning for other foolish invaders. The Edelényi was impressed how they have not only released the captives but also gave them guides through the mountains, so they could enter our side of the Hatvani Mountains. The Sensenites merely wanted left alone. This is how King Pécsváradi of the Dorogi, and my daughter handled the Sensenites. They never crossed the line. My wives invariably practiced a changed version of the Master protocol. They never called, me by my first name, therefore unfailingly called me Master. The wives drew the line on this. Even in disregard to my pleas, they would not surrender this right. They had to have a Master, and I was the one they ordered to be their Master. My wives continued this practice even in the presense of Edelényi and always recommended to the future brides they taught to practice this. They believed it showed others the respect they had for the father of their children. It also reminded them of the security their relationship provided for them from this evil world. My wives also told these brides that this showed the world the pride and honor they had in their mate, and that everything must always glorify their mates.

They have been the source of so much happiness in my life. The wives created the rules for our childcare. Gyöngyösi always searched for a vision for how to name each child. No other wife ever challenged her decision. The lives of these children always verified their names, so something among the Great Spirits helped keep her on target. Nógrád was our primary contact with the Edelényi. She spent as much time with us as possible, even resigning her position in the Edelényi society. Queen Csongrád met with the elders and told them on the mountaintop she could no longer live. She could no longer live, unless she had her, 'lady of the bed-chamber', she would have to return to her palace. The Queen requested that she commission this position and title to Nógrád, citing that it grieved our family too much when she was not with us. The elders agreed, knowing that a Queen was entitled to many ladies and women of the bed-chamber. Nógrád was very happy with this, and when the Edelényi brought all her belongings, reconstructed Brann and Baranya's room to include an extra door. This door leads to the next floor above, and remolded a pleasurable living area for Nógrád that pleased us. She had two nice bedrooms, one for her and another for guests, as she often boarded her parents and other friends for her visits. She had a luxurious cooking and dining area, a large family room and a playroom packed with children's toys. Nógrád explained they included this for when the children in our family would stop and visit. She also had extra rooms for her private use and ability to tailor itself based on her future needs. We were impressed with this setup. The Edelényi also included all her furnishings. We asked them to leave her clothing and small personal items in our room and when the construction was finished, we would place it in her apartment. Nógrád was pleased that Khigir possibly would let her carry them up. However, Khigir would not bend on this subject saying, "If you are to live with us, you will live as a family member and as a family member, your family will help you every way it can. We would have had the silly boy remodel your apartment; nonetheless, we were afraid he would destroy the mountaintop."

Khigir then hugged her and commented, "I never heard you talk about your Master like that previously." Khigir explained that all those comments were in joke only and a sign of her love for the freedom I gave my wives. She added, "We never joke like this unless alone with our family. Do you understand what I am telling you?" Nógrád questioned why this family is being so kind to her and actually wanting her to live with them. Gyöngyösi entered the conversation by telling Nógrád, "You have been so kind to us, and have always worked extra hard to care for us. We have grown to value your advice and enjoy your kindness. Everyone in the family wants you to live with us, as this cannot be a home without you." Nógrád downplayed the extra credit by responding, "I was only doing my job, although I will confess that I always went home sad because I missed you people." Khigir revealed, "It was the way you did your job from your heart that made us feel special. Even so, we missed you tremendously when you left us, as the silly boy would sit and cry, 'where is my Nógrád?'" Nógrád looked at me, and I simply winked back at her, causing her face to blush and my two jesting wives to laugh. Any attempt of wiggling out of this would burden me with more incriminating accusations, so my only hope is to put the stone back in their yard. I simply tried to get past this before Brann and Baranya jump into this game. I decided to slip Hevesi in my pocket and do this exploring in the safer wild wilderness.

That day turned out to be special in that this Edelényi was exploring our unique peak to the top of Lamenta. I told Hevesi to tie herself in with the extra strings the Edelényi had sown into my shirt pockets and up to, we went. Fortunately, we went up on the side facing our living areas. I could not imagine going up this on the cliff side. I never did adjust to such a monstrous cliff and divide on the adjoining ridge. That opening magnified our enormous elevation and the sight of the lowlands before us always traumatize me. It was like us living in the clouds in that one wrong step will take us back to where we are supposed to live, and this return trip would be fast. I considered how this trip looks horrifying from our homes. The trees hid the large secure paths, and tunnels flow under the bare rock parts of its cliff, because of that made this journey very much safe. The open top of its curved peak established protective walls around all its limitations. The Edelényi had guards posted up here that can see for at least eighty miles away. Moreover, these are mountains miles, which give us a one to two-day warning, which is plenty of time to set up their traps and ambushes. They spied closely on them before being able to show them as friend or foe. If any doubt, they would pose as Messengers from the Dorogi. If they saw this messenger receiving maltreatment, they raided. I can still remember the first visit from King Pécsváradi to be with our children. The Edelényi claimed to be from the Dorogi. The guards escorted the Messengers into the King's tent and introduced them to 'the King of the Dorogi.' The King was not angry as he simply explained he was here to visit his daughter and the children of Siklósi. The Messengers asked for a white flag and ran out of the King's tent waving it for the defenders to come in peace. Any ways, back to this view of the Heavens, I had not noticed before how the clouds hid us from behind and on both sides. The split ahead of us on our lower sister mountain range drains the clouds. This is why we can see down through this pass to the junior lands. The clouds covered the subordinate valleys in front of us. The many miles that the mountain slopes, puts us well behind the giant rock walls that seal this land inside. In addition, with the clouds hovering over the lesser mountains, it is almost impossible to see our peak. It took the Dorogi one century to carve out a path to this place. When they first saw this peak, they labeled it as the home of the gods. Thereafter, all Kings of the Dorogi protected it from evil invaders. King Pécsváradi saw it first when he was a child and declared that part of his soul lived there. He could never have known that his daughter would live her remaining years at the heavenly peak. His blessings for honoring the tradition of his fathers to preserve this peak provided his reward when his grandchildren were born here. I can only fear the hand that tore our sister mountain apart. Legends tell that the original species lived in this area split that mountain into two with great fire and winds. They wanted to see the lower mountains below them. Legend or not, for this is the greatest view that my eyes have ever seen. The power of this beauty tied my feet to this ground. I once lived beyond those giant rock walls. I had a good life and so much missed my parents and brothers. I was wise enough to know my wives and family were tremendously safer here. With the Edelényi technology, our lives on this peak in the Heavens not matched anywhere else on the surface of Lamenta. The one big event of that day started when Hevesi begged me to let her stand on the rocks that formed the fence that prevented us from falling. I told her to be careful. She smiled and told me not to worry about her. She slowly worked her way past me staying in the middle of the ledge. She walked carefully and precautions across what appeared to be a road for her. I was enormously proud of her attention to her wellbeing. In a surprise flash, she yelled out "Master, watch me!" Over the ledge, she jumped. I froze in absolute shock. My mind needed to know why she would kill herself is such a sputtering method. We all glorified her in so many ways, especially my Queen, who always had a way out of any situation. Hevesi had her feet painted the night that Csongrád kissed them. She never wanted anything else ever to touch her feet. She cherished this title more than any other titles because it glorified the aggressive warlike part of her personality whom, she accordingly cherished. Hevesi had shown me on this day that she was a daring warrior even to the death of her and my son who nourished inside her womb. I went to the ledge and cried. I lowered my head into my arms on top of the ledge crying, "Hevesi, why?" A few minutes later, I met yet again with another shocking surprise. I felt two soft hands on my shoulder, and this warm yielding voice asks, "Master, why do you cry?" I at once turned around so fast that I almost caught her head, which would have thrown her across the ledge. Before me stood my Hevesi, who looked exceptionally sweet and innocent. I could not be angry because the celebration flooded me from head to toe. She placed her palms on my face and rested her pointed ear against my chest. I told her, "I cry because one whom, I loved so much jumped off this ledge to what I thought to be their death."

Hevesi, still talking in her soft voice, which all my wives did when a danger of me becoming angry was possible, "Master, if the one who jumped was the same species as me, they would have become wind and blown back to where they came." I rested my palm on her head and then told her, "Will the one who jumped promise never to share me in such a way again?" Hevesi answered, in her challenging fashion, "Oh no Master, for that would cheat the one who jumped out of the joy of seeing you so happy when they returned." I knew that even if I slammed her to the ground and threatened to twist off her arms she would never say yes to my request. She was right, since she did get some special attention afterwards. I kept a strong hold on her hand to make sure she did not get away from me again. Hevesi was always so special to me, especially as she could shrink into my pocket and go everywhere with me. She surprised me many times with her wilderness skills when I would go on hikes with my wives, children, or family, or alone with her. She was always there. We totally lost time up here today, as I spent most of it in Hevesi's arms. I believed that she was missing something to play such a mortal joke on me, so I flattered the living daylights out of her. We soon heard a familiar voice calling for us. Hevesi shrank and jumped into my pocket. I at once woke up our hosts, and down this peak; we went. They ran with me as we rushed before Khigir, and I answered, "We are here dear. That is so heavenly up there, almost as if we were in heaven." Khigir continues her quizzing by asking, "Was our

Master playing with his beautiful hosts?" Hevesi answers, "Oh no Master, I kept my eyes on him all day." Khigir afterwards tells Hevesi, "Oh, how I thank the Great Spirits that I have you to keep an eye on him." Hevesi reports to Khigir, "My greatest love, we do have to keep our husband out of trouble, so he will not be a dirty boy. Sometimes it is hard for me, but today he did exactly what I wanted him to do."

Khigir tells her, "Maybe you are getting stronger in your duties. I am proud of you, and as for our Master, it is time for your cleaning. Your wives are waiting for you." I never did get used to my wives scrubbing me. They scrubbed as if the dirt on my skin were another species trying to take me with them. Hevesi laughs at me and says, "Time for you to pay the piper Master." I complained to Khigir that Hevesi was at the same places as I was. Khigir responded with her same answer, "Master; Hevesi is a woman and knows how to clean herself, unlike you who is and always will be a dirty boy." She unfailingly leaned her face toward my ear, uttering the 'dirty boy' in her soft sensuous voice, and followed it with a kiss. She won every time, as she knew I would not do anything that would make her change that mood. Nevertheless, all my wives changed from their sensuous patronizing tones when this finished cleaning, me. I never openly rebelled when they did this, because I always saw how happy, they were when that had again perfectly cleaned their Master. I valued their happiness and sense of accomplishment more than anything else did. Later, in my golden years, I realized how right they had been with all this cleaning. My wives had always cleaned their Master is if I were a King. We belonged together, and as far as they were concerned, my babies belonged to their wombs. They treated the Edelényi teaching about caring for babies while still in the womb as if these teachings were a great law. Because we already knew the sex of each child on its way, they could trade with the Edelényi prepare their baby's room. The Edelényi and some colleagues of Gyöngyösi could determine how many children each wife would bring before me. We would not know the gender of the child until after conception. The final number equaled the number of children's rooms we had. The wives afterwards voted to keep all their children's rooms in the same section. They believed this would make it easier for the mother to check her children at night, and would help her if more than one child was ill at the same time. Moreover, for accountability, as no child can ever go unnoticed by their mother at bedtime. My wives sewed cloth seats in my shirt pocket so Hevesi could sit down as much as she needed while in my pocket.

I always received a thrill when I would look in my pocket and see an expectant Hevesi. I often teased her. She could only get with child if she expanded to my size. She would fire back at her darling; I am afraid of nothing more by saying, "I hope the next time I expand you know what you are doing!" Considering that in her current pregnant condition, I could be more daring, I would respond, "I must have done something right by the size of your belly." This was one of the few times she would let me win by saying, "Master, that you did and thanks." Her life as a mother was much harder than the other mothers were, in that her children did not get her shifting powers. To combat this, she would always go with me on my daily security hikes bringing her large spear with us. Once out of sight, she would shrink, and I would put her in my pocket. She had to have enough shrunk time each day. When we would retire at night, we would add to this sleep time by having her sleep in the pocket sewn to the back of Khigir's night garments. Once our children were older, we revealed to them how four of their mothers had special gifts. The children saw how excited we were about having these gifts in our family. They accepted it as normal. In the later years, Hevesi's daughters would carry her in their pockets for special family fun as she taught them how to survive in the wild mountains. Her daughters would return to our home and teach my other children during their playtimes. This worked well for us, in that all my children had a good grasp of survival in the wild. Stephana, Csongrád's oldest daughter taught all her Dorogi Armies these skills, which turned out to save many of her soldiers and defeat more aggressors. Hevesi could detect movement hills beyond us and could hear for miles around us. Her pointed ears helped; but, she had the feeling of Lamenta that told her. A movement constantly caused something else to move, and that something was identifiable. The movement of birds always alerted her. She advanced my wilderness skills beyond my wildest imaginations, even though I thought Grandpa had taught me so greatly. Evidently, he also learned much from her. We asked the Edelényi to rearrange our dining room adding tables that would fit all thirty-seven of my future children. The wives determined that seating would be by the age and not mother. They believed that because the same age groups would be learning the same subjects from the Edelényi schools. They would have more to talk about, as they would do their homework during this family time.

My wives promised to reward me if I occasionally joined our children and check their homework progress. Because I was a slave for their love, and secretly had a concern for my children's progress, I accepted my wife's brides. This also maintained a belief in my wives that I was still weak with their charms, which made them happy. To keep this effective, I had to pretend that it was a burden, which fooled everyone except Khigir and Hevesi. Those two could unfailingly read my mind as if it were naked. Even though Hevesi, at times, could come through as tough toward me, she always stood fast to the wishes of Khigir. Khigir could tell if Hevesi had been coaching me, as certain things I did become a matter of habit. This gave my precious Khigir a great respect and love for Hevesi, as I never tried to put Hevesi between us on any issues. Hevesi and I would constantly agree with Khigir, and then when out of sight, Hevesi would declare 'dirty boy time'. This meant that what I did during that time was our secret, bound by blood. I constantly complained to Hevesi that 'dirty boy time' was too short, and she would always tell me she needed extra time to clean my mind before we faced Khigir. She was put right on this, therefore to argue would have been senseless. Each evening, after we all cleaned, and I mean 'we' all cleaned, we would go to our dining room and eat our evening meal. Nógrád, Brann, and Baranya joined us, as we discussed how our days went to any problems that needed that required her attention. Nógrád found some Edelényi songbooks, and we would practice singing the songs together. My wives were very good singers, and when I missed a note, I would feel a hand on each side hitting my leg. They were such Masters of disguise, as they would be singing with a smile and in perfect key when the other arm under the table would hit me so hard that their little bodies would bounce. Rather than embarrass them, or more like make heroes of them, I sang along as if all were normal.

We would often talk about the future problems that would face us, such as finding mates for our children. Nógrád always carried a special board shaped pouch with her that she kept her things, inside so they would unfailingly be available for her. One dinner, about one Degi Moon before our babies began to arrive, as we were discussing this issue, she handed a paper to Khigir and asked her to read it aloud. The paper declared a special new law that permitted our children to marry and mate, in that order, with the sons and daughters of the Edelényi. We actually got to our table and danced to a song that Nógrád had taught us in celebration. Our servants come rushing in, fearing they did something wrong. Nógrád explained the new law to the servants who also rejoiced. We always loved the way that the Edelényi could feel the same joys we felt. I was equally impressed because the Edelényi was a homogeneous species and that the injection of our children would change that forever. Nógrád told me to erase such thinking from my mind in that the people had wanted to mate with other species on Lamenta for ages. They believed that it would help their future generations. We all knew that Stephana would never betray the people of her brothers and sisters and having her as the Queen of the Dorogi Kingdom gave a whopping advantage to the Edelényi future. Nógrád added that because these children were born in the Edelényi delivery rooms and would grow up beside the Edelényi children, and in essence, be one of them that it would be unjust to cast them among the Lamentans and their possible evils to mate. They grew up here and as such deserved the same rights as the other children. My wives asked the servants and Nógrád to express our deepest thanks for giving such a gift to the loves of our lives. Which they also shared, their love, hopes, and dreams with our Edelényi family, for now we felt so much more like being their family. News of this revision to the law spread fast, as we begin receiving petitions from parents whom we would consider their children as possible mates. The wives met with these parents and explained that our Great Spirits forbidden us to choose spouses for our children. Khigir explained to them that even though her Master had kidnapped her from another land with the help of his father and Grandpa. Her Master could not have her until we decided we loved one another.

She then joked with them that she was actually the one that decided and threatened great harm to me if I did not marry her. The Edelényi at first thought it was a barbaric thing to steal wives from other lands. Nevertheless, because Grandpa was involved, there must have been a moral reason for this custom. Grandpa could never do wrong in their eyes. The elders, rather than create hostilities between the people, reemphasized the need to keep the mating by mutual consent and love. This must be without influence from parents not only for the Edelényi but also for those, they invited to live among them. We stayed in the front rooms for a few weeks, until the servants informed us that life was back to normal. The wives requested that we take a family walk and see all the wonders that Hevesi, and I discovered. Hevesi then fell to the ground and began to beg for mercy claiming that every time she went on a hike with the Master, he demanded they have dirty boy private time. Khigir told her to stop faking, and told her that the Master would not trade dirty boy time for playing during the dirt time, except on occasion. Hevesi jumped and laughing said, "Just playing." I looked at her and said, "Oh no. You are not going to make me play dirty boy again with you."

I remember what happened next as if it were my yesterday. Khigir punched me in the stomach, followed by a kiss, and said, "Lead us into danger our strong and mighty Master." I thought that this could be a good time to face danger. Instead, if any foe were to see six pregnant women and me with a big bulge in my shirt pocket, they would run as fast as they could to escape. We walked down one of my favorite paths down the hill that ran our house descended through miles of wooded land with meadows and wonderful ponds. Hevesi and I took them to our beloved meadow and pond. This day we beheld an unusual sight around the pond, as there were ten large white horses and one very small white horse drinking the water. We tried to stay noiseless, so as not to spook them. Brann who can walk about on inch off the ground, which she does most times unless around strangers, because the ground hurts her style of Lamentan feet, approaches the horses. As she walks toward them, one of the big ones spotted her, and they all come walking to her. When they spotted us, nine of them came to us. Two of the nine came to me. One was large, and the tiny one came to jump on my boot while yanking my pants with his mouth. I figured this out; there was a horse for each of us. I took Hevesi out of my pocket and sat her on

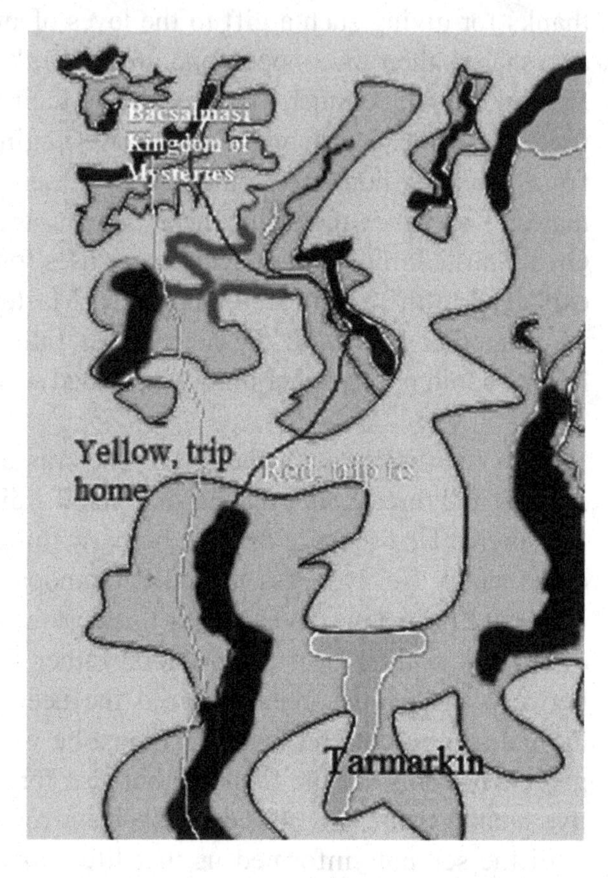

the tiny horse who then calmed down. I walked to my horse and jumped on his back. They had a bridle on their necks because of their wings. We had to lay on their backs and place our feet into the feet holsters strapped to their back. Finally, we had to tie the bridal around each arm, so that we were secure on them. Truthfully, I was watching Hevesi, who seem to have a feel for this. When she was strapped on, I asked her to check my wives, Nógrád, Baranya, and Brann. She flew where they could all see her and told them what they had to do, and afterwards inspected them and then told them you did not have to use your bridals to guide these horses; all you have to do is speaking the command. Therefore, I said to my horse, "Please fly me over to my wives." Up in the air he immediately went before my wives. I then told my wives, "I believe these horses want to take us somewhere? Consequently, off we will go. I ask for Gyöngyösi and Khigir to ride at my sides and the remaining to ride in rows of three or four, just so the last row has four. Hevesi is riding above us. She dashes around in her security precaution defensive posture. I cannot really see these horses taking us into danger. We all feel so much better with that little person watching out for us. Therefore, we will ride wide and visible, while also being able to defend each. The horses reformed facing the meadow and spread their wings to their extended position. They next began their takeoffs, which was an uplifting experience.

Their feet beat on the ground as dirt and dust flew everywhere. It sounded as thunder with the dirt crushing beneath their power. Then those mighty wings expanded and starting, flapping rapidly and up over the trees we went. I looked, saw both Gyöngyösi and Khigir at my sides, and smiled at them as they smiled back. I knew they were watching the other wives and our three friends. I saw to my right above Khigir a heavyset dove with something on top of it. This is the last place that I want to have trouble. The dove flew behind my head, and I could see it no more. The winds stopped their howling noises as I heard an old voice say, "Dirty boy, why do you have your lovely wives up here?" That voice is so familiar, and thenceforth I realize it is Szentesi. We did not see her for a long time. She faded out with Hevesi, Ajkai, and Makói became wives. I answer her, "Szentesi; we have not seen you in a long time, therefore we came looking for you." Szentesi responds, "Siklósi," as a consequence asks me, "Why are you then riding the Horses of Чекудаев (Chekudayev)?" Gyöngyösi followed by inquiring, "My fair and dear Szentesi, we know not of what you speak of, although our Master did sorrow for your return, for fear we might have done you wrong. If we did, should not we talk about it, rather than being enemies?" Szentesi tells us, "I am not your enemy. I just need some time with my birds, and when I return, I want to see Hevesi with an apron on doing some work in the house." Hevesi responds, "If that is what it takes to bring you back into our lives, that I shall do that for you my lifelong and dear friend." Szentesi replies, "Oh my, you have changed so much Hevesi, anyway if you think I will let you clean the house I live in you are foolishly mistaken. I have seen how you clean. I believe the only reason dirty boy married you is for your love of dirt." Hevesi and I both answered, "That is a truth you speak Szentesi." Khigir enters the conversation by adding; "Now you see why we so dearly need you back in our lives Szentesi."

Szentesi then qualifies, "I will return because you all are begging so earnestly; however, I will not marry the dirty boy, therefore, get that idea out of your heads now." I reply, "Szentesi, because we are all truly begging and want you back so much, I will in great pain and sadness forfeit you as a potential wife." Szentesi than calmly revealed, "Be a strong Master for your wives and I will help you get over me." To keep my wives from punishing me I respond, "Szentesi, I so much hope you can help me not suffer so dearly." Khigir asks Szentesi, "Szentesi, will you please tell us about these Horses of Чекудаев (Chekudayev)?" She answers, "You are in no danger for they live in the Bácsalmási Kingdom of Mysteries, where so many great wonders exist. Do we still live in our cabins?" Khigir tells her, "Oh no, my dear we now live in the houses." Szentesi asks, "So the Edelényi have no accepted you?" Gyöngyösi spoke, "You understand the Edelényi?" Szentesi answers, "I was the one who introduced Grandpa to them. I think that I will go back and settle in one of the front rooms before they add me a room at the end of the children's hall." Khigir probes, "How do you understand the children's hall?" Szentesi counters, "They all know you have played with dirty boy, so that means babies will be on their way. Therefore, if they want you to stay in the houses, they would have also to provide for your babies. Mothers stay with their babies, yet for my fear that silly boy has corrupted you. I will sleep in their hall and make sure they are watched over." I tell her, "Szentesi, I can think of no one more qualified than you, thus it will be a great blessing for you. Tell them to start working on it immediately. My seal is in a blue box under our heart bed. You should be able to push it out easily. Now you need to go, before I get tempted to propose to you." She disappeared instantly on her dove. We continued to travel above the clouds. We flew hours over our mountains. Gyöngyösi looked at the suns, recognized some of the land features, and told us; we were going farther north. She told us that the saddle on our continent had grasslands, a sea that divided the saddle from the four islands above it. One of the islands was as huge as the remaining three. Soon we passed the green lands, crossed the sea, and traveled some time on the large island, passing mountains and over a river.

Afterwards, we passed over another sea, which was about the same length of the first sea. We soon were flying over another island, which also had rich green land, a river that flowed to our east to west, and subsequently into some strange-looking mountains. I was saying to myself, 'horses, keep on flying,' yet to my displeasure they had other planes. While the evening was approaching, our horses began to decrease their flapping as if they were descending. They maneuvered around, in a smooth fashion, until we were flying just above another large mountain range. I could see a small pond ahead of us. It had a rock wall around it, therefore appeared to be manmade. Our horses fly over to it and then head for the large hole in the mountain wall. I can see the green water also covering the surface of this pond. We fly into the surprisingly well-sunlit hole. I could feel some heat in here as well. Hevesi has now switched to fly between Khigir and myself, as the hole was not high enough for her to fly over us. The walls of this cave revealed colors that I had never seen from the rocks. There were streaks of blue, brown, yellow, gray, and shades of purple. I could see some special circles that resembled knots in a tree.

A couple of times I saw small mounds of salt. Usually, when I am around water such as this, insects bombard me. Conversely, this hole has no insects so far; even so, with light and water mixed they should be here. I look over and ask Hevesi if she thinks this to be strange. Hevesi tells me that she knows of waters with no insects. She directs my attention to the brown puddles in the water and reveals to me that is my oil, and insects avoid oil. I once more marvel at her wilderness skills. We continue out of the hole into, absolute beauty. The horses land us in a forest, coming in from our stream. We get off our horses now, and I reach down, grab Hevesi, and put her in my pocket. Hevesi, looking around, cheers and says, "Master, it is, get dirty time!" Khigir grabs me instantly and says, "I think not!" She was serious, and I was delirious and responded as a man who wants to sleep in peace does, "Yes dear. Now Hevesi honey, we have to be good, okay sweetheart." Hevesi then replies, "Anything for my Master and Khigir, my love." I think that we are pardoned for now. I never throw Hevesi under our floor, when we are in trouble. She is my wife, also carrying a child whom, I fathered. Therefore, as in this situation, I included myself with her, and she cleverly repented to Khigir and me by showering us with her love. Khigir gives me the serious stare, bends over to my pocket and whispers, "You know I will always love you, right my Angel?" Hevesi jumping grabs her shirt, climbs up her shirt, and gives Khigir a big kiss. Khigir thanks her and puts her back in my pocket. She reaches over and gives me a kiss. I thank her, as for a while there I was puzzled. I said nothing and was the guilty one. I enjoy my glorious life with my loving wives. Although I enjoy so much kissing them, we now have important opportunities, ahead of us. We are sitting in front of an extremely long, yet low waterfall. As far as our eyes can see the water is falling; nevertheless, it falls into a stream parallel with the falls. This stream is wide, although it has many branches from trees hanging over it, which creates an appearance of being a small stream.

I can see trees growing out of the falls. Moreover, these tall trees must have their roots locked deep into Lamenta. The leaves from the trees in the waterfalls and hanging over its stream have stunning bright grassy leaves. The water on the falls is shiny blue, while the water in the stream is green. The horses placed us where this stream makes its next dissension. The pureness of this water makes it look soft and approachable. I decide to wade in it. Hevesi tells me not to, "Master, you must test it first, throw a branch in there, then rocks, and see what happens." I pull a branch down from a tree beside me. I use Khigir's knife to remove the branch from this tree. Into the peaceful water before, I threw the branch. It landed on the water floating peacefully for a few minutes, and then it started spinning and down it went. It stayed down well outside our vision. Ensuing more verification, I tossed a rock into its peaceful looking water. It went down fast while we could hear it hitting other rocks. I looked at Hevesi and said, "We can wade some other day. I would like to see what is behind the yellow glowing trees before us." Hevesi looked at Khigir, who shook her head yes. We, therefore, went along the banks of the waterfalls. We were lucky, in that the horses placed us on this side, which makes it easier for us to move forward. The beauty of this place is the lights from one of our suns propagating through the trees flooding this land with yellow illumination. This luminosity consumed everything it touched. We walked up the hill where the water was stable. This stream was by four small rivulets joining. We could cross each of the brooks easily. We discovered that this forest was not that deep. We were now standing in the open above a rolling valley. The surface resembled large rolling rocks covered with grass. The bottom of this gorge had the only trees. The rest of the land had grass covering it. We could see golden grass before us followed by a large patch of dark green. The other side was very much different giving us an idyllic rich buttery view. The trees slowly filled its peak. I really hate to be out in the open not knowing where we can go, and with darkness approaching, I would prefer to keep my girls somewhat concealed. I ask my wives what they think we should do. Gyöngyösi recommend we sleep along the tree line here, so we will have to cover and be able to detect any movement to our front. She also recommends that we sleep in groups of two under separate trees. If danger approaches, we can quickly go up our trees. Khigir points her finger at me. Therefore, I walk over to the tree beside her where she is preparing the ground, removing rocks and branches. We sleep our ordinary way, as she is so protective of me. I continue to marvel at the sacrifices that daily she is willing to take for me. We put Hevesi in Khigir's pocket where she will be able easily to detect any movements. Khigir had to remove her shirt and put it on backwards, using me to button it on for her. This provided the pocket on her back for our little wilderness woman to do her thing. She is a very light sleeper, yet keeps her long pointed ears up to catch anything. In addition, this was the night that we all caught more than we expected. It turned out to be visions of events in these mountains. We were entering our sleep when Hevesi gave me the warning that something was walking toward us.

Khigir rose and I at once grabbed Hevesi. Khigir took one look into the naked valley before us and instantly went to awaken the other wives and our friends. We saw what appeared to be white wings with sparkling white sprinkles dancing everywhere. There was another bleached, lower light contained by golden beams. Brann, Baranya, Gyöngyösi, Makói, and Ajkai stand ready to transform and attack if needed. I never before knew that Gyöngyösi could fight; however, Hevesi tells me she can become fierce when protecting her family. My two Tamarkins, Khigir, and Tselikovsky stand ready with their bows, arrows in place. I now realize that I have a powerful army with me, as a ten-foot bear, a fire woman with a fire horse, followed by a sky dancer who can do many stunning illusions with her sky, creating a spellbinding blood bath. This Angel supplemented with swirling pinpoint attacks, and my Tamarkins, which can hit the trees on the other side of this valley with dead-on precision. The lights come nearer and closer. Hevesi's miraculous night vision tells me that it is a type of Angel woman and has no visible weapons. She now stands about four feet from and informs us, "Fear not, for I come in peace." She wore a velvet nightgown with a conservative low cut front that, corresponding to her trimmed golden lantern. Her skin was actually a light-gray tone, while her expanded bright white wing with beautiful white sparks dancing throughout it. She had dark eyes and hair. Her highlighted face included ruby-red lips. She introduced herself, "I am called Kapuvári, a messenger from the Kingdom of Mysteries, Bácsalmási. I have come tonight to reveal a great truth about your seeds." She now paused and looked at each of us. She leaned over to Khigir, who had her bow and was beside me, and offered her the lantern that she was carrying, "Here Khigir, take my lantern." Nevertheless, this is something that will wake you up fast.

She knew Khigir's name. That, within itself was enough to convince me that this woman knows things about us and may have some inspirational information for us. Khigir reached out her hand and took the lantern. She laid down her bow and said to Kapuvári, "Kapuvári I thank you for giving us this lantern and have laid down my weapon in trust for you. We want to hear your words." Kapuvári thanked Khigir and continued her message. "All you shall have sons, except to Hevesi, who will bring forth five picturesque daughters. The Bácsalmási spirits heard the cries in your heart for daughters and consequently, blessed you with five daughters. Siklósi, you are the progenitor for thirty-seven children. All seven of your special wives shall bear children; as follows, Khigir shall have three sons and four magnificent daughters who will look like their mother. Many will declare them as having the beauty of the Heavens. You, like your sister Tselikovsky shall have seven children and twice have duplicated blessings. Tselikovsky, you also shall have three boys and four gorgeous daughters and twice be blessed with double babies. Gyöngyösi, the Angel from the Great Spirits shall have one strong son and four divine daughters. Queen Csongrád of the Dorogi, you shall bear two daughters and three mighty sons. Your sons will do great things for their sisters, which will add to the reign of your daughter. Ajkai, you shall have two sons and three beautiful daughters. Makói, you shall be the mother of one daughter as your reward and four strong sons. You will be the mother with the most sons, having four of the sixteen sons of Siklósi. Siklósi, as you are a savior for the beautiful, the Great Spirits will give you twenty-one daughters with your sixteen sons. Your daughters will all have a special beauty, and your sons will all have strong bodies. All thirty-seven of your children will have the choicest spouses from the Edelényi as spouses. Strong wise men to care for your daughters and the daughters of the Edelényi with the greatest beauty will marry your sons. Not all your children will stay in Baktalórántházai, as nineteen will have their father's and Great-Grandpa's adventurous and roaming spirits. You will not be alone in your later years as eighteen of your children will remain with the Edelényi. Your thirty-seven children shall follow your numbers, as your grandchildren will just fall short of 200 at 187.

Your grandchildren shall also follow your numbers because of that raising the numbers of your pedigree to 988. The seeds of the one's in your wombs shall reach considerable numbers and do so many great things during the new days ahead of you. I have not the permission to reveal all things to you about your pedigree; nevertheless, I may reveal one. Because Khigir shared her, most prized possession that she created and that being her love with Siklósi and created what is now the richest and most dynamic family of sister wives she is to be blessed. We know of no other marriage that was composed with five species, the fifth since of Khigir and her Master, with three more species, including Szentesi, who love being with your family, something divine happened here. The dynamics of having so much diversity are still the talk of the great mysteries. You are now the greatest mystery ever to come forth on the surface of Lamenta. You have a species that killed Lamentans on sight with her mighty ten-foot bear power, simply to stay alive. A sky dancer also joined your love. In your family, we also find the Connubial Angel; with her over one million years of dedicated service, throughout the dots in your high sky.

Accordingly, many loved her, yet chose to surrender herself to your family. You have shown how deep and innocent your love is by allowing Hevesi to find her first love. You have a fierce fire woman joined by a fire horse, which now are friends fixed to your family with the elements preventing them from mating with you. You also have the precious Nógrád who may not marry into your family because of her nation's laws, yet gives her life sharing her love with you. You will discover the wisdom in your coaxing Szentesi back into your family. She will be loved by all your children and be instrumental in their social development as ladies and gentlemen. Nevertheless, I cannot stop here, for you have two prized Tamarkins, who all those who were not married in your village would have competed hard for their favors. Last, but in no way least, you have a reigning Queen, who serves all in your family with a heart filled with unspeakable joy. All the hearts in this family pump rivers of love into Lamenta. This is the miracle of our ages.

You are wise enough to know that life among Lamentans would be too dangerous as the evil spread throughout the lands is too great and has a pronounced thirst for blood. Your finest legacy shall come from a son of Khigir. For from her seed, shall come the great King, who shall rule the greatest kingdom in this neighborhood of galaxies. After your seed comes forth three kings and one Queen. They shall forcefully rule, or be allied with all Lamenta. The reign of the great King shall have its obstacles as its birth comes from the Armies of the savages as they face the greatest trained Armies of the profoundest kingdom of evil ever to exist on Lamenta. They accomplish the impossible and give a safe world for all Lamentans to give their children in marriage. Nevertheless, the King faces another extreme challenge in facing the Queen of evil, as she even reproduces his daughter through her wicked ways. The Queen attempts to destroy all Lamenta by casting pronounced stones from the high skies on Lamenta. All vegetation on Lamenta vanishes; however, the King holds on and eventually defeats this evil Queen as a greater spirit casts her into a lake of fire for one millennium. She returns to beginning her long hard readjustment to serving for the good, and in the deep dark, future creates the greatest Empire that serves in Righteousness. The King finally meets his daughter from Lamenta, and she establishes a pronounced Empire on the great continent that you now reside. Therefore, one with your seed shall also have the blood of the great goddess always who will rule more galaxies than all the stars in our skies counted and recounted for one hundred years." She now bows down and tells us this is the greatest honor that she has ever had bestowed on her. Khigir motions for the other wives to join her in comforting, this strange Angel. As I move toward this sensuous bungle of great news, Khigir motions for me to stay put. She is not being possessive, although sometimes I wonder, and even if she is, she has that right by being the first wife. She is being protective, as she will never let me close to Kapuvári until she knows absolutely I would be safe. Kapuvári exchanges a hug, kisses with my wives and our friends, and bid her farewell telling us that we shall have many visitors tonight.

Khigir hands her back the lamp telling her that she needs it while walking over the grass and rolling rocks. Kapuvári thanks her and tells us while leaving, "I have felt your love here tonight, and it felt wonderful." She slowly fades away. We sit and look at each still in shock at what all she said. We now know so much about our children and our great legacy, she revealed to us. Our seeds will eventually rule this entire giant world. Csongrád tells us that she once heard a soothsayer tell her mother that in the end a seed from her daughter's husband will rule this land in peace and sharing. The sky now turned green before us with giant lightning beams flooding our right side. We could see a partial world with small and large stones flying in all directions. We also saw the light of two suns, as one followed the destroyed world, and the other lay deep before us. All manners of chaos reigned on our left as a red eagle with a wide white tale flew over this area. Purple lightning flashed from the destroyed rocks lost from the disintegrating world striking at the pandemonium below. It was as if even in its death it was trying to destroy something. The stomach ripping smells, that none of us had smelt before. We saw the giant red eagle eat the body of a dead person floating in space with one bite. The world to our right began decaying again, as we could hear the screams of people begging for mercy, as if we were beside them. All around this destroying world was destruction. The air straightaway became cold as the pains of death filled all around us. Gyöngyösi cried out, "What way of evil is doing this to us? I command you to come forth and reveal yourself. The sky turned dark at once, as a giant skull with gray-scaled teeth was lying in the same sort of purple flowers that were on our bed above with the Great Spirits. What was even more mystifying was what sat on it? This skull was directly opposite of us, which meant that with the sloping valley below us, it was resting on air. I asked Gyöngyösi, "My Angel, have you ever seen one such as that?" She told us this was also new for her. Gyöngyösi asked, "My dear child, why are you here?"

The child answers, "Because you commanded me to come forth and identify myself." Khigir, now trembling for joy because what appears to be a child is before us questions, "The nice woman wished to know your name little girl. Will you tell me your name?" She responds, "I am called Pápai." Khigir says in her soft voice, "Oh that is such a pretty name." Pápai responds instantly, "I hate my name." Ajkai, practicing her future mother's voice replies, "Oh, Pápai, I truly enjoy your name." Pápai that tells Ajkai, "I know you since I have seen you many times, you are a wonderful sky dancer, that I used to watch constantly. Are you now a Lamentan?" Ajkai, "Oh little Pápai, I know it is hard for you to understand the ways of adults, especially since you most likely are as old as Lamenta; nevertheless, I currently serve my Master of love and strive diligently to bear him children who may call him father." Khigir quizzes Pápai, "Because of your age, why do you still appear as a child Pápai?" Pápai tells us, "So that I may catch my enemies easier." Pápai wore dark black boots the rose beyond her kneecaps, such as Hevesi does. She wore a short silk shoulder less loosely tied dress that joined by strings. She allowed her left shoulder strap holding her dress up to hang down similar to the way that Gyöngyösi does. Her wings were clear as crystal with many sets on her back. She had both red and pink long hair. Her slanted eyes were such as is Ajkai's eyes. Of special interest to us were her ears. Her ears were much like Hevesi's, except they estimated horizontal in length, whereas Hevesi's were projected vertical with her head. She projected herself as an easy target. It was my turn to ask some questions, "Pápai, I must compliment you on your ears, for I have a wife, who is in my hands now that also has similar ears." Pápai answers, "I have heard of you. You are the dirty boy who forces so many women to marry you." Khigir responds, "Oh Pápai, he is sometimes a silly boy; however, he has always been respectful, caring, and loving with all his wives, each of which begged him for permission to marry, except for me who had to tie him to a tree and beat him to marry me." Pápai responded, "I cannot envision a man not wanting to marry one as beautiful as you."

Khigir, "If you want to envision one, look at my Master." Pápai, "Do not be angry at me Siklósi, as I was only teasing, for now man can hold a Mezokovácsházi in his hand with force." I winked at Hevesi and carefully put her pregnant body back into my pocket and asked, "Pápai, what is a Mezokovácsházi?" Hevesi instantly yelled out, "It is my special Master." I continued, "Oh, excuse me; we do not talk about our different species because love has made us one species. Pápai, "What is your mission, then you would leave yourself unprotected? My wives worry now so much for you." Pápai revealed to us that her mission was to capture the evil spirits that hid inside destroyed worlds, and take them to be judged and if found guilty vanished. Gyöngyösi then with tears slowly going down her face tells her, "Oh Pápai, that mission is too dangerous for you, come to me, and I will beg the Great Spirits to find you a new mission. Now come to me." Pápai answers, "I know you as well. You are the Connubial Angel, for I have watched you care for so many knew lives. How can you be here serving this normal Lamentan?" Gyöngyösi explains to her, "It is a thing called love that took all power from me, leaving me before my Master begging for his mercy. He allows me to serve him and bear his children, making me the happiest Angel in the Heavens. Now please come to me, so I can care for you. As you know, I am much older than you are." Pápai explains, "My true friends, I have not been sent by your Great Spirits, but by a goddess in the ages to follow. She rules for the righteous and once lived in this world. I rest on the Skull of Fonyódi, which is stronger than all the evil spirits in this galaxy. This Skull could distort all spirits and make them weak enough for me to toss them in one of the cavities in his head. My goddess gave me a special message for you in thanks for a considerable deed that one of your pedigrees did for her. Once she became healed from the curses of evil, your mighty descendent and a great supreme Queen gave her another chance with her daughter through their grace. I can tell you Khigir, because of a son that someday shall come from your womb, Lamenta will be spared from you have seen before you, for if that child would not have lived, Lamenta would have fallen while still in its early ages, as you see before you.

All the mothers today are a part of this blessing, for their children will do many deeds in the future to keep this chosen seed alive. Without each of you, Lamenta would not receive the great gift from Khigir and her Master." Khigir then asks while crying, "I appreciate your words and know that the children of my sister wives will always be of one family. I wish so much that your goddess would give you to us so that we may care and protect you." Pápai reveals to us that she can feel the great love in our hearts. She continues by telling us this meeting will always be special in that she got to see the womb that was carrying her inordinate King and the father of a daughter belongs with her momentous goddess." She currently asked Khigir if she could touch her womb. Khigir now opens her arms and wiggles her fingers, as she warns Pápai to be careful with her Master of, "He enjoys capturing little girls and kissing them." Pápai then laughs saying, "I am not afraid of kisses, because, if his kisses did not harm all you women, subsequently it cannot harm me." She gives me a daring look and responds, "Come on dirty boy; see if you can handle the best." I explain to her, "My wives tease you for they know I cannot kiss you in front of them for the danger of their revenge." Pápai smiles, getting bolder by the second and says, "Your loss and not mine." She places her trembling hands on Khigir's belly. Khigir slowly massages her hands while the other wives massage her shoulders and comb her long pink hair. Her trembling continues until she faints and falls to the ground. The wives rush around to get what they need to bring her back to consciousness. Without any sort of warning, a large pink beam shoots out from each of the eyes on the Skull of Fonyódi. The beams pick up the little precious Pápai, as all children look cherished when they lay asleep, and pull her through its skull to protect from within. Afterwards, in a flash, the skull vanishes. Khigir now tells us, "Well, at least we know that old woman is truly protected. I worry if, because of my womb, we could be in greater danger."

Hevesi shouts out, "You fear not my great love, for you will always be safe with us." As Pápai told you, your sister wives will invariably protect you. As we were trying to regroup from our visit from Pápai, Hevesi warned me that another light with a white cloud was approaching. I asked my wives to take a comfortable position, figuring if whatever controlled these presentations wanted to harm us. They would have by now. We had enough emergency firepower to stun any deceivers before we give them their final blows. Peacefully, and with grace, this new presentation appeared before us. Another beautiful Angel stood in front of us. She appeared to be shy as she had her right leg ahead of her left leg. She wore a beautiful long flowing silk gown that had a fancy green trim across the tight shoulder less top and a four-inch mating piece she wore on her right arm. Her patterned wings contained detail and consistency that added a greater warmer aspect of her appearance. We all merely took one look at her and relaxed. Gyöngyösi reveals to us, "I have never seen wings such as these. They look so warm." She stood before us with her looking down toward the ground to her left. Her right hand rests on the top of her right leg with fingers extended. She kept it aligned with the special matching trim, which also matched the trim that sealed the top of her breasts firmly show she could comfortably secure this shoulder less gown. Her lower trimming formed a V with both upper ends hugging her hips just below her well-formed waist. Her top also formed the V gives her extra exposed skin, most like for if she wished to wear a necklace.

Both of her shoulders were abundantly and socially acceptable exposed. Nevertheless, her long shiny red hair lay peacefully on her shoulders. This hair highlighted the precious scarlet freckles that covered her shoulders and face. Behind her was a large powerful looking white cloud that I can only believe it is on the far mountainside before us. What also catches our eyes is the gold fence directly behind her. It has sectional's rods that have the head of a spear, and small yellow flowers along its top connecting golden rod, which secures all the remaining rails. This shows us that someone is worried about her security, as I can only dare to imagine what is in the cloud behind her. She continues to stand in her humble position not moving her frozen face. She should know not to be shy around my wives, because Gyöngyösi and Khigir walk out slowly to calm her. Gyöngyösi metamorphoses into her Angel body therefore comforting this beautiful redhead. Hevesi, tells me to calm down as my heart is beating faster. I tell her I think about the next private time we will have together. The little runt just bit me. What kind of wife bites their Master from inside his shirt pocket? I will never ask that question from my wives, because every one of them would forever, bite me. My two wives now have this red-haired doll baby in their arms comforting her. She tells us she is ready to talk as Khigir asks for her name. This shy beauty lifted her head and told us, "My name is Pásztói, and I am an Angel for the caring of children. I have been sent from the deep future by the goddess Lilith, for I am to protect the seed of Siklósi" Tselikovsky asks, "Why would she send one with your beauty to preside over our children?" Pásztói then answers, "Among her unending legions of angels, I am not considered beautiful. She created us to care for children and as such not to be pleasing to the fathers." Gyöngyösi next, with her arms still around Pásztói tells her, "Oh young lady, then you must keep away from that dirty boy there. He will put a baby in your womb, as he has done to so many, you see here now" Pásztói responds by saying, "Lilith told me your Master was a good man and care with all his heart for his wives and children. How could that be?" I then got up and moved toward her saying, "The Lilith goddess, she would certainly not lie to you would she?" Afterwards stood all with great confidence, "Oh no, Master she loves all and would never lie to one who is doing a mission on her behalf." I followed up by asking, "Moreover, is not this Lilith very wise?" Pásztói reveals, "Oh she is the wisest of all the wise. Because she said I was a good man, should not you be sitting beside the father of the children you will be protecting?" Pásztói answers, "Master, I can see where the great King got his wisdom, I shall sit beside you where I will be safe." She at once walked straight to me and sat extremely close to me. My wives were laughing, as Khigir said, "The wolf has taken that poor lamb to its slaughter." Pásztói began talking to me about everything, as if she had known me her entire life.

She was no longer reserved. I asked her, "Pásztói, why were you so shy when you arrived?" She explained, "I have a great fear of women, for so many have tried to do me harm through the ages, yet man has always been very kind to me like you. Do you know why, my Master?" Khigir whispers to the other wives, "He knows, for he wrote the book." The other wives begin laughing. Meanwhile, I answer Pásztói, "No, my dear. I would not know of such things, for I am an excellent boy." Pásztói tells me, "Oh shucks, I should have known that only pleasant things come from a Saint such as you are." The wives are now on the ground laughing so hard and bashing the ground with their hands and feet. Pásztói asks me, "Master, why are your wives acting so strangely?" I tell her, "They are now falling into ill minds from the marvel at our great wisdom." Hevesi currently told me I needed to slow down before I completely kill all my wives. The wives soon formed a circle int the company of us, as Pásztói explained all the wonderful things; she wanted to do for our children. She also explained that our futures would face some surprise torments. However, her marvelous goddess programmed her to be prepared before these events occurred so we will be safe. I had my arm around her, just to torment my wives and said, "Will you be staying with us now?" She tells us that she must return to worship her wonderful goddess as much as she can before rejoining us at Baktalóránthházai." Csongrád asks a special question before Pásztói departs, "Pásztói, I suspect that this question has been asked before, yet as I am recovering from when our Master beat me, may I ask you again?" Pásztói afterwards freezes for a few seconds and next regains her senses saying, "My great goddess tells me that your wonderful Master never hit you, so why did you say such a terrible thing about such a wonderful Saint?" I told her, "Pásztói, Lamentan women are about as smart as a horse's but, and sometimes they say cruel things purposely to hurt those who love them the most.

However, I know the importance of forgiving in a loving relationship, so I forgive her for being a foolish woman." Pásztói then tells me, "You are every bit as wonderful as my goddess said you were. My beloved Csongrád, I also forgive you now will you tell me how I can serve you and answer your question?" Csongrád then answers, "Thank you so much for forgiving me honorable Pásztói; however, I am still discombobulated on why your goddess, who is so many ages after us and rules so much would have an interest in Khigir's son?" Pásztói, "Yes Csongrád, even I was so confused on this issue at first." Khigir interrupts by saying to Pásztói, "Oh Pásztói, I cannot believe that this would have been confused about you." Pásztói then confesses, "Well, it did not actually bewilder me. I was attempting to make her feel better as it is not your faults that Lamentan women as so far lower intellectual beings than your great wonderful Masters. I hope you have the capacity to understand. Any ways, Siklósi's and Khigir's pedigree shall include a pronounced King, who has his seed, stolen and placed in my goddess womb, creating the finest daughter among her 5001 daughters. As even this daughter shall rule a great Empire on this continent and shall create the greatest secret undersea Empire." She now walked over to her fence, turned around to look at us, and with tears in her eyes told us, "I am so sorry, that my wives hate me this much." That literally woke up my wives' brains in what damage their games and antics can do to another. They all ran fast to catch her each fighting to find a place to hug her and smother her with kisses begging her to forgive them. Pásztói told my wives that if they hated me, her goddess would not let her return. My wives all swore as loud as they could that they truly loved Pásztói. They continued as she hung her head down and departed slowly. Then everything turned red and a strong female's voice spoke, "Fear not mothers, for I shall send back my special Pásztói to serve you." With this, my wives ran out in the field after Pásztói cheering, "You will come back our love." Pásztói then yells back, "My loves. I heard you now; please return to your safety, so I have some children to return to."

The wives all stopped and began to blow her kisses. Pásztói was simply shy around women, as she most likely lived with billions of them and naturally for her beauty received red flooring fabrics from all who met her. I must also confess some wrong in this, as I could manipulate her innocence, yet I dare not confess to my wives, or they will punish me severely, so I will attack first. My lovely wives, "Why did you treat that poor Angel so cruelly?" Their heads are down as it looks like I have two solid arrows on the target for today. They come walking around me, and then, without even the hint, start kicking me. I pretend to be suffering and ask them why. Khigir, "For thinking you are a smart boy, and you cannot blame us, because we are females and do not know to a greater degree." I told Hevesi we had better been on our way, and I shot out across the dark field, then stopped and turned around and lay quietly on the field. Soon, they began calling me for us, hoping to get Hevesi to reveal our position. Then the sky began to turn different shades of purple, and a giant tree appeared in the flat naked mountainside meadows not far from where Hevesi and I were hiding. Now my wives and friends started toward us with a burning Brann leading the way. However, my minute loyal pregnant wife who was in my pocket jumped out onto the ground, which lay next to her and began to run screaming, "Help, he is hurt, please help." Oh, this little darling will get double private time this week. She could think so fast and form workable solutions. Brann immediately dropped beside her and asked if she was okay. Hevesi said she was; even so, "Our Master stepped in a hole while running." She pointed to where she could find him. Brann yelled back, "I think Hevesi is okay. She is worried about your Master being hurt." Meanwhile, I was rolling in the grass and digging up dirt to rub on my ankle. I then removed my shirt and wrapped it around my ankle. Brann floated above looking her, me. I lay on my belly so as not to be looking up and moaning. Brann heard my moaning and roared like a lightning bolt. She looks at me and says, "Oh the mighty big boy is lying here as an animal, so you most likely currently have the same intelligence as a woman from Lamenta." I then tell her, "Now is one of those times I am glad you are not a woman from Lamenta. I ran in fear, because when they get angry like that they could seriously hurt me." Brann says, "You should know that they would never hurt you, they were just releasing tension. My question was how much tension they were going to release.

Do not believe that your games will shame us, for order us to walk in front of all naked, and we will if it is in your heart." I told her, "I could never order that for your shame is my glory. Why would I cast before others what you gave to me in love?" I was milking this up as well as possible, for they are such angels when I maneuver the situation to where I can flatter them. They got me up to the top of our mountainside, as I had kept enough pressure on my foot so as not to put too much pressure on their little limber bodies. When we got to the top Doctor Gyöngyösi and Nurse Khigir, sprang into immediate action, running around like chickens with their heads removed. They were determined they would save my life. They did, as they removed my tied on a shirt from my foot and carefully massaged my foot rubbing some lotions on it. Khigir then tells me, "Master, you were fortunate for the hole you stepped in having loose dirt on the side which protected your foot. You will be able to run the meadows in just a few days. I tell her, "With suffering such as this, and to prove that you all do not hate me. I should get a warm hug and long kiss with each of my wives." Khigir approves this only if she may go first. We all agree and while kissing the sky turned a brighter purple. When we finish, I whisper into my pocket, "Do not worry honey, you get two." Khigir says, "After the way she saved you this morning, she will receive three private times extra when we return, and they may be forest private times. Hevesi you proved today what a great value it is to have you in our Master's front pocket. Hevesi declares that she now hears the sound of water from a sea. We look out in front of us and see the purple sky becoming lighter. Ajkai jumps up and yells, "Look, there is a sea before us!" We all look and a shiny light now light currently reveals that a sea does indeed exist before us. I can see where some of our mountain peaks are sticking up out of the water. We have an enjoyable sandy beach facing us, where before it just sloped down. My wives go out to lay on the sand.

To our amazement, a giant stone bird comes to the high sky in our front. Two large black piles of smoke rest on its sides. There is something inside them; however, I cannot make it out. Consequently, a white beam shoots out and from this beam, appears a pink Angel with some light-blue patches coming at us carrying a bag. She has blond hair such as my Tamarkins. She lands on the beach and walks toward us. We all sit and smile at her; we have no fear of her, as it is that big stone bird above her, which is confusing us. When she is near this beautiful spirit tells us, "Do not fear, for I have not come to harm you. I have arrived to bring you food that you may eat." I could now see that she had a large bag, so I got up to help her. She stopped walking, and three bright lights appeared from the black clouds above. I now asked her, "Sweet Angel, may I help you carry those things to show you are kindness?" She laughs and tells me, "Master, I am a spirit, thus to carry things can give me no pain. You may rest for I have come to serve your family and you on this wonderful day." I sat down, and the three lights went out. She has my attention now, although I can understand why the skies would want to protect her. I tell her thanks for my wives, and friends were becoming low on energy and would soon need food. She laughs and says, "I did not see them laying on the ground this morning or being helped to your camp, would you agree?" Khigir tells her, "Our Master suffered from stepping into a hole while running." The Angel looks at her, looks at me, and says, "You are fortunate to have their love." I tell this Angel, "I am not lucky. I am very lucky." My wives begin to chuckle and start rearranging our things to make room for this new food. Gyöngyösi now asks, "We are thankful for the gift of food that you give us, may I ask why we are being rewarded?" The Angel then smiles at her and says, "You are truly as beautiful as so many have told us Connubial Angel." Gyöngyösi smiles and responds, "That is a wonderful compliment. May I know your name, as you are truly a wise and kind Angel?" The Angel tells her, "I am sorry. My name is not for you, or any here to know for my time in the foreground has not arrived." They then gave Gyöngyösi the two large bags of food. Gyöngyösi immediately fell to the ground, and I ran over to her to help her.

Gyöngyösi tells me, "Sorry to scare you Master, I thought it was light as it glided on air for her." I kissed her and helped her stand back up again. This beautiful Angel told us, "Enjoy your time in Bácsalmási!" She turned around, and the sizeable rock bird took her up into the light on its head. The large rock bird and the surrounding smoke vanished within an instant. Once she was in the light, we could not see her anymore. We had never seen this type of food before; nevertheless, it did taste very good. After we finished eating, we got our wake up call. Out of the water came an ugly beast, with a woman in his six feet long arm. They stood on the purple water around them. The beast had a sizable bone skull head of a flesh-eating animal at least three feet long with no eyes. It also had a large jaw with razor teeth that could easily eat the woman's head in one bite. Its humped body looked like a snake. The woman's shoulder less white gown was in shreds and filthy. Her long black hair hung from the back of her head to the sea as the creature was vomiting a white substance on her hair and dress. She appeared to have no life, until we heard her cry in pain as the milky vomit rolled past her ear. Makói yells out, "He is digesting her. We must save her now." She turns into her ten-foot bear and jumps into the sea. Brann and Baranya turn into fire and fly out to attack and burn the beast. My Tamarkins start shooting arrows into his snake body. Ajkai dives into the water turning into an illusion and reappears before the beast as a giant whale. Gyöngyöre appears as an Angel with her sword and flies out striking the beast cutting off part of his jaw. Hevesi returns to her normal size and throws her sword hitting the beast in his left arm, pinning this arm to his body. Csongrád and Nógrád swim out to the woman and pull her back into the shore, now that the beast is burning in flames. I just stand her looking like a fool. My Tamarkins (Khigir and Tselikovsky) start preparing a place where we can tend to this woman. Csongrád and Nógrád get her to the shore. I grab her feet, while they grab her arms, and we rush her to Nurse Khigir and Dr. Gyöngyösi while she is transforming back. Everyone has returned to normal now and I now, put Hevesi back in my shirt pocket. We notice this woman has many soars on her body. Looks into our food basket and pulls out some creams and lotions that they did not know what they were.

They begin cleaning the wounds and apply this cream because it immediately is healing the sores. The other wives are trying to repair her gown, which Khigir completely removed so they could get as much of the white vomit away from her body as possible. The wives sow her old dress, making it small, yet more stable. We have tried for an hour to bring her to consciousness. Gyöngyösi tells me it will be soon. She awakes in a few minutes as Khigir asks her, "What is your name friend?" She looks around, sees her sores are gone, and her dress repaired. Her voice squiggles as she painfully whispers, "I am called Fomenkov, and something evil was after me." I ask her, "Fomenkov, do you know the creature that was trying to eat you?" Fomenkov tells us, "It is a Kisteleki, who lives hidden in the seas ready to kill to eat. However, they only kill women, and can exist for hundreds of years without eating any flesh, living in the dirt from the bottom of the sea." Makói, who is interested in another hunt, asks her, "Do you know if there is more?" Fomenkov reports to us, "There are more somewhere in this sea, I do not know where for I only know that there are very few women in these mountains and what they hunt first." I stand up and stretch my arms, releasing a yawn, ask my wives if they want to go skinny-dipping. They all look at me as if I am crazy and tell me, "Master, that thing is after women? Do you want us to be eaten?" I confess to them that it was a poor joke, and that I will try to keep them from the water of this sea. Hevesi alerts me, "Master. Something is flying toward us." It was a bright verdant horse, with people's skulls, which stuffed it. It was a thing that looked like a person, except for his skull face, and wore a green custom and hood. He carried a giant weapon in his left hand whose bottom had released a bright blue beam. A black blob with many legs conceals the back left of the horse that is flying from our right to left. We can see and hear screaming skulls falling out of the horse. The thing that rides this looks at us also had blue flames spraying everywhere behind him. I exclaim, "What is this terrible thing?"

Fomenkov tells us, "It is called Orosházi, and is the sprayer of plaques and diseases. Do not fear what you see for it is only a vision. He rides through our mountains once or twice a year. He never stops and talks. Instantly, he stopped before us and looked. Khigir immediately jumped on my lap almost crushing Hevesi. By some unknown power, Khigir is always able to get close to me and not hurt Hevesi. It is as if they have some special power. We have a more pressing issue before us. He comes up before us and turns his heart pointing from our right to our left. Somehow, that is telling me that he has no wish to attack. Therefore, I ask him, Are you the one that is called Orosházi?" He affirms that is his name. I then ask, "Why do you come before us now?" Orosházi tells us, "Children and Fomenkov, have no fear of me for I am merely a vision. I have come today to tell you that I shall flood over the enemies of your seeds, which your seed may prosper and the evil ones not to harm them. My plagues shall be great, and many of your enemies will perish." I then say to Orosházi, "On behalf of my pedigree, I thank you so much." He shook his head and turned around riding away. Tselikovsky confesses to us that he was a strange thing. I agreed with her saying, "I would not want to invite him for dinner, which is for sure. His news disturbs me in that I wonder why our seed will have so many enemies." Ajkai said, "Master our answer may be coming." Before us, the sky turned mahogany. Then a light began to shine as the brown sky winds began to spin. A woman afterwards came forth, who walked up to stand in front of me. She had a tree branch that floated in the air to her left side. On this tree branch, sat a large red birth of a species I have never seen. This bird sat looking at her as if they were talking. She wore a gown made of this fur that had a large white trim around the top. Her eyes were hazel with a light-green ring circling within it. Only being able to see her right hand, I noticed six silver rings on each finger, and her long sharp fingernails were the color of a knife blade. Her right lower arm had eight hard steel braces, and that was merely above her thick fur coat. When she touched this red bird, small cherry drops began to fill the air. Her skin was darker than mine was, yet lighter than Gyöngyösi's was. Her right cheek looked like a cracked bowl with small cracks running everywhere. She had ruby-red lips with a metal ring pierced into her lower lip. She wore a necklace, made of large red pearls that she wore above her forehead and throughout her hair.

She had long brown hair with thick streaks of white running through it. Her most distinctive feature was the two large ram's horns that grew from her skull, which formed giant sixes on each side. The way she stared with her eyes and held her fingers showed to me that she was no danger to us. She smiled at me and walked pass me, with no acknowledgement that I even existed. She walked toward Khigir, who stepped aside as she also passed her. Kisteleki then spoke, "I am so glad to see you Zalaegerszegi. I did not know how to contact you. I truly need your help now." Zalaegerszegi sat down beside Kisteleki and asked, "Who cut your dress so that your legs can be seen, and if you are not careful other things?" She gave me a dirty look. Kisteleki then said, "Be at peace Zalaegerszegi as the Master you just gave your evil eye and seven wives and three other women here. I do believe that he knows what this is." She had spread her legs and pointed to her seed catcher. Khigir immediately put her hands over my eyes. My other wives instantly surrounded her, and Gyöngyösi said, "Kisteleki, you should not do that since we had to become married and promise to serve our Master for life before being permitted to share with him what you have just flashed." Zalaegerszegi said, "So true Kisteleki, you cannot flash like that until you are wedded and preparing to mate." She pulled out a new gown from her bag and said, "I will occupy the Master of these women while you later put this on yourself." Kisteleki said, "No one cared when I exposed myself when he carried my legs to this resting place. I know that he got a peek." I then said, "Kisteleki, fear not for it still looks the same." Zalaegerszegi smiled at me and said, "I am sure we would like to keep it that way, right Siklósi."

I nodded my head yes, especially because every female, here was staring at me with serious eyes. I think to myself, 'why are they so excited about me seeing something that is not there as the true parts of it are deep inside them on the road to the womb.' Whatever they think there is to see. They want to make sure I do not see it. Zalaegerszegi tells Kisteleki, "Kisteleki, it is the way of men to peak and the way of women to make it impossible for them to see." Khigir currently said, "I believe Kisteleki called you Zalaegerszegi, we so much thank you for your support as our Master is truly a kind and honorable man." Khigir looked at Kisteleki and said, "Now make it impossible, okay dear." Zalaegerszegi turned and looked at us and spoke, "I am so sorry children. My name is Zalaegerszegi, and I know all of your names. I am the medicine woman in the Kisteleki's family. I was sent to make sure not only is she okay, but also you, since Orosházi was here." Gyöngyösi thanked her furthermore caring for us. Once she acknowledges this, we all relaxed and went about our normal activities, which for me is taking another nap. Sometimes the life of a Master can be so tiring. Zalaegerszegi found small traces of Orosházi's plague, which must have fallen loose with the light wind when he stopped. She gave us some of her special tonics that would save us. Zalaegerszegi felt around my wives' bellies and asked me, "Master, have you planted any seeds?" I told her that all seven of my wives would be blessing me with eight children. Zalaegerszegi now congratulated me. As she felt each one's belly, she told these the wonderful blessings would come forth with that seed. Hevesi yells out to her, "Touch my belly, please," then she ducks. Zalaegerszegi gives me a funny stair, as I pointed into my pocket. She walked over to me and looked in, seeing Hevesi, said; show me your wonderful looking little belly honey. Hevesi lifted her shirt and Zalaegerszegi touched it saying, "Oh my precious, Hevesi. You will have five beautiful strong daughters to give your Master." Hevesi thanked her as we all cheered. Zalaegerszegi tells us, "Now, you all need to get relaxing for you have a special guest arriving next." Soon the waters became peaceful and rich blue and small parts of white flowers began to blow in the air. Light natural fog began to lift off the water, as flower trees began to spring up out of the water, and white doves started to land on their branches. It looked so relaxing and peaceful we all just lay on our backs and gazed with a smile. Hevesi afterwards tells us that something is coming. We soon discover that something indeed is coming and that something is someone.

Once we can clarify what it is, my wives sit up quickly, locking both eyes on her and me. I can understand why they would be concerned, for what is in front of us is the beginning of the river of beauty. This Angel is the cream of the supreme. Her hair is as white as her wings. Everything created about her face was to perfection, especially her large black trimmed eyes. She wore a long flowing silk gown that also floated on the waters behind her. She had her fingers peacefully and gracefully extended. Her waistband, headband, necklace had a special distinguished design packed with diamonds that shined as much as her inner self who was expanding with peaceful and loving glows. Although now as great as my Gyöngyösi's, her body was among the best for women. She peacefully glowed from the sea to the ground before us. We all were looking at her, which I believed scared her. She stops, froze, and her eyes became larger. Gyöngyösi, who is our official spokesperson to the angels, told her, "Young lady, do not be afraid as we will not harm you. Come in peace." She smiled and fell to her knees, as tears began to flow down her cheek. I subsequently told her, "Young lady, none among us will harm you, so have no fear and come be with us, so we may get to know you and you us." Khigir who is as weak for tears as am I asked her, "Oh beautiful Angel, why do you cry?" She tells us, "I have longed-for ages to see you, yet when I served for the kingdom that rules here they would not allow me. Now that I serve for a new kingdom, she has permitted me to visit you." I asked her, "Would that be the same kingdom as Pásztói serves in?" She answers, "Yes, my lord." Csongrád asks her, "Do you know why your goddess allowed you to visit here?" The Angel answers, "No I do not know for sure Queen Csongrád." She gives a respectful royal nod and then continues, "Notwithstanding. I know that she understands my heart, and that I share the same love for what is happening here." Ajkai asks her, "Oh beautiful Angel, may we know your name and will you tell us what is happening here?" She answers, "While living on Lamenta, I was called, 'Supreme Queen of Mempire, Lablonta, Queen of Cumber Lablonta Empire, Queen of Onivac Lablonta Empire, Hersonia 8$^{th.}$ While serving in the fresh Heavens for this galaxy, they called Supreme Queen of Heaven Lablonta. Now for my new goddess in live in the Meshcheryakov (Мещеряков) Palace, and am called, Lablonta, the Mother of Mercy. You are the ancestor of my children; thus, please call me your servant Lablonta.

The pure purpose of this visit is selfishness on my part. To have a dream come true to see the Progenitors of my husband whom will love forever much, and just he as my Master for eternity. I am so sorry that I have angered you. I shall tell my goddess that she must punish me." Gyöngyösi and Khigir ran to her grabbing her gown begging her not to tell her goddess such a lie, swearing, "You have done no wrong. We did not know you and was merely curious. You come over here and enjoy our kisses and a hug, for you are part of our family, for if you took a seed from one of our sons, you are as our son. This is the way of things in our world." I look at her and smile, "You are clearly the most beautiful of my sons." Lablonta begins to laugh, and tells us this is the greatest joy that she has had since the wars in the Heavens. Gyöngyösi asks Lablonta, "Should we worry about this great war?" Lablonta tells us, "We could save all who are here, as I personally saved you Gyöngyösi, for you were too much beauty for the enemy to take from us." Gyöngyösi then says, "Mother of Mercy, yes, you are truly a Mother of Mercy. Lablonta, can you tell us more about the life with your husband?" Lablonta confesses that she has no permission to reveal all; nevertheless, she will reveal some of what she did with her husband. I was to be the next Queen of the most evil Empire ever to exist and as my reward; I could take your son as my husband. Men could not rule in those days. My husband hated the ways of his mother, the current Queen, and he decided to escape to the savage lands. I had a choice, to rule the most powerful Empire on Lamenta or hide in the mountains in his arms. I could not bear the thought of even one day without him, for I still gave myself to him the first time we met, a legal right of the next in line for the throne. I followed him to the land of the savages, not knowing if this was an evil scheme to lure us into their death traps. We were so shocked at how much they loved us, and gave us the same honors out of love that our Empire gives us out of the law and fear of death.

They hunted down these people, as soon many from your shores will be, and tortured them without mercies to death as their only redemption. Your son, known as King Mike, worked hard training the savages trying to create many strong Armies to fight his mother's Empire. Then the day came that shook the foundation of Lamenta, as our Armies invaded this Empire of death. We fought strong, and after years of hard fighting destroyed all that we could find from this old Empire. I have heard that the Love spirits took you to this time, and you could see firsthand some of the death of that terrible time. I was the last official Queen of that advanced Empire. We worked hard to build hospitals, schools, public buildings, and roads. We loved our new people, as they also loved us. We were advancing to a great new era on Lamenta, until one day, something we thought was dead came out of our pass and killed me. That person was King Mike's mother, whom he at once killed in revenge. I watched our new Empire grow from the Heavens, only occasionally to intercede. One such time was to intercede for my current goddess so that her daughter's Empire would follow her. That act of love on that day is one reason why my goddess allowed me to have a dream come true, and that is to look you all in the face and say, "Thanks to my husband." I could take one look at this heavenly creature and know that she indeed truly loved our son. Lablonta now walked over before Khigir and once again dropped to her knees and asked Khigir, "Oh great mother, may I kiss the womb that my husband's pedigree will come forth?" Khigir pet here hair and said, "If that is what you wish, my child?" I then thought how lucky I was she forgot where the real beginning of her husband's line began, for because of her beauty. I would have to deny her that request. All the women in this group formed a close circle around her, and everyone told her how much we loved her. She then stood up and looked at me saying, "Actually, dirty boy, I do know where my husband's ancestry truly began." This entire uncontaminated thing just blasted me so efficiently, since I cannot ever bear the thought that this idea would be in her mind. My face is pure red and my body trembling, although I am working hard to control it. I do feel sorry for Hevesi, who is bouncing all around in my pocket. Khigir asks Lablonta, "Did our bad boy do something wrong?"

This bit Csongrád, as tears were flowing from her face, she hugged Lablonta hard saying to her, "This is the greatest story that I have ever heard, and to be able to hold another who also chose this path is a dream among dreams." They finally released, each other, as Khigir and Gyöngyösi wiped the tears from their eyes. This was a true meeting of genuine Queens, an amazing sight to me." We all stood in a line watching her slowly walk away. We knew that her leaving was painful for her as it was also for us. She comes in humbling and left in our hearts. As a father, I was so proud that someday my seed would take her as a wife. We would then have two Queens who left their thrones. She finally stopped, 1,000 feet away and turned around. When she did, we all waved and cheered. She waved back with both arms as she slowly sank into the sea. We all had to sit down and talk about this visit. Csongrád tells us, "Today I got to hug the supreme greatest Queens of History. The thought that she used my life as an example has brought the greatest pride for ever in my life, for I know that if I ever become weak, I can think of her words and carry on strong on my knees serving the Master I love so much." Khigir confesses that the intensity of the honor that she bestowed on us now has her visualizing the greatness of all our seeds. Brann adds, "I cannot believe what we saw today, it must be an illusion, for no son of Siklósi could ever have a wife with beauty only possessed by the great goddess." I looked at Brann and responded, "Brann I just about have to agree with you on this one. If it were not for the testimony given from her own mouth, I must believe what she said to be true. The fact is that I would take my life, rather than call her a liar. The simplicity and consistency of her beauty are what brings it to the verge of being impossible." Gyöngyösi adds, "Like our Queen, I also met a supreme Angel who apparently it is one of the elites for she clearly lives among her goddesses chosen. Her love is so humble and flows into those she wants as they lower their defenses to get every drop. Family, greatness abounds around us here today, for from us, chiefly Khigir, which rightly all should have come, will see many great deeds and people. Our love will flow through the generations creating much better for Lamentans." I now told this family, "Great things are happening today. This may be a good time for us to share our love with one another." Brann then aloud laughs, "See Khigir, I told you that dirt would try to mate with us."

I smiled and said, "All except for my Khigir may now hug one another. Come here Khigir . . ." I thought we could take an enjoyable walk and try to absorb what is happening here today. As we began to walk, Hevesi tells me, "Master something is going on with the sea." We look and see that it has completely turned purple once again. This time was having some sunlight to help us see what is happening. Fortunately, for us, the waves are splashing from our right or left. These waves are not life normal waves in that they are also splashing white water. The splattering water is so high in front of me that I cannot see what is happening on the other side of the mountain range that was there yesterday. I next look up and see a wonder, which at first stuns me. I think that I may be having an illusion. I therefore, ask Hevesi, "Hevesi, what have you seen before us besides the sea?" Hevesi reports to me, "Oh, I see something I never knew existed, "I see a woman in the sky that you will not be able to try to mate with." I look down in my pocket and say, "Well smarty pants. I got you did not I?" Hevesi then recommends, "We should ask Kisteleki, and by the way, about, mating me, thanks Master." I smile at her and say, "Only four more times to go." I now ask Kisteleki if she told me who that woman in the sky is. She walks back with me, as I help her keep balance as she is hurting still from that terrible beast. Kisteleki tells me, "I have never seen her before, however; I have heard tales about her. Her name is Berettyóú, as she is the purple eyes of the waves. I ask my hop along friend, "Do you think she will talk with me?" Kisteleki tells me, "She should. I have never heard anything bad about her and a lot of good."

I now complain, "Kisteleki, why did you put the long dress on yourself. I wanted you to keep the short one, on so I could sneak some more peeks at you." She answers, "Siklósi, I would be glad to and maybe give you a few more flashes. Let me go to get Khigir to help me change and ask her if she wants to play also, okay dear?" I tell her, "Honey, the day is growing old, and I am afraid that your legs could get cold. We will play this game later, maybe even never, okay dear." Kisteleki then accuses me of being psychotic and thinking that she is ugly. I tell her, "Oh no Kisteleki, I could never be mad at you, as I am holding your last flash dear to my heart. And you know you are not ugly, all right my dearest, now go sit anywhere except beside Khigir, okay dearest." She then says, "I will do this only for you, although I am so sad, because I do believe the three of us would have; therefore, much fun playing this." As she walks away, Hevesi tells me, "Master, you have better been careful with the woman up here, for they are not as easy to trick." I agree with Hevesi and now turn to the purple sea. I walk over to the sea and call out, "I call out Berettyóú, and can you hear me?" She answers, "Siklósi, I can hear you plainly, Kisteleki kind of outplayed you on that last move did not she?" I say, "Berettyóú, there is always a first time for everything." Berettyóú then warns me, "Young man you do not want to get me all choked up, because it might not be good for you." I ask her, "Advice well taken, anyway, is there a reason for your visit with us today?" Berettyóú answers, "No my son, I am here now to take you to another place. I am bringing your small ship now.

Chapter 02

Berettyóú gusting through the mysteries

Afterwards, I questioned her, "Advice well-taken, anyway, is there a reason for your visit with us today?" Berettyóú answers, "No my son, I am here now to take you to another place. I am bringing your comfortable small ship currently. Do you have any questions?" Then, I asked her, "Please answer this question quietly, do you come in peace?" Berettyóú answered, "Yes; I am your friend." Instantaneously, I asked her, "Will you help me trick my wives for sport?" Berettyóú answers, "Okay, I will play along with this tide." Khigir has arrived now with the wives and at once laughs at me saying, "Master. You finally found one you cannot get into your love chamber." Looking at her, I reply, "Does not a love chamber have the wind. Hold on, let me ask her." Looking at Berettyóú, I say, "Berettyóú, can you join me in my bedchamber?" Berettyóú answers, "I can go wherever you wish and be whatever you wish, my handsome dirty boy. Tell me what to you my precious lover." Khigir immediately hits me in my arm and screams, "You stay behind me." She looks at the other wives and tells them, "Keep him from looking at that monster in the sky!" At once, Ajkai comes forward and calls out, "How are you today Berettyóú, is my friend, the Móri Wind been? I wonder how he is taking this news about you and my Master." Berettyóú tells Ajkai, "I have not heard from Móri Wind for many years now. If you find him, let me know so I can blow my dirty boy to him and display how my taste has improved. This lover boy has utterly a collection of wives; however, do not worry, I can blow him away with my powers." She then blew us all to the ground. Khigir looks at me and says, "You have to be careful about whom, you pick up now Master," and give me a soft kiss to my cheek. Berettyóú at once asks me, "When do I get the two blonds you said had been bugging you?" Khigir looks at, and turns and looks at Berettyóú and with a laugh says, "Busted, you are not as good in this game as my Master is." Berettyóú responds, "That is what I get for listening to Lamentans laugh at the foolishness of their women with blond hair. Darn!" "Berettyóú," I cry out, "Do not be distraught, because many, a good man has changed their idea of blondes when they have run into my Tamarkins." The mighty wind, Berettyóú thus exclaimed, "Oh no. You have another one?" "Tselikovsky," I cried out, "Come sit beside me and bring your kindness please."

Tselikovsky has constantly been my special one; she is the one that comes through for me no matter what, and invariably in good style. She comes up next to me on the opposite side of Khigir. Then she bows to her knees and wraps her arms around my leg. Thereafter, she reports, "Oh, Master, I thank you for allowing me to serve you, if your hands are dirty wipe them in my hair." Berettyóú whistles aloud, "Siklósi do not touch that precious little adorable innocent creature's hair, stick your hands up, and I will clean them. If you took her hair, I will blow you into the highest tree." Tselikovsky cries out, "Oh; so kind and caring spirit into the air. Please do not make my Master angry least he beat me once more Khigir instantly falls before me crying out, "Oh mighty Master, please do not beat my poor sister again, I still fear for her current wounds may take her life." Berettyóú looks at me as her eyes begin to flair, and pupils dilate I sense that someone is in trouble and unfortunately for me, that someone has two Tamarkins holding his legs. The sea now begins to pull toward her as she is slowly preparing for a big blow, which I hope does not come my way. What makes this so hard is that I can only see her eyes, eyebrows, and the upper part of her nose into the sea, which is withdrawing. "Khigir," I speak quietly so the wind does not hear me, "Tselikovsky, you girls must tell the truth fast. Otherwise, we are going to take a trip to a place we do not want to go. Look at how the sea is leaving us. It will return, and when it comes backward fast, we go as well." Tselikovsky slowly looks to the rear and recommends that Khigir look back quickly. As she does, she tells her sister, "It lovey dovey time." They both jump up and start hugging, kissing, and crying out, "We love you so much!" Berettyóú coughs and flash flood passes by us as we hold on to the nearby trees. My other wives and friends ran for higher ground earlier, knowing that we were messing with the wind. It is not respectable to mess with the wind. Berettyóú moves her eyes closer to us and asks, "Do my precious little blond darlings need help from that bad dirty boy?" Tselikovsky answers, "Oh Berettyóú, I fear you do not know our Tamarkin customs." Berettyóú replies, "We are comfortable little darling, please explain." Khigir works her way under my arm and takes my hand while she is kissing and playing with it."

Tselikovsky continues, "As a Tamarkin, if we fear someone is deceiving our husbands. We will pretend to be abused and weak. The enemy most times turns the deceit into fear and go, or they foolishly try to attack us Tamarkin women, who never lose in a battle, unless, as here, we are fighting a loving confused wind." Berettyóú looks at both Khigir and Tselikovsky and asks, "Has your Master ever beaten you?" Khigir answers, "Oh no Berettyóú, he is the greatest Master in all our lands. This is the reason he has so many wives. He has so much love that he gives to us. If any of us were to lose him, we would take our lives to search for him in the land of the spirits." Khigir and Tselikovsky start kissing my cheeks and massaging my next as my other wives and friends judge us. Hevesi sticks her head out of my pocket and says, "Berettyóú, please do not hurt our kind, loving Master. We need him so much." Berettyóú then responds, "Oh, he has one of you as his wife. I always thought your species gave little attention to love." Hevesi answers, "That is true Berettyóú. However, when I met this wonderful man, love completely erased my mind and only allowed my Master to live there. He keeps me next to his heart, as much as he can safely. Naturally, if danger is around, I return to his size and sling my sword prepared to die for him. Berettyóú looks at me and then sees my other wives rushing to make sure I am okay from the flash flood. Each is kissing whatever part of my arms or legs; they can grab. This causes me to feel like I am the meal for a pack of wolves. My wives always compel me to marvel at their organization. They have delegated which one will do which task, and work as a perfect team. Berettyóú asks my wives, "Do you all love this man?" They respond, "Yes Berettyóú, not only we do, but also the three friends we have with us." Berettyóú looks at them and then chuckles, "Brann and Baranya. I have not seen either of you dashing through my skies lately. I feared you had left me." Brann answers, "Now Berettyóú; we would never leave a wind that has helped us as you do. We are just taking this Lamentan time for our friends. Yes, we also love their Master.

If not for the elements such as you and I are being incompatible, we also would have joined this compassionate family. I marveled after these wonderful special creations since the first time we met and would challenge the greatest glacier to free them." Berettyóú now looked at Khigir and me and with Khigir, giving me her 'tremble demble' her eyes began to have a life again. I call this extraordinary public emotional release by Khigir her 'tremble demble' as she melts against me with her dazed eyes like the children in my hometown village would do when they saw their fathers bringing in the wild beats from the fields. When Khigir puts her 'tremble demble' on me, I am completely helpless, for I can in no way disappoint those stars gazed eyes as they penetrate my soul to the love her heart needs to survive. Berettyóú tells us now, "I do believe we may have ruffled each another's waves, so here are two peaceful waves on your journey before you." Straight away, the sea turned into a tranquil calm as toward our shore came a beautiful ship, the greatest that any of us had ever seen. My seven angels looked at in veneration, for none of us had evermore saw such as this. Brann burning to say flames, "I have never seen one such as this, even in the seas of the Sensenites, or the evil lands of the flesh eaters." Hevesi springs up and asks, "Flesh Eaters." Ajkai calms her down, 'Do not worry Hevesi. They are looking for larger meals." Makói now roars, "Wow, when Berettyóú apologizes, she really works hard to gain our forgiveness." Berettyóú slowly losing her temper started to draw back the waters as she was filling her lungs with seawater. Khigir quickly confesses, "Berettyóú has won the love from my heart forever, especially how easy she forgives." Berettyóú coughs again and we travel back to our camp. While in our camp, I enlighten my wives, "It may be best that we consider that Berettyóú can be touchy at times. If we want to stop these free rides, we need to take this into deep deliberation. Please remember that we have not a good example of her full wind yet. Now, let us pick up our things, because something tells that ship is not here for our amusement. Let me talk with, Brann jump in if you feel it would be best that I shut my mouth." We now take our things and put them on the sand beside the sea. I ask our touchy wind, "Berettyóú, can you keep a secret."

Berettyóú, "What you say will be as safe as the wind." I continue, "Berettyóú; I enjoy your eyes best when they are soft and happy." Berettyóú now confesses, "I admit that I do have a temper, for when Móri Wind angered me, I blew him off Lamenta. He is out there in space somewhere and should return in a few years. I shall control myself better for you silly boy." I gaze at her and ask, "How can everyone know my wives tease me with silly boy?" Berettyóú tells me now, "I do not understand everyone, for I only know that I heard it in the wind." Ajkai currently shares with us that she believes this the largest sea vessel she has ever seen." We are each dying to know what this sparkling white gigantic boat, is with all the large fabric blankets tied to giant trees that have grown from within it. Therefore, I plead to Berettyóú, "Oh loving eyes of Berettyóú, will you please tell us what this ship is to do? Berettyóú finally shows to us, "I am here to take you to the Land of the Celldömölki, which will later be called the Islands of the Mystanites.

The Celldömölki are holders of the greatest mysteries of Lamenta, and you must see these before you start delivering your beautiful babies." That was all she had to say to line up my wives. Anyone who claims their babies to be beautiful automatically controls them. Berettyóú explains to us that she will send two smaller boats that will take us to the ship. Questioning her, I ask, "My Grandpa once spoke of seeing a large ship, although it only had one tree growing from within, and had many men working with ropes. Who controls this ship?" Berettyóú squalls, "I will control this ship, as I control all ships within my area." Khigir clarifies, "My precious new friend, what do you do about those bad people's ships that are beginning to invade my Tamarkin homeland and even my Master's earlier homeland." Berettyóú gusts back, "Khigir, there are so many evil winds that flow across the skies of Lamenta, many from the Island of Death, which is in the southern lands of this world. These winds love to destroy and help those who are wicked to flourish. My hate for these winds is unmistakable, as I fight them every time I see them. These days, I must be careful, for these winds now travel in considerable numbers, which I cannot stop. Except for this mission, I spend most of my time trying to catch them in small groups where they can be demolished. They seldom travel through this part of Lamenta because of the extreme mysteries in this area, many of which fight these winds, gaining great victories. With that all to our side, come now to the greatest ship to sail these northern seas. You will have a host on your ship to explain more to you. My temper forbids me from spending too much time with you. In addition, I must concentrate on getting you to the Mystanites so you can discover your adventures." Berettyóú turned the ship parallel to the shore as we rowed our two boats toward it. We sat in our boats alongside this giant ship and looked down the two rows of windows that ran from the front to the back of the pure white ship. The top row of circled windows ran to the top of the ship only on the front third and back third. This ship has three extremely high strait trees with five rows of straight branches. The giant pure tied on white furs are catching the wind. When we arrive, I ask Hevesi to expand again and send her with her sword and Khigir, with her bow up first. I must stay here until all my womenfolk are safe aboard the ship.

I notice something strange when Hevesi and Khigir climb the ladders on the side of the ship. Our boats are beginning to rise slowly. Next I send Csongrád and Tselikovsky, and as they get out and step on the ladder, our boat now rises above the first row of windows. We are about halfway up to the deck currently, and I would say trapped. I next send Makói and Nógrád, keeping my girls who can fly on with me. They quickly get on the ladder, not looking down, and begin to climb toward the top of this ship. Our boat now rises at least five more feet; therefore, I send my angel Gyöngyösi, as I help her get up the ladder and Ajkai jumps onto the ladder before her boat. That woman has no fear of this ladder, and considering how long she danced in the upper skies. I am not surprised; nevertheless, I must say something. Therefore, I report to her, "Now, sweetheart, please be careful with our baby, okay my love." She slows down and blows me a kiss, with a delightful big smile. I smile back and give her thumbs up for approval. They both now go up their ladders giving their special wiggles. When they are close to the top, they look down to me to see if I am still watching. Of course, I am watching because I know my wives. When they are doing the wiggles, I had better been watching, or I will get an extended cold shoulder. I sometimes wonder why whoever is up there just did not make all men or all women. I will admit that once a woman has trained her man, life gets somewhat easier. The one thing that has saved me is that my wives have worked hard to standardize my approved behavior. In the early parts of our relationships, I had difficulty figuring the different rules from each wife. They each, naturally kept a few specialties. Hevesi is the most dynamic between them being totally in accord with them when among the wives, and once we are out of sight, she turns into my wilderness pal, mouth and all. She could hang with any of my friends and teach them a trick or two about surviving in the unknown. Nevertheless, she is a woman also, and can comfortably allow that part of her to shine. Before, she had it locked tight, yet now her eyes can sparkle like my other wives. Besides, she knows how to cultivate that sparkle. I am completely pleased that she is to give me five daughters. Her children will give me no problems in loving them. We may have to get the unique hats for the little things until their hair grows long.

It is the special differences in them and by being my daughters will help me to keep a good strong eye on them. Their ears will not be a thing of shame among our families. I will work hard to help my other children be comfortable with their siblings having pointed ears. I just cannot see what the big fuss will be, except it could be a target for hate to divide us. Any ways, they did their wiggle. They verified that it pleased me, and our boat jumped higher. Baranya solicited Brann and me to get off now. She suspected the ships will stop in their storage positions, and that I needed a good jump to get aboard this ship. What could be a better thing to jump across the sea than a fire horse? I had to agree with her, considering the firepower she has for her defense and looking down at the sea below us, would truly like to get these feet on a ladder. Brann and I board our wooden ladders and begin our short walk to the top. Within a few steps, I feel a flash go past me as I watch a fire horse diving over Brann. I brace myself for the shock of this. Nevertheless, I feel two yielding hands wrap around me, and a soft voice say, "Fear not, my Master, for you are in my hands." My Connubial Angel is kissing me on the back of my neck. I can recognize her kisses anywhere. As I near the top of this ship, I am flooded with many sets of hands coming out toward me, grabbing whatever they can. So many voices, "We have you Master, do not fear." Now this is the time to use my brain and not my pride time. With the love of my wives controlling me, these words flow from my lips, "Oh, thank you, wonderful wives, for I thought that fish may be enjoying me for their evening meal. How can I ever repay all you?" My Queen surprises me with, "What about the group private time our Master?" The other wives, after shaking off their first confusion begin to plead as well. Therefore, I say to them, "I must admit loving such beautiful women is much better than being eaten by the creatures from the sea." I then ask them, "Did I just agree to group private time?"

They all, standing while their ground, not willing to sacrifice their newly gained reward, say with a big, "Yes." I then ask, "What about this private time with our group?" They all start hitting me saying, "No. We want this private group time. You promised?" Realizing that I am dealing with seven women here, I follow the road my Grandpa taught me, "Oh my mistake, will you please forgive me? However, I worry so much about Nógrád, Baranya, and Brann. Who will be with them, for we are on a strange ship in a weird place?" I can see the excitement of my wives dry up now, as they pair up as best, they can with our three friends. Then a soft, sweet voice calls out, "Siklósi, I will host your friends while you care for your wives' hearts." We stop and look over at a woman who is the same height of Gyöngyösi and has the same type of eyes as Ajkai. She is wearing beautiful red with yellow emblems repeated throughout her long gown. Unlike Gyöngyösi, always shows her left shoulder, the woman reveals her right shoulder. Her wrappings are loose around her, not bringing any attention to any part of her body. This allows my wives to be more at ease. She wears no shoes as we can see her clean soft feet. Her wrapped hair forms a large ball over her head, which grabs my wives' attention. She has bracelets, necklaces, and special jewelry to hold her hair as she wishes. She has élite paints on her face and eyes that reveal a true beauty. My wives will be exploring that. She walks on her toes toward us as every female in this group rushes around her smiling and firing off great compliments. She stops and gracefully opens her arms, and exchanges hugs with my womenfolk. They dare not kissed her, for fear of messing up her perfectly applied facial paints. Khigir asks her, "Oh beautiful woman, what can we do for you and please tell us your name?" She pauses, looks at Khigir and replies, "I am called Abaúj and I, have been put here to serve you wonderful creations.

Now, go to receive your reward from your Master for saving his life." She looks at me, releases a graceful laugh, and continues, "Because he appears to fall into danger exceptionally easily." At this, she gives me a wink, which almost floors me. Gyöngyösi answers quickly, "We will receive our rewards later, for he is sometimes weak, and may need this rest. We want to know more about you and your beauty."

Darn, they just dumped me instead of a stranger. This bouncing from mountains to valleys can be confusing at times. Nevertheless, I would also like to know more. Therefore, I will just step off to the side. Abaúj will have no part of this, and tells my wives, "Precious wives, I will tell you everything as we will be on this ship for many weeks. Now go to collect your reward. Follow me to your special room, while I show your friends where they will be staying. Follow me." My wives look at her and notice, although she has a peaceful disposition when she says something in her manner that others will follow her wishes. She is the type that would stand her ground peacefully until others grant her request. Anyway, she is only guarding their reward, so the wives fall in line behind her as Khigir grabs one of my arms, and Hevesi grabs the other and pulls me with the group. I know not to look too excited about what they have planned for me, or they will tighten my reins. They are feeling pretty much in control of me now, so things should go smoothly. Abaúj further explains, "Your great love is why you may see many wonderful mysteries that so many others are forbidden. Please keep your love as a priority." Gyöngyösi jumps behind her, as all the other wives, except for my two guards, leap behind her. When Gyöngyösi follows a request, we know there is this somewhat spiritual meaningfulness, which we should honor. I actually suspect that she is just enjoying another as small as she is. Nevertheless, her heart is always in the right place, as I cannot believe she can do wrong. The white furs look so much larger from this wooden floor. The large trees run through the woody floor on this ship. Berettyóú is giving them this good wind now as we are moving out into the sea. I ask Abaúj, "Abaúj, why is the time with my wives, and I so important to you?" She lowers her head and says, "My Masters told me that a thing you called love was the power throughout the universe. I do not want the universe to crumble." Khigir looks at her and says, "Have you ever seen love Abaúj?" Abaúj began to cry, saying, "I have never seen it, nor, as my Masters tell me, as this is so much better felt." Khigir looks at me and I tell her, "Honey, it is against our loves." Gyöngyösi slaps me and says, "No dirty boy, just to see and feel it."

I tell them, "What if you guys get carried away and scare her?" Khigir gives the perfect answer that all seven of my wives agree with, "We will blame it on you." I then reach over and kiss her and say, "At least you all still love me." Abaúj afterwards looks at my wives and responds, "I do not understand this, for you are going to accuse an innocent of doing a wrong, and he is going to allow you." Makói examined her and said, "Abaúj, that is my love, for our Master understands our ways and loves us for these things." Abaúj responds, "It almost sounds like foolishness." Brann then says, "Wait until they do their show for us." I look at Brann and ask, "How do you know, have you been peeking?" Brann joyfully confesses, "We three, sometimes stand next to you, and you do not notice." Hevesi tells me, "Yes Master, I have seen them in our room with us." at once; I ask Hevesi, "Why did not you tell me?" Hevesi answers calmly, "And stop all the fun, are you crazy?" My remaining loyal and honorable wives clap and cheer her answer. I ask them, "What? You all have the same style bodies. Mine is the one that was illegally shared." Brann looks at me and says, "Is it okay if you illegally share it, watching only, again tonight?" I reach over and kiss her saying, "Anything for you my dear." Khigir jumps between our faces looking at Brann and says, "Remember girls, watching only." We hear a whistling voice ask, "May I watch and touch my friends?" We are looking around and startled, notice two large purple eyes looking at us. Khigir answers, "Of course, sweet and kind Berettyóú, and if he does not obey us, you can spin him around in the clouds for a while if you wish." Berettyóú jokingly replies, "Khigir; your generosity is taking my breath away." Abaúj now appears flabbergasted and asks Berettyóú, "Oh mighty wind, please keep your breath, so we may continue our voyage." Berettyóú then cheers Abaúj by saying, "You never cease to amaze me Abaúj." I must now confess that I feel somewhat awkward about this, since I know my wives will be showing off, and I could get hurt if they make a miscalculation. Who ever heard of seven wives bringing in four female friends as an audience?

I have created this strange family that. A quick deeper reflection reveals to me that they are proud of their servant skills they have developed and want a chance to get this respect from their peers for these talents. As for me, I am not inviting any of my friends to adore my talents. If any challenge me, I simply invite them to look at their smiles and happiness. This is a victory for me every time. I am at the mercy of my wives on this adventure. If I create anger in them, they will have a female wind bounce me off the clouds. I never really worry much about Brann and Baranya, as they are accordingly special and have been in my heart for so long. It is the innocence of Nógrád and Abaúj, which worries me. I cannot see what is in this for them, except if they enjoy it; they might give themselves too quickly to the first deceiver who promises them love. The other extreme would cause even worse damage in that they consider it not to be for them and when their true man arrives, they would chase him away. Why does Khigir always get me in these situations? I wave for Brann and Baranya to come over to me and ask them if they take care of Nógrád, and Abaúj during this exhibition. Khigir sticks her beautiful, gorgeous face in from behind them and tells them thanks for helping us. Each of them pops her with a kiss on the cheek, while I grab her and kiss her powerfully on the lips. Hevesi cheers and screams, "They cannot make it. We must hurry." She grabs hold of Khigir and me and starts pulling. Abaúj asks, "What is happening?" Gyöngyösi tells her, "We must get into the chamber you have chosen fast because love it burning them up too swiftly." Abaúj tells everyone to follow her, and those soft little feet begin moving quickly across the desk and down the lovely steps. We did not expect steps like this one a ship. This thing must be of a greater luxury than we suspected. The steps even have a fabric attached to them. What a novel idea. Abaúj rushes us down a wide, floor also covered with fabrics that have strange lights on its walls. These lights have many different colors and emit no smells. I will ask her about that later, for now I had an entire ship filled with women in heat floating over a sea I never knew existed and a wind that wants to give me a trip I will not forget.

Oh, where is Grandpa when I so vitally need him? I will do as I always do when they all decide it is smoke Master time. This requires me to kiss the beautiful face, which struggles, its way through to me. This torments me that a woman would have to struggle with other women to kiss her husband. Another factor that pesters my soul is the woman who is struggling to kiss her husband has our baby in her womb. This is why I am so much more comfortable with our personal private time. During this time, the participating wife receives the care and attention that she rightfully deserves. How in the heck did Khigir get me into this situation? She could reject so many begging candidates until she got her clutches on me, and now it is, 'look what I have, do you want to share this with me?' This is at the expense of Hevesi, and I am exploring in the tamed wilderness around our mountain peak. I just lay and kiss and what they do to the rest of my poor innocent body is up to them. As any try to regulate, their behavior is going to put me personally with Berettyóú in a place I would prefer not to be. Especially considering that, my sky jumper could be an ally with her. I am so confused; I had a wild notice that we were going to go on a peaceful sea voyage to a mysterious land. I did not know I was the mystery that was going to another land. Confused or not, I hold my marriage vows strongly and have always, since the day Khigir tied me up and kissed me, considered that if they gave me their body than I had to give them mine. The logic of this is the couple forms one, so something from each must be provided to fulfill a need on the other's or in my case another's needs. So what the heck, as long as they clean up my blood and wait until I die before they feed me to the dogs, or on this boat to the sea creatures, I should have no concerns. I just hate the idea of getting blood on this comfortable fabric floor. We are in my chamber now as Brann and Baranya have secured our two innocent, and currently looking terrified observers. At least, I am not the only one terrified. It is not fear of the physical here; it is fear that one of my wives will have an emotional need left unfulfilled. That scares me the most.

My wives are now spreading out the super-high quality luxurious blankets keeping me in the center as Hevesi has her sword resting against my shoulder where I can see its razor-sharp Boshi or curved edge tickling the hairs of my neck. Abaúj has jumped twice currently to save me, yet both times Brann and Baranya pulled her back. I am trying to look like I am suffering; however, I am now worried that Abaúj may harm one of my wives trying to defend me. I ask Hevesi, "Hevesi; I know how to speed my wives." Hevesi asks me how I can do this. I tell her, "Put your sword over against the wall and come backward here jumping in my arms, and we will get a jump on them, sounds good." Hevesi tells me as she is pulling back her sword, "Master, you know I trust you, so please do not cheat me out of a strong hug and kiss, okay my Master." I tell her to hurry, so I will not hurt myself standing in one position without making a move. She jabs me in my rear end lightly with her sword and says, "Do not move dirty boy." I start to laugh, then quickly pull myself together. Abaúj watches with somewhat more ease as she sees me laugh and Hevesi takes her sword back to the wall. What she sees next shocks her. She tries to explain to Brann, "Oh Brann, look at what she what looks at '*she dropped a no her she dropped my dress,*' no her dress and she is walking to your Master. What can she do if he sees her? Oh, no she is jumping into his arms; he is now holding her with her specials touching him. Which one is holding whom? Is he hurting her? How can they breathe? The other wives see these and gowns go flying as they all fight for a position against me." Khigir yells, "Timber," which means I am going down fast. Moreover, as the Lions take down a grazing animal, down I go. My wives do not know of anything else in the world now. They are where they want to be, while taking complete advantage of this. I am so proud that they are taking what I promised them. My sweet babies are not organized creatures of prey, and this prey is defeated. Without notice, our ship begins to rock hard to one side. We can feel wind pushing us in a strange direction. I look over and see the door open and a breath-taking special purple eye looking in at us. Berettyóú's wind knocked Abaúj to the floor, inviting her to ask, "Berettyóú, why did you knock me to the floor and the wives across the room?"

Berettyóú looks around and sees us reforming for another round, confesses, "I thought the way the wives were locked onto the Master whom he was using this strange force to hold them against him." Gyöngyösi roles over and explains, "Berettyóú, the force that is locking us is our love, as even our Master cannot move for its power." Berettyóú informs Gyöngyösi that she may have accidentally blown off all their gowns, and if we want her to put the dirty boy against the wall until they redress. Gyöngyösi tells them, "Oh you who are learning of love do not understand." She stood up and continued, "When each of us pledged our love, we also pledged our body to our Master. What you see of me now, is not mine it is my Masters. It is his garden for him to plant his seeds. He has planted his seed in each of his wives you see fighting to love him the best they can. He is a living new life in each of our wombs. What we do here is the battle of our hearts wanting so much to thank him for all that he does naturally for us. Our Master is unlike the other Masters who only take, beat, and abuse. Our Master gives us power over him, when in private of course, because in our homelands, if the Master does not rule his wives with an iron hand, the wives are executed. Our Master truly cares for each of us, and that among the power of our love. We joke and play games, as you already know, from the beach, because of our love. We will never live without our Master; therefore, our love is in every breath we take. Abaúj, do not be afraid, the only hurting, you see, is the struggle to get more love, what you see as painful is actually incredibly exotic and an experience that makes a woman's body stronger and complete. Nógrád has heard much louder and crazier than this tonight and can attest, we are all normal within a short time. Fear not, for inside us exists the rage for the wild and free. During our sanity, we simply work to find the protection we need to have a place for our freedom to fly free. I now return to my freedom and do not care if any, approved or not, for I search for my Master who I have sealed in the heart that feeds blood to my body." This time was different from so many of our other times, and I believe this is because they were on a ship the host and winds were protecting them. Naturally, we probed Berettyóú if it were okay that we close our door, telling her it was our custom. She agreed to consider because she had seen this so many times from the Lamentans. We truly just wanted to close our doors so as not to arouse or scare her, because with temperament, we could end up traveling to one of our moons. When my wives had finished, they cleaned each while dawning their gowns. I will confess that I had no remaining energy. I just lay here without moving, as is our normal procedure, as my wives always take me, cleaned me, and reward me with a, much-needed massage. Abaúj and Nógrád, not knowing this rushed to me throwing a blanket on my different body parts and started crying softly over me. I asked them, "Why do you cry?" They answer, "We had before believed you to be the abuser and never dreamed that our sisters could be so horrid toward you." I told them, "Abaúj and Nógrád, you are innocent of these things. My wives did no wrong. I promised to be a well of love for them to drink and receive the love that makes them thirsty. I take great pride in that my wives may feel free to take from me. What is theirs?" Nógrád further adds, "All this time living with you, I believed your wives to be happy by disposition. Now I know that come to their Master who cares for them. Abaúj continues, "Where can I find a Master as great as you?" Khigir places her hands on Abaúj's shoulders and answers, "I do not know sweet Abaúj, such as men are so hard to find. Sometimes when you see them, you must take them by force and keep them by love. Our Master does not have seven wives because of his ways with words, but because of his way with deeds. He does not take love, but as you have witnessed, gives love. Where are your cleaning rooms?" Abaúj told us to follow her. She took us down this more steps and into this empty room through a window. She then gave me a floating device that has a long rope attached to it. Abaúj opened the window and told me to get on top of the steps and to step out into the large string and wood container. I stepped into it and the cold seawater of the northern waters. Abaúj told me to move around to keep warm.

She pointed at a bucket attached to the ship. She told me to remove it, fill it with water, and dump in on my head. This was instrumental in adjusting my body to this water, for now I could whiz around having this fun. Abaúj yelled out for me to return with the ship by walking up the row of steps that she extended out from the ship. She had a wheel in, which would crank out the steps. Amazingly, this is such a simple design and extremely clever in its role. I walked up the steps, climbed back into our ship. Abaúj removed my buoyant device and asked if some of the wives wanted to practice attaching the floating devices and spin the wheel to control the movement through the steps. She also told them never to go in when the window has the red board over it, or when the water is above the black line along the outside the ship. If you do not see the black line, stay aboard the ship. Tselikovsky had a confused look on her face. Abaúj gazed at her and continued, "We do this because of the danger that a current through the water could pull you out of our flexible container." Tselikovsky smiled, as she now understood this. We have to believe that if sweet little Abaúj tells us something, it is for our good. My wives now hover over me as if I am the honey, and they are the bees. As they are drying me, and making sure, they cleaned every little inch, including behind my ears. While they were working on me, Abaúj called for Khigir to join her. She gave her a bottle of superior oils to rub on my skin. This oil actually felt decent as it released some heat throughout my body. My wives next gave me a pleasurable massage, and afterwards, I felt as if I was brand new. Now that we had all my womenfolk both educated and rejuvenated, we might be able to focus on this journey. Abaúj sits down with me to show Khigir, and me where we are going. Khigir is sticking unusually close to me. I wonder in my mind, what she expects, she shows this pure little innocent woman a presentation that is supposed to glorify Carnal Knowledge, and expect her to stay reserved. Abaúj is acting different around me, and the difference is more of a feeling of being in tune with me. If I ask her a question, she strives hard to answer it. She may actually be in love with me; a love that developed from seeing how controlled in was in defying every idea that she had of man and woman.

Abaúj now lays this large piece of blue and green something on the table before us. She tells us it is paper, which they made from trees. Hevesi feels it and tells her it does not smell, feel, or even tastes like a tree. Abaúj tells her that is because they have changed it through their magical equipment. I tell my wives, if Abaúj calls it paper, and we have never seen it before, then we will call it paper, until we find another word. Abaúj winks at me and continues. When she winked at me, Hevesi kicked me in my chest, and Khigir jabbed me in my side. Abaúj began to laugh at us. Khigir asked her, "Why do you laugh?" Abaúj tells her, "You protect that which you cast out for all to enjoy so short of a time ago." I told Abaúj, "Abaúj, it was okay because they are really telling me they love me. That is the way married women show their love for their husband." Abaúj looked at Khigir

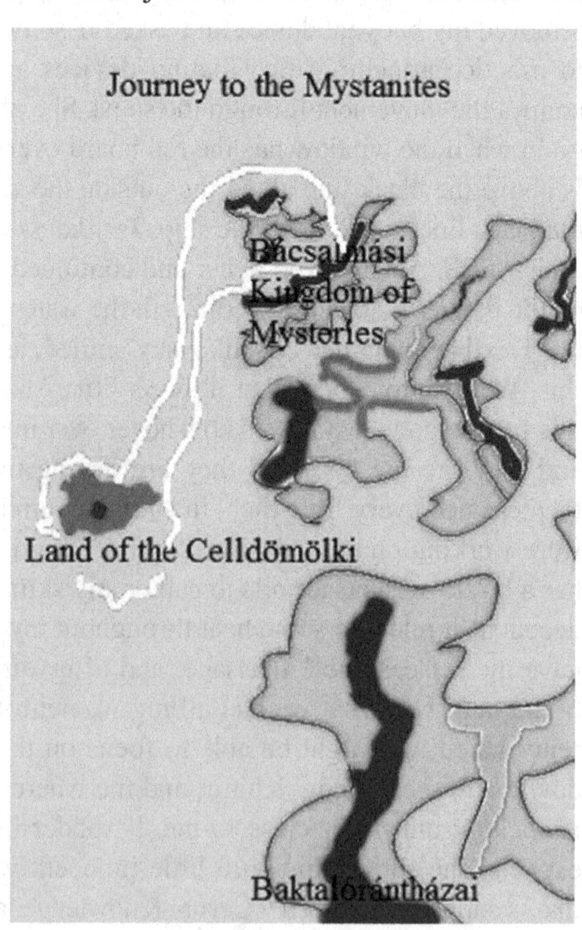

and asked, "Will you be offended if I do not take part in this version of your love, for I prefer to keep your husband strong in case of danger." Khigir began laughing, since Abaúj caught her then replies, "Sure Abaúj." Abaúj displayed painted objects that she said were islands. She revealed chestnut markings that identified mountain and the blue to symbolize the sea. She had light umber to represent desert. She showed us Baktalórántházai at the bottom of our map. She ran her finger to her right to the small green patch. Then across the blue to a spot where the desert and green met the sea, looked at Khigir and said, "This is your Tamarkin homeland." Continuing, she moved her hand back to Baktalórántházai, and ran it up to the second island from the top explaining that this is the route; we took to arrive where she had joined us. Resuming, she ran her perfect finger across the blue showing us how we would sail around the top island. Afterwards, we would then cross the sea to a secluded island called the Land of the Celldömölki. Later, it the Lamentans called it the Land of the Mystanites. It was in the alone on the sea. Resuming a liberal circling of the island telling us there were the important small islands we must visit. She finished by showing us, with her finger, our journey back to the Bácsalmási Kingdom of Mysteries and then to Baktalórántházai. I looked at her and asked, "What is a paper that shows the lands of Lamenta such as this called?"

She smiled at me and said, "Master; it is called a map." Hevesi asks her, "Abaúj, our precious love, why do you call him Master?" Abaúj responds, "Because this is his ship. Does this offend you?" Khigir comes over smiling and hugs her saying, "He is your Master also Abaúj." I gave Khigir a curious look as I wonder, 'did I propose to another woman?' Abaúj looks at Khigir, "Khigir, do not fear me crossing into your territory, for as Brann and Baranya, I am furthermore, from another element. I only want to behave as you do, so as not to be weird or foreign. Does this reduce the tension you have inside you?" Khigir looks at her and massaging Abaúj's face gently with her hands apologizes for her behavior. Abaúj conveys to Khigir, "That is fine Khigir; there will always be adjustments that must be made when different elements are working together."

Hevesi asks her, "Abaúj, what element are you?" Abaúj smiles and Hevesi and says, "My dear, Lamentans do not know of our element, as soon we will be leaving for a new world. I cannot show you my element, for to do so would destroy you." I confess to her, "Abaúj, whoever designed your Lamentan body did an excellent job." She affirms that it was hard to pick a body, and they want it pleasing enough as not to be able to gain respect, yet not so pleasing that it distracted the Lamentans and create unnecessary strife." Khigir tells us she needs to get back to the wives. I tell her that Hevesi, and I am going to explore this ship. She gives me my good-bye kiss and asks Hevesi, "Are you going to keep him in line?" Hevesi pulls out her sword and affirms her purpose. Khigir laughs and tells us they will be waiting. I look at Abaúj and ask her to stand beside me. This is because I want to touch another element to discover how it feels. She assures me that it will feel Lamentan as it did, even though I have Hevesi jumping in my pocket. Abaúj laughs and tells me, "I would think your wives would not need any more attention for a long while." I told her, "Abaúj this is not for attention; it is for retention. They have that right, considering they have played by the rules in getting their property." Abaúj looks at me seriously, and now asks, "Do you think they would be more comfortable if I asked my rulers to send another to host your family?"

Hevesi screams out, "Oh no Abaúj, We have nothing but great love and admiration for you. We just have to work harder to make sure the dirty boy does not do anything he is not supposed to do." Abaúj then smiles and says, "So you are telling me that if I get a dirty boy to do something he is not supposed to do that you will punish him and not me?" Hevesi smiles and sighs, as she shares, "Oh Abaúj is not love such a wonderful thing?" I jump in now crying, "Hey wait, where is my justice?" Abaúj comes over exceptionally close to me, scaring Hevesi and says with a newly released voluptuous voice, "Oh, is not love so wonderful dirty boy?" Hevesi yells out, "Hey seductive woman. You are squashing me." Abaúj jumps back looking down my shirt pocket and pleads, "I am so sorry Hevesi did I hurt you?" Hevesi, while laughing, remarks, "Not as bad as you heated up our dirty boy." I tell them, "Hey angels, I am more interested in my ship than women now, so let us begin the tour." Abaúj agrees and walks in front of us. I cannot believe this. She is doing a wiggle in front of me. Hevesi tells me, "Hold on Master, this could be a rocky walk, of which your clumsiness could put us in the sea." Abaúj looks back and asks us, "Is everything okay?" Hevesi tells her, "It could not be better for dirty boy. He is enjoying your wiggles when you walk." I look at her and say, "I was not Abaúj; do not believe everything they tell you." Abaúj looks at Hevesi and explains, "This is the way I saw Ajkai and Gyöngyösi climbing the ladder, and our Master appeared to enjoy it. It is good or bad that I copied this walk so our Master would enjoy it?" Hevesi warns her, "I would not let Khigir catch you walking like that, because you do this walk much better than us, and we fear silly boy will walk off this deck into the sea." Abaúj thanks Hevesi for her honesty and good counsel and asks her if she helps do the acceptable behaviors among our complex family. Hevesi agrees and I reveal to Abaúj, "Abaúj, Hevesi has saved me accordingly much heartache, and I value her recommendations to such a degree that I follow them, even when I feel awkward doing so. That is why I keep her as close to my heart as Khigir will allow." Abaúj now asks, "As you are married to all your wives, do not they all have equal positions."

Hevesi explains the Abaúj, "Ordinarily; however, this family would have formed in a distinctive fashion. Khigir is the wife. She was the one that forced the Master to add his other wives. We are all so thankful that she shared what was hers that we strive hard to give as much back as possible." Abaúj shakes her head and remarks, "Your group is destroying all that we knew Lamentans." Hevesi and I laughed as I told Abaúj, "My dear, we are only scratching the surface." Abaúj rebuts with, "I have seen how you scratch the surface." I smile and say, "We will reach our destination before I know anything about this boat." Abaúj shifts our discussion reverts backward to this ship telling that this style of ship will first appear on Lamenta after the great Empire of the justice rules most of

Lamenta. We pulled this ship back into this period only for this trip. We will return it at the completion of our mission. They built these ships during the last parts of the great raids to transport troops and supplies. They use these ships for humanitarian purposes after the great wars. You can see above us the twelve large sails made from special fabrics that are difficult to destroy. They can capture about everything that Berettyóú can blow on them. This ship has a bladed frontal appearance. This design allows the ship to flow faster into the sea. We will use the deck for catching the rays from our suns and this natural outdoor time. The circular windows that you see along the sides are for combat operations. Our forces remolded the lower decks in this vessel for this journey. The first deck has the luxurious gathering room in which you all behaved as animals last night. I told her that I had not behaved like an animal. Abaúj smiled and winked at me saying, "Whatever. You were the sneaky little devil that was tormenting those poor helpless women." Hevesi told her to add, "Love depraved." Abaúj looked at me and said, "How could you deprive such angels of the love they need to survive?" I respond saying, "Abaúj, because I want a tour around the ship. I am now a beast to my wives; here help me through this one into the sea." Hevesi cries out begging, "Oh Master, forgive me. I am innocent. I think that different element junk from Abaúj is altering my senses. Relax, I can help you figure out a way to punish me and forgive me."

I reviewed her and said, "You actually think that I would throw my heart into the sea?" Hevesi said, "I worry that Abaúj's beauty will turn your mind to be mad." I told Hevesi, "Honey, you were one of my wives, actually the latest one, and in your case, we saved the best for last, will you agree?" Hevesi answers with a question, "If I agree will you promise not to throw me into the sea?" I winked at her and Abaúj as we each had our little chuckle. Abaúj continued, "That same deck has an enjoyable dining area. The remainders on the floor are composed of individual rooms to be used or recreated based on your needs. The design of the second deck is for hosting any who boards this ship as your guests. We have another dining area, plus a large entertaining area. The third deck is our sleeping area, fantastically comfortable rooms and your marriage sleeping room, as your family has the curious sleeping habits." I asked her, "What is so strange with my wives sleeping with me?" Abaúj then tells me to calm down, that was just some injection of humor. She further explained the fourth deck was for storage, and the cleaning room that I have visited today. I asked her, "As for the dining room for us and for any guests, how does that work?" Abaúj looks around and tells me, "Oh, I forgot to tell you, we must start fishing fast before we enter the no fish areas." I looked at her and laughed, "Okay, funny bunny, come on over here and let me give you something to make you laugh." She innocently, apparently not having solid grasps on the functions within the body she is in, comes over to me, and challenges me. "Go ahead silly boy, and give it a shot, okay," not knowing the consequence flows from her mouth. Hevesi tells her, "Wrong move girl," and lays securely down in my pocket. I begin to tickle her. The first few tries did not produce any results as she looked at me and asked, "Is this one of your sex things?" Subsequently, I hit one of her spots, and she began laughing, as I continued to find her spots.

She lay over my arms begging me to stop, while laughing hysterically. I finally stopped and lifted her soaked body back up so she could breathe. She looked at me strangely, as Hevesi also was laughing. Abaúj asked me, "How did you do that to my body, and what did you do?" I looked at her with a grin and responded, "Now, you know why most of the women on this boat call me Master." I did a changed wiggle and went to join my wives. I must not have walked fast enough, for she caught up with me and wrapped her arm around mine and said in her soft voice, "Are you mad at me dear?" I informed her that I was just tired from such a busy day and asked her how long before we made it to the Land of the Mystanites. She told me, "Almost two weeks to arrive there; however, the return trip will go much faster." Our remaining womenfolk were waiting on the deck for us. As we arrived, Khigir came rushing over to hug me. She freed my arm from Abaúj sense she had not stepped aside.

Abaúj looked confused as Ajkai explained, "Once again, we will tell you the Master is Khigir's husband. Step aside when she claims her prize, jump in when she walks away." Abaúj asked us to follow her to our sleeping rooms. She opened the door to the grand bedroom on the second floor and told Khigir, "Take what is yours and sleep here." She looked at Brann and said, "You others, will you please follow me? Now tell me how you want to use all these rooms?" Brann, Baranya, and Nógrád each selected rooms at the end of the hallway. Abaúj went to the room with the red door. As my head hit the cushion, I dropped into a deep sleep, thinking that a night of rest was ahead of me. Our ship began to rock strongly back and forth halfway or so through the night. I could hear the waves bashing hard against our ship. Special dishware that came from the future began to bounce off walls splattering everywhere. A big wave hit us head-on and almost had our ship sailing vertical in the sea. I was trying to see what was happening and was in the hallway when our ship began to stand. I yelled for my wives to stay in our room. Fortunately, Abaúj's red door was in the hallway above me. She released a rope ladder down to me. I grabbed it and began climbing to the lavish entranceway to our floor.

Brann and Baranya came up beside me floating in the hallway and asked me if I needed a hand. I told them, as our ship was beginning to lay in the sea again, "We need to discover what is happening. Go check Abaúj and we will meet along the entrance step way for this floor." As I was entering the entranceway, my two Tamarkins jumped beside me. I looked at Khigir and said, "I asked you to stay in our room for your safety." She explains, "Oh Master, I had to bring Hevesi for you. You forgot her." She turns around, and I pull Hevesi out of her special back shirt pocket. I slide her in my shirt pocket as she is yelling at me, "Why did you forget me, do not you need me to protect you?" I told her, "I was wrong honey; the emergency of this situation confused me." Brann and Abaúj go forward and try to open one of the doors that led to the first floor of the deck. As they are pushing it, we hear a familiar voice blowing for us, "Keep the door closed children, I am in a big battle out here against the evil winds that are invading." Abaúj thanks her for helping us. Khigir then yells out to Berettyóú, "Please protect yourself and do not get in over your head where you can endanger yourself, because we do love you so much." I later told everyone, and yes, I mean everyone is here now, "We need to fight these wicked spirits with love, so we will all scream out to give our love to Berettyóú." Unfortunately, the evil winds are gaining strength as Berettyóú is fighting with everything she has. The evil winds are bashing us harder and harsher. Berettyóú yells for us to get into the closest rooms because she is going to send our boats into the hallway. Abaúj rushes us to the first room she can find, as all doors open with her voice command, although she had to yell because of the raging sounds of the winds. I go in last and when starting to enter the floor doors come crashing unclosed. I can feel the wind sucking me. My wives and the other women are all holding onto me as best they can. Berettyóú yells for me to hold on and then coughs. Into the room, I go flying as only the Queen may hold onto to me. We can hear the boats clattering as they go down the hallway. I ask Abaúj why our wind sent in these boats.

She tells us, "As a precaution, if she cannot win this fight. We need to work our way to them now, so follow me, and everyone hold onto someone." Khigir asks Abaúj, "Honey, who will clinch onto you?" Abaúj tells her not to worry, for nothing can destroy her elements on Lamenta. Down we walk this hallway, although not vertical, nor horizontal either. We dive from door-to-door until Abaúj hooks us to a rope she has. She gives us belts, which can attach to her rope. Tselikovsky takes a hit with her head against the ship. I can see her blood splattering as she drops to the floor. I release my belt and dive back to her, pulling off a big piece of fabric from her gown to wrap over her head. My heart is pounding in shock. I get up and run toward Abaúj telling her we have an emergency. She opens the next door, and I jump around the room. I order her to get the other women to safety. A lay my blessed Tselikovsky on the bed and began trying to discover how bad her wound is. I lightly shake her head yelling out, "Speak to me my Secret Dove, and speak to me." My body is trembling; I am panicking as I feel across the top to her head. I cannot feel anything broken as I hear a soft voice with warm fingers touch saying, "She will be okay my husband." I turn around, and see my angel. I impart to her as tears' jolt from my eyes, "Gyöngyösi, I can now understand how Grandpa felt when you said the words, 'he will be okay.' I look about the room, and every female on this ship is in here. Khigir and the Queen jump ahead of me to start treating my Secret Dove. I ask Abaúj as she is now rushing into this room, "How far are the boats?" She hands a bag with oils, lotions, and tonics with rags to Khigir and tells me, "Master. I have secured the boats. When danger hits, I will save all you." My wives are treating Tselikovsky by pulling everything from Abaúj's bag and finding a way to use it on my Secret Dove. As Gyöngyösi opens a small bottle, Abaúj yells for her to put in under Tselikovsky's nose and let her smell it. As Gyöngyösi goes to do this, our ship starts to lift out of the water and begins to spin. Tselikovsky starts to choke. We rejoice, as Abaúj asks us, "Why do you rejoice as our ship is now out of the water and spinning?" Ajkai tells her, "Because our sister coughed, she is still alive. We only care about this. Our ship drops hard into the sea. I can hear the boards on the side of our ship starting to wobble. I ask Abaúj, how much will this ship take?"

Abaúj informs us, "The truth; I do not know how much longer I can hold it together, since I am growing frail." As she says the word for weak, we hear a big thunderous burst. The waves start to calm down just a little. We can now hear rain pouring, and Abaúj gets excited. Makói asks her, "Why are you excited over the rain?" Abaúj explains that she heard that evil spirits do not like the rain. As she is speaking, once again our ship lifts out of the water. The winds blow us to one side, and then our ship tosses to the other side. We go through this, a couple of times, and subsequently we hear another large thundercloud, so loud the looking glass in this room shatters. Gyöngyösi tells me that Tselikovsky will be okay, and we rejoice. We now can feel hard pressure against the ceiling above us as another wind is pushing us down fast. Slowly, we are sinking.

We stay cautious because I can hear board snapping on our deck and see our ceiling beginning to bow. We hear a strong wind rush below our ship as it rattles again. Then steadily our ship sits back in the water. The winds are making crazy noises now as we get a good jolt when one of them shoots from the water. The noise continues as our boat rattles. I run over and give my Secret Dove, a big kiss. She yells at me for having blood all over my clothes. I tell her, "You may punish me privately tonight; I will have Abaúj get the whips." Abaúj yells at me, "Are you crazy; I will never give her whips to beat you, which will simply cause more blood." Abaúj is extremely furious now, so inflamed that Khigir goes over to her and tells her, "love. They are purely joking. We will not hurt your boy, okay our love." Abaúj tells her, "I would be even angrier if one of you were to be whipped. I saw the beasts doing that to wilderness people on your other continent, and it was terrible." I notice something strange now. Therefore, I ask my other shipmates, "Has anyone noticed the winds are quiet now?" Abaúj being overwhelmed with great joy shouts, "Berettyóú is saving us!" Thus, another wind pushed hard against our ship. However, this time, another wind pushed back from the other side of our ship. Eerie voices whisper, "Wives, prepare for your raping . . . S . . . *'oooohwhew wwwooh."* Instantaneously we heard some more thunder, yet this time lightning was also striking all around us. We were looking out the two circle windows along our wall. The winds have changed into vicious ball balls of concentrated cloud and striking at our ship.

Even so, as each almost made contact, lightning would strike it, shattering the ball. Shortly after that, another would follow it. Another lightning bolt would hit it. The thunder had already shattered all that it could in our ship. Smaller winds would permeate into our hallways whirling everything unattached item. Abaúj told us to put blankets over us, for she could not guarantee how long our windows could hold. We immediately wrapped ourselves in the available blankets. Just as I had done this, our ship received two hard hits from the black winds. Our windows shattered as our door flew open. Astonishingly, another wind from our hallway entered and pushed the broken, window's pieces back into the sea. Lightning whizzed from this wind, one at each black wind ball as they beat against the walls in our room. The lightning hit the first one. It exploded, blowing a wall of our room through the hallway shattering the wall around the room across from us. The second black wind ball escaped into the hallway. The 'friendly wind from our room chased after it shooting its lightning until soon we heard a large explosion. We escaped from what remained from our room and went into another small room. As Abaúj went to the room, the walls exploded. I grabbed her gown and pulled it toward me. My wives grabbed what they could as we could, though struggling, pull her back to us. Abaúj became angry with us saying, "You should not have endangered yourselves for me." Khigir told her, "Shut up before I hit you. We love you now and as such will die with you!" Abaúj currently looked puzzled and confused. I shook her and gave her a kiss, hoping that maybe I had this magic in my kiss. Her body turned green then slowly regained her normal color. She sprang up and commanded that we follow her. She took us to her red door and flung it open telling us to jump through the door. The strange purple smoke-filled room prevented us from seeing inside the room. We trusted her and thus two by two jumped into the room. I went last with her. As we went to jump in, I could see our ship fragmenting and the sea swallowing it. The last blast knocked both of us down from the door.

Abaúj began floating on the sea. I jumped in, grabbed her, and swam quickly to the red door, which was sinking. I was a great swimmer, from trying to wear out all the swimming trunks my mother had made for me as a child. The red door went into the sea, and as such I pulled Abaúj under with me and we dashed through the door. When we went in, the inside water rushed back into the sea, closing the door behind it. Abaúj told the purple smoke to vanish. I counted my women, and all were present. My wives cheered when they saw us. Abaúj, while giving me a kiss, asked us, "Why are you such fools always trying to save me?" Gyöngyösi explained to her, "We have covered you within our blanket of love

Abaúj. Like it or not, when you are with us, you are us." Abaúj looks puzzled and asks, "I did not know such actions were included in love. I believe that love is only for pleasure." I asked her, "Abaúj, when you saw my wives seeking their love, did I look as one who was receiving pleasure?" Abaúj answers, "Tricky boy, I always believed you to be an actor." I ask her, "Was I acting in the raging sea?" Abaúj, "Actually, no, where did you learn to swim so well?" Khigir tells her, "His mother would make him swim in the special swimming trunks that she made for him, hoping that he could have luck with the possible mates. I will confess that I liked them." Abaúj shakes her head as says, "You Lamentans are strange." Tselikovsky, looking out the windows that are now visible throughout this 'round' room, shouts, "We are in the high dark skies again!" Abaúj asks, "How do you know of the towering black skies?" Khigir tells her, "The love spirits brought us here once." Abaúj exclaims, "I should have done my homework on your people. There shall be many legends flowing through the ages on your adventures." Khigir tells her, "Let the wives put you into something warm and sit beside our Master while we try to figure out what is wrong. They will take you into the corner and change you." Abaúj complains, "Why not change me here?" Khigir warns, "Our Master will see you." Abaúj replies, "Have not I seen him and most all you here. If he wished to do me harm or shame, why would he have risked his life to save me, not once but twice? Change me here, where this blanket of love can warm me."

I went over, with Hevesi in my pocket, to stand beside Khigir and study these skies. Abaúj worries not about me seeing her; however, I have seven wives and three of their friends who are concerned. Therefore, I have the security of Hevesi in my pocket who is watching both my eyes as if she were a hunting bird, while also monitoring my heartbeat. Abaúj enjoys the concept of a love blanket. The same blanket wrapped tightly around me. Khigir directs my attention to the violent spinning spirals below us. Abaúj reveals to her that these are winds fighting. The black winds are evil winds, and the large one in the middle is Berettyóú. Another wind lifts from her shooting its lightning at the dark winds, as we see them beginning to explode. Khigir comments, "Wow, I did not know that Berettyóú could divide herself." Abaúj tells us, "She cannot. Something else is happening. Meanwhile, we need to get her this help." She calls out, "Guiding spirit. We need your help." A spirit answers back, "Why do you have Lamentans in this room. You know this act is forbidden." Abaúj answers, "Where is the ship you gave them, for you know the water making these bodies stop performing. These allied winds are losing to the black evil ball winds, as a few are trying to reach us now. Berettyóú and the other wind are fighting for us, yet they are slowly losing. Will you help them and get us another ship, so I do not have to dress in front of that man who is with us?" The voice speaks, telling her, "Abaúj, why would you fear changing before that man, as we created you exactly as the women who you are among?" Abaúj explains to the voice, "I fear not the man, for he has twice prevented me from stopping to perform. I fear the women who own this man." We hear chattering, which ends as the voice demands, "Abaúj, explain it in your reports. We will now destroy the black wind balls." We watched in our windows as thousands of lightning bolts struck throughout Lamenta. The explosions were so loud that we could hear them from our room in the high skies. Our room begins to descend slowly, and soon we are back into the lighted sky. Two large purple eyes look into our window as Khigir shouts, "Hello our friend."

Berettyóú asks, "Are all your family with you?" Khigir answers, "All, including our newest member Abaúj." Berettyóú replies quickly, "Are you telling me you loosened up hard heart Abaúj." The girls all began laughing as Abaúj jumps up into my arms. I hold her as I will soon hold my children. She reaches up and starts kissing my neck. Berettyóú cheers, saying, "Wow, that love virus that you produce must be contagious." Abaúj leans her head back and asks, "Speaking of friends, where is the wind that helped you?" Another voice spoke, saying, "Hello Ajkai, how are you?" Ajkai looks out the window and answers, "We are doing great, thanks to your friendly winds Móri." Móri answers, "I wish I could have been here sooner; however, for this strange reason, I ended deep into the dark skies. I am back now so I will be with Berettyóú as we protect you during your sea journeys." We laugh, knowing how he ended in deep space. We elected to keep this secret to ourselves. The bright, peaceful sea was growing larger. I saw another ship that resembled the one we had lost, except it was grander and had four large poles growing out of it. As we approached the sea, our room stopped descending and started moving toward our ship. As we got closer, the ship opened while our room went gently into place. This ship closed behind it. Abaúj told me to open the door. I opened it and before me was our brand new hallway. She asked me to stop and spoke to Khigir, "Since I got you a new ship, should not he carries me across the threshold?" My wives yelled at me, "Master, where are your manners? You saved her from the sea and now rush to your newfound bounty. You are being a bad boy!" I look at her and say, "Jump in my arm's sweetheart. She glides up and drops perfectly in place." I whisper to her, "Hug me tight, and start kissing me as much as you can." I walk slowly; despite, these strange creatures called women are cheering her, "Show him what you have Abaúj!" Abaúj asks me, "What do they want me to do?" I tell her, "They want you to show me what you have, so I guess you must remove your garments."

Hevesi yells up, "Abaúj, He is trying to trick you. The wives want you to kiss him harder." I look down at Hevesi, who is now sitting and looking so innocent and blinking her eyes at me. Somehow, in the process, my Tamarkins went down the hallway ahead of me. My first step puts me head-to-head with them as they, both help to ease Abaúj to the floor and tell her that her performance was outstanding. Khigir asks Hevesi, "What was all that whispering?" Hevesi tells her, "She was muddled over what the wives wanted her to do. I explained the situation to her as best I could, because even our Master and I, were disarrayed." Khigir tells Hevesi, "Wonderful job my best friend." She reaches over, gives me a kiss, and says, "So you are going to be a good boy, I am proud of you." I tell her, "My love, so much as happened, I wonder if we are who we are." Khigir tells me not to worry, for she will take care of me. I wink down to Hevesi as I truly gain more respect for this little genius each breathing moment. She told the truth, or a truth, which is possible to disprove. I got a kiss rather than a kick. Abaúj could not refute this answer and just accepted it as what had happened. I shudder to think what would happen if she were in Grandpa's shirt pocket. No one would be a match for that duel. As it stands now with her in my pocket, Grandpa would have to think long about how to pull tricks on me. Abaúj told us she smelled food and confessed, "I think this love blanket is making me hungry." I told her, "Now, you understand, do your wiggle, and get us to that food, okay princess." We were all famished as most of the wives, except for Khigir and my pocket friend had worked their way around us and found the dining room. Khigir was hanging tight beside me because Abaúj has a wicked wiggle. Hevesi yells at me to slow down my heartbeat because she is taking a beating. Khigir instantaneously elbows me. Oh is not love a wonderful thing, once you get over the pain. I believe that she might have cracked my rib. I must pretend as if nothing is wrong, so I may eat. The alternative is my wives' doctoring me for hours. Oh, is not such love a wonderful thing? I ask Abaúj, "Will you sit among the wives and try to loosen them up, because they have been through a lot today?" She winked and began wiggling to the dining room.

Khigir tells her, "Abaúj, you must not forget to eat plenty because your flesh has also been stressed and will need nourishment to restore itself tonight." She winks at Khigir and replies, "Sure thing sugar." We laugh as Hevesi tells us, "At least she is trying." Abaúj asks, "Did I do wrong?" Khigir tells her, "Oh no sweetheart, you did perfectly." Abaúj smiles, then joins my other side, clamps onto my arm and marches proudly with us to the dining room. When we enter, the three of us go in opposite directions. I stop and put Hevesi on the floor, so she may expand. We always have her expand when eating. After all, we want our daughter to be well nourished. Our food providers offer a feast for us tonight. Abaúj sits across the table from the wives who decided to sit in a row tonight. She starts joking with them about the events of the day. Abaúj is completely relaxed and appears filled with much joy. She jokes about her love learning experiences today. Our women are biting off on this as I can see their backs beginning to relax. One by one, they begin jabbering. Hevesi asks us if she can join them, because they are having all the fun. We nod yes, as we grab an arm, swing her back, and rush to the other table laughing like children. She comes running and screaming, "I have been abused. Someone save me!" This was the crowning spark for our family, as even Berettyóú peeks her eyes in our room and asks, "Are you okay?" Abaúj stands up, with food all over her face and replies, "We have never been better!" Berettyóú comments to Móri, "Now do you believe me. She is so strange currently. Those Lamentans have washed her mind." Móri tells her, "She needs the happy times for all the ages she has served so sternly." Berettyóú agrees as they rock the ship once for us and leave laughing. I cannot imagine how I could ever explain these events to Grandpa or for that matter, anyone. It will be best for me to continue with my mind diary that Gyöngyösi is helping me compile. Khigir looks at me now with her tender look and her sparkling eye's. I instantly tell her, "Oh honey, you promised to stop at seven, and six, and five, and four and . . . ." She interrupts, "I know Master; however, she is so special to us. See how your other wives fancy her." I look over and respond, "Yes the other wives that you gave me do fancy her."

Hevesi interrupts and reminds us, "Do you not remember that she is from another element?" I called Brann over to explain these elements to us. Brann tells us, "There are four elements, Lamentan, air, water, and fire. You are Lamentan. I am the fire, and Abaúj is aerate or air." I ask her, "How do you know she is air?" Brann answers, "By the way; she way, she controls the wind, thunder, and lightning. It is the air that gives her the extra spark in her wiggle that you adore so much." At once, Khigir elbows me. I ask Khigir, "Why did you hit me. Brann is the one who said it?" Khigir answers, "Because she is my friend, and you behaved in that manner in front of her." I began to defend myself catching her elbow preparing to hit me again and at once said, "Yes dear, I was wrong." Khigir lowers her rib buster and bends over instead giving me a kiss telling me that she forgives me. I thank her and then thank Brann and suggest that she go burn someone else for a while. She laughs and does her wiggle back to the table; she was eating with her clique. Khigir looks at me and I quickly respond, "Oh no honey. I do not mess with fire." We laughed and returned to join our group. Brann was only wiggling to celebrate getting me in trouble, which since it is in sport. I have to congratulate her. I will ask Baranya the next time, since a focused horse is safer than a woman is. Abaúj now pops her head between us and thanks us for wanting her. I wave for Baranya to join us and ask her, "How did Abaúj know what we were saying?" Baranya answers, "My friend, you spoke using her air." I looked at Khigir, "You know, even though we cannot marry, she would go exceptionally well with Brann and Baranya as a member in our family. And with her among us, you might be able to improve your wiggle." Ouch, her elbow got me again. I am beginning to think that whoever made women gave them this special capacity to afflict pain on their men with the speed of lightning. Because they consider me to be domesticated, I sit here and smile, receiving another kiss on my cheek. We finish eating, joking, and our food fights of which I could not pass. To show there is no justice anywhere, I threw the grapes at Makói hitting four of my wives. Tselikovsky grabbed an apple and fired it at me hitting Khigir instead. I believe her recent head injury has temporarily altered her precision. The apple spins through the room, at a woman's fast speed, and then surprisingly splashes off Khigir's head. Khigir shook it off and started hitting me.

As I turned my face the opposite way, Tselikovsky slapped me. This time something else happened that made all the wives begin laughing and saved me a few weeks wrapped in beds while my injuries healed. Abaúj was pounding on my back yelling, "Bad boy." When I heard her laughing and realized she was hitting me, even I burst into laughter. When she realized we were all laughing at her, she stopped and put her hands over her face and started to run to the door. I jumped at her catching her gown. That gave my Tamarkins time to grab her arms. Khigir asked her, "Abaúj, what is wrong?" She, as tears are flowing down her wonderful unpainted face because our little swim washed her face completely, "I am a fool, and you laugh at me. I now am filled with shame." I pick her up, even though she is trying to kick me my wives are holding her feet, and sit her on our table. Gyöngyösi, who helps me with emotional issues, starts wiping her tears while kissing her cheeks. The other womenfolk, or should I say potential women arrows, surround us looking sad. Gyöngyösi places her soft palms on Abaúj face, shifts her head, so they have eye-to-eye contact, and asks her, "Why do you cry my friend?" Abaúj confessed, "I acted as a fool, and now you think of me with shame." Khigir moves in from the right as I move in from the left. We both start kissing her, and I say to her, "Abaúj, could those around you, kiss you like this if they thought you had brought shame on them." Abaúj answers, "I do not know how you Lamentans think anymore. My mind is so confused." I then ask her, "We laughed because you were behaving as one in our family, and this made us all consequently, happy." Abaúj looks at each one speedily, "You do not think of me as a fool?" My baby dolls poured it on this with all denying her charge. I would perish entering a store in which they were the venders. They would get every coin I could gather. Charmers with innocent eyes can melt the most hardened of hearts. I know to stay on their good side.

I walk to the other side to the table as Khigir is chatting with her ensuring her. We are enormously fond of, and think she is especially special. I now put my hands on her shoulders. I get up on the table and sit down, putting her in my arms releasing a warm hug. Khigir invites everyone to join us. Afterwards, she asks, "Abaúj would you like to be an unmarried member in our family such as Brann, Baranya, and Nógrád. We really want you to be a part of us." Abaúj asks, "What is the difference between being a married or unmarried member?" Brann tells her, "You do not have to let the dirty boy grunt over you." I look at Brann and say, "You talk big, yet I know you would like to have some of that grunting." Khigir looks at both of us with a stern face, which means to stop it. We smile at each other, giving our silly 'we like you' gestures. Khigir explains to Abaúj, "We only marry with those who can reproduce with us. We add our greatest friends as our unmarried family, which allows you to find one of your elements and marry creating your new happy lives. The freedom to mate with reproduction is an enormously important custom for our peoples. We will love you as one in our family, and because we know, you are eager to learn much from us. You will continue to enjoy our show as you did last night. Baranya is not so greatly interested because we are not horses, and Nógrád has deep conservative values that we are slowly trying to melt. We would allow Brann to watch us more; however, every time she does, she gets starry-eyed around our Master following him and making strange sounds. We fear her excitement could burn him." Brann jumps off the table and begins kicking the cups to the floor screaming, "I never did anything like that. After I saw his pitiful performance last night, I could not sleep for laughing all-night. Never have I burned for that dirty boy!" Baranya speaks out, "Hey Brann, cool down, I told you they would catch you." Brann dives across the room, landing on Baranya who holds her tight telling her, "Now be a good kid, after all we are in public." By now, we are all laughing and some beating their heads against the table. Abaúj is petrified and walks over to Brann asking her if she is okay.

When Baranya pulls Brann's face from her chest, Abaúj discovers something she did not expect. Brann is laughing hysterically as well. Abaúj looks at her and asks, "I thought you were filled with anger?" Brann tells her, "Oh Abaúj we are a family. I was having fun, and our special air, was that funny?" Abaúj confesses with a chuckle, "Oh yes, it was funny. I did not want to laugh for fear of shaming you." I tell Abaúj, "Abaúj, you had better let those laughs out before you damage your body." She starts laughing and then loses control as the entire room guffaws riotously. Once again, our ship starts rocking, although this time, we hear the voice in the wind warning us, "Children, pull yourselves together because we have company coming." Abaúj accepts our request. Each of us gives her a fast hug, and we follow her to the deck. She tells us as we go up, "My family, I have never been on this ship previously." Khigir tells her now to worry, for we will improvise along our paths. We exit into the deck. This ship has much better stairways than the earlier one, which also was luxurious. The deck, covered with shiny square marble rocks, and covers all that we can see on this ship. This reminds me of the Edelényi dining and dancing rooms. The sky presents a bright blue, sunny, and cloudless view. Berettyóú is giving us a soft wind, enough comfortably to cool us. We lean against the side of our ship while looking toward the sea and the clear blue sky. This is looking into infinity, as we can see no end. Csongrád alerts us that she sees a small black ball coming toward us. I ask Abaúj if we should do back under deck. She tells us, "We need to wait until we know for sure. You can go under deck or wait by one of the exits. I am waiting here." Khigir and I with Hevesi in my pocket went up to stand beside her. Abaúj queried us why we were not going to safety. Khigir tells her, "You are family now. We stand beside you." Abaúj said, "I almost had the love blanket figured out, and now I have to learn this." I whisper into her ear, "You have plenty of time to learn it." The black light became larger until one side of our ship had a dark sky, while the other side was bright and empty. We were in the clear sea now, for no land appears for at least one week, unless Berettyóú decides to expedite our speed. We could feel a whirling wind going around our ship. Abaúj tells me, "Whatever is trapping us, it docs not want anyone to leave. Oh where are our winds when we need them." Our ship was now sitting still in this sea, as our giant sails hung straight up and down vertically. Afterwards, we heard a large crack in the black and something come crashing through with white, yellow, red, purple, and orange lights flashing everywhere. We could see its mangled body going in many distorted ways. An orange ground appeared on the black sea. Next, we could see beginning to form feet, legs followed by a contorted torso, waiving arms, and then a head. The lights now performed a dazzling dance behind her. She also was dancing. We could only see her silhouette, even though her twirls sometime revealed more legs at both a side and front torso. Our lookout group began to notice the four strong white lights were flowing from her back. Abaúj tells us that these lights are a good sign. These lights now float onto our deck. A voice speaks out, "Who speaks from this giant beast in the sea?" Abaúj gets ready to speak; however, first Khigir and I pull her down and give her a kiss wishing her good luck. Abaúj looks at us strangely and then begins to smile, "You know. I might start liking the family thing." The voice rocks the ship and asks again, "Who speaks in this giant beast from the sea?" Abaúj walks out toward her as I walk from one side and Khigir on the other side. Abaúj answers, "I am Abaúj of the Zalaegerszegi, and I am to take this family of love to the Land of the Celldömölki, as the Mystanites want to visit this love formed beyond all the rules to be." The body and voice stood still for a moment. Abaúj tells us, "She is verifying our story. We will be okay now." Abaúj speaks again, "Is it not customary for those who use my air to tell me their name as well?" The voice says, "Just a moment more Abaúj, I am receiving my orders now." She straight away stood still and said, "My name is Letenyei of the Celldömölki. The Mystanites failed to tell us that you were coming to visit our lands. We welcome you Siklósi, Khigir, and little Hevesi in your pocket. Stand up honey and please wave at me. I will not hurt you." Hevesi stands up and waves saying, "I took one look at you and knew you would not hurt us, so I was simply catching up on some sleep."

Letenyei, "I am told that you are incredibly sage. Now I know you are wise. Is it veritable that you can expand to the other's size and are with child?" Hevesi tells her, "Letenyei that is true; besides, my children will stay the same as the other babies from my Master's wives are." Letenyei then sadly asks Hevesi, "Will not that be a burden on you to provide care?" Khigir went to talk; nevertheless, Abaúj interrupts her, "Oh no Letenyei, because I will do all the work for her as she wishes for me to do." Letenyei challenges Abaúj, "How can you do that for you said you were of the Zalaegerszegi, which we have corroborated." Abaúj responds, "That is true, for

I have yet to tell the Zalaegerszegi the mystery, love family has also adopted me." Letenyei tells Abaúj, "Abaúj, you are from the element air, and they are Lamentans. Leastwise four of them are. Air does not mix with Lamentans." Abaúj tells her, "I know that; however, they have two fire elements as members from their family. Moreover, we are in their family; at the same time, because of the elements may not reproduce and when we find one of our elements and wish to mate we may do so." Letenyei updates us, "I have just been told that nowhere in all our universes has there been a family comprised of three elements." I then tell Letenyei, "My friend Letenyei, we are known for our union of the different species within the Lamentan planet. We begin with my two Tamarkins and myself, which represent the most beautiful from their tribe. After that, we added the Connubial Angel, who has served in the universe for over one million years. Our complete family was on the deck now working their way to us in their nonchalant style. Letenyei looks over and yells, hello Gyöngyösi." Gyöngyösi comes running, screaming, 'Hello Letenyei, sorry I have not visited in a while, the Great Spirits are allowing me to live in love and bear children." Letenyei tells her, "Gyöngyösi, you have earned this privilege considering how many of our babies you have saved. We will never be able to repay you." Gyöngyösi tells her, "I believe when I see their beautiful little faces, I will be completely rewarded. I hope that I did not interrupt anything." She fell in beside Abaúj on my left side, which is close to her position giving me my kiss on the way. I next invited Csongrád to stand before Letenyei.

This wonderful wife is The Royal Highness Queen Csongrád is reigning Queen of the Dorogi. Our baby daughter, once of age will receive her throne. Letenyei then comments, "I have dealt with your father, King Pécsváradi, who has always been honorable with us. His or your kingdom is one of our greatest allies, and we will honor that agreement with you and your daughter Queen Stephana. Are you his daughter who spent most of her time on the sky bridge?" Csongrád answers, "Yes, that is me, and we will honor all my father's pledges. I waited at the sky bridge knowing that true love would find me. One day, from the sky came down Siklósi, Khigir, Tselikovsky, and Gyöngyösi. Khigir had mercy on my pleas. She allowed me to join this family as a wife, and bear children for our Master." Letenyei replied, "If you are his slave, I will free you and take you back to your father. Run, for I will save you." Csongrád immediately fell to her knees before me and grabbed my legs begging, "Save me, my Master." Letenyei pulled her lights back and questioned asked, "My allied Queen, stand so I can save you." Csongrád responds, "Letenyei; you do not understand as my father has given me into married with my Master, so I may produce more Queens. This daughter of mine that you call Stephana, who currently lives in my womb father, I currently hold on to for my salvation." Letenyei looks puzzled, "How can he be a Master of a reigning Queen?" Abaúj answers, "We live under a blanket of love and are a family. We call him, Master because that tells him how much we want to serve him, and the great joy that his love gives us. He is kind, sometimes silly, and sometimes dirty; however, all the time loving and caring." Letenyei, "So my ally's Queen does this for her satisfaction." Csongrád stood up kissing and hugging me, turns her head to Letenyei revealing, "Letenyei. I searched too long for true love to give it up without laying my life down first." I gave Abaúj a quick tight hug and a kiss on the head. She looks at Gyöngyösi and asks her, "Why did he do that?" Gyöngyösi tells her, "Because you described your family and your love so perfectly." Abaúj confesses to Gyöngyösi, "I did not know if what I was saying was true. I was listening with my heart.

Afterwards, I felt foolish and feared you would hate me." Gyöngyösi tells her, "Sweetheart, when you talk from your heart, you will always be talking within the protection of our love blanket. I know it can sound and feel strange. You must stay under that blanket of love, and everything will be good for you. Think about how we feel about the other night behaving like animals. We do not care and would do it again by the name of love." Abaúj confesses, "I never knew this love thing could be so powerful. The Mystanites have good reason for wanting to see this." Csongrád now took her position beside Khigir. I continued, "My next wife is also fantastically special." I waved for Ajkai to come forward. Letenyei shouts out, "No way. I wondered where you had been. Are you telling me you are in with this group also? This is too amazing. How are you Ajkai?" Ajkai tells her, "I have been so wonderful since I have discovered true love. I have my Master's growing son in my womb. I am so happy every day now." Letenyei adds, "I never thought I would hear you confess to serve a Master." Ajkai clarifies that, "I do not serve a Master. I serve my Master who lives within my heart and grows in my womb." Ajkai takes her position beside the Queen. I now motion for Makói to come forward and introduce her, "This one is my special wife, for she has spent most of her life in hiding. She can use metamorphism to change into a ten-foot bear." Letenyei asked us, "I was told you were from Baktalórántházai, is that correct?" I answered, "Yes." Letenyei probed Makói, "I know your species lives on the upper lands on this horse continent. You are away from home are not you?" Makói confesses, "I slipped off to be alone and rather got lost. I stayed in the southern mountains, believing I would be safe. One day, some Sensenite hunters began chasing me as I accidentally ran into their territory. I ran north and as close to the high peaks to such an extent possible. I discovered the secret caves and saw an elderly man appear. I switched back into my human female form and scratched my leg so blood appears. I lay on the ground crying for help. The old man, who turns out to be my husband's Grandpa at once took me to his village at the top of the world and nursed me back to health.

I do not know how he knew what I was; however, he told me I would always be safe in his village and they all welcomed me to live there. Then one day, this family came to our village. Their love spread everywhere, to include me, destroying all my foolish defenses. My Master forgave my ugliness and gave me his seed. I shall give him his son who now grows in my womb." Letenyei appearing to have been sobbing tells her, "Makói, your story is so heartwarming. I truly wish you to keep the great love that now fills you." Makói thanked her and went to stand on my far end. I reached out and grabbed her, while asking Abaúj to make room, because I needed this Makói time. I gave her a few kisses on the face and looked at Letenyei confessing, "We have all searched so hard for this ugliness that she speaks of, yet can never find it." All my wives started clapping saying, "Beautiful Makói," repeatedly. Letenyei says to Makói, "Makói, you have found your family. You no longer belong with the Tapolcai." Makói agreed. I had to hand Hevesi to Khigir and hug Makói so tight. Makói is one who subsequently easily slips through our cracks, taking the back row. I mean to keep her in the center as much as possible, yet events usually progress in an opposite direction. I now motioned for Tselikovsky to come forward and introduce her, "Tselikovsky is the blood sister of Khigir and is also a Tamarkin brought across the sea to mate with me. She holds a special place in my heart and my son and daughter in her womb. We kissed, and she worked her way in beside her sister and the Queen. I now motioned for Nógrád to come forward. "Letenyei," I explained, "this is the one who gives us the most grief, as her species and mine can mate, especially since every one of my children will mate with them, as the Edelényi had enacted new laws to allow this. They may not grandfather any law, which would allow her to marry with us. Their customs dictate that the law at birth remains, in effect, until death. We have made her a part of this family forever and give her what we can, plus the extra privately of course." Letenyei tells her, "Nógrád, we have a great working relationship with your mother nation as we have joined with them fighting to get your supplies and transporters through safely.

I will introduce a political request for your exception, even if we have to link you with our judicious force, which of course gives you diplomatic immunity." We looked at her and cheered fighting to hug her. We love her, and she needs to be a part of us. That could be why she has so many extra rooms on her floor. This always puzzled me. I waved to my fire girls to come forward. Letenyei asked them, "Do I know you, for in your Lamentan form, I cannot recognize you?" Brann tells her, "We are acquaintances, using only passing through to make sure everything is okay. I am Brann, and this is Baranya." Letenyei responds, "I always believed Baranya to be a horse." Baranya tells her, "You are correct Letenyei." Letenyei continues, "You both always go so fast that I can never catch you to chat." Brann tells her, "Oh Letenyei, we have much work to do throughout Lamenta." Letenyei tells her that she understands. I conclude by telling her, "This is my wonderful family of love." Letenyei also adds, "This is an exceptional family. I shall brief the elders of the Mystanites and tell them they shall see something that has truly never existed. If it were not for me knowing so many of you here, I would have declared myself a fool in the early parts of this introduction. I shall go to see how to recruit Nógrád. I confess that I do not know for sure how to do this; however, that does not mean we should not try. I now big my farewell and welcome to the waters of the Celldömölki. Oh, before I leave, I wonder if you well all enjoy dancing to some music on this ship's lovely marble deck." We begged her to provide this for us. She dropped a soft ball onto our deck. Letenyei told us to speak the words to a song and a sample appears. Select what we wish to hear and tell it to sign and play for you and enjoy the richest music performed for the Lamentans throughout your world. The sky returned to its normal condition. Khigir spoke the name for a Tamarkin song, and it began to play. She grabbed me as I grabbed Tselikovsky. The three of us began dancing it the traditional Tamarkin way. My mother taught me this song as a child and how to dance it like a Tamarkin gentleman. The rest of our family began dancing it; however, quickly discovered it was harder than it looked.

My Tamarkins and I had years to practice this great song. My wives were tripping over each other, yet their laughter was filling the great seas with joy and love. I truly never suspected to enjoy such a song like this again. Each of my wives began picking songs, and naturally; they grabbed me to join them. My glory of expertise dwindled quickly as the three of us joined the clan of the fumble feet. That brave, tough Hevesi shrank and had Khigir drop her into my pocket. I enquired from Hevesi, "Honey; you should be out here having fun as the rest of us are. Why hide insecurely when you could be proving to the family that you are truly more foolish than they ever believed?" Hevesi tells me her species have no songs. I instantly looked over and saw Makói sitting at a corner laughing at everyone. I told Hevesi, "Honey, I bet Makói's species also has no songs. You should go join her, and between both of you harmonize the best you can. She needs you." You never tell Hevesi that someone needs her, for she will instantaneously jump to the challenge. She asks me, "Master, as this is your will. I shall obey with my heart. Will you please put me somewhere that I may expand?" I put her on a nearby stool and up she sprang to run over to Makói. She soon began pulling her up, and they began to dance, tripping over each other, more from laughing that trying to dance. My loners were finally enjoying themselves. We danced the night away. We finished by collapsing on our marble deck. A happy family sleeping beneath the stars as Berettyóú and Móri pushed us through the sea. I know Berettyóú believed she was delivering deranged people to the Mystanites. Crazy or not, she liked us. They would push extra hard at night while pushing any potential trouble away from us. We finally made it halfway through the sea. I wrongfully hoped that peaceful sea would be ahead of us.

Chapter 03

Voyage in the sea to Celldömölki

The sea appeared as the clouds do in Baktalórántházai as they cover the lower mountains. They look so calm and inclusive; even so, they are covering up another world. I can only wonder what lies below us, as I do know we have not met one element. This element controls most of Lamenta and even within our own bodies. My mind begins to wonder, until, as in a flash, bombarded with such the peaceful sound of an Angel singing. Her harp is ringing each note so perfectly that even with my eyes closed I can see them floating across the water and embarking within our vessel. This voice harmonizes with the air, sea and, without question, me. She once again sings the words that she once sang for me during our private time when she was blessing me. I must hold tight to the rails here, least in the sea I go. Every time my Angel sings, I feel as if I am with the Great Spirits. I understand how those Great Spirits must enjoy this so much. Each word in the song chases something bad making it leave me and fills me with so much love. I never thought our music ball would know such a special heavenly songs. Except for of an occasional disturbing splash in water, I would have no idea where I was at this time. She is now singing the second verse. My Angel has made a revision in her performance, because the first time she played for me, she would pause between the verses and kiss me gently on the neck. That was private time, so this must be her public performance. I can still hear some mountain ballads playing on the other end on the deck. I can only suspect that one of my wives or the other element is not in the mood for this heavenly harmony. I do recognize how they are being quiet while she is singing to me. My appreciation ends when two little hands touch my back. I know these hands.

I am bewildered and confused in how she is playing the music and touching me at the same time. Curiosity forced me to turn around and open my eyes. Painfully, this soul strengthening heavenly nourishment stops. I have in my hands Gyöngyösi and I pull her tight in my arms. I kiss her on her angelic neck thanking her for giving me water in the middle of this desert. She asks me to show her the secret ball that Letenyei gave me. I fight hard to let the words escape from my mouth as I am cherishing the greatest gift that I have ever received from the spirit world. I manage to get them out by offering a deal, "First, you explain where you have been hiding your harp." Gyöngyösi chuckles in here; I am going to straighten you out boy manners, by responding, "Okay, funny boy, do you want to play games. Why do not we play silly boy gets thrown into the sea, and Angel falls to sleep?" I tell her, "I would rather play, 'Angel makes and creates a dirty boy." Gyöngyösi then hits me and sternly demands those special balls that play Angel songs so the other wives may also enjoy this. Dumb boy instantly discovers that his Angel is going crazy. I look at her and declare, "You know I have no ball. Every move I make when leaving you watch me. My love, come on back into my arms before that wonderful music you were playing seeps out of my body." She touches my heart and with her other hand, rests it on the side of my face. After that, she closes her eyes and then opens them claiming, "Something is wrong here my Master, for you are telling the truth."

I look at her and say, "Look here Angel; you know I never would lie to you. Partially, from my love of you and from fear, your Great Spirits will cast me into a burning fire somewhere." She moves back into my arms, which elicits my immediate hug. She has hung with us much better than I had ever expected. I originally feared that every time we passed a temple, she would make us sacrifice everything. The opposite has been the case. She accepts and adores Khigir, as the head wife and adores everyone in our family. It is nothing to wake up at night and see her massaging someone. Gyöngyösi has a capacity for sensing the activities in our flesh and when she believes her efforts will help make us better; she is there. She has fallen into the emotional and mother role.

Whenever one of us needs a shoulder to cry on, they can depend on her. I find myself the most helpless in her arms. I can think that part of us that sailed from the land of the spirits returning to my cold infant body. It is this bond, which will make me forever her servant; therefore, I could never lie to her, not try to trick her. I know when she gives me advise, it would be best if I followed it, because the alternative not only hurts me, it hurts my Angel. I cannot even imagine any of my wives hurting, as despite the recent incident with Tselikovsky's blood on my hands. This is the worse part, by far, of love. We put ourselves in something else that faced danger also. I always fear a terrible gang trying to harm my wives. I find myself feeling sorrier for the evil ones, knowing that my wives can jolt a force as great as an Army can. This may be the reason that I can rest at night. I charm them about their power. When the danger approaches me, those little soft arms are ready to save me. With their fighting power, so I often wish they would not make me lead them. I would prefer to be in the back of the gang rewarding them with praise. Their devotion and love for me has placed me on a pedestal so high, I fear that if I fell off, death would follow. Her heart is beating the song we just heard while she holds herself tight in my arms. The moons are reflecting their lights of her angelic hair. This must be by design, as the moons and suns' creation was that while in the presence above her hair, they might enter within the Great Spirit's euphoria. Khigir now comes out and asks me, "Hevesi is getting tired, and do you want to keep her in your pocket currently?" I tell Khigir, "Tell her in just a little while; we have a problem we are working on, so for now continue to play with Makói." Khigir then complains, "If you two would stop playing around and playing your music again. Therefore, many of us would once more become happy." Gyöngyösi reports, "My love Khigir, that is our problem, for neither of us played our secret song, yet we heard it somehow." Khigir now explains, "Well, maybe we have a stole away on board." Gyöngyösi further clarifies, "Or we are receiving a visit from the only element that is not represented in our family." I ask Gyöngyösi, "Honey, what are you saying to us?"

Our Angel explains, "My Masters, I saw what appeared to be the music note's silhouette flash before the Cegi Moon. I believed it to a strange bird of the seas. Even so, as I think harder about what I saw I can now certify clearly that it was a music note. We may well have enjoyed our first visit from the water element. Come and stand beside me, and we will sing this song together, and it may reappear." Khigir asks, "Who was this thing playing for?" Gyöngyösi answers, "Clearly, it was playing for silly boy here. Did you see anything?" I confessed, "The music was accordingly refreshing to me and gave me so much peace. I could not open my eyes until you touched me." Khigir follows up with her question, "Why whatever this would is, sing only for Siklósi and run from us?" I then broke loose from the warmth and heavenly peace gained from holding Gyöngyösi and moved a few feet into the open. I flexed my arms, did a little wiggle, and afterwards answered Khigir, "It must be a, she that is clearly intelligent and has good taste." I braced myself for their retaliation. Within a flash, I was down on the deck to the side rail. My wives know every vulnerable part of myself. They knew how I would respond to any situation. I sometimes wish all I have to do all-day were planning how to torture my Master. My mother never told me about this when we discussed married life. She had to wait until I was much older before we discussed it seriously. When she tried to explain this to me as a child, I would run away from her crying. She did not know how to tie me to a tree and scare me as Khigir became a Master. I am waiting for tickling. Light tickling. Light bites, my hair pulled, or any of the other new torture skills they have devised. One time my wives thought they would torment me by taking my clothes. I simply headed for the Edelényi sellers naked. It took all seven of them to circle me to the stores. They begged me to put my clothes back on my body. I tried every way to break free from them. When women, older serious looking ones, and young beautiful ones, passed by I would tell them, "Hey honey, today is your lucky day, for my wives have taken my clothes?" We got into the store, and I picked my new clothes. They knocked me to the floor and dressed me. This must be a new method today, as they, each grab one of my arms, wrapping it around them putting themselves each facing me. They are now moving their mouths toward my ears. Oh, man this could really hurt.

Subsequently, I hear each telling me, "Of course handsome Master, for if she thought that wisdom would be inside her, to go with that good taste." They are kissing me. I tell them, "I thought you were mad about me boasting and were going to torture me." Gyöngyösi answers, "Oh, silly boy, if we did not believe those things, would have your children in our womb?" Gyöngyösi freezes and whispers to us, "I hear something." Within minutes, the three of us hear angelic music once more. We stop our playing. I shake my head, because now this music is taking away my fun time with my wives spoiling me. I join them as their scanners are scanning the sea. I am always impressed with how they can scan detecting any abnormally and its intents. We can be walking among the crowds shopping with the Edelényi and one will say, "Those men over there are bad." Every one of them quickly corroborates this, and they clamp around me like scared chicks to their mother hen. I ask them, "Where is this crime?" One will answer, "The man with the green shirt beside the shoe store." I then realize that this shoe store is at 2000 feet behind us. I glance at them one-by-one and notice their hearts are pounding so I tell them, "Okay, stay close to me." Now, they return to normal. I will never figure them out; however, I am learning how to soothe them so within itself, stabilizes our harmony. What is happening in the real world is what decides the importance? Significance is what exists between their ears. This significance will allow me to sleep at night. Their scanners are scanning our seas currently. Makói joins us now as she slips tired little Hevesi into my pocket. Makói explains to me, "Master, she is so tired. I felt sorry for her. I look down in my pocket and see what I expected to see, and that is Hevesi looking at me with a big smile. I look at Makói and tell her, Thank you, really much. I was on the way to get my little friend, as we had a mystery we would need help. Can you hear that music?" Makói affirms she hears the music, and congratulates Gyöngyösi for playing so well. Gyöngyösi spins around and tells her, "Sorry love, it is not me this time."

I tell them, "This is our mystery, for its source is the sea." Makói asks if she may help in the search also. The wives who are already searching nod their heads yes. I then ask Gyöngyösi, "My Angel Gyöngyösi, I have heard that voices from the sea like little tiny people, is that true?" Gyöngyösi answers, "I think that I might have heard tales about this, although anything that attacks from the sea will naturally consume the easiest to digest first." I follow up asking her, "Gyöngyösi, would some bait help us catch this easier?" Khigir answers this, "Master; bait will help you catch anything faster, do you have some hidden bait?" Hevesi has slipped under pocket chair and is kicking my chest with both of her feet. I ask Khigir if Hevesi made good bait. These three wives turn around and start yelling and hitting me saying, "Never, not our beloved Hevesi. We love her too much. We need her." As they are hitting me, the sea music becomes louder, and I can now see a beautiful woman sitting on the sea playing a strange-looking harp. I ask my wives, "Who is that woman of the sea?" Believe me or not, because I said a woman, they are going to study. Even my precious Hevesi has her head poking out of my shirt pocket trying to verify if this woman exists. The woman playing the harp stops for a second as my wives turn around. Her eyes are looking into me, and I smile and shake my head yes. She begins to play again. Gyöngyösi remarks, "I believe she likes our Master." Khigir follows up with, "Therefore, the sea does have intelligent life." I tell them, "Smile and move slow, so you do not scare her." The woman looks at me and begins talking, "Siklósi, why do those women hit and kick you so viciously?" Khigir asks, "We were only hitting. No one was kicking. The sea woman quickly rebuts, "The little one in his pocket was kicking." I say to her, "Do not worry my friend, because your music takes away pain, because you know my name, may we know yours?" She smiles, while playing her music softly replies, "My name is Bélapátfalvai, and I am of the Mysteria Seas." Gyöngyösi tells her, "That is a lovely name. I notice you are playing a harp. In my species, we play the harp. Your beauty is more prodigious than I would expect from regular sea women. Are you an Angel also?"

Bélapátfalvai responds, "Gyöngyösi, as you are an Angel for air and Lamentans, I am an Angel for the aqua element. We have no need for wings in the seas, where all may swim freely from our sea surface with the surface meeting the air." She begins playing again as the notes appear on the air and drift off toward the Cegi Moon. Khigir asks her, "Why do your notes appear visible and drift away?" Bélapátfalvai explains, "That is from the air element, which traps all things from the aqua element and takes them to the dark skies." Above her head, I see a smaller moon inside a golden octopus. This thing is shooting so many coin-sized stars down to Bélapátfalvai. Makói questions, "Bélapátfalvai, what is that above your head, which is offering you smaller stars? That is the good news I bring to you. That golden object is a Kisteleki, which is a special ship that can host Lamentans, who survive from the air. I am also surviving beside you in Kisteleki. Do not fear him. You are my guest." I asked her, "Bélapátfalvai, your fingers sing in my heart. Some in my family are from fire, and one from the air. May they also join us?" Bélapátfalvai confesses, "I am glad my fingers sing to your warm heart. Any among you that survives as you do, will also survive in Kisteleki. They are among the reasons they sent me to you, so the four elements may exchange our welcomes. Another reason was to explore your famous love. Although, so far all I see is these wives hitting, kicking, and screaming at you." I now confessed to Bélapátfalvai, "Bélapátfalvai, you saw us playing with one another, for I was pestering them. I love so much to tickle their anger. Search our hearts, for you only will find love." Makói, who was securely behind me, climbs on my back and sticks her gorgeous face toward my cheek kissing it. Khigir and Gyöngyösi turned their backs on Bélapátfalvai while standing in front of me and began kissing whispering their 'I love you' to me. Bélapátfalvai comments, "I can feel their love now, even that little one in your pocket. Watch role does she perform?" Khigir turned around and told Bélapátfalvai, "That little one we call Hevesi, and she can expand to our size. She has a daughter in her womb that belongs to our Master.

Hevesi helps protect our Master when he explores the deep wildernesses as he enjoys. She also provides him valuable counsel when meeting new people or experiences. She behaves like a challenging friend whom, our Master enjoys so much." I jump in and add, "Hevesi is extremely dear in my heart and knows many of my foolish secrets. The one behind me is special in that if it were not for me, she would not be in front of you now. I am her rock, and she is my love light. I love all my wives as they, each have such a special gift. We call the beautiful dark one Gyöngyösi, and she fulfills my spiritual needs. The wonderful blonde-haired person you see before me; we call Khigir, and she is the head wife, and attends to my wives' emotional needs. Without her, I would most likely be insane." At this time, I asked Khigir to gather the other members of our family. Bélapátfalvai confesses to me, "I know all members on your new ship, as I have followed you since the beginning of your trip. I pretended not to know while testing if you were true. I told her, "Bélapátfalvai, as every one of my picturesque wives will tell you, 'I never lie to a magnificent woman." Makói says, "He only lies to me when he says that I am beautiful." Bélapátfalvai responds, "Makói, You are exquisite. I often watch the Szabolcs playing on the northern seas and in the fall waiting in the rivers for the fish to return to their birth waters." I ask Makói, "Who are the Szabolcs?"

She responds, "Master; they are my people." I respond, "Makói, your people have the air and currently the water elements that love them and understand, as do I, your wonderful beauty. Now come stand in front of me so your new fan can appreciate your beauty." She lightly trembles and scoots out in front of me, immediately turning her back on Bélapátfalvai and wrapping her arms around me. Hevesi then squawks, "Makói, you are squeezing me honey." Makói steps back and begins laughing, "Sorry Hevesi." I place my hands on her shoulders as Gyöngyösi helps me spin her around, and she sees Bélapátfalvai and releases a timid smile. Bélapátfalvai begins playing her music again, and I can feel Makói's body start to relax. I whisper into her ear, "See, I told you that no danger existed. I am proud of your bravery Makói." She turns around and gives me a wink.

Consequently, I whisper to her again, "Wow; I am married to a Szabolcs. I must be exceedingly lucky" She turns her face around to kiss me, waiting for me to lower my face. After we kiss, she responds, "Or you must be a senseless man." This experience is making me feel compassionate. Consequently, I inform her, "Makói, if being foolish provides me kisses and love such as this, and then I will remain foolish." Bélapátfalvai interpolates, "Siklósi, you say superbly kind words to your wives. I feel like finding me an aqua man and teach him your words." I pull Gyöngyösi closer to me while rubbing my hand through her hair. Informing Bélapátfalvai, I confess to her, "Bélapátfalvaim, I do enormously love each of them." Khigir arrives with the rest of our family. She returns to standing in front of me. The members who came with her, all crowd behind me. Bélapátfalvaim asked Khigir, "Why do you stand in front of Siklósi?" Khigir discloses to her, "Because if something were to attack my Master, the pain of seeing him suffer is so much greater than the pain of my suffering." I disclose to Bélapátfalvaim, "If danger comes, I will break free of her and struggle to gain safety for my wives once more." Kisteleki hovers over us now, while Bélapátfalvaim begins playing her music again. My family is terrified, from here Khigir, Gyöngyösi, and I turn around and

Hevesi yells out, "Do not worry. We are safe my loves." Khigir and I laugh as Gyöngyösi blows Hevesi a kiss. Bélapátfalvaim is now requesting permission to board our ship. Khigir grants it immediately. Bélapátfalvaim releases her harp into the sea. She stands on the water and walks to the side of our ship. Kisteleki releases a blue beam over her, and she rises to our deck and sticks out her hand. Khigir, Gyöngyösi, and I grab her hands and pull her to our deck. Khigir compliments Bélapátfalvaim for her soft hands. Bélapátfalvaim confesses, "We did not know how you felt while living, as the few samples we have, always die within a few minutes of entering our world. I am sure you realize that this is not my real appearance. We struggled hard to produce an appearance pleasing to Siklósi and not threatening to your wives."

Khigir responds with, "Bélapátfalvaim, your wonderful appearance would place fear in many wives; however, you are safe with us." She elbows me next and questions me, "Right dirty boy?" I cough and then readily agree with my 'I am innocent' smiling.' Bélapátfalvaim walks over to my other wives and our friends and begins introducing herself by telling them things she knows about them. Within a few minutes, she has everyone loosened and feeling relaxed. She tells them, "We have planned an exciting discovery adventure for you. We are excited to share our wild with Lamentans of many species, fire, and air. This will be a memorable experience for you and remember, if you must cool down dirty boy, we can have our water help you." They are swarming around her now, especially Brann. Bélapátfalvaim clearly is feeling comfortable currently at least with me by adding her sense of humor. She, like the rest of the universe knows our inside joke of calling me dirty boy. To me, it was strange hearing those would come out of something so small and beautiful. Her hair is fashioned perfectly above her head, which must be a popular style for the other elements when they visit us, as our Abaúj also wears her hair in this style. Her skin is flawless and darker than I would have expected from someone that lives in the sea. The fabric of her dress matches the best silk fabrics available from the Edelényi. Kisteleki moves closer.

My family flinches at his movement. Bélapátfalvaim tells them to have no fear for Kisteleki is merely positioning himself, so he may bring you safely into his under the sea ship. She continues to reiterate the beauty and novelty of what we are to witness. Kisteleki pulls us slowly into his shell. This place is so large inside. I ask Bélapátfalvaim, "Why does this appear small from outside, yet is so large on the inside?" Bélapátfalvaim explains that they had to reduce the size because of the ship's sails. Notwithstanding, once we were locked-in his power beam, Kisteleki shifted over the sea away from your ship. He was then able to expand again. He is now repacking his air reserves, thus you will breathe much easier. Go ahead and sit in your comfortable rotating chairs.

You may turn around and watch the ocean from your wide windows, or swing back, and we can talk, while you watch the ocean from above us or across from you. I then asked her, "Bélapátfalvaim, how long will we be absent from the ship?" Bélapátfalvaim comforts me by saying, "We will have you back on your ship as you are approaching the Land of the Celldömölki. Berettyóú will be in contact with one of our emissaries who will warn us to return you. Thus, sit back and learn, as I apologize that this trip will be much shorter than the proper time to give it justice. We are so proud finally to visit some fire and air and our prize, you Lamentans. Our philosophers can find not explain this, because we have always believed air and fire to be unfriendly to the Lamentans. We know the Lamentans must have air and us to survive. Our historians have never found an event such as your union, even during the great civilizations that existed on our lands before our arrival." Brann now comes over, sits on my lap, wrapping her arms around me, and explains to Bélapátfalvai, while giving me a soft kiss to my cheek, "Baranya and I could not live without this family. Besides, this ménage cannot survive without the dirty boy. Therefore, I am forced to soothe dirty boy for the sake of his wonderful wives." I was extremely surprised when Brann began by treating me pleasantly. However, once she got our attention and relaxation, she plundered me at will. Either way, I do love her tenacity against me. Nevertheless, I kiss her and tease her, "Are you ready for some real heat sugar baby?" She immediately jumps and hides behind Khigir. She swings around, placing Brann in front of me once more. Khigir, while holding Brann informs her, "We think it is time for you to get some real fire from our Master." Brann looks at me as I am licking my lips. She yells for Baranya, who is with the remaining group lying on the floor laughing while also kicking it. Baranya, while still laughing chokes through, "Brann, you have been wanting our Master to heat you up for a while. Take advantage of it now. Hurry and remove your garments and get some real Lamentan heat."

Baranya put the final pinnacle defeating our attempts to hold on to reality as we all drop laughing. Khigir releases Brann, while joining our hysteria. Brann looks terrified, so I add to our summit, "Do not worry Brann because you are so inexperienced. I will go slow and tender for you since we are not married as of yet." Oh no, Tselikovsky is laughing so hard she is urinating on the floor. I remove my shirt to help her. While removing my shirt Brann drops on the floor crying, "Oh, please not me, I promise to be kinder to you my Master." I rush over and tend to Tselikovsky to prevent any embarrassment. I quickly finished, especially as Khigir came rushing to her sister's side, who was still laughing. I do not think that she knew what was happening. I walked over to Brann and wrapped my arms around her. I asked her if feeling my bare chest was exciting her. She told me, "Master, I do not want to anger you. Nevertheless, I am not ready. I will be polite to you from this day forward if you forgive me this one time." I gave her a kiss on her forehead and told her, "I will release you only if you promise to be the same way to me that you have always been." Brann lifts her tear filled, face to me and quizzes me, "You mean you enjoy my hostility?" I answer her, "Oh Brann; I could not live without it. Honey, we were playing with you. I hope you know that I never take an unwilling unmarried woman. You are always safe from me." She tells me, "It is time for us to play. I will take off my gown and lie on top of you. Therefore, lay down now and let me do all the talking and begging. You must continually deny me. Okay, my friend and Master." I wink at her and lay down on the soft, fabric-covered floor in Kisteleki. Brann slings off her gown. My wives and other family friends stop laughing in absolute confusion. Brann dives on me and begins begging, "Oh Master. I burn so hot for your love. Take me and do as you wish." I tell her, "Oh Brann, I am too exhausted to do this now. Maybe we can later, okay, my love." Brann yells out again, "Oh Master it must be now. I burn with lust for you too much. I can no longer hold the secret of my great want for you." I tell her, "Oh Brann, we are not married, for me to do this now with you could anger my gods."

Brann begins crying as she is rolling her body over mine. She begs again, "Oh Master, please take me. I burn too hot. Please." She now turns her face toward our family members who all soon look so gloomy. She begs to Khigir, "Please Khigir, make him take me. I have no shame now. I burn only for our Master." Baranya rushes over beside her and tells her, "Brann you are my love. Come with me and I will help you recover." Baranya and Khigir lift her up and pull her away from me. Brann is really putting a show on tonight. She kicks her legs in an attempt to break loose and return to me. Brann cries out again begging, "Please do not take me from our Master. I must be his now. I must allow him to enjoy me, so my great fire of lust will be cooled down." Our entire family was puzzled, except for Hevesi, who is laughing in the pockets of my lower wrappings. A couple of times she got too loud, so I tap her with my hand. Our family looks so sad now, as all feel accordingly guilty that they had offered something to Brann that we could not give. Worse of all, we offered herself, and she really so much needed this. They rush to give her some wine that is one of the tables. Bélapátfalvai stands beside me and hands my shirt back to me. It is perfectly clean. I ask her how she cleaned it so fast. She explains that they can extract anything with water in it from our fabrics. She laughs and adds, "Even smelly water." I hand Hevesi to her and quickly put my shirt on and small at Hevesi. She is doing well now as Bélapátfalvai is playing lightly with her. I place her in my pocket. Bélapátfalvai complains to me, "You are all behaving so strangely. Moreover, to tease poor Brann and then humiliate her in front of all, taking from her what you promised. She must be so heartbroken now. I never believed your family to be this cruel. I tell Bélapátfalvai while smiling at her, "Hold your judgment until the story ends." Brann at this time stops, breaks loose from our family. She runs back to me jumping and clamping to me. She afterwards climbs up on me resting her legs on my shoulders. She continues by yelling out, "Master, do we make a great team or what?" She is presently laughing and rubbing my hair, completely messing it up. Hevesi starts to laugh triggering me as I laugh also. Khigir and her family walk over to us with a disoriented look. They are completely befuddled. Brann is swinging her legs and laughing harder now than before. The strange looks on everyone's face is feeding her fire with perfectly dried wood. Khigir asks me, "Was this a joke?"

I tell her, "Khigir, I felt so guilty for us humiliating her as we did, so we decided to fight fire with fire." Baranya rushes over to Brann and reaffirms, "Are you okay, my lovely flame?" Brann confirms by saying, "I have never been happier before, leastwise what I can remember." She yells to me, "Dirty boy, put me down, and do not be peeking while you are doing this." I tell her, "Fire face, you already showed us your glory. Therefore, if I peek what can I see that is new?" Brann then tells me, "Okay, dirty boy, you might as well be allowed to see the best." I now tell Brann, "Honey, hold your gown up, so I can lift you over my head." She laughs and tells everyone, "See, dirty boy is a Master of this craft is he not." I can now lift her over my head and slowly lower her until her feet are almost on the ground. In stopping I tell her, "I get a kiss before releasing you." She tells me, "You get two, one for lifting me and the other for peeking at me and not getting caught." Hevesi yells out to Brann, "Brann; I caught him." Brann tells Hevesi, "The next time you expand I owe you not only a kiss, but a giant hug, my dear." Brann now gives me the two kisses. Afterwards, I drop her feet to the floor. Brann looks at Bélapátfalvai and asks, "Did you pack our music ball, because I feel like dancing with Makói? Makói lowers her head and tells Brann, "My dearest Brann; I am a poor dancer." Brann tells her, "Do not try to trick me Makói, because we were watching you dance with Hevesi, and you did a wonderful job. We have some work to fine tune Hevesi." Bélapátfalvai tosses her the ball and tells her there is a large dancing room through those doors. She is pointing at the doors. Brann grabs Makói and heads to the dancing room. Her comrades ask her, "May we also dance?" Brann yells back, "Every one. We must have some fun." They all rush into the dancing room. Khigir, Gyöngyösi, and Hevesi stay with Bélapátfalvai and I. Bélapátfalvai asks me, "We both are playing a trick with your family?" I told her, "Brann was, and I simply supported her. My heart believed that she had a right to redress." Khigir and Gyöngyösi both gave me a big kiss. Gyöngyösi responds, "You have such a wonderful heart, my Master."

Khigir is holding my hand; she gives it a slight squeeze, and as I look at her, she gives me a yielding wink. This soft wink means I may be in the clear on this one. I realize Brann really is a fantastic, completely believable performer. Hevesi tells me, "You think you are going to get away with this?" I tell her, "You think you are not going to get fed to one of those large sea beasts who surround us now?" Hevesi reveals to me, "I can see in the future, and you did get away with this, my loving Master?" I winked at her and told her, "Above all else; you are my trusted friend." Khigir asks me, "What does that mean my dear?" I explain to her, "Brann whispered the concept of a pretend play, for we did not want to wake up Hevesi. Because she did not know it was fake, she also was crying. I needed to reinforce to her that she is my trusted friend, and if she would have been awake, we would have been included." Khigir blows a kiss to Hevesi, who is smiling and looking so innocent, because she in no way wants the family to think, she was also involved in this hoax. Hevesi released her unimpeachable chuckle. Bélapátfalvai confessed to me, "I am so captivated with the way fire, and you worked as a team. I was also impressed with the tenderness your family expressed when believing Brann to be emotionally hurt." Khigir reveals to Bélapátfalvai, "Our new friend, we are completely covered by our love, which is the blanket that holds us together. We play hard, and we love hard." Bélapátfalvai agrees that what Khigir has told her matches what she has seen. She suggests that we allow the family to enjoy themselves while she gives us our tour. Kisteleki has many decks. However, she can only guarantee our safety on this floor as the other floors has the life-support and transportation devices all geared toward making this deck as glamorous for us, which is reasonably possible. We are on the highest deck so more of the deep sea will be visible for us. She shows us the two bedrooms and our 'married' bedroom has a giant heart-shaped bed. The unmarried room has extra furnishings for private eating and other single's activities.

She showed us our dining area and explained that Kisteleki did all the cooking and cleaning. Bélapátfalvai showed us the rooms; we could clean our bodies and remove any body wastes. Our tour included a room with many, what she called books. These were interesting in that they had words and pictures. The words were in their languages, so of no value to us. Bélapátfalvai told us that they would put a machine in the forests beside a little stream by our home in Baktalórántházai with a map to a side cave in their entrance, which has a small stream and fills it with paper and something she called 'inks' inside special devices she called 'pens' so we could record our history. This was indeed a blessing for us, as once we returned to Baktalórántházai we recorded all our events from these miraculous adventures. She told me that Kisteleki would provide us an inscribed report of our sea adventures, and the writing would be in our language. Because they had been watching us, he would also add those summaries in his report. Khigir remarked, "Who knows, maybe someday some books, like those in that room, will appear telling of our tales." I gave her a strange look. Our guide showed us some recreational rooms. We now walked back upstairs to the viewing room. The floor was made of a strange material like the viewing wall that allowed us to see through them. We noticed that our bedroom and the cleaning room had their views blocked. This gave us some relief. Just as we were beginning to sit at the table in the middle of this viewing room, our family members came running up the steps telling me, "Master there is love outside our window." I got up and walked with them to where they saw it and sure enough. Love was outside as a giant water heart that was splashing into the sea sending soft ruffles across the water. I yelled for Khigir, "Everyone, come over and look at this. It is wonderful." We stood in a long row before our window so everyone could get a good view. They had made a fine ledge along this never-ending window, which would be perfect for Hevesi. I put her on the ledge and saw her face also enlighten. Anything that has to do with love or hearts these women adored. In front of us was a giant heart that controlled everything around it. Bélapátfalvai explains, "This is another one of our welcoming's for you. Your clan represents the greatest summit of love for us, and we are so happy that you are showing your true selves during this adventure."

Csongrád warns Bélapátfalvai, "If our Master is showing his true colors, then a beautiful really sexy woman such as you should be careful standing next to him." I look at her and respond, "My Honorable Royal Queen. I am only filled with uncontrollable lust when standing next to you my love." She comes running to me as we hug, and I swing her around. She leans her head back, and her gorgeous hair floats in our air. I see a wonderful human being laughing and extremely happy presently. I slow down and release her as we both rush back to gaze at this giant heart. Gyöngyösi informs Bélapátfalvai that this is the best representation of loved, she has ever witnessed. She further explains that this tells her the sea people have a great grasp of the concept of love. Baktalórántházai then explains that love is extremely important to her nations. They only suffer from seclusion from the other elements because they are the sole elements that does not need air. Lamentans and fire cannot survive in their water. Thus, through the ages, their expansion has changed the makeup of Lamenta. As we created more water, we caused added cities and civilizations to fall into the water. The earliest civilizations lived-in the lower lands so they could recover water that was inside Lamenta. Tselikovsky, in thinking woman asks her, "When you said, 'we created more water,' what did that entail and why did you create more water?" Bélapátfalvai explained, "The way we formed ourselves on Lamenta was through a long yet simple process. We collected dark matter and dark energy from the space materials, and brought them here. Dark is not evil in this process. These materials could produce hydrogen or specifically H2 that combined with the oxygen and made water. Lamenta was an extremely hot world during that time, too hot to sustain your life. The mighty spirits of this galaxy wanted to plant your species on this planet. Therefore, they provided us with much more oxygen and H2. Slowly, the species that were occupying this world without permission either exited or died. Once they planted the vegetation and beasts, after the planters planted your species.

Your species, with Hevesi's Mezokovácsházi, Makói's Szabolcs, and many other new species began their lives in this world. We provide much food for many species on Lamenta, to include the Szabolcs and yours. We also feed the air with our oxygen and H2 as it breaks apart and helps clean the air by washing it with rain. Our rain equally important feeds the eating beasts and vegetation that keep you fed and healthy. In addition, by controlling the temperature range, we keep you from burning up or freezing. Every drop of water that you witness in this sea has at one time, and some many times floated through the air. The only element that does not directly depend on us is the fire. Nevertheless, we sustained the fuel and air that fire burns. Fire burns the wood best when we do not exist within it. Lamentans have more of our element, then any other substance. You are virtually more of us than you think. Do you have any more questions for me Tselikovsky and did I answer your question?" Tselikovsky told her she had completely answered her question. I then asked her if we saw some of these pre-age sites. She assured us we would see everything, and recommended we go to enjoy the fresh meal that was waiting for us in our dining area. We were hungry for sure for both food and adventure in learning about worlds we could never have dreamed that lived with us. Kisteleki rotated himself around so we could see the giant heart while we ate. They were all enthusiastic and excited. Air had previously entertained us, and now the water was. Fire could carry out one of the most dramatic hoaxes in our family's history. I call Abaúj to me and ask her how she feels about this water adventure. She confesses that her views of water are changing drastically. Our wonderful air family member never realized how water was cleaning them and floating among them. Abaúj agreed with the rain cooling everything; however, she reminds us that air takes water out of objects and dries them. Bélapátfalvai sits down with us and explains to Abaúj, "I hope not to offend you or make you feel uneasy in any way. I want to emphasize that there is more the same about us than different, as not only has all water existed in your air, yet all water has returned from your air. You have been with us, as we have been in you.

So many of us have traveled through the Lamentans, as they breathe you constantly for survival, our water fills all parts in their bodies, and helps preserve their internal temperatures. Brann asks, "What purpose do I serve?" Abaúj tells her, "You provide the lifesaving heat, so they may endure during cold conditions. Without your heat after Siklósi's birth, he with all in his village would have died as most Lamentans did before springtime. You are the only defense against the cold for them. We are all needed in order the keep the Lamentans on this world." Khigir thanks them and asks, "Are we not going to enjoy this beautiful blue heart that shines through our windows. I notice it is beginning to shrink now. Bélapátfalvai explains that they merely created, this as an introduction or a welcoming. They had not designed it to keep pace with Kisteleki, who is taking you to a special area for a visit." I asked Bélapátfalvai, "Bélapátfalvai, so we may talk simpler with you, would you be angry if we gave you a nickname that is so much easier to pronounce?" Bélapátfalvai answers, "Oh that will be quite fine as Bélapátfalvai is not my real name, you may pick my new Lamentan name." Khigir rushes into the conversation by saying, "I really like Béla." I agree with her, as she is the one that handles my affairs with another woman. Béla chuckles and responds, "Yes; I also like Béla." Gyöngyösi tells us that she will now go tell the rest of our family. Béla confesses that her feelings with our group are not what she expected. She expands on this topic, "I cannot believe I am sitting with fire, air, and Lamentans while feeling this comfortable. I am glad that you gave me a new name as a feel like a fresh person. I remember the warm thinking that flowed through me when I saw you saving Abaúj. I could feel your determination to succeed or surrender your life trying. It was so special. She was helpless in your arms, and you would not let go of your belief that you would save her. She also did not attempt to break loose, for in the short time you were together; she trusted you with her life." Abaúj leaned her head on my shoulder and said to Hevesi, "Do not tell Khigir." Hevesi looked at her and laughed, saying, "Abaúj, you are family now, so you may also kiss him and talk dirty if you want."

Abaúj looked at Béla responding, "Since then, I have no fear for my life, because, if our Master is around, he will save us. I believe that with every drop of air inside my body." Brann explains that she watched Siklósi stumble around the Tamarkins, who tagged along with him. I noticed something strange about the way they were with each other. They were burning inside to give birth to their love. I could think that this was a true love. When they became married, they behaved as newlyweds. The love spirits met with them. They came back, glorifying them for the way they controlled their love, not knowing the power that it had." I asked her, "What power?" Brann answers, "The power that keeps us altogether, my dear." Brann continues her story, "Then one day my friend the fire horse that we call Baranya came and told me she had met this family, and that they wanted to see me again. I was so excited. We returned to them and have no plans to leave, except for some temporary missions for our species. Baranya and I have decided this is the place for us." I give Brann and Abaúj each kiss and hug, thanking them for the joy and happiness they have brought on our family. As Béla feels the joy in Brann and Abaúj tears slowly roll down her cheeks. Hevesi asks her, "Béla, why do you cry?" We stop and turn around looking at her, and I ask, "Béla, are you feeling okay?"

She tells us, "I feel so lonely presently. I cannot explain this. What is wrong with me? I may have to tell my leaders that I am too weak for this mission." Brann explains to her, "Do not fear Béla, you have no defects. What is happening to you, also happened to me?" Abaúj tells her, "Béla, nothing is wrong with you. Do not fight what is happening inside you. Nor should you try to determine what is happening. The same thing happened to me. Enjoy this feeling, and cling to us to fight the loneliness caused by your emptiness." Béla divulges to us, "I never knew of this loneliness inside me, how this torment dared to reveal itself to me now?" Brann explains, "Because before you denied and depressed it.

Because you have seen love, you are releasing all the hurt and pain inside you." Béla asks, "Why now, during such an important diplomatic assignment, which requires me to represent the best I can for my species?" Brann kisses her and tells her, "You will soon understand." Abaúj also kisses her and informs her that is going to send a ten star rating to her people concerning the great loving Béla." They wave good-bye and return to the wives. Khigir now walks over to her and kisses her, informing her, "You are the greatest host that we could have ever dreamed to have." Béla looks at me and asks, "I am so confused. I behaved as a result weak before them with me being defenseless as they praise and kiss me instead of grabbing such an easy victory for their species to glorify. I explain to her, "Your people have welcomed us and do not seek an easy victory over three visiting species. Béla, what would we have to gain by hurting one that has shared her heart with us? Would that not be foolish? You have shared your heart, we may relax and share our true heart with you? Would that not be greater for your mission?" Béla tells me, "I fear that would show them you are weak?" Béla, "Then you teach us how to act in front of them, and when we get back to our private places, we can act freer." Béla agrees that would be accordingly much better. She asks me, "Why do I feel so comfortable around your family and you?" Hevesi explains to her, "Because we are tremendously much fond of you, our new friend." Béla looks down at Hevesi and reveals, "I am truly fond of you my special friend and envy the way they love you." I tell her the two, which Khigir allows me to love the most, are Hevesi and Makói. They worked us so hard to get their love, Hevesi for her dedication to fighting and her terrifying meanness ouch. Stop kicking me, dear. Makói was so different, as she had trapped inside herself and did not know how to come forth. Every step that beauty has taken is always in the faith she has in her family. The true reason that we keep Hevesi in my pocket is to make her be good." Hevesi starts yelling, "Khigir. He is trying to kiss her, help." Khigir comes running and looks around asking, "Did someone call my name?" Hevesi said something. Nevertheless, whatever she said confused me."

I then ask Hevesi, "I did not understand what you said, so why not say it again slower, and maybe Khigir can translate it for us." Hevesi tells Khigir that she thinks I hate her as she begins crying. They always have to toss that crying in there to increase the drama. Khigir reaches in my pocket and takes Hevesi saying, "I think someone is tired and needs a nap. I will return after I get her to sleep." Béla and I laugh. Béla looks at me and asks, "Why did she say you were trying to kiss me? Is my curiosity showing that much?" I tell her, "To be curious is natural, as I am the only male on this ship so come on over here and get your first kiss and hug." Surprisingly, she rushed into my arms we shared a wonderful kiss. Afterwards, she slowly steps back and tells me, "That was extremely stimulating; I can now understand why your wives follow you with so much loyalty." You could be correct; however, even I do not know they answer for that. Nevertheless, what exciting things do you have for us to see today?" Béla tells me that soon we will arrive to see the Esztergom, who has some amazing likenesses with the Lamentans. You should begin gathering your family up around these windows and I will go gather some special eating treats. I went down and gathered my family for a viewing, a few of which I had to wake up including Hevesi and Khigir, who were both in a deep sleep. Tselikovsky tells me, "It is time to do to her what she always did to me," and pounces on Khigir. I get Hevesi in my pocket quickly making sure no one rolls over her. Khigir instantaneously grabs Tselikovsky and wrestles with her. Their laugher draws our family back into this room. Béla enters and sees them fighting and asks, "Is everything okay?" I tell her, "They are reliving some exceptional memories from their childhood." After a few minutes, I tell them we have to go near the viewing windows for a special treat. They promptly stop and kiss each other as the other wives pull them up and straighten out their gowns. They both blow a kiss to Béla and start walking around the viewing room holding hands. Béla shakes her head, "Do you think I will ever figure your family's behaviors?" Hevesi asks her, "Why would you want to do something such as that?" Béla laughs and then tells me, "We should go to see some sights, I believe a dirty boy like you will enjoy." I think to myself, 'wonder what joy it would be to live at a place that also had some men. Do I not only have Lamentans, air, fire, but also now water calling me a dirty boy?

This is such an unjust title for such an Angel, like me." Béla asks me, "How can that be an unfair title when you have seven pregnant wives?" I tell her, "They made me do that?" Béla laughs and tells me the watermen say the same things. I enquire from her, "Do you also read minds?" She tells me, "Only simple ones." Hevesi is laughing so hard in my pocket now that it draws Khigir for us. Khigir asks her, "What is therefore funny?" Hevesi points at me and I instantly point at Béla. Béla looks at Khigir and innocently answers, "For some strange reason Hevesi became amused when I told Siklósi he had a simple mind." Khigir has now started laughing. I latch on to Béla's arm and start walking with her, handing Hevesi to Khigir telling them, "At least there is someone around here who does not laugh at me." Khigir, never failing to take an opportunity to respond adds, "Yes, the one who thinks you have a simple mind." Béla asks me, "Siklósi, did I offend or shame you?" I told her, "Oh Béla, how could one who is as adorable as you shame or insult someone?" Béla looks at me and answers, "By being ignorant." I look at her and say, "Mam, would you do the honor of escorting me tonight?" Béla answers, "I guess because you cannot find a wife that will not stop laughing at you, this would be appropriate. Now lead me." I shake my head no; a Gentleman allows his Lady to lead the way. Béla laughs, adding, "Not in the water worlds," and begins walking up the steps. My remaining family claps for us. I can see Béla becoming blush. She tells me that such a little event as this is becoming extremely exciting. Khigir comes up behind me tickling me. I tell her replacement is beside me. She looks at Béla and tells us, "At least I was replaced with a wonderful beautiful woman." Béla smiles while staring at Khigir and responds with, "What an enjoyable compliment, my Lady of honor." Khigir then asks her, "If you want to ditch this simple-minded man and be my escort, I would be honored." Béla looks at me and says, "I am so sorry. This is just too great a deal to pass." I say that I understand, and if I had such an opportunity, I would not pass up on such a wonderful deal.

I turn to Gyöngyösi and Makói and invite them to join me. My special loves rush to me after, which into the viewing area we go. Béla stands up to address our group, "I hope you are all having as much fun as I am. Even though I am not here to have fun, you people have a way of rubbing off on a person. Either way I ask you please to forgive me for my foolishness, as I am growing too tired to play the serious diplomatic role. All things aside, we are approaching Esztergom, which our closest species to the Lamentans. If you turn around now, you can see them as they appear currently. Kisteleki will stop moving so as not to scare them. He will also release some foods they enjoy. We have never had a physical incident with them in our recorded history. They do not fight, and they are favored among our species. Hevesi yells out, "They are half women." All my clan immediately turns around as my special Gyöngyösi and Makói rush to cover my eyes. I say to them, while being extremely calm because I never want to hurt any of my wives, especially these two, "My loves, do you not believe that I have seen what women appear as under their garments, thanks to both of you and the balance of my wives. If she looks as you do, then what harm is there, if she looks different, subsequently what harm is there. Either way there is no harm." Khigir comes over, gives me a kiss on my forehead, and then tells the young women to release me. I naturally pretend as if they used excessive force. My captors, in haste, massage and kiss my eyes. I tell them that I believe I will see again. They rejoice over this pronounced news. I must pretend as if they met a great physical challenge in restraining me successfully. They walk away with their happy wiggles feeling proud of themselves. As I watch them Khigir comments, "Lovely deed my husband." I thank her for this compliment and ask her to show me these Esztergom. She guides me to the window, and I have trouble believing my eyes. The first thing that I notice is that this area is shallow, maybe twenty feet at the deepest part here. I ask Béla and she explains that this is an unusual plateau in the middle of the sea. Any ships that have discovered this sailed around for fear of grounding their ship.

Their ships need deeper water for sailing. The Esztergom are warned far in advance if an intruder is heading this way, so they all leave this area, leaving it to appear as a lifeless desert. I can see many half-human females with a lower fish's body. They are beginning to swarm around Kisteleki, who is feeding them plentifully. There are so many of them, young, old, and our age. They all look so happy and appear not to be worried about us. They are actually coming up to the window and placing both hands against our see through walls, as my wives are rushing up to match them. Hevesi expands to enjoy this with our clan. Béla asks me to enjoy this fun. They match her hands and then she moves along the wall to kiss them. They match her kiss, which excites my wives as they always enjoy meeting kind things. I place my hands up against the window, and they all avoid me. Brann laughs and ensures all my clan understands this. Tselikovsky yells out, "Look; the women under the sea are much wiser than us." Brann adds, "They have a strong willpower." I look at Brann and comment, "Oh. That is a relief; therefore, I do not have to worry about them lying naked on me begging to be seduced." Gyöngyösi and Makói both come rushing to me as Makói says, "We will hold our Master's hands. They play with me, as we pretend we have a wall between us. We meet our palms as the others are doing with the Esztergom. Gyöngyösi claps my hands while rushing to me for a kiss repeatedly, as Makói repeats the same process repetitiously. This cyclically process is confusing the Esztergom causing many to form on the window beside us. Gyöngyösi guides us to the window as she puts up her left and holds me with her right while Makói holds my left hand and places her right hand to the window. They rotate, placing their face against this water wall and as one kisses an Esztergom, they will immediately turn back to kiss me. Soon, they will have me stand at the window while each kisses their side of my cheeks. Shortly thereafter, they put my face to the window and waved for the fish women to kiss me. One, trembling while three others were pushing her, came to the window, and we had a quick kiss. Gyöngyösi and Makói clapped in excitement, as soon our whole clan and Béla stepped back joining in the clapping. Afterwards each returned to their posts. However, something different happened this time.

I now had a large line in front of me. Béla stands behind me and tells me, "They are not fond of men. I believe you are the first one they like. Congratulations my friend, for they apparently sense, your love." I tell Béla, "I will wait until later to analyze the whys in this, for now I want to present a good diplomatic appearance to them." Soon, Béla asks us if we would like to meet these Esztergom. My clan goes crazy with excitement. Béla yells to Kisteleki to open the doors to the bottom bay and open the bay. Kisteleki uses his golden octopus legs to raise our ship about ten feet, which now puts our top deck well above water. Béla tells me that Kisteleki's eyes can see for three hundred miles in all directions. He could see more; however, the curvature of our planet prevents this. She apologizes and asks me, "What do you know about Lamenta and the skies above it." I tell her, "I have seen the Lamenta is a giant round rock and the two suns, three moons and so many stars have many cold dark skies between them." Béla tells me this is good, for she heard that most Lamentans believe Lamenta to be flat. I confess to her that I also believe that until I was above this world. That is where

I met my Angel Gyöngyösi. Béla asks me, "Am I to believe she is a true Angel of the Great Spirits?" I tell her that if she accepts this as authentic, no one will prove her veracity false. I call my Angel to my side and ask her, "Do you think it would be special for the Esztergom if they were to see a real Angel flying over the water?" Gyöngyösi answers, "I do not think on such things, if you wish it, I do it. Do you wish this my Master?" I continue, "I think it would be virtuous if they could see a special beauty reserved for the Great Spirits." As I finish talking, she had already transformed and Béla has dropped on the ground with her head lowered into the palms. Gyöngyösi tells Béla, "Béla, do not fear me, for I am the same, so rise and kiss me as you did my Master." Béla begins begging for forgiveness for kissing her Master. Gyöngyösi then asked by, why did you not enjoy his kiss as much as I do? Béla afterwards asked, "What do you want of me?" Gyöngyösi answered this almost immediately, "That you love me and my Master with the same heart, now rise, and give me my kiss and hug."

Béla, not knowing what she was doing rose and kissed Gyöngyösi and with trembling arms as her mind was returning to consciences wrapped her arms around her." I easily massaged Béla's back and neck. Béla, surprisingly become calm quickly and feeling her oats, asked Gyöngyösi, "Do his massages always feel this pronounced?" Gyöngyösi answered, "Great enough to justify leaving the heavens." Gyöngyösi took Béla's hands and had her, touch her womb. She tells Béla; in here is my Master's son. Béla looks seriously at Gyöngyösi and answers, "You truly love your husband." Gyöngyösi tells her, "I have loved him since then I put his soul into his infant body." Béla confesses, "I have never heard of such a pronounced love." Gyöngyösi tells her, "My Béla, all in this family have a great tale about their love and sacrifice to be in our family, as married or even unmarried. You should ask each one of the wives to share their story with you. I tell you, you will be impressed with what you are among in this clan. We are all simple, yet sacrificing and live under the harmony of a loving, caring, always giving Master." I tell Béla, "Be careful Béla, as my wives will try to recruit you as a wife also, and soon you will have my baby in you." Béla tells us, "You have already recruited me. Sadly, I hope you understand that because of the elements, we can never have children." I now tell Béla, "That is the only reason Brann, Baranya and Abaúj cannot marry me." Béla asks, "Why cannot Nógrád marry you? I have noticed how she loves everyone in your clan so much, and each one loves her. She is Lamentan." Gyöngyösi explains that Nógrád is not Lamentan; she is Edelényi who had laws forbidding her to marry with us. The Edelényi had graciously agreed to allow our children to marry their children. Their laws are effective based on the date of birth, for that she can never receive an escape clause. Abaúj is asking her leaders to issue a diplomatic plea on Nógrád's behalf. We can only wait." Béla speaks into her shirt and appears blank for a few seconds. Her mind returns, telling us the water nations and species shall also issue a plea to the great Council of the Edelényi. Gyöngyösi and I thank her with hugs and kisses. Béla laughs while telling Gyöngyösi, "There, he kissed me again." Gyöngyösi tells her, "Béla, I would expect my husband to kiss such a beautiful person, such as you."

Béla immediately blushes and then reminds us the Esztergom are waiting for us, so we must hurry. We rush down the steps following Béla. I wonder to myself, 'how my wives knew where to go.' Béla, our resident mind reader, tells me that Kisteleki guided them. She leads us to another set of stairs that take us down to the bottom of Kisteleki. We enter a large room with plenty of indoor light. I joke to Gyöngyösi, "Even since we left Grandpa's modern village, we no longer have to wait over a day to see." As we get closer to the water, I notice the water strays in the hole. I ask Béla why the water is not flooding the room. She looks at me and says, "Silly boy, I told it not to." That made, sense to me, as she was water and why would water destroy itself. As we were walking to meet our clan, Khigir and Makói came running to us asking why we took so long. Gyöngyösi tells Khigir that Béla was flirting with our Master again, to no luck. Khigir looks at Béla and offers to give her some important tips. Béla shakes her head and cries out, "How have I lived this long without you deranged lunatics?" I look at her and say, "Darling, as I am an insane lunatic, I would not be able to answer that question." Khigir wraps her arm around Béla and asks her, "Can you think of any solutions?" Béla tells her, "I am still searching. I may need you to help me find an answer." Khigir hugs her saying, "I will be here if you need me, as I do understand much what you are undergoing." Béla thanks Khigir and now asks our clan to join her. She begins by saying, "I so hate to spring this on you currently. Notwithstanding, I am sure you noticed that our fish women naturally have no clothing on their Lamentan half, as they have no clothing on their fish lower half. Traditionally, when we meet with them in a large ground as this, we remove our shirts, so they may be more comfortable. Believe me, after seeing how Brann looked so wonderful when she shared herself with us, I now feel inferior. I have such a hard time fighting dirty boy off, who will be feasting today, with my shirt on. I dreadfully fear him when he sees my top half that he may want me to perform as Brann."

I looked at her and said, "This time only. You are safe. Because the one I shall enjoy today is that one. I was pointing at Makói, waving for her to come to me. What was so funny was when I said this one; Brann went diving on the floor. I could not let this slip, so I said, "Brann, just as Béla said, "We have already had our fill of you. You are yesterday's thrill." Béla looks at Brann and argues, "I never said that." Brann tells her, "Béla I know. Silly boy is just angry with himself for not taking me when he could." I look at them and say, "Get your shirts, for I want to compare you against the Esztergom." Makói was beside me now. I know that she is comfortable unclothed with my other wives in our bedroom and with them bathing. She had not been topless before the other unmarried in our family or Béla. Moreover, now to be bare-breasted in front of, among her favorite foods, fish women, could be traumatic for her. I will keep her beside me and help her if she gets the trembles. The last thing I want to this time is for her to turn back into a ten-foot bear and devour as many Esztergom as she can. Therefore, I have her beside me, especially since she believes in me. I unbutton her shirt buttons, while leaving her shirt in place. Going slow and careful always works on my wife Makói. I have for so long wondered why she puts as a result much faith in me. If she can hold my hand, she will do things she had never took on before. Today will be one of those times. Kisteleki removes his outside fences and leads his bait into our viewing area. A few pop up to explore what is above them. When they spring up out of the water, my wives are standing waving at them. Béla pulls Khigir to the side and tells her not to stand too close to the pool. She is afraid that because Khigir has so much water in her blessings, that the Esztergom may become scared believing this to be a trick. Once they are relaxed we will introduce you. Kisteleki began lifting buckets up from under his floor packed with the seafood these Esztergom craved. My wives began by tossing the bait into the water until Béla told us to hold it and have them take it from our hands. This is when it became fun, and my wives began talking to one another about how enjoyable this was. We slid Khigir in as I stood beside Makói.

The three of us joined the bait feeding my hand. Makói really began to enjoy this. My wives were yelling back and forth to one another about the events that were happening on their side to the pool. Within about twenty minutes, they packed before us, and thankfully, Kisteleki was creating the enticement for our sea women's large appetite. Our sea friends decided to rattle our brains and began to talk to us. We were astonished. I asked Béla to explain this strange phenomenon to us. She reveals to us the Esztergom can talk with all the species in the seas they desire. After a few minutes of hearing the other species talk, they can learn the complete language. This is the reason the sea protects them so much. I look over at some of them and ask, "How are you ladies doing today?" They want to know what species I am and why I look so much different from the women in our group. I tell them I am a male. I ask them if they have men in their species. The Esztergom denies having any males. I ask them how they reproduce without any men. The female fish tells me that they simply bury their eggs in the sand and return later to collect their children. They keep all their children together as all the adults help in caring for them. Béla tells me that their eggs decide most of their standardized appearance. These eggs are incredibly popular among the sea fish and have a stimulating effect on male fish who spawn them. The spawning merely activates the eggs; they provide no exchange in the biological matter. I look at Gyöngyösi and convey to her that I did not understand a word she had said. Gyöngyösi notifies me that she will explain the details later. Nevertheless, she tells me that their eggs include all the things needed to form their bodies, which is why they all look the same. The fertilization provided by any other species in the sea simply starts their eggs. They return just before the eggs' hatch and collect their daughters. I told Gyöngyösi that this did not make sense. When I think about it, our way did not make sense in so many of my shots dying before hitting their target. A woman, who is wading in front of me, lefts up her hands toward me.

I might as will say they are women, as the fish bottoms are in the water and the only thing before me is their skin from the waist up and light brown hair, which dried extremely fast when out of the water. They all look the same, with their red lips. They are beautiful, and I would feel sad if we hurt any. Ajkai yells out, "Khigir, please help us. Our Master is trying to pull one of them out of the water." Khigir comes running to me, as I am currently sitting on the bottom floor of this ship holding hands with one of these curious angels. I ignore Ajkai, as Makói is perched behind me with her arms holding my chest. Her beautiful face swings around my body where she can see everything. I tell these female half-fish, "This is my special love Makói. She will answer any question you have." Khigir asks Makói, "Our lovely icing, is our Master being good." Makói looks at Khigir and says, "No Khigir, he is being . . . . Great." Whew, I thought she was going to pull a Brann on me. Khigir begins laughing, comes and shakes Makói hand with a kiss, my hand with a kiss, rubs my hair while laughing, and gentle rubs the new acquaintance's hands as they smile at each other. Khigir returns for the rest of the clan. I ask this new contact if she knows the origins of her species. She tells me, "I do my Master." I now realize that since everyone calls me their Master whom they think it is my name. I then also realize that one should deny a giant school of topless women, at least from the waist up, the right to think of me as their Master. If only such a magnitude as this had not bored me. The same thing in such a mass number defies my logic. She tells me that they created them to swim in the pools of a pronounced space King, who has access stately to magic. When his kingdom was defeated, the conquerors considered them to be from evil, thus brought them to Lamenta dumping them in the great seas. I asked her if they had any enemies. She told me that all snakes and eels hated them and when seeing them struggle to kill them. Even the ones who are not poisonous will choke them. All carnivorous species in the sea who cannot communicate will also chase them. They prefer to stay around here, as many killers do not wish to get this close to the surface. The sand makes it harder for the snakes to get closer to them. The largest problem that they have is seeking food, which many times involve eating other sea life, which can cause problems.

They are lucky because many larger species are friendly to them and help them hunt. They fear that since some Lamentans have sailed across the seas that someday they will bring many hunters. That will require them to relocate to the bottom of the sea and live in caves. I ask her why they have grown so fond of us. She explains that they feel something special in us, which tells them we will not hurt them. Makói confesses to her that we will work exceedingly hard not to hurt them. She holds Makói's hand and tells her. We believe you, even though you are a Szabolcs. We have brought Szabolcs food many times in the cold waters when they were starving. The Lamentan side in us always wins in our kindness to each other's species. This made Makói so happy that she slid through the water and gave her new friend, a giant hug. Tselikovsky yells out, "Oh no; our Master has poor Makói recruiting for him now." All the Esztergom looked over when they heard the splash and froze for a fraction of a second and responded in unison, "Your Master has already recruited us. Show us where we will be staying."

Béla goes running across the floor screaming, "How could you?" The Esztergom are laughing currently as my wives quickly discover the Esztergom hoaxed them. Soon all were laughing, and we tossed them in the last of our food. They thanked us for our kindness. Kisteleki warned us that we were running late. Thus, our new friends excused themselves as we slowly departed so as not to hurt any of them. We felt accordingly sad when we saw them crying at our departure, as we were also saddened. I had so many complaints about them initially. Nevertheless, they grew on me. I am now fantastically fond of their dedication to survive after they suffered such a great disaster and end up in the wild ocean. Soon Kisteleki was returning to his normal speed. Then about ten minutes into our trip, Kisteleki made a sudden shift and we could see him shooting powerful light fire that was zipping way ahead of us. Béla came out handing us weapons and told us to listen fast while she explained to us how to what she said fire them and reload them.

Kisteleki had risen out of the water, and his golden octopus arms were shooting his weapon far ahead. Abaúj now claims to feel something certainly wrong. Kisteleki is making an extremely loud sound currently. There is an intense uneasy feeling among us. A few of my wives begin crying. My Tamarkins pull out their arrows and put their deadly razor multi-sharp heads on their arrows. We have the feeling of a big fight ahead of us. I just wish I understood what was happening. I ask Béla what is wrong. She begins crying, and tells me it is too terrible. Gyöngyösi and Csongrád while looking out the window asked Béla for two weapons. Brann and Baranya hand them their weapons and turn into blazing fire going down to Kisteleki's control room to find a way to exit. I look out the window and see them flashing off into the skies. Khigir and Ajkai begin screaming now. I look down at the ocean, we were just in, and see so many mangled partial parts of the Esztergom floating on the sea, which was now red. We saw a few hideous beasts lying dead among them. These beasts were twice the size of cattle, had wings and large powerful legs and arm with petrifying claws. Their heads were large as they had a large flat bone that ran from their nose to at least two feet past their heads. With jaws packed with meat cutters, which based on what we see, no flesh can survive. What made them a threat in the middle of the seas were the twenty-feet wide span of their muscle packed, feather-free compound boned wings. The ones, who were dead from our previous friends, were now covered in blood and crushed bones, It must have taken so many of them to pull down one of these beasts. Béla, Abaúj, and Ajkai now rush to Kisteleki's control room and soon vanish. Kisteleki calls over his ship wide speaker devices that he is converting our upper deck to battle stations. He asks that those among us who are fighting to prepare to fight as the Hegyközi. He warns that they can also live under water over long periods of days. We are doing everything to round them back to us for their destruction. He also explains that all the sea beasts, after receiving the news, are in this area trying to secure the few Esztergom that are hiding and most likely terrified. We can see what must be hundreds of thousands of large sea creatures. Many are species we have never yet seen. They are rushing to this area to secure the Esztergom body parts. This will not permit one more bite of their flesh to fall into the grasps of the Hegyközi.

Shortly later, as the clean sea sand is beside us, we see our first live Hegyközi when they come darting out of the water. They chased by everything possible in the sea, as jellyfish of all sizes stung them without mercy, and even the snakes are pounding them. The Hegyközi must be shoddier enemies than the Esztergom to them. As they leave the water, my Tamarkins and the Queen are hitting everything they can. They are trying to destroy their wings and by it force them back into the water for a cruel death. Nógrád is providing us all the supplies, especially extra weapons as we are burning these quickly. My greatest surprise is what I have on each side of me, as I am fighting them in the open and close to the edges, any way to get a good shot. I like to work them from behind so as not to scare them too bad. I always believed a greater pain thought you had escaped only to discover you would be in the numbers of the lost. Back to my greatest shocker is how effective and patient that Hevesi and Makói are fighting. Hevesi is no surprise, as I know she will get as many of them as any of us do. Makói is my pride today. She is in no way shy or showing any signs of fear. She has a death stair in her eyes, as I would not be surprised if she does not change into her ten-foot bear if one of the Hegyközi were to stumble on this deck. The richly populated sea tops with dead Hegyközi, as so many are also dropping out of the sky. I am noticing that many of them have completely burned faces. Kisteleki tells us that we may stand down. Our ship is going to do some sabotage work now with his octopus weapons. I hear a faint cry for my name. I ask Kisteleki, if he can identify the source, and he tells me to go down to the pool. Makói follows beside me. She is sensing the same wild notion that I am. We rush into the bottom pool and see an Esztergom in the pool now calling for both our names. We walk over to her as Makói pulls out her knife and dives in. She stays under water for a few minutes and then returns to the surface, throws her knife across the floor to me and wraps her arms around our guest and starts kissing her. Makói stops, gives her one more sniff, and tells me, "Master, this is our friend."

I look at her and tell her I am so sorry that so many died, and that I feel it to be my fault. She tells me, "Oh, no it was our fault for we knew to be more careful as we had spotted them in the area. Fortunately, only about ten percent of us showed up today, and more than half of us got away. We actually lost so many trying to get our injured out. Yes, we do have many hurt." Makói declares now that we will not release her, but take her with us. She looks at me and I agree, of course. Those sweet milky bear eyes got me again, as I cannot believe what I see. I see a large bear saving a big fish. Where is my consciousness? My mind is going to lose it. I look down at her and ask if she has a name. She tells me she does, and that we call her Dabasi. I tell Dabasi that we are in the middle of killing those who hurt your people, and as many will be arriving, not knowing they will die. We need to secure her. I yell to Kisteleki to ask him where we can put our friend. He opened two sizable doors that are enclosing a large water tank. He also sprays water on our floor.

Makói and I dragged her out of the water. We then slide her scales over the wet floor, going into the next room with what appears to be small people's pool. We easily drop her into the water. Makói asks to stay with her to insure her safety and help for a smooth transition into our world. I go back up to the blazing war. I barely make it to my battle station because of the wind. I yell out, "Is that you Berettyóú?" I have been appearing before me now two purple eyes, and a voice saying, "I am sorry." As the wind is slowing, I ask her, "Will you be able to tell me what is happening in our war?" Berettyóú apologizes for being so busy and informs me she will send Móri, who will be here as fast as the wind. I laugh and say, "Very funny our wonderful friend Berettyóú." Away she blew, as Khigir tossed me a weapon and asked, "What did you do with my bear?" I looked at her and laughed reporting, "I do believe your bear is taking after you more and more each day." I looked above her and saw a burning Hegyközi coming at her. I instantaneously lifted my weapon and fired a beam into him as Khigir dived to the floor. The beast, now a blazing fire crashed into Kisteleki dropping to the sea, where a large group of carnivorous fish began eating away at it.

We went to our battle stations and began firing away beside my Queen and Tselikovsky while Nógrád continued to provide us with energized weapons. Shortly thereafter, we felt a new breeze begin to blow over us. A voice informed us, "Soon this will be finished. We have blown every Hegyközi we could find from around Lamenta for this final destruction. They are enemies to all and kill too much, to sustain themselves. Siklósi, you should be proud of those who are fighting with you. Many of the Hegyközi are arriving in this sea dead. Abaúj is taking the air from them, forcing them to die instantly. Bélapátfalvai or Béla as you call her is drawing the water from their bodies and blood, which kills them quickly. Amazingly, to include the smoldering touch, Brann and Baranya are burning them alive. Ajkai is surprising us as she is performing great mysteries in the skies. She is changing what they see. Therefore, many are destroying one another in hysteria. Berettyóú is attempting to blow as much as possible back to this graveyard, so the Esztergom can see how their friends avenged their massacre." The smell was beginning to make us sick; as a result, I asked Móri if he would blow this stink away from us. He then bid his farewell, feeling it important that he helps Berettyóú after he removed this vomitus smell. Kisteleki asked us to stand down or stop fighting. He was going partially to raise our windows, leaving the top open for the time being. He lifted himself about one-hundred feet higher and hovered or remained at this position. I enjoy the little monitors beside our chairs that tell us what is happening. I now know that hover means to remain in a higher position. Kisteleki has all his golden legs stretched and firing his weapons spraying the incoming zone. He has powerful beams, when they contact one Hegyközi; they bore straight through hitting any in that target trajectory. He gets five kills from each shot. As these are line wounds, the Hegyközi kept most of their flesh, when they die crashing against the sea. This provides more feed for the sea beasts.

As these beasts are feeding on the Hegyközi, we can only hope that they will develop a taste for them and as such, begin hunting and feeding from them. It astonishes me how many of them exist. I have never seen these creatures previously. We receive some more peace within our hearts as we see these things dropping. Brann and Baranya are near now. I can see long flames of fire moving in front of their target's faces. This is amazing, watching them fight for their fallen friends. The Esztergom clearly made a favorable impression on them. The way their flames burn in the faces and chest areas with pinpoint accuracy excite all who see it. They have added the chest burning most likely to destroy their hearts, so they will not be able to live in the water. Those who hold onto their hearts fall to the sea blind and by it become easy prey for their new neighbors. We can see Abaúj now as she has collected dust to spin in her sphere. She is suffocating them, as so many continue to drop to the sea. Kisteleki announces that we can see Béla working at 10:00 o'clock high. Béla's large target is swirling with red. We can see water pouring down from these compressed flocks. Just as in Abaúj's zone, they are dropping by the droves. Khigir yells at me to see Ajkai. I look to our left and see a giant wall of fire, running from the sea to the sky. She is displaying an apparition, which resembles reality so much. Looking at the sea before us, I see a sea packed with open mouths and jaws, including rows of razor-sharp teeth. The Hegyközi are piling up on one another. They do not want to enter the wall of fire. As the Hegyközi are now sitting targets, Kisteleki is blasting them and filling these open mouths waiting to feed on them. Berettyóú and Móri are preventing the Hegyközi from retreating and going higher to avoid detection. Kisteleki is sealing our ship and announcing his concern about some Hegyközi entering and harming us. I look at Khigir, Tselikovsky, and our Queen and ask them to bring Nógrád so we can watch her. I snuggle with my three wives I am holding and of course, Hevesi, who is asleep in my pocket. I complain to my wives about them always taking, me to threatening places. My Queen tells me there is no place too dangerous for her Knight of greatest honor. Khigir, who is laughing with us adds, "Oh, Royal Highness, now your nights are dangerous."

The Queen looks at Khigir and replies, "Oh my lovely Khigir. My nights are not dangerous. What can I do?" I tell her to be thankful that her Knight is protecting her nights. She assures me that she considers herself truly blessed. I hug them and recommend we talk about what happened today. Khigir takes the lead on this one with anger in her heart. She claims that many of the Hegyközi should have alerted someone who could have monitored and help fight them. Kisteleki intervenes trying explains the group, which attacked our Esztergom, was not that large. He estimates maybe around one-hundred, which is their normal raiding numbers. We know that they hide deep inside caves and sink to the lowest parts of the sea waiting to attack. They can reassemble within a few hours and slowly kill getting to their target. Kisteleki agrees that something may have seen a few of them as chose not to investigate in more detail. Tselikovsky thinks that we are in the wrong place at the mistaken time. She changes the subject and asks, "Where is our lovely Makói?" Khigir and Csongrád also begin to panic. I tell them not to panic; she is doing something she loves to help work off the pain and suffering she saw today. They look at me trying to decide if I am telling the truth. Khigir relaxes and reports to them that I am telling the truth, especially because of my deep love for Makói. Tselikovsky inserts that our Makói really fought hard and openly today. She could see no ounce of shyness on this day. I added that we had seen a different person today. I feel her confidence and ability to care with compassion flowed through today. Nógrád turns the fire up on this conversation by claiming how much she is now missing Makói. Khigir asks me to take all of us to our special Makói. I tell my wives and Nógrád to follow me. Down the steps we go, to the pool on the bottom floor. Khigir wonders why she would be down here. Tselikovsky reasons that she is holding on to the fond memories of the Esztergom compared with a sea filled with their torn body parts and blood. As we start for the pool, Khigir worries telling us, she cannot see her precious bear. I tell her to be patient, as we will soon see her. When we walked past our pool a twisting and rising force of water sprang us, terrifying us.

The water stopped spinning and walking on top of the surface; we could see Béla. We cheered and opened our arms causing her to run toward us. It feels as if she was gone for such a longtime. Our room became dark as little stars were floating around us. The light reappeared, and the stars vanished as my wife Ajkai comes running to us. At this time, two whirling streams of fire came rushing down the steps and appearing before us, were Brann and Baranya. The mysteries continued as the bubbles began rising from the surface of this pool. Shortly thereafter, the bubbles rejoined and from that came Abaúj. As her feet hit the ground, she came running for us. Makói opened her door and asked if we would join in her room as it had seats to sit on. In we went in with Khigir following Makói and me. Khigir stops and asks, "Siklósi, do you know what this is?" I told of course that she was an Esztergom. Brann adds, "Khigir, she is one of the many reasons we fought today." Béla asks Makói if she knows anything about caring for an Esztergom. Dabasi tells Khigir that she will soon learn. Makói asks Béla if we can keep her. Béla tells her that she will ask Kisteleki to find her school, so she will be able to tell them this is what she wants. Béla asks her, "Is this what you truly want. As you know, the numbers of days are few that you may live on the air, before being unable to return into the sea." Dabasi confesses that she wants to belong to Makói, our family, and I. All other things no longer matter. Abaúj sits in the water, behind her massaging her shoulders, and asks forgiveness for not detecting this savage massacre. Dabasi explains to the entire family that it took them many months to figure out what they could be planning. She confesses that they misjudged this one, figuring instead that they were waiting for a large festival, which would take place later in the season. However, we alerted them not to assemble in a large group. Therefore, so many went back to their living places, leaving only around ten percent to welcome us. We figured that because we did not know they were coming, they sure did not know. Our resident Queen asks her about what she felt today when she saw this. Dabasi told her it was something she never wanted to think about again.

That so much hate and greed could do that to others is a hellish thought she must burn from her mind. Csongrád reveals to us that this is the thing; she fears worst for her daughter. She may have to fight wars to save her people or punish other nations for doing her kingdom's wrong. She may have to decide who dies and who lives. War, she added, is a truly terrible thing, because the innocent on both sides must suffer. She jumps in beside Abaúj helping to massage her back. Soon, we are all in the water playing with her. Ajkai, after having so much fun playing with Dabasi cheering saying, "We have a new family member?" I put my arm over Béla and ask her when Dabasi becomes acclimated to the air, will anything different change with her. Béla tells me that nothing else will change; she will have to have water on her scales as much as possible to prevent them from shedding. She asks me if her being half-fish bothers me. I tell her that this is a reason we love her so much. My problem is I think that being on land she will want to be like all the others around her. Béla asks me if she can find a solution for Dabasi, what I might do for her." I tell her, Béla why you would care because you are leaving us soon. I mean that we tried to please you. Nevertheless, you had to throw away our affection and kindness. She puts her hand lightly over my mouth, thus I stop talking. She testified that her problem is the opposite, and the final proof for her today was the way this family fought so hard to obtain justice for the Esztergom. She claimed that we had the real love, and not the pretend or fake love, then to return and see an Esztergom under our permanent care. I interrupt, “Her name is Dabasi.” Béla comments, “Oh, so you give them names also?” I inform her that Dabasi told us that was her name. Béla compliments me on teaching her something new about this wonderful species. They always assumed that since they all looked identical, they thought of themselves as the same. Béla, if my family chooses to add you as an unmarried member, what all would we have to do to keep you in our family. Do not be concerned about the unmarried, as Brann, Baranya, and Abaúj are because different elements cannot mate. Béla understands this.

She explains that the water has never lived among other elements and that ordinarily to entertain such a notion would be frivolous. Nevertheless, as all the other elements represented in this family, they should approve, based on how much we plead to keep us together. Béla asks me how I knew this is what she wanted. I tell her the way she responded when I had my arm around her shoulder. She now asks to be forgiven if her response if it was inappropriate. Béla, I told her you did respond appropriately. It is because you were so relaxed when I was touching you, which told me how comfortable you were around us. I now inquired about what she had in mind of doing for us. She told me that it was just as important to her as it was for us. She would search for a wizard who tales speak of being able to change Esztergom into Lamentans. Béla told me she could not guarantee this. She promised to ask the mysterious ones to help her. They are notorious for their warm hearts. I told her we would help also in any way we could. Water, I asked why you want to be with us and give up so much. Béla explains that she is not really giving everything up, because some water from a stream or raid will always be near. She confesses that much of because of for selfish reasons. One such reason is being so close to strong love. In addition, she wants to have others to share her life with through the years before us. She asks me if this is wrong. I tell her it is not wrong, now we need to go to sell this to our family. Béla asks me how I will vote. I ask her, "Do you really not know my heart by now?" She tells me that her feeling is that I will support her plea. I tell her, "Girl, you are absolutely right." Before we return, she pushes a button on the wall and talks to Kisteleki first asking him if the Hegyközi were demolished. He answers that they are shattered from the sky and currently digesting in the stomachs of the sea beasts, who will now search Lamenta for their new prey. It will be at least one thousand years before they are raiding anyone. Béla asks him to take us to the deep-sea bottom, so we can request permission to keep Dabasi. Kisteleki asks who Dabasi is. She tells him this is an Esztergom, who met our guests. She finds herself desiring to spend the rest of her life in this family. Kisteleki then comments how strange women act when they feel a little love.

They appear to give up everything and follow that fancy. Béla asks Kisteleki to take us to the high Council so she can make a plea before them. Kisteleki questions her about why she would have to make a plea to the high Council. Béla tells him that she also wants to be a member of this family. Kisteleki asks, "They got you too?" She tells him that they stole her heart also. Kisteleki tells her to be patient; he will find her heart and give it back to her. Béla tells him, my Kisteleki, I am telling you that I find myself in love with them. My heart is still in this body. Kisteleki finishes this conversation by telling us the missions with men do not have these strange problems. We begin our journey to meet my family. As we open the door, Khigir takes one look at me and comes running to me asking, "Another one Master." I tell her if our family accepts her love, she will give it to us, as much as she can based on the laws of the elements. She will be wonderful to have around for our Dabasi. The Esztergom will most likely approve our plea for Dabasi if they know that Béla wants also to join with us. Khigir asks me if I am trying to sell her on having Béla in our family. I tell her that she wanted this long before I was. I am only giving you some ammunition to help win over the rest of this clan. Khigir walks over to Béla and confesses that she had dreamed of having her in our family. She thought that Béla would never consider it. Béla explains that during the battle today she had fought so much better than previously. This she attributes to the peace and trust, she had in Brann and the rest of the fighters. Trust was automatic. Béla tells her that this was the closest that she felt connected with others throughout her entire life. During the fighting, she cared more for her comrades' lives than hers, as they were concerned more over her than themselves. Moreover, that felt good with her. We enter the room now as the family is spoiling the daylights out of Dabasi. I noticed that they had put a sleeping shirt on her. Khigir asks the family to listen to her for a second. She asks them if we can bring both Béla and Dabasi into our family. Ajkai asks Béla if this is what she wants. Béla moves out in front of them, removes her clothing and falls on her knees, saying, "I come before you begging that you let me serve you, even as your dog if you so desire.

I promise to serve and love all in this family, if you have mercy on me." Brann and Baranya come up to her and put the clothing she had thrown on the floor and then lifted her up. Brann looked her in the eyes and confessed to have never dreamed of saying to the water element's representative that she truly loved her, and would always serve with her. Ajkai came running up, as all the wives did. They all dropped on their knees and declared their love for her. Khigir sat down between Béla and Dabasi and asked them what we had to do, rather than steal them or fight for them to be forever with us. Khigir put her arms around them and turned their heads, so they were facing her. She looked them in the eyes and told them. You are mine now, and I will not give you up or release you. Dabasi asserts that she will die with them. Béla acknowledges that she will die with, or for them, as she knows Dabasi would also if given an opportunity to do so. Dabasi confesses that she never dreamed that someday an aquatic diplomat, such as Béla would share her family with her. I sit down behind Khigir and wrap my arms around her waist, asking, "How is my daughter doing in there?" Khigir tells us, "She is so proud of her daddy." Béla asks Khigir why the other wives follow her decisions. I tell them, because just as you, no one came to our family unless through Khigir. She is the number-one wife. Béla adds that she is also the most beautiful. She adds that Khigir must also be the greatest creation among the women. I tell them that once she knows and loves you, she will worry much that you enjoy a great life. She is extremely shy around those whom, she does not know. In addition, when we are riding on horses, she also rides facing me with her arms wrapped tightly around me. Dabasi asks why she behaves like this, because, if she were as beautiful to the same degree of Khigir, she would want to show off that beauty. I tell Dabasi that those Hegyközi are not the only evil things that roam over Lamenta. Many wicked Lamentan men who see Khigir, desire to have her, and then would destroy her after they took her body from her. She has a cold heart against men whom, she does not know or suspects are lusting after her. Béla looks at us and reveals that she thinks I lust after Khigir.

Khigir tells them, "Oh dirty boy is always in heat around me." Dabasi eager to know more about this relationship asks me, "Why does Khigir allow you so many privileges with her body?" I tell them, "My fresh loves, this is because she trapped and captured me." Khigir adds that love made her do it, reporting that when love, captures you, all old things pass away, and new things move in to take their places. Béla ads, you are saying the same thing that has happened to Dabasi and me. Khigir shares with them that love does not care who it captures, when it captures there is no escape. Your heart destroys all logic. Just as Béla stood having nothing on before her family tonight, love takes away your shame. Dabasi asks, "Has our Master seen you unclothed?" She adds that our Master has been with all his wives bare. Sometimes when I want him to look at me when I am naked, he ignores me. Those are the times I walk up to him and hit him while screaming at him. He now knows to watch me when I am sharing with him. Béla asks, "How many of your wives are with child?" Khigir tells them that our Master has blessed all his wives with the gift of his child, or children as in my sister, inside our wombs. To have borne a child is extremely important for our nation. Once we are with child, we have fulfilled our duties as laid down by our ancestors. We may become part of our social order. Kisteleki summons us to our dining room. Khigir asks me to speak to our clan before eating. We could not bring Dabasi up all the stairs because of her size. She is one long muscle packed fish. I begin by thanking all in our clan for the hard fighting today. Continuing, "We showed the Hegyközi whom we are, yet no one has thankfully been alive of them to remember. We showed each and ourselves what we are made of inside. Elements or species do not matter in this clan, what binds us is our love. We know wrong when we see it. The massacre, we saw today was wrong. I have always held that to kill for survival is often justified.

To kill for the statement or installation of terror as those beasts did evil. Leaving their blood and body parts on the surface above the sea was appalling. No predator will leave as much of their prey behind as these beasts did. I know that this was the first time all four elements joined beside one another and fought for a common cause. We can stand for something or fall for everything. I vote that we stand for something. We can stand for our family love and clan." Every one cheered at our table. The girls were excited now as the sense of belonging was bonding. We were even tighter. Kisteleki had two of his mechanical people bring our food in on trays and place it on our tables. Kisteleki recommends that we eat faster than normal as he is scanning our area looking for the highest concentration of the Esztergom. Béla explains that they had never been this deep and the sea creatures sworn to silence who have been down here. I ask Kisteleki to get the directions from our Esztergom, especially since we want to go straight to the appropriate authority. A few minutes later, I could feel our ship turning as we begin heading into the deep dark blue. We now return to take some food back to Dabasi. She eats some of it and afterwards asks us to lay her beside the big pool, so she will be able to go out and meet with Szatmár her Regina. I ask Kisteleki if he displays our windows. As the windows become clear of their metal covering Esztergom tells us, her Maison or home city is before us. We look out the window and see a bright shiny light. Three lit towers with beautiful windy roads swirling around them are now visible. I ask Esztergom why we did not see the lights from above the city. She explains that they have a solid water shield above it that reflects the light back. No one above it can see them. I ask her if they minded afterwards if we looked at it from the outside. Dabasi promised to ask Szatmár. She now pointed her hand to the redheaded Esztergom sitting on the large rocky ledge. She has so many Esztergom swimming around her. Evidently, she occupies a honored position. I told Dabasi that her Szatmár had red hair and looked much different. She explains that they are all from a different creation. They are incredibly wise and able to solve various difficult situations. She is looking at our window as our complete clan is looking at her.

The sea waters lifts her red hair fluffing it to create a glamorous appearance. She has a light that is shining on her Lamentan half, while she tucks her fish section away in the sea floor among its striking flowers. She is looking at us with a warm, gorgeous peaceful smile. Dabasi asks for permission to go to Szatmár and invite her into our pool. We yell at the same time, "Go, hurry . . . ." In the water she goes, shirt on, and her circular lower trunk with a large, wide bottom tail fin sticking straight up and down it goes. Within an unbelievable instant, she is out into the open sea heading directly for Szatmár. At present, is the time for our faith in her. I can see how the clan is uneasy concerning her return. This is when I inform my clan that if she leaves us, she will be returning to her people. Khigir tells our clan that she has faith that her love for us will bring her back. We watch as she stops swimming about ten feet from her Regina. Szatmár opens her palms motioning Dabasi to move closer. Dabasi goes directly to her, wrapping her arms around Szatmár's waist. Dabasi places her head on the Regina's stomach. Szatmár wraps her arms around Dabasi's head and lowers her head to rest on Dabasi's head. We can see how there appears to be a loving relationship between the different versions of the Esztergom.

The Regina acts more like a mother than a leader. The Esztergom, who was paused during Dabasi's move to her Regina, are now swimming once more. All seems to be okay. We know that such affection as this will sway Dabasi to return and be with her people or species. After just a few minutes, Dabasi released her Regina and slowly turned around. She paused as Szatmár mounted on her from behind locking her arms to Dabasi's arms. They were swimming this way, and we were all so happy. Dabasi was bringing her Queen to us, so we knew it was, time to do some begging if we wanted to keep her. Shortly thereafter, two beautiful heads popped up from the pond. At this time, we were sitting on the floor at our feet below the water from the sea. Dabasi turned around and waved at us. We waved back. Makói drops into the water and underwater swam to Dabasi and came up in person with her.

Makói was crying and said to Dabasi, "We love you so much, and I was afraid you had left us Dabasi." Dabasi started kissing Makói and told her, "I could never leave my best friend, not at any time ever, because I love you and our clan too much." Makói looked at Szatmár and smiled, saying, "We truly welcome you, and I beg with all my heart that you not divide Dabasi and myself." She raised her hand out palm down, and Makói drifted over to it and kissed her hand. After kissing Szatmár's hand, she drifted back to Dabasi. Makói began to move toward where she had been sitting. She was holding Dabasi's hand. Dabasi was holding Szatmár's hand. Szatmár seemed to be at peace with this and kept her glorious smile as she wades with her servant and host. When they were close to the pool's edge, Dabasi dropped to the water, came back up under Makói, and raised her up to where she could walk across the floor. Makói quickly sits down and sticks her legs out as Dabasi floats in backward against the pool's wall wrapping her arms around Makói's legs. She is leaning her head against Makói's stomach relaxing it completely while staring at Szatmár with a large small. Khigir waves for Szatmár to join and tells her, "Szatmár, come to me, and I will help protect you." Szatmár asks if they can hold one hand first. Khigir approves this invitation instantly. Szatmár begins her introduction, "I believe that Dabasi has told you some about my responsibilities. So many of our women have reported how hard you avenged our foolishness. I am so sorry that you had to witness the blood bath as so many of our cherished schools gave up their lives. Thanks to you, the Hegyközi will no longer be a threat to us during my lifetime and the lifetimes of our fingerling. My sibyls tell me that your clan is the first union of all four elements. My spiritualists cannot explain such a wonderful union. I shiver in thinking how that great union helped save the future of our nation. The horror you saw today caused by the Hegyközi was merely their introduction to our demise. They were attempting to instill terror in the sea beasts and thereby remove any allies we had. They would have collected in the numbers you destroyed today and invaded our cities in the deepest lands across the sea. Once again, I am thankful. I feared entering inside your pool today at first.

Many of our women testified to me that they had enjoyed their visit to your air. Now the big question, as you wish for me to break a serious commandment from our creators never to allow one of our women to live with those who walk Lamenta. I see the intense faith that Dabasi has on your relationship. Your love is evident, so I ask you what I should do. Should I break the laws of our creators? Should I fall to the temptations of love? What would you have me do?" Khigir begins crying and tells Szatmár, "It is just that we love her so much and want to have her as a part of our wonderful family." Csongrád explains to her, "I am also a reigning Queen of the Dorogi. I will tell you as Queen to Queen that every time I gave into love because of temptation, the results were always to my benefit. In addition, I plan to break any law from my ancestors, which are my heritage and blood, if that law takes away from their divine right to the pursuit of love. My daughter who is in my womb currently will always rule with love within her heart, or I will not give her my crown." Szatmár responds, "Your Royal Highness; I have heard that a great ruling Queen was in these islands now. I simply, naturally believed you had your Armies and advancing your borders. Your words have taken the crushing chains of this decision from me, for I will always rule my people with love being my law. Dabasi go to those whom, you love. I ask that your family care for her, as she is so special and brave to live within that world so far above us. If you want Dabasi, she is yours." Our clan, except for Brann and Baranya jumped into the water to hug Dabasi. I rushed as fast as I could to get a good place to hug and kiss, as I was a madman. My wives, without hesitation pulled me off and shared their love with our newest unmarried family member. Khigir was now hugging Szatmár, as Csongrád sat down with them and hugged Szatmár for ruling in love. Szatmár looks at Brann and Baranya and asks if everything is okay with them. Khigir tells her that they are from the fire element and attempt to avoid water when possible. She continued by requesting that she not fear for their love of Dabasi, and have promised her some exciting adventures. Szatmár asks if we can send back some reports about what she is doing, as she will quickly become a hero, especially for the fingerlings. Khigir reassures her that Béla should be able to perform that for us. Szatmár in excited that her little Dabasi will be in the same family as Béla.

Khigir tells her that we are going to make that request after leaving here. Szatmár freezes for a moment, and then becomes conscious again. She tells us that she asks the other representatives to go before the Council and make the petition. Szatmár smiles at us and explains that it is important in issues such as this to know the answer before putting yourself in a trap. They may not let her go with you, so if they are not, then why go to them. Szatmár now wades over to Csongrád and tells her. I have never touched a land Queen. Csongrád rushes her hands out and adds that she has, at no time touched the hands of a water Queen. Csongrád asks her, "How did you become so beautiful?" Szatmár laughs, saying, "I was just about to ask you the same thing. Instead, I will ask you why you stepped down from your throne." Csongrád tells her that she can advocate, as the King, her father, will never allow it. He holds his peace because my Master and I have agreed to give one of our children to the throne. We cannot think of a better gift to our child than a powerful kingdom. I was so lonely among our palace wanting only someone to love, especially after my mother's death. My Master arrived one day with his three wives at that time. A crazy thing called love put me on my knees begging him for permission to serve him all the remaining days of my life, and for him to plant his seed in me, so I can bear his children and surrender them to him. Szatmár tells us that she has always dreamed of that sort of love. She also congratulated Csongrád for giving her people a Queen filled with love and not greed or lust for glory. Szatmár furthermore enlightens us about their servant days, when she must serve all who aid her. She loves those days as it provides her with an opportunity to work industriously proving to her subjects that their Regina also knows how to work hard. Khigir, while hugging this wonderful creation, tells her she could always join us. Szatmár thanks Khigir for the greatest invitation in her life.

Nevertheless, she must stay with her school. Her world will turn out rattled enough with Dabasi leaving and will need a strong leader to keep them from going after her. Szatmár waves at Brann and Baranya while thanking them for their support today. She now hugs the Queen and Khigir and asks if she can hug each of the remaining ones to include the tall ugly one. Khigir tells her the tall ugly one loves it when you lightly bite his neck. Szatmár tells us, those ones must be dreadfully strange; no wonder our creators freed us from them. Khigir told our clan the Regina wanted to hug them in saying good-bye. She had to add in, "And the tall ugly one must go last." All my women laughed at this one. Therefore, I gather this must be one of those insider jokes for those who have nothing inside their heads. Either way, they have my heart so, once again; I must go with the flow. Szatmár, whose tear filled face, is leaving all my women in tears also. It baffles me; they have just met each other and to create this much emotion. She must give wonderful hugs, as I shall soon will receive my treat. I brace myself against this pool's wall and open my arms to hold her tight, so she can know how those tall ugly ones hug. She comes up in front of me, and I pull her into my arms, enjoying the beauty of her red hair and the softness of her skin. Notwithstanding, unexpectedly, she bites me on my neck. I am wondering if all the hugging from my wives made her hungry. I yell out 'ouch' and Dabasi rushes over, and pulling her from me tells her not to be biting our Master's neck. Her face turns red as all the wives are laughing. She asks, "Did I do wrong?" As I slide back into the water, I tell her, "Nothing that a wonderful long hug and kisses would not heal." She pleads with me, to forgive her and starts kissing me everywhere feverishly. She is truly embarrassed, and her soft body is trembling. I ask her, "Did the one with the hair color as the sun, and the enormous breasts tell you to do that?" She confirms this explaining she must have done it wrong and that Khigir was only trying to help her.

I told her, "Szatmár sweetheart, you did nothing wrong. In our family, we love to pull tricks on one another, and these tricks are to add joy to our lives. You are so innocent. Now relax in my arms because the only fear you will have tonight is escaping from being next to my heart. You are so innocently wonderful and perfect." Szatmár asks once more, "Are you sure I am innocent?" I told her if she had any more doubts she could spray my face with more kisses. Besides, if you want to play a trick back on Khigir, put some emotion in your kisses and hugs. She will not be expecting that. Szatmár looks at Dabasi and asks what she should do. Dabasi tells her to show him how a Regina can burn a man's heart leaving pleasant memories until he dies. She then says, "Okay Dabasi, I will do as you recommend." She looks at me and says, "Hold one little boy, because the Angel of the sea has you in her arms." She was so wonderful, shocking me that a fish woman could be this sensuous. As this was clearly one of my best friend-to-friend emotional exchanges, I passed out. My woman dragged me to the floor where I lay unconscious. Khigir apologized to Szatmár, saying it was all for fun. Dabasi tells Khigir that Szatmár understands. Khigir and all our women, consequently, congratulate Szatmár as the undefeated Queen of the Hugs. They all agreed that never before had any seen such a wonderful, powerful heart throbbing display of work released on a poor defenseless man. Szatmár asks whether he will get better and worries about doing me permanent damage. Khigir reassures her that I will recover, most likely with a giant hug. Szatmár reports, "You are a strange but extremely loving family. I will miss you." My wives told her how much they would miss her. Within a flash, hundreds of Esztergom appear asking their Regina if she is safe. She tells them she has never been safer in her life, and the one in danger with her being here is the sleeping one on the floor. Szatmár wades back to Dabasi, gives her a warm, soft hug, kiss, and wishes her the greatest life filled with love. Makói tells Szatmár that she will care for her as if she came from her womb. Szatmár tells reveals her faith in Makói. Szatmár waves good-bye, and calls for her protectors to follow her. She returns to her rock, as the sea light once again shines from her perfect female fish's body. We, except for dirty boy, waved good bye to her. She waves back with both arms, and Kisteleki now heads for my Council. Khigir decides to have some fun, so she has the wives take off my clothing and for Hevesi to seduce me.

She picked Hevesi because she has special physical properties that pull my seed out amazingly fast. She has Hevesi spread my seed over my groin area. Hevesi runs over to Dabasi, whom being shocked at what just happened, appears to be in a daze. Dabasi confesses that she had never seen anything such as this in all her days. She asks Hevesi if it hurts to put that thing inside her. She reassures her that it is among the greatest experiences for Lamentans or compatible species. Our laws require us to be married first. This means we in one body unite, so the joining in this manner is more in line with that. She asks Hevesi to tell how many are married to the Master. Hevesi tells her seven are married, and all seven are expectant. Dabasi asks her how the Lamentans become pregnant. Hevesi told her that what she just did would make a non-pregnant woman carrying offspring. Dabasi clarifies that it is one-on-one specific contact. Moreover, this triggers some babies who grow inside your womb. She likes her way far better, drop an acceptable load of eggs into the sand. Cover them up. Come back a few months later and wait for them to dig their way out of the sand, helping if they need assistance. This is so much easier. Hevesi explains to her that she prefers feeling her Master's child growing inside her. Makói has arrived now; therefore, Hevesi returns to Khigir. Khigir tells everyone that she will inform our Master that Szatmár turned to a wonder woman and seduced him. I woke up and could not understand why my clothes were laying on me, and I felt so yucky and smelly. I ask Khigir to tell me what was going on. They were all sitting around a circle with Tselikovsky in the middle laying on the floor. They had put a rag over her head. I asked, "What is wrong with my secret love?" They said that she fell down after Szatmár froze all of us, and you then got on you and seduced you. She is a Master, and you missed the best experience in your life. I felt around me and told Khigir I felt like Hevesi had seduced me. Yes, it was Hevesi, no doubt in my mind. Hevesi then stares at me strangely and asks me, "Why do you say it was me?" I ask her to join me and have her press a certain 'factious spot on my lower belly. I tell her that only she can stimulate that spot and leave it excited for a couple of days. Hevesi asks me, "Does it hurt you my Master?" I explain to her, "My sweet love, it is a great feeling, and right now I feel great. I will go swim in the small pond beside Béla for a while to clean myself. Oh, and once again, thank you so much my special wife." You should know that it is impossible for you to touch me in love and I not to know it. Khigir never said a thing as they were pretending to work on Tselikovsky.

I called for Tselikovsky to join me, so we could wash her and discover why she had no blood from her injuries. Tselikovsky got up, with the help of Khigir of course, and tried to walk to me. I told her to stop since I would carry her. When I got her in my arms, carrying her as I would have an infant, she apologized to me. She told me the only reason they did this was to get back at me for the longest kisses and hard hugs with Szatmár. I told her not to worry about it and asked when she was going to compete against Hevesi and see if she could give me a unique pain. She looked at me and said, "Dirty boy; I can give you a real special pain that you will remember for a longtime." I revealed to her, "My Tselikovsky, I believe you could truly do that, and when will we see Dabasi's city?" Tselikovsky tells me that if I had not played my games,

I would have seen Szatmár's city. I guess that she is right, so I received my reward now. I asked Tselikovsky what you are going to do with this dirty boy. She perked up and said she was going to give me a fast cleaning. Tselikovsky ordered me into Dabasi's pool. She also requested that Dabasi watch how they clean the dirty boy. Makói became excited to reveal to Dabasi that this was playtime, as she grabbed some rags and oils. She continued by asking our new family member if she wanted to help. Béla came running and asking if she could also learn. I agreed, since I was going to keep my special parts clothed. They splashed me and dried me off as Makói explained in detail how to apply the oils. She knew how to do this, as I once again realized how dedicated, each of my wives was in taking responsibility for my personal care and appearance. Béla is working, especially hard as the water does amazing things for her. Instead of dripping to the floor as it runs off me, she commands it to go from me, releasing any dirt and back into the pool for Dabasi. Self-cleaning water, this is something I never expected to see. I now ponder to this about how much around me; Béla's species have controlled the objects of my life.

Abaúj's species flows in and out my lungs and Béla's species runs through my blood, and both keep me alive by the minute. Now that is a mouthful and then to think how Brann and Baranya's fire adds to this. I never realized so much how important their species was for our suns. Without our suns, we would have no food, and life would soon vanish. All three play important roles for our existence. I feel honored to show my thanks by enjoying their wonderful gifts they give to our clan. Béla stands up in front of us, as the water from her clothes begins to return to the pool and begins to cry. I rush up to her, with my bear to discover why she is crying. Dabasi asks her if she can help in any manner. Poor Dabasi who must watch from her laying position in this small mini pool that would be great for children. Béla confesses to be extremely scared about meeting the court, as she does not know what to say. Khigir is running fast to join us. Our Master wife can sense when someone in our group is sad or suffering and will always when possible rush to their aid. We explain to her why Béla is suffering. Khigir offers an immediate solution, which shows that large breasted blonde-haired people do have their minutes. The wonderful times we enjoy together appear will never end. She has matured so much with my baby inside her womb. Khigir tells Béla, "If they ask you a question that you are not comfortable in answering just do not answer it. Simply look for us and someone in our group will respond. We will keep you between us, so you will never feel alone. Do not be afraid of quiet time, as this is important for our presentation. We will speak at the appropriate time. Above all other things believe that we want this as much if not more than you do. We are not pretending. Our hearts have you in them. This is real love and we will not release you, unless we discover that you truly want to be separate from us. We will fight over you and for you. Blood or no blood is a decision they may have to make. We have secured Kisteleki alliance, if he can do so. Gyöngyösi suspects that they may have some secret abilities to control him.

Berettyóú and Móri will help us, as our ship is waiting for us. We can get to them without Kisteleki through Ajkai. I am still working on some contingency plans and need for everyone to contribute; therefore, we will all sit her around our lovely Dabasi. You are a member currently, and we will try to get you involved in any way we can. Now back to our Béla, will you please stand?" Béla stands as Khigir motions for the clan to surround her. Khigir continues, "Béla, look around and tell us if one is here you do not like." Béla looks at each and blows them kisses, and then she looks at me and tells Khigir, "My Master Khigir, what about the tall ugly one?" Khigir and all the clan begin laughing. Khigir walks up and hugs Béla. She presently tells Béla, "Honey, we are yours forever and ever. We will give you your freedom when you mate, and if the new Master wishes to take you away. Let us now rush, and put on the pleasant gowns that Kisteleki has selected for us. Furthermore, you, silly boy, come with me." I jump behind her as we rush to our clothes the robots have placed on separate tables. The clan helps one another, as Khigir and Béla assist me. Khigir always teaches the new family members how to care for me. Khigir gives her a fast overview based on the limited time that we have currently. Gyöngyösi asks Kisteleki if he is serving any other masters. He tells us his only instructions come from us. Gyöngyösi now tells Kisteleki that she fears something may try to change his instructions and asks him if he can block any changes and merely take instructions from those who are on this ship. He agrees. Kisteleki notifies us that we are at the Council's court. This is a dreary place, which are mainly ancient crumbling buildings. Lights that make it impossible to see above cover it. The wide front steps had a large statue of an ox that had sizable horns. The steps are of no use down here. The door has two large, strange circular emblems on it. The top one is the only hallway visible to its upper part is above the floor of lights. It has traces of division into quarters by the crossing large engraved lines. The area is swarming with small fish. Béla begins to tell us about this place. She mentions that they do not permit large sea beasts here. Therefore, the small fish uses this as a sanctuary. At times, this fish packed this area so tight that no one can see before them.

This central city created by a powerful species that once lived on Lamenta, remains advanced for what the land of Lamenta has to offer. Our civilization moved this part of their city down here. We did this for our private use. We also wanted to conserve it. The Council stays in their private chambers and is visible only through false lights elsewhere. Lights will escort us to the judgment hall. I ask Kisteleki not to unload us or enter an enclosed area before I contact them. Kisteleki tells me he now has contact. A large voice currently comes over our ship as it rattles from the walls, "Welcome before the Council of the Pásztói. Why have you come to this forbidden place?" I told this voice, "Oh Council of the Pásztói, do you not know why we are here?" After a pause, the voice repeats itself, "Welcome before the Council of the Pásztói. Why have you come to this forbidden place? Please state this for Béla's official request." Gyöngyösi is now answering this question, "We are the clan of our Master Siklósi, home of the four elements.

We put ourselves at your mercy because of the love which, we cannot escape from your wonderful creation that you call Béla." The voice answers back, "We do agree over her love, which is binding. Kisteleki, you may enter through the gateway to the Council of the Pásztói." Kisteleki reports to me that he is now disabled, and they are pulling us in through the gateway, which is the only permitted method of entry. Khigir thanks Gyöngyösi for her wonderful diplomatic and emotional answer. We know that when kindness and love can be an issue, she is the one to lead the way. Khigir tells her that until we become more aware of their tactics, we will have her lead the way. It sometimes is better to enter with a small stick with your big stick tucked away from view. Gyöngyösi asks Béla if the Council of the Pásztói is spiritually enlightened and if her appearing as an Angel could help. Béla tells her that the ancients recorded that Angel once lived on Lamenta. The Council would be impressed if she could do that. Gyöngyösi instantly turns into her beautiful real self, the Angel who took our hearts and filled our dreams. We arrive at our docking ports, and some armed guards greet us.

Kisteleki allows us to see what is outside our door to greet us. We take our secure armed positions as Gyöngyösi spreads her wings as our doors open. When the guards see her, they drop their weapons and fall to the floor wrapping their heads inside arms. We drop off our weapons and follow our Angel. I can see through their little vision boxes astonished people. Khigir tells us to stay here. We will wait a few minutes and then return to our ship. I tell everyone to go into the protocol overabundance mode for our Angel. I direct everyone that when she turns around, we are to bow freezing, until she turns back around. We must do this to perfection because they are watching us. I ask Gyöngyösi to turn around and look at us. When she turns, we immediately drop onto the floor and hide our faces. She walks over to me and touches my head saying, "I command the dirty boy to stay with you continually, especially when around me." I whisper to her, keeping my head down and say, "Forever and ever my love." She smiles and now walks out in front of us. The giant doors open and rows of unarmed guards come out, and as they take their positions, they instantly go onto the floor and bow their heads with their hands wrapped over them. Gyöngyösi walks among them giving a few of them small kisses on the tops of their heads. She is injecting them with her spiritual bliss that brings peace and happiness. She touches every one of them shooting her love and peace within them. We know these legends will abound about this day. As she touches each one, she gives them a blessing. When she has touched the last one, a voice comes out in the air again, saying, "We welcome the great clan of Siklósi and all the elements and powers to which he had bound. How may we serve you?" Gyöngyösi asks them, "Come out before me, as I have shown myself to you, should not you show yourself to me. I have come in peace. Will you receive me in peace? A few minutes later, as if they were seeing if we were going to kill them, a small old man comes walking out to us. Béla whispers so Gyöngyösi can hear, "He is King Rogov." Gyöngyösi speaks out in a loud voice, "I am blessed to have King Rogov come out to meet me." The King looks at his soldiers and tells them to retreat. They all go walking slowly back through the doors they entered. King Rogov comes to about ten feet and bows to the ground asking, "What may we do for you great Connubial Angel. Gyöngyösi tells the King, "I did not know my fame was so inordinate that you would understand me."

The King answers back, "We have many volumes on your great deeds throughout the ages. Our scanners have verified it is you. We hope that you forgive us for our introduction; it is that verifiable we heard Siklósi was going to take our Béla by force. Why have you come?" Gyöngyösi begins by saying, "I hope you do not think hostile to my husband and the father for the baby in my womb Siklósi. He sometimes becomes too zealous to please me. I have come to beg that you give into me Béla that she may serve with me as we try to help those who need such help, and love all who need love. Would you grant me this plea?" The King, still bowing, promises to vote in favor before the Council of the Pásztói. He also claims to understand that if Siklósi made those threats in an attempt to please the Connubial Angel, he was fully justified to do so. He tells us we must appear before the Council at this time, and that he will stand beside us when submitting the plea showing it, likewise, to be his plea. Béla comes running before him, saying, "Oh, thank you father for your great love." She stunned us by her words. Kisteleki tells us not to be concerned, for they call all leaders their father. Kisteleki had us each swallow a small berry size device that he said that would allow us to communicate, and help him find us if an emergency exists. King Rogov lifted her up and then asked her if she brought the reigning Queen, who was with them, so he could extend the proper protocols. He figured that we had some an important person securely hidden. Béla asked in her mind for the Queen to come forward. Csongrád, who had been standing beside me in the open, came walking up to Béla, and after they hugged each other and extended the courtesy kiss on each other's cheeks Csongrád asked her, "How may I serve you my love?" The King interrupted, "Will you go inside and bring out the Queen, so I may greet her?" Csongrád asked him, "How do you plan to meet our Queen? The King subsequently becomes angry tells her, "Look here, what I say to a Queen is my business, and not a commoner's business." Béla shrugs at her King's shirtsleeve. He looks at her and asks, "Is it your turn to be strange now, who do you want?"

Béla, not fond of the way the King was acting answered, "I would like to introduce you to the reigning Queen of among the most powerful kingdoms of Lamenta, The Royal Highness Queen Csongrád, Queen of the Dorogi Kingdom." The King's face turns red, and he begins to stutter. Csongrád tells Béla, "Béla, remind me the next time I come here to bring about twenty of my Armies." King Rogov now offers a curtsey and says to my wife, "Your Royal Highness Queen Csongrád, Queen of the Dorogi Kingdom. I did not expect you to be among those who were welcoming and standing in the open unprotected." She answers him, "I am a commanding Queen, and I do not run from anything that could hurt any of those who serve with me. Love protected me and evil will not hurt me." King Rogov tells, "As was I, when a young prince. Siklósi has an amazing clan. We are not skilled in the manners of those who walk the surface, yet I am sure there is something I can do for you. What would that thing be?" Csongrád opens her arms to Béla and replies, "That I may have Béla to love the remaining days of my life. I know my daughters, who will be powerful Queens need her love and wisdom." King Rogov tells her, "Your Royal Highness, I will do all that I can except for ordering my Armies to fight, to gain the favors needed for the Council to grant this request." The King tells Béla to bring her comrades into the judgment room. He asks Csongrád to walk with him. We could hear everything that they discussed as Kisteleki. The King asked her how she would handle many different types of situations. She answered each question with her conviction and wisdom. The King finally as they were walking into the judgment chamber, told her that he valued her wisdom. She told him a final thing on ruling. She told him, "My friend, remember to love your servants more than yourself, and they will love you further than they love themselves." The Council heard this and spoke through her walls saying, "You are truly among the wisest rulers in the history of our worlds."

She extended them a royal nod. When they walked down the judgment hall, the King asked her if she joined him in giving the petition. Csongrád told him she could think of no better place to be. They walked to the center of the room, in the wide open where Csongrád always enjoyed standing. Gyöngyösi leads us into the judgment chamber. She stood a few feet behind Csongrád. We lined up in the same row as my Angel, half on each of her sides. This chamber was much larger and higher than we expected it would be. The walls and floors were a polished white marble. Every five feet are a large red column with many detailed faces sculptured on it rose toward the ceiling. The ceiling had rows of columns without designs running between the two end walls acting as support to the ceiling. We understand that this species has remolded the outside to prevent the tremendous water pressure from destroying it. I suspect that they can have themselves (water element) work around this pressure somehow. The walls have so many wonderful paintings than to look at them is to experience how they lived. These advanced people were amazing, as portrayed in these paintings, many of these paintings illustrate that they had machines working for them. They had strange bridges and ships in the line of Kisteleki; however, more mechanical in appearance. They also appeared to be short on garments as so many were no clothing in these works. Breathtaking, as each painting releases a new secret. They had books such as Kisteleki has in his ship. They must have enjoyed sitting at tables staring at the books, for some strange reason. Their children look well cared for, and happy. Their vegetation looks poor, brown, and thin in most places. I see in one painting where they built a house without walls with planting and growing under its roof. They look like a peaceful species as no weapons appear in any of the paintings. I notice a few paintings have groups of people talking. Eight colored lights currently appear in this room, two along each wall. Now a small group of women enters the room with instruments. They situate themselves and when the eight lights flash, they begin playing. I am not that impressed with the song, as it has a dull beat and constantly hitting the same note and small series of notes. I notice the King bowing to this song. Csongrád does not bow, as royal customs will not allow them to bow before any other nation's national anthem. I guide for us all to bow.

I tell Gyöngyösi to do what she feels is appropriate. She elects also to bow. The Great Spirits answered my silent plea in that this song ended and we stood again. Csongrád told me once during our private time that her mother taught every royal courtesy to her and would practice with her repeatedly until it was second nature for her. They presented moving images of events in our lives. They were all fine, happy events. They stopped the events, and all the lights around the room banished. We were in absolute darkness. I could feel Makói becoming uneasy. Afterwards, the lights, to include the Council came back. We could see again. I was having trouble figuring out why they were doing this. Kisteleki tells us to be calm since they are testing our patients. I finally stood up to one of them and said, "How much longer are you going to play these games?" He went to shoot a light beam at me; however, Ajkai could absorb it. She overshadowed all the lights around the room, as she danced around the room above us with flashy lights doing many strange things. Shortly thereafter a voice spoke, saying, "Fear not Ajkai. We were only testing." She changed back to be a Lamentan and allowed the Council to shine again. Gyöngyösi now declared, "Council of Shame, I am appalled and saddened by your inappropriate behavior. I hope you do not force me into seeking restitution for your awful behavior." The lights now assumed Lamentan form and apologized to Gyöngyösi. They did not want the people to know they had angered a popular legend in their history. One of the members, who was the only one dressed in white asked, "Who brings this petition to the Council?" King Rogov stepped forward and declared, "I King Rogov do bring this petition before the Council as my petition." The Council, who each had a door in the wall behind them, went through the door leaving the chamber. They returned in just a few minutes and asked, "What is the petition?" King Rogov spoke, "I petition on my honor the Council approves the assimilation of my trusted servant Béla into the clan of Siklósi." He had to say my name, for they would never allow her assimilation under a woman, even if that woman was their cherished legend Gyöngyösi. Kisteleki thinks that because I stood up to a light, they will be impressed that Béla will be secure.

The Council now asked, "Why should we make the first exception in our long-standing history?" The King answered, "Because all in Siklósi's clan love her. Our legend Gyöngyösi loves her through her divine rights, and wishes to make Béla her sister. The Queen of the mighty Dorogi has made a personal royal request to have her to love and as a sister. The lights that overpowered you would be her sister. She would also be a sister to an Esztergom, as Queen Szatmár released one of her servants to them signifies the first release is the history of the Esztergom. I understand the mind of Queen Szatmár, knowing the importance of her species to become more in tune with the universe around us. This clan is the first ever known the union of fire, air and a wide assortment of Lamentan species. We have the chance today to do the right thing and to blend with the other elements. We saw today how this clan destroyed a painful predator of innocent Esztergom. They are a force of love, and with my Béla, they will be a greater force of love. We cannot go down through history as the fools who cheated our species their due representation in the universe." The Council thanked the King and told us they had to deliberate. Meanwhile, the soldiers brought in tables and food for us. Béla sat with our women, and they talked about women's things. I noticed my women eating from Béla's plate and offering her some of their food, which she naturally selected what she wanted without giving this much attention. They were behaving as natural sisters. As they talk with each other, they always have the tendency to hold each another's hand. That tradition is alive and well with them. I know if the Council sees that, plus Abaúj running up to hug her and do their cheek kissing ritual. I still have a hard time accepting the division between water and air, and as they closely mingled and integrated not only their history but living cycles, such as evaporation. Khigir is not trying to play poker today. Her face displays worry and anxiety. The poor little thing could hardly sit in one spot. I am working hard to calm her, and to my fortune, Tselikovsky is here helping me. The Council member with the white robe comes back out his door. King Rogov rushes to him, and they speak quickly.

The King turns around and points at me, waving that I go to them. I hope that they did not want me only, because I have a Tamarkin hold each arm as we go forward to the King first. King Rogov tells me not to worry; he simply has a few questions about any release clauses. He feels this is a good sign so begs us to be relaxed and mature. Khigir, Tselikovsky, and I go to the Council member. He invites us to sit with him at a nearby table. This Council member asks, "I hate to burden you during your meal; however, we wish to know if you have any release clauses for Béla, or is this to be considered as marriage and forever binding." Khigir looks at him, and speaking in her sweet female tone tells him, "Mister Chief, Council member; our agreement with Béla as to be in accordance with our divine laws. These laws forbid any marriages between the elements, as they are not able to chemically to reproduce. We hold the ability and freedom to reproduce among our highest values. My life and future are now being lived to its fullest with my husband's baby in my womb. I can only tell you that this joy is the greatest joy to my life, and we can never take that from one whom, we love so much. The Béla we share, as with our fire and air have the right to leave our clan to mate at any time and with their sole right to select that mate without our approval. If after being married, their husband, and her desire to stay with our clan, they may do so. We enjoy our lovemaking too much to cheat them from this. She may also leave our clan at any time for any levelheaded reason. Moreover, by reasonable, I mean if we know or can be commonsensically be assured the decision will harm Béla; we will return her to you for you to decide. We have not met with any fire councils or air councils to establish a return clause. We honestly love her too much cheat her from a good life. I hope you believe me that we will care for Béla using our love as the guideline. You can search Béla's mind to confirm this, as our clan has explained this to her."

He paused outside a moment, looked as Khigir, and smiling, told her, "Future mother, I have just confirmed this to be true. I must return to the Council now. We should finish soon and notify you of our divine decision." We returned to our clan and shared with them, what we just testified concerning. Around two hours later, the female musicians returned and began to play once more. The King stood up another time and bowed. My Queen stood beside him. Gyöngyösi returned to her position as we quickly returned to ours.

This was the critical moment in our relationship with Béla. Would we cry each time we saw the rain because we missed our beloved element of water? The music has stopped, and the musicians are exiting through the doors they entered. All are quiet now as the nine doors open and Council returns. The chief has four to each side of him as they represent the two against each wall or eight members not counting the chief. Another man enters the room wearing a half-black and half-white robe. It is black on one side and white on the other side. The chief has now ordered the man to shake the hand of the color, which represents the decision. If you shake my hand, then we approved the petition. If you shake any other hand, afterwards we disapproved the petition. The man began to march around the Council. He came around and passed the first four black robes, creating excitement in us. He then marched past the chief, as my girls began to cry. The man stopped as he passed the sixth black robe, turned around and came back and shook the chief's hand. Gyöngyösi begins to cheer, telling her sisters, "The petition is approved. Béla is now our sister in love." The King and Csongrád walked up to thank the Council members, who appeared to be more excited in visiting with her than with their legend. Csongrád looks to be in peace as she is walking beside the King. Her royal moves are much more impressive than King Rogov's moves are. She looks like she belongs to be there, and to be entitled the addressing as Your Royal Highness, as I hear each member address her. She thanks each one and renders her hand, that they may kiss it. Béla is excited and asks Khigir if she can bring some personal things that Kisteleki may store in his storage places. Khigir tells her to bring whatever she wants. She also tells the bobbing Béla to ensure she avoid the sanctions permitting her to bring questionable items.

Béla provides Kisteleki with the information; he needs to find the items she requests. The room soon fills with the soldiers who are drooling over Gyöngyösi and Makói. Makói appears to be enjoying this extra attention. I tell my Tamarkins, they should mingle and meet some water people. They choose to stay beside me. This many males make Khigir feel uneasy. I tell her, "Now, you know how I feel with so many women around me." She tells me that this does not count in that I can abuse, and have my way with in such a manner for personal pleasure with the females being at my mercy and command. I ask her, "Khigir, when have I ever commanded you precious little bundles of love?" She explains that she did not say I did it, but that I could do it. I look over at Tselikovsky and ask her, "How is my special love today?" She tells me that this has been a long day, and that she fears it may continue to go on. I explain to Khigir that I believe most of us are tired, and we need to get out of here before someone does something stupid, and we lose Béla. She agrees and begins to go around collecting our clan. They begin to march in by twos, as I do not want any of my women walking alone among this civilized chaos if such a state were possible. Tselikovsky, who has received many second glances tonight, joins me as I collect Gyöngyösi and Csongrád. I thank the Council as take my clan back into Kisteleki. When we walk in, we only can see bodies lying on the floor. We do not see this for long, as we also end passed out on the floor. Khigir had previously asked Kisteleki to assist Béla in collecting the things she wanted to bring with her. Off we went into dreamland. Béla had to use Kisteleki's receiving door because scattered out all over the place are we. The last thing I saw was Abaúj passed out on Brann and Baranya. Yesterday's foes are today's collaborators.

Chapter 04

Revenge of the Rétsági

I cannot figure out what this strange crunching noise is that keeps me awake. It is cold in here, much colder than the season of nights, which is a not at hand. Even today, as I was fighting those killing beasts, our suns remained strong. I should not be this cold. Now, I am really becoming confused, because when I came in here, what could not have been a few short minutes ago, my wives were piled up with half on top of the other? Some were even holding on to one of their sister's feet. They were tired, yet now they seem to have gone to their rooms, which is where I should also go. I cannot remember Kisteleki ever being this quiet. Usually something produces a noise, except today I hear only that strange crunching noise, which is bugging me. I never heard a noise such as that. Kisteleki has left our windows, as he calls them open. We must be in a deep part of the sea because everything is so dark. I want to see what Kisteleki is doing, so I call for him. He gives me no answer. That is a first. His calling box usually has lights shining. Dabasi must have told my wives, there are no women down here. That is the only reason I can think that they would be leaving me alone like this. I do not even have a little Hevesi in my pocket. It was for times like this that I married her. I am a man with seven wives and alone. That would be a joke for Grandpa's joke book. Kisteleki's box lights are gone. He usually shines light through his box, so we can see where to go if we want to talk with him during the night hours. I at no time asked him if he also sleeps. We never needed him at night before considering this is our first night with him.

Because I am the only living man in our clan, I will go and see what that crunching noise is. It is coming from our dining room. I wonder if some of our new family members have some strange eating habits. I know it cannot be Dabasi, unless her species can walk at night. I have heard of stranger things. It could also be Béla; however, I always picture her as eating gracefully. What if one of my wives is a secret night crunchier, and only now I am discovering it? Nah, they are perfect. It is some secret machine that Kisteleki has, which helps him to clean around his ship. He could be crushing things he no longer needs. Ouch, I just stepped on something. This has to be some trash Kisteleki forgot to pick up. This is times such as this, which I wish I would have invested a few hours with Béla and learned how things performed inside a golden octopus at the bottom of the sea. I just heard something hit the wall in our dining area. At least, I now know which way to go. Like a goofy head, I was going the wrong direction. I now smell something that is bad. This stink is making me want to crawl. I must be careful now because this floor is wet. Whatever it is, it smells and is sticky. I lower my hand to the floor to touch it. It is some mangled flesh. I also feel some bone chips. It is not the flesh or bones of fish, who have a different structure. I have cleaned many fish and wild game in my life with Grandpa. We always collected enough for all my cousins and everyone in Grandpa's clan. This flesh has a strange smell to it. The thing that is eating it may be putting digestive enzymes into it, as my fingers that touched do feel slightly different. I should be okay, as I have wiped my hands fast. I am now sliding my feet so not to create any noises. Something strange is going on around here. It is hard to think that all my wives vanished from me, and I not know it. I always figured to be more in tune with them. Now is the time to concentrate, because I am at our dining room door. I kneel lower in case something wants to take a whack at my head. I can never accurately describe the emptiness of the dark when something in that dark could be a danger. Apprehension coupled with pressure hitting every spot of mine, and for what could be an incredibly simple explanation.

For all, I know, they may have received an invitation to go play somewhere and elected to let me rest. In goes my head. Outcomes my head fast. I saw something that should not be in there. It is too dark to get the details. I do know it was not a female, and it was big. I will describe it as an insect of some sort. I saw many different and most ugly species today. I am still stuck on the amazement that so many things live down here. Now where did Kisteleki keep our weapons? This will not work. He secured them in one of his special places. Since he has them secured, I will try to find something else, like perhaps a piece to one of his machines. I can only hope that if I take a piece off one of his machines, it does not scream or do anything weird. I know that my body needs some more sleep. I am still groggy, and about as alert as Khigir is when riding with me on horseback. I think this sweeping robot might work. He is tall, round, and sturdy, and has many ruffled edges. I can swing him hard and get a good hit. He is sturdy enough, that as long as I keep him in front of me, I should be able to escape in one piece. Come on, mind, stay with me. We can pull this off. I cannot sneak quietly in that room, as this robot weapon rattle; therefore, I will throw something in and hit the window. When it turns to looking at the window, I will design a straight-line charge. I am pulling off the robot's head, since Béla told me; they had no brains in their heads. I need some sharp points this can cut. Oh yes, it has many pungent points here. I will throw a head inside that room and be sure I do not hit the window in case it shatters. Okay, here it goes for my clan. It is spattering against the wall, and the thing is retreating right in my path. This robot weapon is cutting inside him as I push and lift up. It is not that heavy, yet when on the floor feels like it can use its claws for stability. Once I get it against a wall, which is now, I will twist this robot around, and then pull it out some, just enough to move it up through this thing's body. The darn thing has many little bones inside. Nevertheless, they snap easy.

The stupid thing now lets out a howl. This tells me that he is not alone. To beat all things, this robot is turning on its lights. They are red flashing and enough for me to get a look at this thing. It is a . . . . a Hegyközi and he is eating on a Lamentan female rib cage. I can feel the life go out of him at this time; therefore, I am pulling out my robot spear. Using its red light, I am quickly looking around for any more body parts. This one must have been hungry. He is cleaning them to the bone and even crunching the bone extra. This victim must have had something inside it that he likes. I am looking for body parts rather than thinking, because by jibber jabber is putting me in the league with, something strange. What kind of hand is that? It has fur on it. Maybe this thing was eating an animal instead. I see a necklace laying on the bloodstained wall. I know this necklace. It was my mothers. She gave it to me after Khigir accused me of kissing her and Tselikovsky. She gave me a big handful of them. She told me they might help to keep those girls fresh. I kept them hot by playing outside when both suns were shinning. Khigir has updated my vocabulary since then. I knew the words I need to know to hang out with Grandpa; therefore, not all that girl stuff interested me. Now, it has hit me. It is the exact necklace, which I gave to my special love, Makói. Therefore, that is her bear hand and this ugly thing was enjoying my wife. She put some deep cuts into him, and two others are lying on the floor. I cannot image that I slept through a fight such as this. I have painfully lost the one that trusted me so much. Okay, I must get in that weapon room now. I have a job to finish. I should have stayed on the roof until the last one dropped. I have to lose this flashing robot. A spear that flashes strips me of my element of surprise. Speaking of elements, where are my fire, water, air, and wind? This is so unlike Makói to be in the open like this without someone near her. After grabbing the necklace, I went out the side door. The robots use this door to bring our food into us. I have not only lost Makói, I also lost our son. My poor little bear is gone. Her milky brown eyes always could glow in the dark. At least, I have the honor to have killed her killer. I wonder whether I will have to avenge any other. There has to be something in here the cooks use in which I could convert into a weapon.

Something, so I can save some of my clan, please! I am taking a chance fumbling in the dark like this. I know the Hegyközi are dreadfully patient hunters and are more inclined to lay in hiding, waiting for me to pass by them. I will pass by them. I will pass them out of this world and into the terrible place, the Great Spirits, or whoever rules this down here sends them. I think I found something. These are long jagged edged knives. They will work, as without weapons this is going to be hand-to-hand for a while. Grandpa taught me a good trick once on animals. I will cut off some fur from Makói and tie it around my waist. It will cause me smell like them. Therefore, they will be relaxed, which I hope gives me the edge to get one of these knives in them. I am cutting off a big chunk. I know they have locked into their positions around here, especially after the large yell that killer released. I can go to the next floor through the robot steps. If any of my wives are hiding up here, I will have to save them later. Now, the thing I have to be careful of is that one of my wives does not mistake me for a Hegyközi and gets me. I am going to have to whisper so they know it is I. My wives are fighters. Three of them cornered my lovely bear, and she got two of them, with the third not leaving. I will whisper for Khigir, since she is their mother and sister. I am crawling on the floor in this darkness, as occasionally something flickers. Hegyközi must have taken a big hit from them. I saw him mow them down by the thousands today, yet now he is a powerless machine, trapping us in the bottom of the sea. I have a change of plans. I will go all the way down and see how Dabasi is. If she can swim, I will pull her to the big pool and send her for some help. Unit I can find Béla I have no other choice as my situation stands at this time. Stay with me, my mind. Trying to walk down these steps quietly is like trying to force Khigir to shut up when she is beside one of her sister wives. I really could use her at my side now. I do not need her for the muscle power. I need to soak up that faith she has in me, so I can do the impossible somehow. The hour has come for the one they call Master to save them. Will I save them, or did their bad decision provide a meal for our enemy such as in Makói. I need to go somewhere and cry. I think I could cry enough to raise this entire sea far past its normal shores. I have trouble with accepting everything happening so fast.

My logic is not tying this journey together. This bottom floor feels so empty. In war, such as this, feels must be used for the foundation of being. This water is so cold. I do not know if one of us Lamentans could swim out of this opening and up to the surface and survive. Dabasi and Béla will have to save us after I clear this place of these beasts. I am crossing the room with my back to the wall, and both knives pointed forward. I can feel them laying on the floor. Somebody put up a good fight in this blood pool. At least by straddling the wall and the large pool in this room some lowlight is making it in here. My eyes have changed to my night vision, which in truth is about the same as my daytime vision is, and that is not good. Into the room with the mini pool I go. It looks like my clan is going to be composed of a lot less members than I thought. The surface massacre has revived itself here, and with a revenge that took our Dabasi away from me. All that stress with her dream baby Queen, who had a dream for Dabasi that sure was not as this before me. These killers must have a plan for this one, because they left her head on the table with some sort of white powder below it, which has made it easily visible. I am staring into her eyes that strangely still have their glow of hope and love. I hope she forgave me before her horrifying death. With the amount of blood around this room, they must have chopped her painful piece by piece. In executing, a brutal killing such as this must suggest the Hegyközi blame the Esztergom for today's massacre, Part One. Two, is unfolding before me, and it is not pretty. They chopped her large foot fin four times. They wanted to ensure she got the pain each time. They terrifyingly have weapons that can chop large widths, as they chopped my love every foot up her fish's body. They did not chop her Lamentan torso, chopping each arm four times and then finally her head. I cannot dream of someone being tortured, such as that, who based their security on my false lies, and keep her smile and eyes filled with our love until the end. I will always love my wife Makói and miss those four sons and daughter whom she took back with her.

I will also love our good friend Dabasi as I was so much hoping to find the mystery man who could give you Lamentan legs, and thus you could live with us forever. There are as well three dead Hegyközi in here. Who is getting only three of them each time, but not saving my women? Dabasi would have been too hard to save, as she was not mobile. They should have thrown her back into the sea, which is here almost beside her. The walls are starting to rattle and leak. Kisteleki is not going to hold much longer. I need to go back to the highest floor and try to gather somebody on the way up to the top floor. I figure that when Kisteleki crumbles, my limited chance is at the surface. I have no idea how far down I am. I would like to be able to say 'how deep we are,' yet cannot because I have only seen one other living thing, and I killed it. One of the beasts has his big chopping tool beside him. I will need that. These things even feel nasty as I try to wiggle this strange-looking ax. I can use this. I am going to use a piece of Dabasi's shirt to tie my long knives to my waist when I need them. I must move fast now, because the water is coming in faster. I hear a small creak by the pool. I know where that spot is because when I was sitting there it bugged me. Okay, here I go. I say medium loud, "Revenge time." This is to warn my clan. My ax goes swinging into the head of a stinky Hegyközi. Off it goes hitting the wall. His wide wings drop fast. This gives me cover to move. I am going out the opposite wall and catch them off guard. First step and I hear one of these things growl. 'Ax swing, head off, wall splatter'. I hit this demon with a solid hit that slung his head to the other end of this room. They will be waiting for me there, so I will switch to the middle of the room. The water is coming in faster than I originally expected. Cracks are now appearing everywhere.

This makes it harder for the Hegyközi to find me. I start walking faster when I hear a faint, 'help me.' I rush to that area and speak out, "Where are you?" A whimpering, 'I am here Master under this thing,' breaks past the crackling of the walls. She wiggles the dead beast enough for me to know which one to move. I lift it up high satisfactorily to slide my ax under it and then use the ax as an advantage to flip it over. I feel around and find what I am looking for. A few quick touches and I say, "We have to go fast Tselikovsky. Is anyone else down here?"

She tells me that they butchered Nógrád not far from the mini pool and were getting ready to finish her off when I came down the steps. She had managed to sneak away when they were hiding from me. Tselikovsky then tucked herself under this thing, as he was laying on his side; afterwards, he unexpectedly falls over on her, trapping her. I asked her, while picking her up, why she did not call for me sooner. She told me the beast I just killed was too close to take that chance. Tselikovsky asked me if I could help her because she could not walk. I went to touch of right leg, and it was gone from the kneecap down. She tied one of her emergency for the way of women rags, as a tourniquet to keep her alive a little longer. When I went to pick her up, they had removed her left arm from the elbow. No time to talk now, she knows they are gone, so I get out of here. I have her ride me piggyback while I run for the door. On the way, I am able to behead two more. The light from the steps made silhouettes out of them easy targets. When we pass the stairway entrance, I close the door and turn the wheel on our side of the door. Béla told me that this would prevent the first floor from seeping water in the other floors. As I go back to pick up Tselikovsky, I hear a large crashing sound below us as our first floor breaks up. Kisteleki rolls like a round rock across the ocean floor until resting against a small ledge. We now have a larger problem. Our ship is upside down, and we are on the lowest floor. We have two more floors above us, plus the viewing floor. Tselikovsky is now crying in more pain. The rolling around as we were bouncing from the walls banged her up some more. I have not heard any moan from the Hegyközi, as there does appear to be many of their dead bodies lying around us. Thus, I tell my secret love, we will take a break here. I massage her easily and give her a hug. Next, I rub my hands on her cheeks and wipe away some of her tears. I can feel her tears, as this place is still so dark. I wish there was some sort of light someway. I tell Tselikovsky, "My secret love, somehow we are going to get out of this, and I will care for you and our children all the remaining days of our lives."

She cries, quieter now, and sobs, "Master. We shall have no children, for the beasts inserted their claws into me and pulled out your seeds and my womb from inside me." My puzzled mind wonders what kind of horrifying evil are these creatures. I do know one thing. A war is on, and until I die, I will hunt for and kill all Hegyközi that I find. There are some new noises, and light monster moans now. I tell my secret love to holdfast, that I must kill a few more Hegyközi and I will return shortly. These will be easy kills, in that they are on the floor injured. I do not know if they are ambushes, so I swing around to the other side and work my way back. I find a cup under my foot. This is a good place to find cups when silence is a serious issue. Picking the cup up, I throw it at our opposite wall. Then slash, slash, slash, bonus slashes, four more monsters dead. I know I must rush back to Tselikovsky as she was really suffering. She was hiding it as best she could, because she always put me before her in all things. I kneel down beside her to see if I can move her, and something is wrong. She is not warm, presently. I hold my hand over her mouth and cannot feel her breathing. Afterwards, I whisper her name and lightly shake her. My secret love, the wonderful gift of deep love my Tselikovsky is laying here dead now. She felt so different when I was carrying her to this floor. At first, I thought it was because she did not want to be a burden. She was smart enough to know that I am not leaving without her. Then I supposed the shame of not being able to walk and have part of one arm missing might have bothered her. This is why I reassured her that it was my time to take care of her. I do not know if I am all that is at issue on this one, for if any of my other wives survive, she would feel so much less a woman. When I add all this up, I believe that she could have with our blanket of love, overcame these issues. It was realizing the final issue we talked about before I went to avenge her torturers. This issue concerns how the Hegyközi took away from her the thing she valued most and lived for. She had her dreams come true by having two babies in her womb, and the promise of five more. She lived for that, as they all hold on much too hard on this issue.

When these things took away the lives that she was creating and her ability ever to create life again, they drained her life. They had tortured her beyond what her dreams and hopes could handle. What I commiserated the most about this special creation was how she stood in her sister's shadow her entire life. She stood her by her choice and conviction. She saw how the misery the gorgeous beauty, which Khigir took from the heavens when she was born, could destroy everything around her and herself. Khigir tried to hide from this attention, as this was the primary reason; they decided to train me to be their mate. These were two sisters hiding behind each other for the opposite reasons. When Khigir is around, no one realizes that other women are nearby. That is one reason that when we ride horseback, she hides her face in my chest. Khigir always wants others to glorify my other wives for the beauty she feels they have. The person she wanted to glorify the most is the one who is lying beside me in this dark dungeon deep under the sea with no life. Khigir knew of the extra secret love, which Tselikovsky and I shared. She even asked me to treat her sister as the most important person in our lives. Tselikovsky always hated the sneaking around for fear the other wives would discover it. Gyöngyösi knew of us and personally asked Tselikovsky to allow her the opportunity to keep us a secret. Our Angel would pull guard duty for us, and tell stories of adventures that Tselikovsky, and she had. Of course, Hevesi knew. Hevesi would rather die than be a part of something that would take this time to shine in the light away from Tselikovsky. During our private time, we always loved and loved hard. I told Tselikovsky that this was the time, which she stood in no shadow behind anyone. This is as if the Hegyközi reached inside me, and torn out my heart. I will cry later, and I mean I will cry for the balance of my miserable days. I have some serious killed to do now. No more will I silently try to sneak around them. I am going face on. If any is still alive inside Kisteleki currently, the last thing, they will see is their head spinning into another wall. I hear a noise to my left. I roll to my right missing an ax that is now lodged in our floor. Up I spring while my ax is swinging and off into another wall goes ahead of evil.

I feel something behind me. Therefore, I duck, and up I come with my ax and this time a head bounces off the ceiling. They are fighting in the open now, so clearly they think they have me. I got another one, and then two more as the three heads are bouncing off the walls. There is no time to think now, it is swing one way, turn to around swing the other way. I am thinking our species reacts to grief differently. They must have thought that my Tselikovsky's death would impede my fighting abilities. Wrong, stupid beasts, it has given me the energy to fight hard, as their heads are flying everywhere. I do know one thing, and that is if I am to see any of my wives alive, I will have to kill these slimy curses from the deep. So much, I do wish this fight were earlier. What sort of man sleeps while his wives were torn apart harrowing piece by painful piece? They are dropping so fast that some of the heads are hitting others who are arriving at the front of this fight. Nevertheless, many of them endlessly keep coming, without any end in sight. Even if the end were in front of me, I would not know because of this darkness. The only thing that must be saving me is the dark reduces their fighting effectiveness more than it does mine. While chopping a chunk of an arm from one I use it to wipe some of the sweat dripping from my body. They have stopped attacking for now. That is good, because I need to swap my ax with one of theirs. I noticed a few had larger axes than the others did. A serious walk-through will help me to wiggle around some of the places where I think I saw a few big ones. I remember they had an extra rank insignia on the right shoulder, and will feel for this. The ax I have is dull, and it was starting to slow me down when hitting their neck bones. So I may kill effectively, I need a sharp entry cut, a fast snap of their neck bone, whacking off their head at a slight angle so the head will get a solid lift and float through the air. My favorite is the bashing sound as it hits a wall. Here is one and it feels like a strong ax. The blade is sharp, so I am back in business.

While I am here, I might as well grab another one because most of my fighting circles a small area, therefore, if my blade becomes dull, I can swap it off quickly. I am not going to live under the illusion that this trash does not know where I am. Too many of them came to fast as me for them not to know, so I will reduce up on my noise discipline. One of my wives should still be around here somewhere, as I am running out of floors. I can feel the damp chill of this deep water as it fights the stick of all these dead carcasses lying around. Our first floor junk yard is out of business now. Therefore, once I have done a scan through here I will find a way to get to the next floor in my path. That floor would have been above me. Nevertheless, it is below me currently. That might explain how the Hegyközi could get to me so fast. They were going down. There just cannot be that many more of them in this dead ship. Consequently, because of the pond floor's deterioration, the Hegyközi cannot board this lifeless ball in the deep cold dark bottom of the sea. The time to concentrate is at hand. I lightly call to my family. When I hear a noise, I sidestep quickly and look into that sound. This has enabled me to slam three more heads into the walls. These last three were injured and by it not able to move. My women at least have a few punches in their behalf. I continuously offer my help. I hear a noise in one of these small rooms the robots kept their supplies. I verify once more if someone is in there, then I tell her to get away from the door, and I fling open the door and dive into the minute closet. Fortunately, it was one of my lazy dives, and I end in person with my Queen. I can barely recognize her face. I always knew the fool who tried to interrogate her would have their hands full. I feel across her body, and she has both hands missing. Her engorged groin area is soaked with blood, so most likely means

I lost another child. My flower of the sky bridge has no legs from beyond her kneecaps. She cannot see, and can barely talk. My love is not going to survive much longer. If I truly loved her, I would cut her head off instantly; however, I cannot let her go. Therefore, I hold her as gently to such an extent possible. I want her cut-up chest against mine, so she can feel my heart one more time.

This is not what her father had in mind when I took her from her throne. You would have thought what the King said concerning our entry before the council would have sunk in my head. A reigning Queen should never be placed in a possible compromising position. That is why kingdoms have Armies. I must keep strength in my voice, because that is what will keep her going and at this stage, it is minute by the minute. She has lost too much blood. I cannot believe she is still alive. The one thing I learned from Tselikovsky is not to mention anything about our dead baby, and the one they took from this woman would have been born into a world as a kingdom was waiting for her. This is such a shame. I was looking forward to her father visiting and playing with our children. I was planning to find a way to keep my other children occupied, so the King could have had some extra time with his granddaughter and future sitting and reigning Queen. I cannot even look into what is left of her eyes. She looked so elegant and every ounce of pure royalty as she graced the council beside that King. He walked and behaved to be proud because he was also in the presence of true royalty. Any soldier who packed that building that day would have given anything to serve her for life. Now even their dogs would have pity to look on her. This is so wrong. I cannot accept that she must pay such a high price for a love she had to share with my other wives. In her kingdom, she could have selected her husband and for how long. When done with him, she could have slain him for virtuous reasons and taken another man. Moral reasons are being justified by execution. Even I have trouble sometimes trying to know the difference between good and bad. These were descent hands, but what happened was terribly wrong. She would have lived a better life being the daughter of a town drunk. No, no, no, this cannot be.

Now time for the empty promises, those that are made intended to keep, yet will never happen. They just feel so good for the soul. I promise to care for and love her forever until I die. I tell her that I can never let her go. Oh, if only she knew how sorry, I am for not being here to defend her. She put her trust in the wrong man. I will have so many questions about what I lost this day will echo through the years about what was taken here today by creatures that should never have been created.

They never could have been created to do anything good. Therefore, why were they created? To torture the good, mangle Queens, who are trying to build a future where the poor can have homes and their children's schools is evil beyond understanding. Is this what my weakness, not to deny her the love she wanted, do for the Lamentans? Hey everyone, there goes Siklósi, the one who destroys the finest of Queens. Why are we plagued with so many curses? These are curses the harder you hit the faster and stronger they hit back. She motions, understandably, shyly with her stub that used to hold hands decorated with the greatest jewelry, yet will now be the source of pity for even the poorest of pawns. I put my ear beside her mouth. She always enjoyed this. I wonder how it feels to know that an activity that you once enjoyed will never be again. I thought the world up there was cold; try it at the bottom of the sea. Somehow, the fear of death no longer binds me. My life is lying in my arms. I had hoped so deeply to give her back something more for all, which she gave up for me. I will always remember our first private time after she became pregnant. She just thanks me endlessly for allowing her to give me that which she wanted most, and that was a daughter. She believed the highest of spirits had blessed her when she discovered that not only would he produce and heir, but also a spare and then three more. She told me that she was the envy of all the princesses in the known kingdom, because she would be able to raise our children like real people and not aristocratic barbarians. Guess what Csongrád. The reward of being married to aristocrats is not what will mangle you. The curse of being married to poor trash like me who promise to defend you is what will destroy you. It is as you are discovering, only to awake to find yourself disfigured beyond what even you would not do to your enemy. Take that, wrap it all up proper together, and call it love. I hope you remember that poison we called love. As if we foolishly thought, love would heal all wounds. I ask her to forgive me for not being here to save her. I tell her that I only blinked my eyes, and all this happened as if in an instant.

Oh, please no my lovely and innocent Csongrád. Do not tell me that you know and understand my dear. I order her not to tell me she understands. I made her a promise and broke that oath. There is nothing to comprehend. I tell her it is time for her to pressure me pay. Either way, I can never let her go. I lost my Tselikovsky by just leaving for a second. I lost all of them for sleeping just a flash. I am not going to lose her. In my arms, she is going to stay. Every time she received a chance to do something for me, she jumped on it, never hesitating. How can a Queen be so smart to sway Kings, yet so foolish to trample through the unknown parts of Lamenta with me? How are they able to hide so much pain? Even with all their hopes shattered, they continue to hold on strong for fear of hurting me. I tell my love, "My Love, show your pain, because if whoever created this had no mercy on us, then please show me no mercy. Show me the woman inside you while I hold you." She started to tremble some; I could feel that she wanted to release this terrifying experience, yet she held on to her control. This is crushing me on the inside. I look at her and cannot imagine or even feel the pain she is undergoing. She tells me her message, "Master, we were entering this ball when you were hit with a small needlepoint arrow. You dropped immediately, therefore we dragged you side with us. I remember Khigir yelling you had been poisoned. Your eyes were rolling. We could see your legs and arms spasm, and you go into convulsions. You stopped moving and froze, eyes open. Gyöngyösi yelled that she thought you were dead. Before we could react, thousands of those Hegyközi invaded us and broke their way into our Kisteleki. They did something to paralyze Kisteleki as all his inside lights vanished and we began sinking. They divided us, taking one each. Brann and Baranya burned their way past them. They sprayed something on them that erased their flames. They had an old magic man with them that did something to Abaúj, Ajkai, and Béla. What he did with them, I do not know. I remember hearing Khigir scream once. That is when I refused to create any noise. I did not want them to feed from their evil to me."

She was beginning to choke now, so I motioned for her to remain quiet as I tore off another piece of what remained to her gown. The other torn parts were on her four limbs. That caught me somewhat off guard so I asked her, "Have you talked to anyone else since this raid began?" She told me, "Gyöngyösi helped me with my wounds and pulled me into this closet, so they would not continue to chop at me. Oh Master, I am so cold." I pulled off my shirt, wrapped it around her, and started telling her how much I love her. I told her, "Now is not a time to become weak my love, now is the time that our blanket of love is going to save you. We are a husband and wife. As such, I will care for you all the days of my life. Have no more fear." My love asked me to touch her face one more time. She always enjoyed this during our private time, telling me that in my hands, she felt the greatest peace. Csongrád began coughing steadily again, as she was fighting for each breath. She stuttered, "I knew you would come back to me my Master. Thanks for our great love. I will always love you." Immediately, her poor beaten, chopped thin body became stiff and cold. I tried to move her hand, and I felt her heart, while placing my ear in her mouth. My Queen was gone. Just as she did each step of her life, she died with elegance and royal grace. She knew one important thing about me, and that was I would come back for her. She graced the sky bridge with an empty heart searching for love. Even though I had her in my arms when she died, I did not see her die for all this darkness. It could be that this darkness is hiding just enough of this devastation permitting me barely to hold on to a shaky reality. My reality now has my second wife died in my arms. Our life together is gone. This is because an uncontrollable evil waged unjustified war against our love. A war they want, then war they shall have. It is time to do some more killing, especially considering I have three more wives to find. I lay my still, and forever beautiful, Queen's body down because I must move on in this battle. I even so have hope in three more, actually four if I include Ajkai. She is a slick one and exceptionally creative. If I ever see the light again, I shall look for dancing stars.

For now, I will kiss my Queen good-bye. I figured someday she would want to spend a few years with daughter Stephana and help her to the throne for a bit. I could understand that easily. This woman loved her husband more than she loved herself. All my wives deserve their own husband. They picked me, and the Hegyközi hit us badly today. At least, I know there was a reason I was unconscious. The timing of these events is beginning to mystify me, and I do not know if they intended this as a special blessing or something else. I spoke to Tselikovsky just before her peaceful death and then to my Queen as she drifted off into the other side. The degree of physical tortures these women went through should have killed them way before I came along. One concern is how that beast was eating Makói; nevertheless, just in time I could discover that before I finished my search. Therefore, the timing of these deaths might be manipulated. I cannot put my finger on it. It could be nothing. Moreover, I should just be glad that they died peacefully and did not have to exist with lives of horrible misery. I am impressed how I was able miraculously to kill an entire floor of Hegyközi many within a split-second timing in the pitch dark. The constant darkness is also pestering me. Kisteleki told me during my tour of his ball that he had a thing called backup power. If something happened to him, this power would take over. This darkness is not natural. Now watch this. I will swing my ax and chop a head off a Hegyközi. Swing; chop heads, now they are bouncing from the walls. Wonder how I knew this was going to happen. Whatever this game is all about, I am stuck in it. I am going up to the next floor. Instead of steps, I will be shuffling above the steps that are now my ceiling. By reaching up and using the guardrails, I can pull myself along the sloped ceiling and reach the next floor. The only thing I like about this if I have to exit fast I can slide down these steps. If my notion is right, I will meet a few at the entrance door. I guess on this one that I was wrong. This floor is quiet, and has only a few scattered Hegyközi bodies. I call out 'love,' as I am walking or should I say stumbling around. I hear a noise behind me, smell a Hegyközi, Therefore, turnaround swinging, and get him. His head bashes of the hallway wall. I have blood over me now. I should find a place and clean up before my wives find me. That would have worked in my life as it stood up to a few hours ago. I have a theory.

Since we each have a private room in this hallway, except for me in which they added my name to each door, I was going to guess I know where I can find my Precious Dove and Angel. Gyöngyösi's room is beside me now, so I open the door and call her name. A Hegyközi comes flying at me and into my kitchen life. I wonder how that became lodged in its neck. As it falls past me, I take my ax and off go the head and my spare knife. A quick scan of the room finds no one. I call her name again and then hear a faint Master. Her voice came from this wall. My hands find what is left of her torso quickly. They chopped all four of her limbs, and gave her a special treat. They took all of her hair. Actually, they burned her head, giving her a crown of blisters in its place. I cannot touch anymore. This is sickening. This is an Angel chopped to pieces. They also destroyed her womb. I do not feel hurt or anger in her eyes and instead see peace and love. They had enough mercy to keep her eyes, although she clearly cannot see. I share with her, "Gyöngyösi, I think we got a bad break on this one." She tells me, "Master, it was worth it to be your servant. I would go through this one hundred times just for a kiss." I reached down on the floor and picked up her gown ripping what remained in two pieces. I used one piece to wrap around her waist, and the other piece wrapped around her breasts. I kiss her bare left shoulder in memory of the wonderful gowns that she had worn. All with her left shoulder bare. I place my hands on her lower cheeks. When I try to touch other parts of her burned head, she flinches. She has had enough pain, so I confess to her, "One soft, warm kiss, for one hundred times, well then my love, I owe you at least ten thousand kisses. You hold on for me, and we will begin each day for the rest of our lives with a kiss that you have paid for with your blood. Okay, my Angel!" Gyöngyösi tells me, "I am sorry my Master, this time their magic has trapped me at the door of death. Its chains are wrapped around me now. You were the greatest husband a woman could ever dream of having. You made my trip as a human an experience. I shall always hold dear to my heart. You are my love. Now, go search for Khigir and save her.

I know that you can climb any mountain, for I have seen you do so. Climb this mountain and enjoy the harvest that awaits you there. Do all things for love my husband." Her body began to become stiff as no breathes come from her mouth. I acknowledge that to have had a wife who was an Angel to love and be a part of was an unspeakable joy and a privilege. I will have to explain to the Great Spirits how something accordingly wonderful, consequently perfect, subsequently loving, and above all so caring had to be in this manner desecrated. Gyöngyösi had her limbs chopped off, womb desecrated, crown of glory or hair burned from her head and still could praise the power of love with her dying breaths. The irony is that over the last over one million years Gyöngyösi helped save the lives of all newborns regardless of their species. It could have been possible that helped save the lives of some who butchered her today. If that we to be the truth, she would forgive them. Gyöngyösi, Hevesi, and Khigir hold the leadership positions in the wives organization. Gyöngyösi always handled anything that dealt with emotions or spiritualism, even on my behalf. She had been through everything so many times. Nevertheless, she always drifted to the back and allowed the others to collect the praise. She was a husband's lover. In this, I mean she loved the role of the husband or Master as they called me, and the joy of belonging to that person. She served with her heart. I thought for sure that she would be staying with me through her spiritual powers; however, these magic men are screwing everything up. Another one dies in my arms in a dark black place, which prevented any image worthy of holding in my memory. The emotionalism of this death is crushing me.

My arms are twinging, feet, wobbling so bad that I dare not try to walk. This death was harder than the others were in that Gyöngyösi felt just as beautiful in death as she did each morning we woke up to meet the new day. I wonder how I can go on without my Gyöngyösi. Every thought in my mind and every feeling I have, was born through her. In the ways between a man and a woman in the sanctity of our wedding bed, she taught us everything. I always joked that we had yet to learn the Carnal Knowledge, because all we knew was the Gyöngyösi knowledge. We have all tried to mimic her soft loving touch and the energy that she focuses in her touch, yet none of us could even come close. I plead that whoever allowed this to happen punished.

I will complain to someone up there someday through my lowly unimportant station. It is so hard to believe that they glorified for her on how great this would be. Then, without notice, just before she gives me our son, brutally destroy her and her baby. As hard as this is going to be for me, I must leave the dead body of another consecrated wife. I wish the evil that did this to them will allow me to collect their remains and put them to rest in a sanctified style. Now is the time to move away from the dead, and find those who still live. I push her door open swiftly as it slams into a Hegyközi for his introduction and here is my good-bye, an ax in his head so it may kiss Kisteleki's wall. Rather than attacking me one at a time, they would do better to form into a small group and think this out. I will meet them one at a time, as this helps me keep my arm muscles flexible. I go straight to Khigir's room to keep in tune with this dark experience. I push her door open, and this time I am in the position to swing my ax. I got a hit. His head goes flying into her wall. This one had a big head. They must have brought their geniuses to this room to reason or fight with Khigir. In I go check throughout her room. I feel about everywhere I can, floor, well, except for the furniture. While moving with my left hand in front, right hand holding my last knife, and ax tied to my waist where I can pull it up fast. My left hand is touching something furry. It appears to be as perplexed as I am. The main advantage I have enjoyed is the ability to smell them. I smell a few of them now. They want to fight in the middle of this room. Here she goes, time to decorate the walls. Each one that squeals, I think of a wife that I lost and the way she begged not to have her life destroyed. These insects simply walk into my blade. I still cannot picture one of them torturing one of my wives. Someone else had to do that. How would they have known all were pregnant? There are no more beasts in this room. I cannot imagine how someone could survive in this room, and then again; I wonder why they guard this is heavy.

I appear to be the Master of more questions. Instead of finding answers, I am finding dead wives. Not the day I had expected when I woke up this morning. I am without question hungry, and I will not eat Hegyközi. I need to find a way to get Kisteleki back up and running. One of my wives today, I believe it was Tselikovsky who mentioned the bewitching men turned him off. I know enough to know that this magic man crap is for the ignorant. Someone must be up to something below me or this floor is working loose. I have been in this room with Khigir every time she has come here, and I do not remember this. I had better checked it out, after all, that power up for Kisteleki has to be somewhere, and Khigir does represent an important leadership role in our family. Ouch, something just bit my finger. I whisper, "Is that you Khigir?" She replies, "Are you alone?" I tell her, "Yes, honey, unfortunately we are unaccompanied, except for a loose straggler here and there." Khigir unhooks something and tells me to move. Up comes the trap door and out, she comes. I ask her if there are any wires or buttons in the compartment. She asks me, "No, why Master?" I explain to her that I want to power up Kisteleki. She slaps me and yells soundlessly, "We can never fire him back up. He ejected his 'special instruction card' or something similar, as I have discovered, they throw these words around as if we have been here our entire lives. He then asked Gyöngyösi and me to smash them to pieces. We put the remnants in his light shooter and 'boomed them. He has special advanced equipment that cannot fall into the hands of the Hegyközi magic men under no situation. We got the bad break; however, our deaths will save so much in the future. It is important that we go down with this equipment." I ask her, "Khigir, you know there is always a solution if we put our minds to it. Now tell me more about these magic men?" She answers, "I do not know everything. I just know the parts that I ask them when one of them takes over my body. Kisteleki had a report hidden deep inside his important 'do not tell' files from the hidden spirit of the seas. I will play it for you now. Here, put this in your ear so only you hear it." The tape was a personal machine message, created by different sources and many from historical accounts, then put together somehow, and is as follows: "When you listen to this voice you most likely have been invaded by one of the worse sarcomas of energy in all of time.

They are the Shelyapin. The Rétsági imprisoned them because they are minus jumpers. Wanting more power in this fresh positive cycle, they reprogrammed themselves with additional destructive abilities. They plan to introduce new diseases, unknown evil powers, and a magnitude of natural disasters such as stars colliding, birth defects, and wide-scale famines. Minus jumpers can jump into the positive and are a precise small select special creation with certain absconds that they have preserved. The Rétsági collected all the minus jumpers and tried to reproduce their genetic instructions, so they could become the jumpers. With their Empire making the jumps, they wanted to remove the Shelyapin from the cycle. Then they could keep them inactive for both the minus and plus cycles. This would be forever, or at least until a technology was created to reprogram them to be contributors in their hosting civilizations. The minus do not die, as the plus do not die. The Shelyapin would therefore, not be in this cycle. The normal species and elements, such as us, simply become inactive until our point in this circle arrives again. The early Rétsági, who tried to jump, caused many destructive problems, disrupting the balance of the energies and elements, to the point that it almost destroyed all who were existing at the time in their realm. They do not have the ability to perform these jumps, e in unison with the Shelyapin. The Rétsági goal was to contain the Shelyapin during this current positive cycle. The ruling spirits blamed the Rétsági for the failed unlawful jumps and forced them to release the Shelyapin, who then set up their death force and started jumping. Time is a cycle or circle that will turn forever. Half is plus and the other half is minus. Minus may never see or touch plus, unless in its nonenergized element condition. Our four elements, as are also in our family are fire, air, water, and positive charged Lamentans (people). Their four elements are temperature or the force that moves the cells fast for heat and slow for cold, antiair or the gasses not found in our air, rock, and negative charged people. The positive side uses energy to create and control heat. The negative cycle h an element, which does this.

A cycle safeguard dilutes, dissolves, or disseminates the gasses, which we do not use for our air, so they do not hurt positive life. Most of these gasses are stored in other worlds and parts of space to reform worlds, preparing for the next time cycle shift. This was a lower life-form over-view. In summary, the Shelyapin is enemies of the positive elements. They also may only exist in the positive cycle in rocks that must be under a deep sea free from any sunlight. Sunlight may never touch them as the heat from the sun or suns, moves the elements within them, and thereby are performing negative element functions. If they touch air, or fire, which is within the same subcategory of elements, they will lose their powers and may set up energy uncontrolled releases of atomically anticharged energy. Fire can control the molecular movement within elements as air can add its gasses to form new gasses, which are damaging to them. The concepts discussed in this fill over seventy trillion gitoconics of electronic data at the national library for the Shelyapin. Therefore, a quick summary such as this presents itself as 'strange' at best. The Shelyapin will take over nonintelligent life forms to perform their killing on their behalf. The mental processes in these beasts quickly weaken to the point the Shelyapin will look for new hosts. The only method available for them to exit a host is the host's execution. They live in the shell of rocks in their sea of sculptures. Cursed are those who touch these statues. Do not destroy these sculptures, for to do so will trap them in the positive cycle forever.

Combining the four elements releases them. This combination may also contain them forever. Once you have contained them, bury the statures so nothing ever discovers them again." I look at Khigir and ask, "Is this telling us we are in trouble. Because it was here, I discovered the burdens of watching my wives die, some in my arms, as their mangled bodies gave up their dying breaths. Yes, honey, we are in trouble, as I am so sick of all this darkness.

We must get some light." Khigir, whose voice came from the other side of our room this time said, "No light you stupid ignorant lower life form." I went to look at her, yet could not see her because of this horrifying darkness, so I spoke back, "Look here you Tamarkin, I am older now, and if you need a Master's discipline, I will discipline you. Do not forget I am the man and as such the higher life form nearby." She retaliates, "Oh, just like all those male Hegyközi laying around without heads." I shouted back, "Khigir. I was the one who chopped those heads." She then carried on how that she had influenced me to do that work for them. I had to know who the 'them' were. Khigir told me that we were fools for believing in love as a blanket to cover all things. She asked me if I knew how she felt trying to keep her sisters alive, as she had to stop the blood from pouring out of the legs, arms, and wombs. Khigir added, "I was the one that heard them beg for their Master to save them, yet our powerful Master lay on the floor by the door sleeping during their hideous screams and pleas for mercy." I knew what sort of an impact my short visit with my loves was, as if I must know that if she was there begging to keep them alive, it had to be a jolt to her also. Moreover, she suffered from the loss of me as that security blanket. Just then, I heard something hit a window. I know our rooms have windows in them, and it did not come from this window. My 'every uses' room is across the hall from me. Privacy is an amazing concept only when applied to wives. When applied to husbands, it means they will ensure everything is for you. Oh, I wish those days were here again. I would give up my privacy for the rest of my days for one more day with my Angel, actually for any of them. I whisper to Khigir, "I think we have some spies. Do you know if there are anymore Hegyközi here, and if so, can they hurt me as so many appear to be lifeless robots? Khigir tells me, "Those are the ones whose mental processes have broken down or are waiting for possession. There will always be some as the Shelyapin can produce them at will. They produce extra that can be used as hosts, if need be. Some are real; therefore, you cannot take a chance on one not being actual." "Khigir," I ask, "Are you telling me there are Shelyapin on this ship?" She affirmed that, "They are on this ship appearing as the Medicine men. They are enormously angry with Kisteleki for trapping them here forever. Those who did not escape with our family will be sacrificed. They will kill us also.

They will only leave one behind, as they cannot touch hands who kill. This is why they have others kill for them." I ask Khigir, "Can you think of any reason someone would kill for them?" She explains, "Somewhere, I heard they do power deals and things along that line. Therefore, hey Dove, hang on, I have to check that noise out." I grab my ax. I go across our hallway, and into my room, I do continue. I have to be careful in here because each wife has their special touch in my room. I always enjoyed that. It will miss them every minute. Since I have accounted for all my wives, I swing my ax in a four-foot circle me and slowed down only twice. I swing it again in case they have any backups. Only get one crack this time. Because, I have heard so many heads hit the wall that I do not even hear their crashing sound. The splashing blood gets me, as I do think; it is a little over dramatic. I rather hate killing these things now, because I am releasing the Shelyapin. Moreover, they are simply creating new bodies to populate. Perhaps, a form of injuring would produce better results. I toss my ax, which bounces off my closet door with a small cracking sound. I am sure Kisteleki will forgive me, so in joking, I said, "Forgive me Kisteleki." I go to stab anymore Hegyközi clones and get a freezing shocker. A voice pops back, "No. I will not forgive you." The voice came from my closet, am speaking in I say, "Why not, my friend?" The voice retorts rather sarcastically returns to me saying, "Since when have we been friends?" My brain comes back on telling me that only one-person talk to me in this manner. How could I have forgotten my best friend? I express my greatest joy, "Hevesi. I thought you were gone. They told me that someone shot poison in me, and I figured you went after them dying in defense of your Master." Hevesi then tells me, "Master hatter. Let us not overdue this. Nevertheless, I am not in the mood to expand and let you play dirty boy." There is only one method to handle this sarcasm and bitterness, "Oh please honey, I will be a good boy for you." Hevesi then tells me to pick her up and listen carefully to what she has to say before putting me in my shirt pocket. She is seldom serious and when she is, it warrants my undivided attention. I say to her, "Okay Love, tell me please."

She begins by saying, "That is not Khigir in the next room with you. Your wives are prisoners somewhere." I respond, in a way, hoping she is telling the truth, "How do you know these things?" Hevesi tells me that the walls talk, and she listens. What if that is truly Khigir in the next room. I need to know without a doubt, so I ask Hevesi to show me how I can know for sure. She tells me that a clone will never speak badly of the Shelyapin nor stay calm when others do. Hevesi also warns me not to let her know that I have her. I hold Hevesi in my hand and say, "The Shelyapin is evil monsters, and should all die." Hevesi yawns and orders me to stop flattering her with my wisdom. I tell her, "If I do not recover all my wives, I am throwing you back into the sea. You are too much for even seven of us to handle." She tells me not to bluff her, she knows that her 'little treats' lead daddy to the water every time. I confirm this with her, mainly in appreciation of the truthfulness in her statement plus her overwhelming confidence. We are talking about a five-inch woman talking to an almost six-foot man and not losing a breath between words. A little, condense package of guts. I do need her positive attitude now. I ask her what she knows about the Shelyapin, and she tells me, "Too much, to include the Rétsági do not like them. You keep me in your pocket, your eyes off the other females. Because for now and only temporary, I am your Master Wife, you do as I say suffer the outcomes." I asked, "Or else what?" Her response, added with a kick to my chest, "Private time could be history big boy." How does she do this? The last few hours filled with watching my wives die and chopped gone and here I am laughing. My Hevesi knows how to get inside me and turn the keys. I tell her, "Well Angel, if you know this much, then you must ensure that the silly boy reaches it, okay my little love." Her mordancy chops back, "I told you dirty boy, I was not in the mood, now get your behind to work, before I have to straighten you out wimp." I laugh and say, revealing my rancor, "Of all things to find today, I found you."

Her swift kick to the identical spot turns my key and off, I go. It amazed me that a five-inch woman in a wobbly pocket can kick the same small without fail. I feel my way back into Khigir's room and now only carrying my kitchen knife as currently I stab in the arm and kick. I will let the Shelyapin suffer in these mind-rotting bodies. Another one charges me, and slash, kick, down it goes. Khigir yells, "Stupid, kill the creepy thing." I ask her, "Woman, how did you know in the dark that I did not kill it?" She stutters for a minute and responds, "Because you seldom do anything right." Hevesi chuckles in my pocket extremely quietly, "I did not hear a head bounce off-the-wall," would have worked enough. I lightly tap her and give her my frown, which means 'please' shut up. She smiles and frowns at me, and bam, another kick to the same spot. Why I love this little pain in my back, or should I say chest, I will never know. I have hundreds of large ten-foot wingspan monsters attacking, and I have to worry more about a five-inch headache. As I continue to step over these things, I get a push from the back, and down I go. As I hit the floor, fortunately I hit the side of a Hegyközi and roll to my right. Khigir comes down directly on the carcass. I grab her hair and roll her. I hate doing this to her, especially how fond I am of her golden sun colored hair. I grab one of her arms and while forming it into an L and holding her elbow steady apply pressure to her wrist. She starts screaming for me to stop. I ask her, "Are you going to give me some answers, or should I give your arm to one of those new hungry Hegyközi's who will enjoy this appetizer." She agrees to talk. The first thing she asks is, "How did you know I was not

Khigir as I did everything exactly like she told me to do?" Hevesi starts to laugh, as we have all been down the road of doing what Khigir said to do like recently having a Queen bite my neck. The impostor asks, "Who is that laughing?" I scratch my throat, wiggle my head, and tell her, "Something must have gone down my throat wrong, as the thought of someone doing what Khigir had told them to do, caught me slightly off guard. Hey, hold one minute. I will ask some questions first, like where are my wives?" She tells me to let her hand to go, if I ever desire to see my wives again.

I shake her lightly and ask her to take me to my wives. She reassures me that her goal was to take me to my wives, as they have some special hand chains waiting for me there. The impostor adds, "You cannot escape from this ship, as neither can we. We may be spending eternity together with your wives and you. The number of wives who survive is based upon your cooperation, so I would recommend you let me go, and do what I say." Hevesi tugs on her little seat, we sewed inside my pocket for her, which means yes. Therefore, I let go of her and try to straighten her hair with my hands. She tells me to stop touching her hair, "You are touching a nonfunctioning unit of this body, thereby wasting our time." I tell her, "When you are cloning the body of my Master Wife, do not tell me what to touch or not to touch." She shakes her head and says, "I never could figure out, you positive cycle psychos. Touch, but do not render nonfunctional." I stand up and offer her my hand to help her stand. She promptly hits my hand and tells me to move away. She can perform this function. She speaks; "Lights" and the lights come on although shinning from our floors since Kisteleki was flipped upside down against a ledge by the sea. The smell magnifies itself with the lights lit; I think this is more from being able to see all this carnage, most without heads. I did most of this in less than one day, which shows daddy came home. I tell this imposter, "All these carcasses need to be destroyed before we are all in trouble." She informs me that they plan to remove all the bodies and scrub the walls as soon as the prisoners receive their orientations. I follow her, as she knows where something is, and I am playing on someone else's mountains, so until I know where their bears are, I will stay in the open area. I ask her to pause for one minute, so we may chat. She wants to know why she would want to talk to me. I tell her, "It is wiser to know more about those who will someday kill you." This pauses her as she turns and walks to a nearby table, sits down, and invites me to sit wherever I want. I tell her, "My name is Siklósi, what is your name?" She answers, "My name is Mórahalmi, and I am a genuine plus time jumper for the Shelyapin. We have three genders in our species, male, female and reproducers. I reviewed Kisteleki's social data files. I am so impressed with you Siklósi, is your question about my name is up with the advanced questions for your preschoolers."

I kept this conversation alive by adding, "Mórahalmi, Which of the genders did you belong to, the male or reproducers? In addition, to clarify, I asked your name for protocol reasons. This was not to display my educational level. Oh, yes, one more question. How can you read Kisteleki's data files?" She tells me, "I am a female, such as your females, except we do not labor in the house, nor bear children. We did not bring a reproducer with us, so you will clean my private area, and with some adjustments, I might even have your bear my children. Now, do want to continue with the insults? Perhaps I should begin the changes currently, because I think, you would form me a wonderful little young woman. Oh, and yes, we can read some of Kisteleki unencrypted data. Do you want me to explain unencrypted data?" I tell her, "Sorry, give me a minute here," as I begin looking at my Khigir's cloned features. "Mórahalmi, it might be delightful having sex and grunting on top of you." Mórahalmi looks at me and yells while laughing, "I cannot believe you all still act like animals and perform in such a degrading manner. We simply take a shot, and honey. I will save a shot for you. Okay, dirty boy." I thought that this one might not be the one to push hard. I could handle every species I meet on Lamenta calling me dirty boy. Then I learned to handle it when the other three positive cycle elements joined them. Do I now have to learn this for all four of the negative cycle elements? Mórahalmi tells me, "We are the sole elements of the negative cycle; you will ever meet, because only we can jump. I wish you would talk with your mouth. Talking with mouths is new for me, and I find it refreshing." I shake my head yes. How lucky for me, she is a mind reader. I ask Mórahalmi, "Mórahalmi, why did you take Kisteleki's ship?" She tells me that, we know the Rétsági told King Rogov many lies about them and hidden some valuable information that they need to accomplish their mission. They have trapped the remaining members of our group, and that information includes how to free them.

We are beings with emotions also. We were created for a special work, a role in which the evil ones have discovered they could profit from being like us. They wanted to come into your cycle and take all that you have. Fortunately, our creators could stop them from staying here too long. They can jump; however, in small groups for short periods, at the cost of much destruction to innocent ones, in the negative cycle. The members of our group that are held captives include my husband and two sons. Somehow, we are trapped together for eternity, and all my leaders can worry about it how to feed and secure you and your gang. In addition, once we get our things in order here, we will prove to you that the Rétsági was the ones who gave you a hallucination induced by their poisons. Everything you saw in the dark was from them. Once they put your torture and the torture of each of your clan except for that little one in your pocket, in motion they had to return. We could break in only one of you at a time so as not to hurt you or demand anything from disturbing the link to the negative cycle. To get you out, I had to jump in here to pull you back to me. Give me the little one for I brought a special container strapped to me under my blouse." Hevesi then said, "I am defeated now, because the dirty boy will be me up just to get under your blouse." Mórahalmi answers back, with a peaceful voice, "Quit the contrary Hevesi. I am putting you there to protect me from that bad dirty boy. Will you help me sweetheart? At least tuck your head up and tell me under my blouse will be defenseless because you hate me?" Hevesi pops her head up starts to talk only to be interrupted by Mórahalmi screaming with some light device that was flashing a light, "Lenti, look how ravishing she is Szerencsi." Szerencsi, joins the conversation, "Oh Veszprémi, look at those pointed ears, she is so beautiful. Can we build her a delightful house to live in? Please. Please." Mórahalmi yells out, "Oh Lenti, will you produce me a house for her also, please, please, please?" A comes back from her flashing device that says, "Wow. Three pleases. I had better get started on that some honey." Hevesi says, "Mórahalmi, where is your husband?" Mórahalmi then comes over to my pocket and in front of Hevesi says, "Oh Hevesi, I would never do any bad around you.

Therefore, you do not worry. Lenti is my husband's father and will have him churn out lovely furniture and everything for you, okay, will you stay with me?" We hear a voice come through that box saying, "Hevesi. I am Szerencsi, and I am right here waiting for you to jump back from the Rétsági link. Will you stay with me some also? I will let you pick out the furniture that my husband's father Veszprémi will manufacture for you. We will do everything you want okay, honey, please, please, please, please." Hevesi pauses a second and says, "Mórahalmi, I hope you are a good-hearted person and likes to share, because four pleases deserves something, if we are going to be good and kind people, do not you think?" Mórahalmi answers quickly, "You are so right Hevesi. I will do what you say also, okay, just let us love you honey." Hevesi, who is standing firmly in my pocket with her chest, puffed out answers, "I guess I should give you a chance and put you on probation. I am sure you would rather be on probation now, rather than, I say a permanent no." Mórahalmi answers, smiling and looking so happy, "Oh yes Hevesi, you can put me on probation, because I promise to be good and do what you say." Szerencsi's voice comes through the box, "Hevesi, little Angel, can I be on probation also. I also promise to be good and do what you say." Hevesi all pumped up now as if she is the ruler of the universe replies as if talking to a longtime friend, "Sure Szerencsi; I want to be fair, so you can have probation also." Szerencsi unleashes five 'thank you s', until Lenti yells out, everyone, get into your positions, our warp drop is approaching.

Mórahalmi asks me to hold her hair to the rear while she ties it because she wants to ensure it does not get into her eyes since she has Hevesi with her. I pull back her hair, and we get another surprise that I did not notice. Hevesi yells to me, "My husband, do you see what I see?" I replied, "Maybe number eight." Hevesi said, "Nah big boy, one of me is enough would you not agree." I said, "Oh yes, my love, Oooooh yes." Hevesi starts laughing and says, "The last ten days have been so long without you." I told her, "I agree honey; I think we are going to create some revisions in our private time, would you agree?" Hevesi sits back, lifts her hands up to me and says, "Oooooh yes." I ask her, "My love, do you want to go to the safety in Mórahalmi container. You know, since it is under her blouse. I will be keeping a close eye on you?"

She stands up and kicks me, in the same spot, which triggers a laugh and question from Mórahalmi who asks, "Did she just kick you?" I told her, "I deserved it because I was being awful." Mórahalmi comments, "Bad indeed, if we were on the other side now, I would have slapped you, but since you have Hevesi, would a kiss work instead." Hevesi then yells, "Hey, everyone pause for a minute. You are all being rewarded based on my work." As my lips met Mórahalmi's for a brief kiss, I answered, "Hevesi, sometimes life just is not fair honey." I take her out and hold her in my hand now as Mórahalmi asks another question as her pointed ears that resemble Hevesi's ears almost perfectly, "Did she say, 'My husband,' when talking to you?" I told her, "Yes, we are enormously in love, as she spends the most time with me. She can expand to our size for small periods of time, and she is carrying our daughter in her womb." Mórahalmi then looks at me and says, "Do you have to marry every female around you. Get me off your number eight list." Hevesi tells Mórahalmi, "Mórahalmi do not be angry with my Master, for he has loved me more than any other in my life. He serves me so well, without him; I would no longer wish to live. Can you understand that I am a grown woman? In addition, we have thousands of young women who could marry and beg that he marries them, who live in our village; however, he chose me.

He gave me a new life, honor, pride, and unqualified love. Please understand that he is my husband." Mórahalmi apologized and said, "I was wrong. He just does not look like the good husband type, especially kissing me, and we have known each other for less than ten years." Hevesi laughed and said, "Mórahalmi, I can see that you are going to take much work getting us in line for the positive cycle; nevertheless, please remember he was kissing you for me. Setting up a better relationship with you for me and the care you are to give me while we jump this link thing." Mórahalmi asks Hevesi, "You think if I told him I was sorry and gave him another kiss, he would forgive me?"

Hevesi laughs, and then answers, "Oooooh yes." Mórahalmi kisses me on each cheek and says she is sorry. I complain to her, "Kisses on the cheek, what about the lips" Mórahalmi looks at me and with a smile lightly slaps me saying, "Oooooh yes. Do not talk about that in front of the little one. I finally could slap you. I am so happy now." Hevesi looks at me and says, "Yes, do not talk like that in front of my tender unimpeachable ears." I look at her and smile, "Innocent, who is the one that has me screaming during private time and limping for days." Hevesi says, "I can find that person and tell them never to do that again if you wish?" I told her, "Oooooh no, Hevesi, tell that person I want to see them twice a week from this day forward, please." Mórahalmi takes hold of Hevesi, who comments, "Master. She has such soft hands. You need to put her back on the number eight list." Mórahalmi turns around and secures Hevesi under her blouse in a special strapped on container. Mórahalmi turns back around to face me again as Hevesi yells out, "Hey Master, you are going to like it in here also." Mórahalmi yells out, "Hevesi, come on honey, you know we have to keep some secrets." Hevesi and I both laughed at this one. I asked Hevesi, "Honey, do you know what we are doing now with Mórahalmi?" Hevesi tells me, "No, do you?" I tell her, "Any ways, I kind of think she is funny." Hevesi tells me, "Do not worry Master, Mórahalmi is a wonderful person." I add, "Yes a lot kinder than the Khigir, who was in the dark." Mórahalmi tells us, "Yes guys, which was a kind and sweet Rétsági. Okay Siklósi, Hold onto both of my hands and keep your eyes on me. We will be doing some twisting and passing through some strange noises and winds. One spot always lifts my blouse. I have a special surprise in their just for you. You had better catch this because that is all you will see for the next ten years in that area. Happy hunting, now we can jump." When she said that, a bright red light flashed and up we went, like a rocket. We were spinning around, and I kept my eyes on her. She has such a peaceful and confident look in her eyes, so I am also appeased.

We do not shoot up that far until we begin to spin in a circle with so many different things that I cannot identify. What is unique is that they never collide; they simply go through each other. These objects continue to change into other objects, which is strange to watch. We pass through so many colors, now the noises, and the giant wind, and it is a note with some good news. That was a fast glimpse; nevertheless, I got it. Now, the rest of the trip will be boring. I continue to look into Mórahalmi's eyes as, she, for the first time on this trip looks into mine. I wink at her, and she smiles back. I do not know if she is my enemy. Something cries inside me to trust her. At least, we are going somewhere, and they did stroke the mountains out so Hevesi. They pumped her up, and when we saw Mórahalmi's ears, it was as if something inside both of us was released. Hevesi was not the abnormal one in our group. It was I. I can live with this. Hevesi knows how to deal. She had my heart on the ground wanting to marry her. She is so wonderful inside and has the childlike quality to influence adults. She is also an adult; nevertheless, we run into groups where the height represents the age. I have never fought with someone so much in my life, even more than having me with my three brothers. Nonetheless, each minute I miss her. Even though I forgot about her while watching, my mangled wives die. It was better than during those times that I did not think of her. Hevesi is only a 'her' around our growing family. When strangers are present, she is a soldier, watching and planning her attack. I can understand why Mórahalmi would have some concern about Hevesi and me. We just do not look like we would compose a couple. Those who think as that, find a great surprise when they run into our powerful bond. Mórahalmi's hands are soft and warm. I can feel her blood flow through them. I am so glad I asked her to sit down and talk, because we almost could have mistakenly fallen in the enemy game, with me joining King Rogov as her enemy. We are slowing now and land on an appealing marble patio. Two men and one excited woman are awaiting us. The thrilled woman rushes to Mórahalmi and starts to unbutton her blouse. Mórahalmi stops her by holding her hand in place, looks at me, and asks, "Do you have anything to say to me?" I simply said, "I am especially glad that you are single."

Hevesi looks at Mórahalmi and asks, "Is that true?" Mórahalmi asks, "Do you think I would be a hot number eight?" Hevesi says please four times. Szerencsi, "Oh, her voice is accordingly soft." I then look at her and say, as I am holding Hevesi, who loves to lay on my palm on her back and so stretching exercises, "Her name is Hevesi." Szerencsi speaks in a soft voice, "Hello Hevesi. My name is Szerencsi and just like Mórahalmi, we love you and are going to help take good care of you." Mórahalmi asks me, "Can we compromise on a schedule with her?" I tell them, "She has to work that out with you; after all, she has me trained. I do know she really wants to see the rest of our family. Do you have any shirts with pockets like this?" I motioned to both to come over and look at my shirt as I slide Hevesi back into it. Hevesi sat on her special fabric sofa or bed and looked up with a big smile and oh too innocent. I saw some slow tears come down Szerencsi's cheek as I took my emergency rag out and wiped her cheek. She said, "Oh, she just looks so beautiful and happy." Mórahalmi said, "We will have the shirts in only one minute, okay, please wait." They both ran to a machine on the wall, touched some things and said some words. They both removed their blouses as their comrades cheered. It did not matter to them, for they were doing something in order to have something little to pour their love into." They put on their new shirts and ran back. Lenti spoke up, "Mórahalmi, do you remember when I used to be the leader here?" She looked at him quickly and said,

"Yes," then turned around to me and asked, "We are going to meet the rest of your family as soon as they return from their swimming. I can ensure she will see whom she wants to see and does what she wants to do until she, or you tell me to give her back. We have a delightful dinner and music show tonight that Szerencsi could host our little Angel if that is okay. Sorry, we do not have her houses finished yet; however, when we do, we will put it in your married bedroom. Is this okay?" I looked down at Hevesi, who was enjoying this too much. I asked, "Well, what do you say boss?"

She shook her head yes, and I lifted her up out of my pocket. I then moved her face beside my cheek, and she gave me my kiss. Szerencsi then cheers, "She gave him a kiss, how wonderful." I looked at her and said, "We are diplomats here, so you are on your best behavior, all right love." Hevesi agreed as I handed her to Mórahalmi who slides her into her remodeled shirt pocket, and as she turned around I heard her say, "You can be bad, I will not tell, okay little Angel." They were out of range for me to hear anything else. Szerencsi had her arms wrapped around Mórahalmi's right arm, as they both skipped to their leader. About halfway there they stopped and Mórahalmi turned around to look at me and said, "Well come on daddy. Do not be a late bug." I could hear Hevesi laugh at that one and off, they went. I picked up my pace and arrived about the same time they got there. Mórahalmi turned around and looked at me as I was arriving, and I answered, "Oh darn, I guess I am a late bug." I could hear Hevesi laughing again. Her laughs are going to put her in control of many things. We each stood in front of a chair, with one vacant chair. Their leader came to this chair and asked us all to sit, as he also sat down. He began by saying, "For those who do not know me. I am called Lenti. I see we have wife number seven, Hevesi, my soon to be replacement and the Master whom the women have told us so many stories about you Siklósi. I regret to have to welcome you under these dismal times. We usually do not start our first contacts with a meeting; however, I did not want to discuss this with your clan until I had your agreement. We understand that Hevesi is your ears; at the same time, attendance is not compulsory, as I am sure Hevesi's two new servants would be glad to join her with your family." I answered, "I think it would be best if Hevesi were here with me. I value her counsel too much." Szerencsi and Mórahalmi both sighed as Mórahalmi said, "If I had her, I would keep her with me always also." Szerencsi immediately confirmed this decision. Lenti then directed my attention to the other individual at the table, introduced him as Veszprémi, and confirmed that he and Szerencsi were the scientists trying to figure a way that they can save us. He looked at Szerencsi and told her he needed her same level of dedication.

Mórahalmi looked at her and promised to work the schedule where she could love Hevesi during her free time. Mórahalmi then looked at me. I looked at Szerencsi and said, "We will endure every sacrifice with our time that Hevesi will allow us. I am sorry; I promised her that I would never order her around; nevertheless, I have found her to be an exceptionally proper, caring, sharing little Angel, so she will with the rest of you be fair. Once you gain her love, you will have her wrapped around your finger, so you will get your fair opportunity to love her also. Do we have a deal?" Szerencsi ran around our table and gave me a kiss on my cheek. Hevesi yelled out, "Hey, I do not let married women kiss my Master." She got all four of them on that one as I watched all four of my hosts laughing. I wondered how could have King Rogov sided with the Rétsági. It could be that having Hevesi with me pulled the maternal fire, if there is such a thing, out of these two loving women and flooded them with love. I know that love erases so much. Any fool can see that Lenti has no control over Mórahalmi and Szerencsi, Hevesi does, to the extent that I cannot see them doing something that would harm her or those she loves. Sometimes in our lives, we have to go with our gut and heart, even though our minds tell us to hold back. My gut is in this one. Furthermore, Hevesi's gut and heart are buying this, and she has never been wrong. At least with this road we have been promised to meet with my family again, and that will be the test, because I will live and die beside them. Lenti asks me a question, which I did not hear and Hevesi yells out,

"Master, wake up remember we are diplomats here." I naturally heard her voice, and I looked at Lenti and said, "Oh. I am so sorry. This has been such a long day, and I have trouble concentrating unless Hevesi is beside me." Mórahalmi gets up and stands beside Veszprémi who is sitting beside me, and asks him to trade seats. He gets up, smiles at her, and says, "Anything for our Angel Hevesi." Yes, he is married and yes; he earned him some points because his wife, Szerencsi is giving him the milky eyes. That cannot be faked, as it was so instantaneous. Lenti tells me, "Siklósi, if we had some time to spare, I would have given it to you now so you can join your wonderful family. I am going to tell you the situation; if you believe this, or not will not matter. There are no guards or locks here. You may go anywhere you want at any time you want.

I am sparing Mórahalmi to help you with anything you need. You may freely ask her any question you want. Therefore, the war with the Rétsági is over. You lost; we lost; they lost. Let me explain the way the universe was set up. It was set up to go in time cycles with each one being one nonillion, or ten to the 30th power. Gyöngyösi will explain that to you. Suffice it to say your grandchildren are not doomed; nevertheless, someone's grandchildren will be doomed. The time cycle runs in a somewhat skinny circle, with positive time expanding and negative time retracting. It is during the negative to positive switch that we generate the fine adjustments and set up the next circle. Whatever created this system has seen its function over 100 times. We have done this all 100 times, each time takes about one year, and then we hibernate in our host rock statue, Whichever side we jump to; we stay in that shell. This time as we departed our shells, the Rétsági could find us, through our high-level codes. They first could capture us. With the help of some old powers, we could affect the jump, but not until the Rétsági had made some illegal attempts. They jumped on our high-level codes and did not include the low-level codes, causing much destruction. They could recapture all our people except for us, as we had some special assignments before our jumps. The Rétsági tried to jump with our people, and after killing thirty-six of our people, could get enough of the code to create temporary jumps, in which they first destroyed our positive statues, which have the opposite effect on us forbidding us to return to the negative side. To construct these adjustments for each cycle, we must jump into our special negative time rock statues we keep deep in the seas. We rotate the planet that hosts them. This time the switch was going to be from Lamenta. I am now also completely confused, so here is the summary.

The switch will not be made this time, as the negative will vanish when the new positive launches. Your universe will notice no changes. As positive expands this time, it will not return and will move into unknown zones. We cannot return, and we have no way to get anywhere. You entered this puzzle when the four positive elements united in your family set of something on the negative side that pulled you in until the Rétsági while attacking destroyed your return. We can and we will return you. We are close to getting us back. When we go into your positive cycle, we go as Lamentans and will age and die in Lamentan soil. Our four statues are still hidden somewhere, as we are hanging on as long as we can jump. This so we can watch and if need to, destroy our statues if the Rétsági finds them and tries to pull them back. We need your help. Will you think about helping us?" I looked at him and asked, "How much time are we talking about here?" Lenti said, "We have about three days. We have been able to plant code disruptors in thirty-three of the Rétsági illegal jumpers, which will destroy them when they try their next jump. Once the remaining three get close to the barrier, we will try to jumble their codes to prevent entry." I looked and asked, "How can we help you?" He said, "We need your permission to send false codes of your genocryatic code, which is the code that contains the specific composition of every one of your cells. We can create exact clones of you and place those clones in other places to spread out and delay the Rétsági. This helps keep you alive longer, because when they find you, they will kill you, as they showed you in their little games, they played with you. In addition, when we take the final jump into the positive cycle, each one of us must have a positive Lamentan hold our hands. This way, when we actually jump, our codes provide the safety, and your codes help create our new positive bodies. If a Rétsági is in the positive cycle when the switch strikes, with their incomplete codes, the positive cycle will also vanish. Remember, if at any time you want to leave, you may do so, which will sign our death as official. However, if you jump alone, you lose your element friends, as they can only return with our codes and your Lamentan codes."

I looked at Hevesi and asked, "Hevesi, what should I do?" Hevesi asks me, "My husband, were you paying attention?" I looked at Mórahalmi's shirt pocket and answered her, "Yes, my love I heard every word. I want to go with your gut, especially since our daughter is in there." Hevesi looks at Lenti and asks, "Lenti, I am confused on how the cycle switch does not affect us, as we are already deep into positive time, yet a bad code, we die instantly." Lenti tells her, "Hevesi, this time cycle is a skinny circle and not a straight-line function. As each parallel and dimension jump on the circle in its own way. You hit the circle past the bottom point, thus you are already in the positive time; however, anything that happens at the bottom of the circle pulls everything above its back." Lenti asks Hevesi if that explained everything to her. She looked at him and that little con artist said, 'Yes, that was exactly what I was thinking. I just forgot about how the parallel and interference are not fixed by the dimensions." Lenti looked at her with strange eyes and said, "I have had trouble remembering that a few times also." She just casually rolled her head over toward me and said, "If I were you my husband, I would do two things. The first thing I would do is stop drooling over this pocket and the way its contours are well defined. Then the second thing I would do is kiss both of these women and shake both men's hands. Afterwards, I would ask them if they could use some news partners." Instantly, I am being kissed on each cheek, and Lenti is shaking one hand as Veszprémi shakes the other. Our slobbering and shaking comes to a halt when Hevesi yells to Szerencsi, "Szerencsi, and married women only one kiss." She jumps up at attention and says, "Yes Master" as Mórahalmi cheers, “That means I get another one.” Szerencsi complains that this is cheating. Hevesi tells me, “Szerencsi it is a strategy. I am working on number eight.” I then look at Lenti and say, “It would be pleasant to have a few minutes to say hi to my wife, before I bring them here to start helping.” Lenti subsequently tells me, “Oh Siklósi, spend the rest of the night with them, enjoy a genteel formal meal we have prepared for you, and someone told us about some music balls we found, which should be instrumental in providing you a wonderful night of dancing. I must warn you that we found mind reprogramming and altering Rétsági code generators in two of your wives’ heads.

We have the video streams of the surgeries and we have the devices they implanted available for you to study. Mórahalmi will provide this data to you.” I asked him, “Is it okay if I have one of my wives research this on my behalf?” Lenti said, “Any or all your wives. However, you want to obtain this information. Khigir and Csongrád had the implants, they tried with Gyöngyösi and Makói; however, their bodies rejected them. They were afraid that since Tselikovsky had twins in her womb, that her body could react outside their zones of acceptable universal risk.” I look at Mórahalmi and ask her if she takes Hevesi and reviews it with her. I asked her to point me in the direction of my family, and I will surprise them. She suggested, with a wink, that I hurry and thereby hide in the brush and surprise them. I shook my head yes, and while preparing to meet with my family, heard Hevesi congratulate her on a great idea. I truly hope that Mórahalmi is not hooked on having ‘a friend in the pocket.’ Even I, while rushing to meet my wives I have not seen in two weeks, am missing Hevesi already. I can hear Tselikovsky laughing in the background; thereby hurriedly hide myself within easy viewing of our flowery camping area. Tselikovsky always talks louder when she is uneasy or upset over something. I usually believed this was because she wanted a stranger to find her, thus she could have a good fight, which she would win. When she is mad, this Tamarkin lion can defeat anything. This tells me that Khigir, and she is not getting along well.

I know my women, especially Tamarkins, as they have a special way of teaching with their fists and claws. I can see that our hosts took excellent care of them. The tents are spacious, and have signs to indicate special functions such a cleaning and eating as examples. They even have a tent that reads, "Cleaning Master." They must have told these people some war stories about my adventures in the wilderness. There are also so many flowers around this area. We have some thick patches in our mountains; however, not so many varieties as these so close beside each other. Now they are rushing in, as Makói who must be hungry looks in the dining tent and yells back, "It is ready." That will be a good time to sneak up. Nevertheless, I would like to talk have some updates, and I know who will tell me.

Gyöngyösi enjoys a fast walk around an area when she first arrives, and this looks like a path she has walked many times. They must really enjoy their privacy in this small-fortified area, which has an eight-foot tall wooded fort around it. I know my wives requested this. Gyöngyösi is preparing for her walk with only her short silk garment that she wears under her nightgowns. She would never wear this if she believed a male was around, except for me. This reassures me my loves were treated with respect and honor. Gyöngyösi will get a surprise tonight when she walks past me. Here she comes. I am now ducking back into this bush. I will pounce on her when she walks pass me. Waiting, waiting, wait this too long. Something is not right. I stick my head out from my bush, and she is nowhere around here. With my curiosity distorting my comprehension, something pounces on me and warns, "If you say a word, I will stab you. What will you do for your life?" I answer, "I am the Master of these women and have returned to caring for them." The voice tells me, "Their Master is gone, and have you come to play with one of them." I confess, "Oh no, not I." This voice responds, "Oh. You think they are of no beauty. If you are their Master, would they recognize you, and you recognize them." I now am putting this puzzle together so I answer, "All, except for that little tricky Angel." She then rolls, pulling me over her and asks, "How did you know it was me?" While holding her firmly I answered, "A gut feeling my love. And how did you know I was hiding here?" Gyöngyösi answers, "I saw you from your tracks that lead under the bush." We laugh quietly as I respond, "I must have been gone for so long that I lost my wilderness skills." My Angel tells me that everyone is here except for Hevesi, Ajkai, the elements, and me. I tell her not to worry about Hevesi; she is okay and asked if anyone is acting strange. Gyöngyösi tells me that Khigir and Csongrád have must bitterness and hate in their hearts for they blame our hosts for your death that they witnessed just before a species that call themselves the Rétsági freed her. I update by reassuring her that I am not dead, and that we have many questions we must answer soon, or we may all be in danger of our deaths.

Gyöngyösi asks me if we have enough time for a short family reunion. I tell her we have this night, with a fine dinner and new music balls to dancing and singing. Her face releases her happy shine as her eyes reveal she is excited, thereby she asks me, "Are you ready to meet us now?" I jumped up and said, "My goodness woman, where are your garments?" She tells me, "An Angel told me I would not need them on this walk." She can think on her wings so cleverly. She grabs my hands as we head for our tent. As we become closer, to our surprise, they are all outside cheering for us. We begin to walk as they begin to run for us. I ask Gyöngyösi, "How did they know I was here?" She tells me, "Because you are their husband and live in their wombs." I notice that Khigir and Csongrád are trailing. This is not the Khigir, which I know. I will see to this later, for now it is happy time. The little bubbles of joy are exploding everywhere. We know there is so much farther to go; however, being together will cause the journey to be less painful. Nógrád is head-to-head mixed in with them, as her lips fight for a cheek to kiss or hand to hold tight. There can be no married or unmarried in this part of the reunion. When things cool down and we prepare for the serious side of this reunion, after the unmarried may have to be segregated. Then another part of me asks, why, for we are at the threshold of losing everything in existence, and we should worry about some trivial formality and not instead, deal with what is in the heart. We here agree that if we were to form the rules, Nógrád would be standing in the married line. Nevertheless, to accept some law from an ancient age, which before we believed to be among the forerunners of time, only to discover that perhaps millions and millions of forerunner ages existed before them now seems foolish at best. She suffered as the rest of have, if not more. I can feel where her pain would be greater, for to want something and that something wants you, but to have another something that has nothing to do with the something to forbid it. I may think seriously about finding a new home if the Edelényi did not give in on this issue. We are all in the fighting mode now, although not all as much as Khigir and what used to be my Queen. I pause our reunion, and ask Khigir, "Are you disappointed that I am not truly dead?"

She flattens me with her answer, "No my Master. I just can never live through that pain again, only to discover that love is but an introduction to hate and suffering." I then ask my family, "Do we still have food remaining in our dining room?" They shouted yes and pulled me inside the tent. I yelled on the way in for Khigir and the Queen to join us. They took me to a special chair at the head of the table that had an empty plate and cups before it. I asked them if they knew I was coming tonight. They denied knowing this; nevertheless, knew a day would come when I would return. I always marvel at their faith. As we sit down, I asked that Khigir sits on one side of Gyöngyösi and me on the other, which was usual; however, next I asked that a seat remains open between Khigir and Csongrád. They objected to no avail because I ordered it, and they obeyed. Grandpa always taught me to divide those who hate you before you convert them. I began by saying telling them that we have all been through so much pain and hurt and that if it had not been for our love. We would have vanished long ago. I then confessed to seeing Makói, Tselikovsky, Gyöngyösi, and Csongrád die before me. I had begged at their deaths for one more chance, as I hoped, many of them had done. I wanted this chance. I have found a way for us, to include our elements to survive. Csongrád then asked, "Master, how did you escape?" I told her that Hevesi had saved me. They all began the cheer and celebrate, "Hevesi is alive," until they slowly began to pause and look at Khigir, who asked me, "Master, where is our precious Hevesi?" Then, our tent door flew open and in came Mórahalmi as Hevesi was screaming, "I am here my loves." Mórahalmi pulled Hevesi out of her shirt until she screamed, "Put me back in your shirt my sister now!" Mórahalmi obeyed immediately, as all the wives cooled down and passed in front of her receiving her kiss and exchanging their oaths of forever love. This little five-inch woman has everyone in this tent doing things, her way and we agree this is the fairest and best way as Hevesi also wants to enjoy the special relationship with each.

I motioned for Mórahalmi to sit between Khigir and Csongrád, knowing that even though they could resist me, Hevesi would control them, if the videos she watched as convinced her of foul play. Hevesi began by saying to Khigir, "Khigir, get over on your knees before your Master and give him your vow of incessantly love again, NOW." Khigir was up and holding on to my waist as tears flowed down her cheek swearing, "Forever and ever my silly boy." Without asking, or hinting in any way of disloyalty Csongrád ran up to my other side and cried the same oaths. I motioned for Gyöngyösi and Mórahalmi to comfort them. Khigir hugged Mórahalmi tight asking forgiveness for all the wrong she had done. Mórahalmi told her that she had always forgiven her, even while she was doing these hateful things. My family is now back on the same sheet of music. I could also see where Khigir's rejections had hurt the other wives, as they furthermore swore their forgiveness as our Precious Dove pleaded for them to forgive her. Hate can deceive the strongest eyes of love. Hate, however, can never kill the flame of a true love. When that true love once again receives its fuel, it will burn the hate away from it. As we settle down, I ignite other fire, "Well women, you have a hungry Master here, now who is going to feed me?" I miscalculated the degree in which they had missed me, as I found myself on the floor flooded with food and an ocean of innocent sweet unending 'sorry.' This was my mistake, so I decide to wiggle out of this gracefully by saying, "Wow, my family did miss me." Naturally, a Master with food over his face and garment is not going to remain dirty long in this bunch, as I see the tent door flap open. The flap opens again and three of them return with rags, clothes, and soap. They even have soap in here. I thought this place was to be as a paradise. It fooled me. As they rush up, Hevesi yells, "Mórahalmi, put me on the table and turn around." Mórahalmi complains, "Why do I have to turn around. You are the little one?" Khigir smiles at Mórahalmi and says, "Because she is the boss and has our Master's daughter in her womb, she must have figured something out." Mórahalmi laughs and as she releases Hevesi and turns around answers, "Oh, how foolish I am, how could I forget that you would need our boss to help you."

Everyone laughs except for me. I killed hundreds of Hegyközi, only to be manhandled is such an unmanly manner. Wish I had that ax again, so I could kill another thousand. They are slashing up their beautiful gowns. Their hair is now undone, and face paint adding streaks to their faces, yet their smiles are chasing away the darkness. Mórahalmi teases Hevesi, "Oh Hevesi, just one little peek would be fair, because he got a peek at me in the tunnel." Hevesi responds, "Number eight." Mórahalmi cries, "Oh Hevesi that is too high of a price." Khigir asks, "Hevesi, explain peek in the tunnel." Hevesi responds quickly, as if she had rehearsed this, "Oh Master, do not worry, it was so fast that even I did not see, and I was watching dirty boy like a hawk." All the wives laugh and cry out, "Hevesi to the rescue." Khigir blows her a kiss and confesses, "The true reason we were all so sad when you and our Master was away from us was not from missing our Master, but from missing you." Hevesi, with her chest puffed up reveals, "Oh, I knew that, now we need to hurry because the crybaby boy is getting goose bumps." I look at her and say, "Thank you my only truelove." Mórahalmi, with her back still turned comments, "She can grow on us so fast." Hevesi, never one known to be conceited, replies, "I know. We need to get him dressed, because I am hungry." When our Hevesi speaks things happen fast, for in a whiff, we are all eating one more, this time I am filling my plate one serving at a time. While eating I asked Mórahalmi, "How much time do we really have?" She tells me, "One stable day and maybe a half a shaky day after that." I ask her if they have a way to show my family our situation. She raises her hands and a giant white canvas, the size of our ship's sail, appears before us with talking and moving images appearing on it. As the video finishes, Lenti comes running in front of us and warns us, "The Rétsági had executed another violation, which is going to shift the cycle today. The good news I have is that we have located the four element statues and made an agreement for the exchange if we go now, as the Rétsági is drawing close to our statues. Can we go at the present time?" Khigir yells, "Time to move out." Hevesi yells, "Khigir." Khigir apologizes, saying, "I am sorry. You have been gone." Hevesi now yells, "Time to go."

Lenti asks Mórahalmi, "Did that just really happen?" Mórahalmi shakes her head yes and warns, "You better get moving, and the boss has given her order." She grabs Hevesi and away we go to their power station. Lenti tells us, "I am sending you back to a newly remolded and confused Kisteleki. I will put together the element exchange, hold off the Rétsági until the elements are safe, and return. See you in a flash." I ask Lenti, "Let me help you." Lenti denies my request telling me this is his mission. I shake his hand only to find ourselves asleep on Kisteleki as Abaúj is yelling, "Who is that peculiar woman beside our Master." 'Strange woman' was the wakeup call for our gang. We all sit up and look around. Abaúj tells us, "You all look as if you are in a new place." I go to shake it off until Mórahalmi rolls over. My clan begins screaming. Abaúj informs us not to be afraid, as she will save us. Khigir dives on Mórahalmi keeping her elbows down so not to hurt Hevesi. Gyöngyösi yells to Abaúj, "Abaúj, it is okay, she is our best friend." All the wives and Nógrád agree as Abaúj dissolves before impact. Mórahalmi looks at us and asks, "Am I gladly received?" Khigir tells her, "You are welcome for our eternity and any other eternities you can jump into." Khigir asks, "Anyone wanting to get up." Hevesi yells, "Not me." The rest of us jumped up and began checking to ensure we are indeed on our Kisteleki. Kisteleki yells out to us, "Welcome back sleepy heads, Dabasi, and I was worried about you." Mórahalmi asks, "Who is Dabasi?" Hevesi tells her, "She is our best friend; we need to tell her we are okay, so she does not worry." Our gang heads down the steps to the floor. It is so much relief once going down his steps rather than crawling up them. As we, rush around our Dabasi, Mórahalmi yells out, "Oh wow a Zemplén." Dabasi then comments, "Only our Queen calls our ancestors from the old books' Zemplén, how do you know of Zemplén?" Mórahalmi confesses that one of the members from a previous jump brought some as a stole away. She lost them in the shuffle of the planets and was not able to bring them back with her. We always wondered if they had survived.

Khigir then congratulates Dabasi as being of the most ancient species of our universe. Hevesi adds in, "And still the most beautiful." My wives' cheer as Mórahalmi looks down and asks, "Hevesi, how do you get so much love in that little heart?" Hevesi blushes her eyes and sits down. Khigir tells Mórahalmi that Dabasi agreed to join us after a terrible battle and lives strongly within our hearts, as we are so eager to take her back to our mountain home. Mórahalmi tells us the Zemplén was created to live in the sea and not on mountains. Ajkai gives her thanks of Lenti's great heroism and then explains that we hope to find a magic man among the Mystanites to transform her into a Lamentan. I ask Mórahalmi, "What about Lenti's great heroism?" Ajkai looks at Mórahalmi and explains, "Oh, I thought they knew." Mórahalmi tells her, "It is okay. Lenti was not able to survive the exchange, and told me to thank you so much for what you did for our known life." I then asked, "What about Szerencsi and Veszprémi?" Mórahalmi explains that they wanted to start life on a planet; we had jumped to a few cycles previously that they enjoyed so much. Seeing Hevesi and having Lamentan bodies now gave them an urge finally to start their family. Mórahalmi looked at us and said that no magic power in this universe could transfer Dabasi, and that those mystics were playing with coding that would eventually leave her in great pain and kill her. The creators of another cycle created her in a previous negative cycle, and when the change mixes the positive cycle of this final leap into her shells, she will suffer sadly. We sat around sad. She said, "However, I might be able to find a solution; even though, before I was to do that I would have to know that everyone loved me." She must not be as bright as I took her to be, by not learning from my food incident. She ended on the floor smothered by all the family with loud kisses and echoes of, "You are loved." A few minutes later, I lifted her up only to hear from inside her pocket, "My turn, now it is my turn." I thus pulled Hevesi out and put her up against Mórahalmi's face as she gave her a kiss and said, "I love you so much, therefore, please help us."

We could see a teardrop fall from Mórahalmi's eyes, which told us that love was melting her defenses, although she never raised her defenses again after our talk at that table. I gently put Hevesi back in her pocket only to receive a, "Watch those fingers' dirty boy." Khigir then responds, "Oh Hevesi, we could forgive an occasional close call cannot we?" Mórahalmi begs, "Please." Hevesi answers Khigir with a yes and tells Mórahalmi, "Number eight." Mórahalmi begs again, "Please." Hevesi then answers, "Okay, this one time and that is only because I have so much love packed in my heart, do you understand?" Mórahalmi then answers, "Yes boss." She reaches in her pocket and hands me a pill saying, "Lenti told me I would need this for something special, as we only receive one each. This is a special pill, which will mix the cycle charges in Dabasi and allow us to shift her shape into a complete Lamentan body. She will be able to live as you, except she is a negative element like me and can never reproduce with the positives. Moreover, I can never reproduce, as I do not belong to our reproducing gender." Hevesi starts crying saying, "I so much wanted someday to care for the babies you would give our Master." Mórahalmi tells her, "I guess you will have to settle with me helping you care for our daughters you are going to give our Master, is that a deal?" Hevesi promises and yells out today is the second best time in my life. We ask her, "When was the best time?" She says, "When our Master kept his mouth shut for two whole weeks while he slept." Mórahalmi tells Hevesi, "That was not proper." Hevesi confesses, "I am sorry, Master." I tell her, "Even though you were breaking my heart, I still loved you." Hevesi looks, smiles at me, and before she can talk everyone yells, "I know." Mórahalmi tells Hevesi, "I think they know little Angel." Hevesi smiles and gives us her melting innocent shy eye, winks. Khigir then tells her, "Hevesi, you win again." Hevesi, having us all off guard fires back, "I know." I frown at her and ask Dabasi, "Honey, please take this pill, because you will never believe where we went to get this for you." That brings a round of laughs as she swallows it and vanishes. Hevesi yells out, "Mórahalmi, what happened?" Mórahalmi answers, "You must have given me a false kick." I see that familiar stare flash back into her eyes, as I see her shirt pocket shake. I look at Mórahalmi and tell her, "Oh, I forgot to tell you to wear extra padding under your pocket." Mórahalmi coughs and says, "Thanks for the warning."

Khigir asks, "What is that all about." I tell her that we are discussing a method that Hevesi uses to keep us in line. Khigir then waves her hands and says, "I do not want to know." She looks at Hevesi and asks, "Why do you not use that on me?" Hevesi looks at her, tells her to look at where her pocket is, and confesses, "You have too much padding for my method to be effective." Mórahalmi and I hold hands and reply, "Oh yes, indeed Hevesi." The water in the pool begins to steam now, and in the fog walks out a nude woman asking, "Will somebody give me something to wear before the dirty boy gets excited?" Wives go flying now as garments fly through the air, as Khigir dresses the woman. Mórahalmi complains to Hevesi, "Why did not you force the Master to turn his back on that woman?" Hevesi confesses, "I wanted to Mórahalmi; however, her beauty left me speechless." Dabasi comments, "Hevesi, you are being too generous." Hevesi yells out, "Someone saves me. I am in love." Makói runs over to her and yells back, "She is mine; I found her first." Khigir then asks Makói, "Would you really refuse to share something so beautiful with your family." Makói afterwards answers, "I guess not, but only because I have so much love packed into my tiny little heart," as she looks at Hevesi and blows a kiss. Hevesi blows a kiss back to her and adds, "Oh, sister. I understand the grief you now bear." Mórahalmi asks Hevesi, "Was that virtuous Hevesi? I must confess to having never seen a bear as gorgeous as Makói." Hevesi adds, "And the only bear I will ever love with all my heart." Makói thanks Mórahalmi and Hevesi. We now walk over and sit down around the big pool. I say to the gorgeous Dabasi, "I remember a special creature who bonded to Makói and me at this exact spot." Dabasi tells us, "I remember my friends telling me to keep away from you, because you looked like a dirty boy; however, when Makói jumped in and offered me to you, I was therefore afraid, and discovered we were so wrong. They could not believe me when I returned. You did notice that they kept the spot in front of you open."

Csongrád finally jumps into our family talking by adding, "Even the fish in the deep-sea know about the dirty boy. Where was my daddy when I needed him?" Nógrád exercises her new confidence by adding, "Very likely with my daddy receiving dirty boy lessons from our Master." Nógrád surprises all of us with this one as the Queen leans over and gives her a kiss saying, "You are probably right." I feel a new family here now as tested, apart we were, and found to be wanting, joined once more. Mórahalmi has blended in so perfectly. We all trust Hevesi's gut and when she likes someone, that person can be trusted. I wonder if she realizes that we exist today because of her and the faith I put in her judgment. Kisteleki announces that he has our things ready for departure, and that we should arrive in about twenty minutes. I ask him if I can create some clothing for the newest members of our family. He asks me to have them stand in front in the open, so he can scan them for measurements. I question him. How long will that take? Kisteleki tells me thirty minutes. I question him, "May we fashion our departure after our clothing is finished?" He confirms; I look out our window and witness the sea moving much slower. We look at our friend who took us to the secret worlds beneath the sea with confused feelings. We have met challenges we could barely overcome. Nevertheless, we also found joys, forever locked inside the sea of our love. Our sea expands from the deepest parts of the sea, the four elements, to the heavens, and the cycles of time.

Chapter 05

The knees of love

We are sitting near the viewing windows on top of Kisteleki staring up at the dark. Then the light begins to shade the dark seawaters, and we begin cheering. Up to, we continue as the light becomes brighter. I notice a dark spot in the middle of the light. I guess this to be our ship. Kisteleki announces, "Ship dwellers, prepare to go ashore." Smiles flood the faces of most of my women. A few will find this as a new experience. Nevertheless, I comprehend my women will help them make the transition. My smile dims because I do not see what lies ahead of us. I am still confused not knowing the reason we are on this journey. I originally thought it was a reward for our love. Despite, watching my wives die can never be a reward. I must also consider this building our confidence and patience. This makes me wonder if we still need building. Hevesi and Nógrád are firing up Mórahalmi. Nógrád and Mórahalmi are becoming great sisters. This bond will bring much glory for the Edelényi, as new tales will travel our cosmos. Makói is explaining to Dabasi the wonderful things that lay before them.

Brann, Baranya, and Abaúj are briefing their new partner Béla about the astonishments she has yet to enjoy. Eyes begin to brighten as we witness the light-blue waters around us. Our trip beneath the sea shall soon end, in a victory. I shudder to think what would have been the result if the Rétsági had made their jumps, and if I had not demanded that Mórahalmi set down and talk personally to me. She now stands to become one of my best friends, as Hevesi will drag her along on some of our wilderness walks.

Hevesi is another source of my great pride. I loved her because who she was, and not what she was. The smallest bundle of love among us made the greatest decisions. I will also add that she made the put right decisions. Kisteleki now wobbles. Looking outside, I catch sight of the sea waves pushing against Kisteleki. The Suns hit my face, forcing me to close my eyes and turn away. I notice many of my wives doing this also, as our cheering explodes. Kisteleki lifts off the water and flies toward our giant ship and lands on our deck between the second and third sails. My women rush to the deck, not realizing we will be on it for a few more days. I walk over to one of Kisteleki's boxes and thank him for what he

had done for us. He confessed that he would be empty inside for a good while. I told him that he was welcome to visit us at any time. Kisteleki assured me he would keep this in mind and asked me to take care of my women. I noticed his exit lights were flashing brighter now, so I as I went out the door, he closed it behind me. He carefully lifted off and after clearing our ship sank into the world, we had just departed. Khigir informs her clan that we have food in the dining room. Being empty-bellied myself, I casually walk behind making sure I can account for my women, as I would hate to lose one now. We should be hungry, considering the great distance we have traveled since our excellent dinner last night, or earlier today. It is difficult to distinguish because both were bound in the dark for too long. Everyone is here, as I witness a wave of rainbows before me. I notice the three of our new sea members have red hair. That makes things easy. I remember Béla had Tamarkin hair when we met. She must on purpose changed it, so we would accept her much easier. The wives have been making a big fuss over their red hair, as each of the hands had touched it; noses smelled it and lips kissed it. I can never see myself touching and kissing another man's hair. If I can sneak past Hevesi, I can imagine myself playing with their red hair, simply for my curiosity, of course. I dare not be caught, as this would doom me to a constant bashing of 'dirty-boys' taking away, my remaining sanity. They are sitting around our newly expanded table talking as if tomorrow words no longer will exist.

I sat down in my chair. As I sat down my wives finish talking, and I begin my dinner speech, "Well, women we are back on our boat, and the sea is now beneath us. We survived some terrifying events, yet from it came the great things. My first gift is from Mórahalmi and her comrades. They trusted and depended on us. Therefore, we continue to live. She adds to the mysterious composition of our family by representing the time jumper creation of the Shelyapin. The second gift is Béla, who lured me into the sea with her Tamarkin hair, yet rises with her red hair, which I will also cherish. Béla adds to the mysterious composition of our family by representing the water element, and because that making our family complete with the known elements of Lamenta. Dabasi comes to us, defeating her fear with the help of a push from Makói. She turned this fear into a wish to be a part of our family. Her half fish's body would present many obstacles in her journey along the paths of our lives. She was willing to accept this as her new existences. We were as a result lucky that Lenti, who died so our elements might once more join our family, gave us a special pill. This pill transformed Dabasi into a beauty that will need much work on my part to protect. Dabasi adds to the mysterious composition of our family by representing a life form from the last negative time cycle. Our Master wife and I will be discussing some equalizing changes to the structure of our family. We discovered how much our unmarried family members meant to us. We know the sacrifices made by our newest family members. I am sure that Khigir will identify the great new ideas. We proved that we possibly would endure unwarranted troubles as I hope we need no more testing. As in everything, we give thanks for the food in which the air elements offer for us today. I especially thanked Abaúj for caring enough for our newest members by having a seat prepared at this table, so they could enjoy this dinner with their family. Thank you." In a speech this long, I know to expect hearing spoons hitting plates as the 'you' is flowing from my mouth. I choose from the bowls of food that we pass around the table.

We enjoy this compared with each going through the bowls choosing their selections. Someone has opened the curtains in our windows allowing the Suns' lights to enter. The heat is in the air, and soaks so deeply back into my bones. Living in the sea contains the cold, damp, and dark air that closed in in line with this tight around and in me. I look for us to spend the extra time laying under our two Suns enjoying their heat. Our future legends will read that Khigir and Tselikovsky called to their parents to return their heat within their bodies. I am also discovering the food above the sea tastes fluffier than the heavy food below the sea. I did enjoy eating the vegetable rich food. They also had meat, from special species, which were cultivated only for eating purposes. I almost forgot how beautiful my women are. Nevertheless, I am relearning an eyeful at a time. They always behave graciously when I look at them, as if they have a special sense that I will be looking. I ask Brann about their experiences with the Rétsági. She explains to us, as my wives are listening in considering they also are curious. The events were no-good. Sucked into a spinning tunnel, the Rétsági went into the center of the time cycle. The Rétsági planned to mix the four negative elements with the four positive elements to end everything. They kept us in solid cages with a five-foot thick transparent wall dividing the negative from the positive. We had no walls to our sides or back, as the charge from the positive locked us against our diaphanous wall. The Rétsági was no longer a normal land species, as they had millenniums earlier developed machine parts of their bodies. Over time, the machines may possibly destroy their flesh components and take over their kingdoms. The people element of this evolutionary process did not develop the proper safeguards and abilities to reason and considering the consequences. The Rétsági truly believed that they would survive destroying both sides of the time cycle because their reasoning confirmed this. They were only missing one element, and those were negative people to stand for the land. The Rétsági's limited abilities to organize and get results. This is why they make so many failed jumps causing so much destruction.

They believed this destruction to be from negative forces fighting them. What surprised us was how they concentrated on punishing and torturing you, instead of collecting one of you and filling our cells, release our wall and end everything. The Shelyapin could give them a strong fight over you by slowing and pulling you out and replacing you with positive cycle clones. One of the machines discovered that one of you would finish populating the cells and pulled a clone into the cage, which of course did not remove the wall between us. They, therefore, believed you to be clones. The Rétsági believed the Shelyapin planted the clones as a decoy to hide the true Lamentans, which was indeed their goal in progress. They can create fresh machines with new abilities in a rapid way. They originally programmed this machine with hair from Makói. This puts them on a false trail once more. They continued to scan for added biological material and discovered the difference between the Lamentan hair and the clone hair. This enabled them perfect their detection machines. However, by this time, everyone was out except for Hevesi and our Master. They were still unable to detect, as another fashion in the Rétsági paradise, foolishly, had Hevesi and Siklósi in their system. They were torturing and fighting full force with them. They had to fight with their loaded force because of the protection the Shelyapin was providing. The Shelyapin suffered two dangerous loses as this fashion could trace them back to their negative cycle statues under the sea. This delay gave the Shelyapin the ability to make the switch off with newer clones that had a special Lamentan compound that would dissolve within a few hours. The Shelyapin at once pulled out the Master and Hevesi finishing the transfer of the Lamentans. The Rétsági right away shifted their efforts toward destroying any additional Shelyapin statues, and optimistically destroying the time jumpers who held our Lamentan clan. They may perhaps only use the clan that belong with us, as once each bottom cycle jump from the positive to the negative a clan comprised of the four elements will form on both sides.

They used their rock tracers to match the rock from the statues they destroyed and could find the statues, except for the four who were hosting you. Lenti pulled a smart move and pulled their four statues to your sanctuary. This was the reason they needed to hold your hands to finish their jump, as he might not risk replanting their statues. They began to suffer extensive losses in their deployed machinery on Lamenta, once again believing the Shelyapin jumpers were on Lamenta preparing for the cycle changeover. This accounts since they stopped scanning the positive side for Shelyapin jumpers. Naturally, not the fashions were on line as a few kept searching the positive side keeping the pressure on Lenti. Lenti sent those who are here back to Kisteleki, who as an intelligent machine was no match for the Rétsági. Lenti came to free us, as he could release our holding charges. The positive elements quickly dispersed back into the positive cycle with only one mission, and that was to prevent the Rétsági from recapturing them. Lenti escorted us through the jump, releasing us and taking a decoy route to draw the Rétsági of our trail. He hoped to keep the Rétsági occupied until the cycle closed, which would destroy the Rétsági who they wanted to catch on the wrong side. Sorry to say, they may well destroy him; even so, he had drawn them too far-off our trail and King Rogov would not help them track us. They went to destroy King Rogov. Nevertheless, the cycle closed just in timesaving the King as Lenti vanished with the Rétsági. We are accordingly honored to be back with those whom, we love so dear." My wives went around our table hugging each of them and thanking them for the sacrifices they made to stay with us. I reassured our elements that they were indeed with their family once again. I can understand where we actually have three sectors within our clan currently. We include the married, the negative elements, and the remaining, too varied to classify. These include Nógrád, Dabasi, and Mórahalmi. Nógrád presents the special challenge in that she is the only one from these last two sectors that can reproduce.

This reminds me of an awaiting issue with Abaúj and Béla. I ask them if we have any status in the diplomatic negotiations about Nógrád. Abaúj informs us that she has the update; however, feels it best for Nógrád to reveal her situation. Khigir asks Nógrád if she wishes to update her or the Master or both in privacy. Nógrád asks to show this to the complete family. She begins by crying, which elicits Gyöngyösi to fall at her side, wiping the tears and humming once of her peaceful tunes. Gyöngyösi recommends that she stand still so the task will flow easier. As she stands, Khigir supports the other arm. Nógrád continues by telling us that when she received the news from the Edelényi leaders, it had not caught her off-guard. Her mother and she suspected this condition for many years. She was too afraid to get the results of the tests. Nógrád completed these tests several times without her collecting and reviewing the results. The Edelényi removed her from the qualified to marry list. She then began working for their special missions. Eventually, she received her assignment among this family. Nógrád enjoyed being one together with our family, and with the laws being so strict about any interspecies breeding. She thought that her shame would stay a secret while she enjoyed being an unmarried member of this family. She asked forgiveness for not telling the complete truth at first and if this condition were unsatisfactory, she would return to the Edelényi. Khigir asked her, "Nógrád, why would we find your condition unacceptable?" I told her, "Nógrád, we would only reject this condition if it caused you to suffer." Khigir asked her, "Would you like to become a married member?" Nógrád asked Khigir if she realized that her seed collecting parts worked, it was just that she had no womb. Khigir told her, "Oh that is great. As you know, we need more help with dirty boy these days. If you wished to help us, we would be so indebted. Please." Nógrád confirms, "I will, if you are sure our Master would want me?" Hevesi adds, "You have two legs and long hair. You are qualified." Everyone laughs as the mini-mouth has struck once more.

I told Nógrád, "Nógrád darling, you realize my fondness for you, why you would ever think I did not love you as one of my wives, cannot be based on the way I have always loved you? Yes, of course, I love every woman in my clan. If I did not love you, I would keep it no secret, correct Brann?" Brann replies, "Come on dirty boy, let this woman give you the fire?" We laugh at this one. The wives now congratulate Nógrád. Béla provides happy news by telling us that because we are on the sea, she has the right to perform the marriage ceremonies. I look at Gyöngyösi who corroborates this by informing us, "The elements may unite Lamentans on the sea and in the air by not being under a roof. Love is within itself an element that fills the airs and seas bonding with the elements." One more mystery unfolded. I then looked at Khigir and asked her, "You recollect any ideas?" Khigir asked the wives to excuse us. We went into the hallway. Khigir begins by sharing that she understands my concerns with some of my women treated differently. We both agree that marriage forms the everlasting bond and, by it, everyone would forever be a part of this small army. It is the fair thing. Khigir is searching for a way to overcome the barren womb issue. She fears this will open a floodgate of potential problems down the line. I think for a moment and tell her, "Khigir. We hold seven reproducers and seven who cannot reproduce." She agrees. Next, I tell her, all seven of the reproducers will bear five children, and my two Tamarkins will bear seven children. Khigir looks at me rather strange in that she can read my mind as if an open stone writing. She tells me to continue. I tell her, "Each of the seven reproducers will receive a barren married sister. We will call that couple, 'sisters of the womb.' In love, the mothers will share my babies among their sister of the womb. Everyone has her hands on the child, which gives me a well-adjusted and nurtured child. We will all win." The sister of the womb receives my child from the womb and delivers my child to me. You and I will then return the baby to both sisters of the womb." Khigir afterwards asks me, "Why do you wish that I help return the baby to its mother and sister mother?" I told her that with fourteen wives, I might have few opportunities to see her. Afterwards, I told her that this was so everyone understands that all my children come from her womb.

We agreed that fourteen was too many for our heart bed every night. We could house everyone for special occasions. The elements will be recharging themselves throughout the night throughout Lamenta. Nógrád has many extra rooms the new wives can use. As your pregnancy's progress, you may wish to pair off with your sister of the womb because of your special needs. All wives are sisters, and therefore, how they wish to pair off for their rest is their freedom. I could never see Makói too far from Dabasi, nor can I see Mórahalmi separated from Hevesi, except for an occasional wilderness trip with me. Either way, Hevesi must always be with me in the wilderness. Khigir asks me if I will explain why. I tell her, this because she knows so much about the wilderness, and I do not really believe I will ever learn it all. Nevertheless, I need to understand these things to teach our sons. Khigir jumps into my arms. It has been so long since we have shared our minds in this way. We click together thus perfectly. I grasp that she will always do the best for our family. She surprises me by her next question, "Master, how do we work out dirty boy time with them, because, as wives, they hold the right to Carnal activities with their husband?" I looked at her and said, "Khigir. I do not even want to think of such an extra load. We must figure another way." She slaps me on each side of my face and asks me, "How dare you downgrade your wives in such a way?" My mind is sincerely confused presently. I just told my wife that I did not want to be intimate alongside seven new women, and I am the bad boy. If I look at one of them, they hound me by the dirty boy jokes. If I refuse them, I am the bad boy. If this the way with seven wives how can, I ever hope to survive fourteen wives. I ask her, "What do you want me to do?" Khigir tells me, "To love them like you do your other wives. Because they cannot have children does not mean they do not suffer the ways of life. This probably means that they suffer more. You must make them feel special as a woman, the way that only a Master can do. Our focus must always be in love and the laws of love.

Our blanket of love spreads evenly. Do you understand? If you do not love them or want them, please do not marry them. That is creating a fire of hurt that will burn our family." I agreed with her. The little thing is truly a bundle of caring and loving. She tells me that for these ceremonies, I will confess my love for them and beg them to join as my wife. They encompass no idea of doing things the easy way. The only thing that I understand to do is comment about what I remember seeing that no one knows I have seen. This should make me happier in that I am receiving some people that I have wanted for some time. We return to our family and announce the news. Khigir finishes through one of her get serious or get out warnings. She looks around at the unmarried women in our group and tells them, "If there is any among us who do not love my husband and wish to be his wife and serve him as I do, you need to leave now. If you do not love my Master, I do not love you. Sorry, to refuse my best gift to you will put a great hurt on me." My wives stand up clapping agreeing. My little Khigir has this punch inside her perfect body. I can see me begging the Mystanites magicians for the extra stamina because these women are in the overdrive mode now. These weddings are going to put them on fire, and I will burn. What a problem, burn me and burn me completely. Abaúj and Béla look around at the unmarried and both stand up as Abaúj speaks, "Master Khigir, we humbly accept your gift and promise to love our new gift as you love him. May we perform the ceremonies tonight in a condensed and consolidated, yet still legitimate way?" Khigir thanks them as my wives welcome our new brides. Khigir tells her the consolidated ceremony will be fine. Nevertheless, their new Master must prove to them, his love before they agree to wed him. Brann lit up on this one, "Oh wow. He is going to beg me?" I told her, "Just like you begged me before, maybe to use the same words." Khigir came over, slapped me, and told both of us to be serious. This was about love and marriage, uniting and becoming as one. I winked at Brann as she winked back at me.

I remember the deck game she played. It tormented me for days knowing the wonderful beauty that she had cloaked. That wall was coming down fast. Khigir explains the ceremony will be the true bonding, and that her ceremony is for an abbreviated consummation. The bride will stand before us; the Master comes forward on his knees and asks for her love. When the bride removes her gown, and gives her hand for her Master to kiss. When he kisses her hand, he will help her back into her gown. This may turn out better than I had originally thought. Abaúj and Béla perform the ceremony, and my time arrives. The first to come forward is Brann, who is acting different this time. I ask her, "Honey, what is wrong?" She touches my shoulder and tells me, "I have waited at this day my entire life." I am accordingly glad that Khigir slapped me demanding that I treat this as exceptionally special. It is their day of love, and that is so important. I drop to my knees, with a tear rolling down my cheek. When Brann sees this, she wipes my face and then explodes with tears all over me. A fire woman is drowning me. Love is indeed strange. I begin, "Brann; I remember the first time that Khigir, Tselikovsky, and I saw you. We had discovered the depth of our pure love, and the sky was a mystery to me. When you arrived and met with us, I saw it as proof that our love was real. You were a powerful force in cementing this family. When Baranya told us, she would bring you back. We were now so excited. Your return told us you also believed in our love. When we played your game on the deck, and you were on top of me begging me to take you, I want to obey you so much. I cried inside for a few days trying to overcome this secret love. My love will never need to be a secret from you if you will give me this plea. Please take me as your husband and love you as my wife. Will you please let me serve you, my love?" She dropped her gown and kissed my hand. I stood up and handed her gown to her. She threw it to the floor and began crying, "Khigir, please help me. I do not want this back on me as I stand before my husband.

Nógrád came walking forward. Khigir has kept these women separate by been removing the ones I have completed and keeping those who are waiting in another room. We are aware that it is impossible to boast the same emotions for each, and thereby wish to provide the protection against someone getting hurt. As Nógrád walks toward me, my heart begins to pound. When she walks past me, I grab her into my arms, and we begin kissing. She is limp in my arms. I can feel her heart beating hard also. I let her down and apologize while getting on my knees, "Nógrád, I am so sorry; your beauty was too great for me to allow you to pass by me. So many times, we almost gave in to the fire within our hearts. You understand how hard I necessarily fought to marry you, and have as my wife. I could always see your love through those lovely eyes. That is why I never worked that hard at not hiding mine from you, actually sometimes striving diligently for you to notice. Nógrád, you belong to this family, and you belong in my bed for to be my wife. I simply plead that you give us a chance to make your life as wonderful as you would like it. Will you let me serve you for the rest of our lives? And please never put out our love okay, my wife." She dropped her rode. I then kissed her hand. I handed her gown back to her as she threw it and pounced on me dropping us to the deck. She was kissing me in a heated rage as her tears were flowing. Khigir and Gyöngyösi came over to help her. She just asked them for an extra minute, saying she had held it in too long. When the minute finished, I told her that tonight we would consummate the way I should with her Gyöngyösi took her to a private room as Khigir brought in Abaúj and Béla. I confessed to both that, "I have not known you in acceptable time to declare a hidden love. I knew you long enough to realize that I will love you, and that I want you to be in this family. You are becoming acquainted inside your new female bodies so do not fear that I will expect ability from you. I will teach you the best ways to enjoy your bodies with your husband. I discern you would not be here unless by your faith in this family. You are now an intimate part of this family. The inside this family has opened the doors for you to stay.

Will you trust me as we develop your love and strive to give you the peace you deserve and the rivers of love to drown?" They dropped their robes and I kissed their hands, holding onto their robes. I asked them if any of the wives had explained how their new bodies worked. They told me they had explained a few things. I ask Tselikovsky if she explained this to them in a private room. Tselikovsky asked about Dabasi and Mórahalmi. I told her that I knew Hevesi and Makói would take care of them. She smiled and hugged Béla and Abaúj welcoming them as her sister. Tselikovsky then grabbed their gowns and said, "We need to get these back on so dirty boy does not follow us down the steps." Béla looks confused and asks, "Would the absence of our gown creates a different behavior in our Master?" Tselikovsky smiles and answers, "Yes, oh yes. I am so glad I got to you before he did, stick with me sisters, I possess a few things to tell you." I thought, of all the wives, I had to pick Tselikovsky; well currently, those two easy private times now filled by means of great challenges, as Tselikovsky is the Master teaching on ways to force me to suffer. Now the two extremely special ones will be joining me. I look forward to these two women in that they have already won my heart. The most beautiful of all women, Dabasi now walks in and prepares for her ceremonial consummation. Lenti's pill did her wonderful. I am extremely glad she is so beautiful, as she deserves this much more than others do. She slowly walks forward, being precautions which each step. Dabasi and Makói are so similar that I wonder if Dabasi has not based her personality from Makói. If thus, they certainly blessed me with double happiness. She reaches me trembling profusely sweating. I tell her, "Dabasi, have no fear, as I offer you something that Makói always enjoys and sometimes asks me to give extra. I will not hurt you, but in time show, you why the creatures created as you have been." She looked at me and smiled. I dropped to my knees. Dabasi also dropped to her knees. Khigir and Gyöngyösi chuckled, afterwards Khigir responds, "I knew someone would do that." I tell Dabasi, "Darling, you must stand so you will recognize I am not here to hurt you. Nonetheless, I am in the front to serve you and your needs. I helped her back up, sneaking a kiss on her cheek.

I felt her become slightly more relaxed. I looked into her eyes and confessed, "Dabasi. I think you realize the first time our eyes met each other that something existed between us. You knew that I would never hurt you. Your heart knew if you became part of our family that you will love you. You are now a part of our family. Makói begged me, in front of so many Edelényi to wed her. I am now begging you to join her as a wife for me to love and to give you the love your heart and soul deserve. Will you let me serve you Dabasi, and may I put my love in your heart as we may currently openly confess our love?" She dropped her robe. I kissed her hand and handed her robe to Makói who had been coaching her. Makói leaped and shouted. "Dabasi is now our sister and my sister of the womb." We did not announce the pairings for sisters of the womb yet. Nevertheless, Makói peeled her eyes to mine, so instead of putting them through any more suffering. I winked at Makói. I told Makói, "How could I ever refuse a question from my hidden love?" She looked at me and smiled, saying, "I see." This response created joy in my heart, for she was coming out of her shell, and there is no one else better to bring her out than the little fireball Hevesi. While holding them, I asked Makói if she would teach Dabasi all the things about her new body that she needed to comprehend. Makói gave me a kiss on my cheek and reassured me. She would obey me. Dabasi rushes to my other cheek, kissing it, and then reassures me that she also will obey. They bobbled off so happy and deep in their chatting that Makói has yet to give Dabasi her gown. This is no harm, as I am the only male on this ship, and we are legally married now; by the air and water, she should be just fine. Now the special one who changed all our lives forever is waiting to come to me. I look over and hear Hevesi screaming, "Master. We do not enjoy all-day." I look at Hevesi and say, "Oh, but we do own all-night little darling." Hevesi relaxed in her tiny chair that Mórahalmi brought along by her. I think that Mórahalmi may allowed more of her articles behind to bring the special items Lenti made for Hevesi.

Either way, so long as she is happy all is going to be well. I stand in position and Mórahalmi walks toward me with stylish grace, with thrilling majestic steps. Csongrád replies, "I declare this is someone who may teach me how to walk." Khigir agrees that she too would love to have lessons. Mórahalmi currently stops in front of me. My disrupted breathing is identifying my increased passion, she tells me, "Big boy. If you want this robe to drop, you had better brought your 'A' game." I tell her, "My love, you only deserve an 'A' game, for any other game before you were so unjust." I drop to my knees and stare into her hungry eyes. She has waited for this moment in her infinite life and deserves my best. I begin, "Mórahalmi, even as my capture and tormentor I cannot hate you. Something happened when we first sat down as our angry words and feelings drifted away, fortunately to a place we will never be able to bring back. My heart almost left me when you told us that your husband and two sons held captive. When I saw on your stomach that you were still single my life returned to me. I hope you understand how my passion for you grew stronger each day. I cannot see how this could necessarily been a mystery with Hevesi reporting every little peek. Hevesi needs you. Besides, I hope, you need her. I can think of no one any better to raise the wonderful daughters whom, she will bear for me. You will make excellent sisters of the womb, if you decide to marry me. You must base your decision on our love, is it real? Your question must be, 'will this love fulfill your needs.' I must ask myself these same questions. However, I think that our love is real; it has a depth buried in trust and in faith. As I enjoyed trusting you among my heart love, Hevesi, I now ask you to let me surrender my heart to you. I want to hold you in my family and life. I want to share our future with you. I want to be there when you are saddened and find a way to bring happiness back into your life. I want my children to grow up around you and for you to be a part of my life. Will you let me serve you? Will you take my heart and hold it safely against yours? Today can be the beginning of our life together." I paused as she dropped her robe. Hevesi screamed out, "Mórahalmi, make him beg more." Mórahalmi answers back, "I cannot Hevesi, as he speaks the truth of our love.

I need his love too much to risk losing it." Hevesi tells her, "I know. He got me also. Hey Master, I told you that she looked good under her blouse, was I right?" I told Hevesi that since we were married now, I possibly would speak the truth. "She does not look good under her blouse?" I saw both faces droop as Khigir yelled out, "How dare you to say that Master?" I looked at Mórahalmi, as I could feel many angry faces staring at me, "Actually, Mórahalmi the truth is that you look great and so wonderful standing before me. Good is an injustice in describing what you are sharing with me." She jumped in my arms and started kissing me frantically. Unlike her normal self, when I said she did not look good. She did not retaliate. Instead, she absorbed the pain. It shows that once they are married and after being, married to depend on their new love to pull them through the dangers of hate. Hevesi yells out, "Save this for me." I yell back, "Too late you let the cat out of the bag." Khigir comes over to us, wraps her arms around us, and tells Mórahalmi, "Remember. I am also here to serve you. I gave my husband and obligated him to you as your husband as well. I will never step between, or interfere with your marriage. Nevertheless, I am always here to help you. Khigir looks over to Hevesi and tells her to take great care of Mórahalmi, and teach her the ways of her new body." Khigir helps me redress Mórahalmi. We slide Hevesi into her pocket. I look at our table, which is now complete with new foods and wines. I ask Mórahalmi to ensure everyone returns to our table for this celebration. After they all sat down, I come to the table and sit. Mórahalmi asks me, "Master. You are the greatest among us, should not you sit down first?" I look at her and all my wives and answer, "No Mórahalmi, for my life is dedicated to love my wives, and serving you. When all my wives are seated, then I shall set, eagerly awaiting your commands for my service." Mórahalmi answers, "You are making me feel so special and loved." The remaining thirteen wives raised their wineglasses. I held my wineglass and looked at Mórahalmi who quickly raised hers. I raised mine and said, "This is so hate will find another place to dwell, for here we are servants to love."

Everyone drank to the toast and cheered afterwards. Mórahalmi looked at Khigir and asked, "Please explain this thing called hate?" Khigir tells her, "It is an evil force which chases after us trying to destroy our love. Each minute of every day, it lurks everywhere waiting for a thought to invade and plant its seeds. Mórahalmi and all the other new wives are prime fresh targets. Therefore, please fight this assiduously and love sedulously. I will ensure that our Master love you as honorable wives. We must make sure that we love each another, for hate will search so hard to a crack and destroy your love. If anyone feels wronged by another, and you will absolutely come up with occasions when someone has, intentionally or mistakenly, wrong you come to either the Master or me. We will strive hard to give you the justice you deserve and resolve any misunderstandings. Forgiveness is what our love is based on forever. As I constantly forgive our Master, I ask that you also do the same." I looked at Khigir and asked, "You continuously forgive me?" All the wives, original and new, responded through a loud 'Yes' and toast. I mumble, "Really women, why do not you tell what I am doing wrong, so I can do the way you wish me to do?" Gyöngyösi answers, "Because then you would not be the man we married? We would take you no other way?" I, mistakenly, responding with joy tell them, "Gyöngyösi, this makes me feel so good that I would not complain, even if you were going to clean me." Ouch. Darn. Oh, heavens no, please not me. Overlook by passion, I lost control of my mouth. They undergo and surround me currently as I found myself helplessly pulled by fourteen wives into the cleaning room. Now gloom filled by face as Khigir smiled at me and said, "This is what you wanted Master, how you could expect that your wives who love you so much would deprive you of this refreshing experience." I realize not to move, because these little bundles of love can punish without a heart. The original wives are explaining everything to the new wives so it looks as if, to my misfortune, this tradition will live. I can only hope that when we receive eight babies in this mix, I will get some relief.

That is a hope they will not honor. These little bundles of love will find a way to keep me cleaned. They were humming yet now Mórahalmi is teaching a song she claimed to grasp and learned about eight cycles previously. We shudder to think of life that deep in our history. I shudder to think how life on Lamenta, as well as other worlds, must create all these things again. I can currently feel a depth of life around our Lamenta and now understand more about the great things we experienced and witnessed. From the top of Lamenta on our Baktalórántházai to the deep dark seas of King Rogov, we shouldered experience and witnessed so much love and pain, and greatness. We shall, within a few days arrive in the Land of the Celldömölki and behold more mysteries. At least when we arrive, washed I will be. Thanks to the longhaired beasts who are at the present taking, no chances that I could become prey for dirt. Now that I am clean and oiled, they give me a clean robe and back to the party we go. This time, I will be extra quiet. We celebrate for around two hours. Abaúj tells us the night hours are here, and that we should get some rest. We look around and see the familiar darkness back on us. Our Suns are now resting and the three moons preparing to share their nighttime lights. I look at Nógrád to stay. Gyöngyösi and I walk over to Khigir. Nógrád comes before us.

Khigir tells her, "Oh Master would like some private time alongside you. Have no fear." Gyöngyösi tells her, "You have seen and heard us many times, now is your time to be blessed. You held on and waited your whole life for this. Maintain no fear for Khigir and I will be with you." We go to a special room in which Abaúj, in her amazing wisdom, has prepared for us. I ask Khigir to watch and tell me what to do. She knows me so perfectly and can read this situation. We appreciate that this must come out faultlessly as this is Nógrád's time. Khigir is an excellent coach as always she did us honorably during this special Nógrád's time. When we finished, Gyöngyösi holds her tight and said, "Nógrád, we are truly sisters of the womb, for we are loved by the same Master." Gyöngyösi now took her consummated sister of the womb to our sleeping room.

I asked Khigir, "How do they all comprehend who their sisters of the womb will be?" Khigir shows to me that she has already made the assignments pairing them off as, Khigir and Brann, Tselikovsky and Baranya, Gyöngyösi and Nógrád, Csongrád and Béla, Ajkai and Abaúj, Makói and Dabasi, Hevesi and Mórahalmi. I tell Khigir that these choices are perfect, and that she must have known their hearts to do this wonderfully. She smiles as I continue to marvel at how hard she keeps our family happy. I ask her about our sleeping arrangements in that fourteen are so many. Khigir tells me that we do not need to worry about fourteen because we retain many who wander throughout Lamenta during the nights such as, Brann, Baranya, Béla, Ajkai, and Abaúj. This leaves only nine, which are two more than before who shared our bed. Our rooms are large enough to handle two more, especially considering Hevesi sleeps in my back pocket. I told her that I could not manage this without her and her wisdom and gave her a long-overdue hug and rash of kisses. She told me that we also had a new custom in our family, to set back and watch this wonder unfold before us. Brann and Baranya came before me and asked, "Master, may we fly in the sky as fire tonight telling all that we are now married?" I told them only if I got a good-bye kiss, and they return to us. They both gave me a kiss and reassured me that they would return to attend to their

Master. I asked Brann, "Would it not bring greater joy to you if the Master you married served you?" She looked at me and smiled, saying, "When I became your wife, the struggles of the past went away. We do as you wish now my love." I held them both tight and said, "I will serve you because you are my wonderful wives and justifiably deserve my best." My fresh Brann and Baranya turned to fire and dashed into the sky as a woman rode on the horse, as a new show of sisterhood. Ajkai now came before me. I asked her, "Is not this first time you were able to return to the night sky?" She told me it was. Nevertheless, she missed it so much and before did not want to be the only one, besides the fire, which at that time were not married, to leave in the night. I told her, "Ajkai, I understand, for if I may possibly dance in the sky at night I would.

Go to enjoy yourself, and bring me back a happy wife, okay my love?" She smiled as we kissed and into the sky, she jumped. Now before me stood Béla, my so special Béla who showed us a new world. Although we had the misfortune in her world, this was not her fault or doings. I hug her and tell her, "I will serve you my love and am so thankful that you chose this family. This family is your family." Béla kissed me telling me, "I would boast no other family nor will I ever serve any other Master. I will return, before you awake and help Abaúj prepare the things you and my sisters need." I thank her walking with her to the ship's side rails. She leaps overboard and before hitting the water turns into water splashing on the surface as she mingles into her home. Now before me stands Abaúj who asks me if she can sleep in the air tonight. I reveal to her, "If this delivers me a happier wife, then, please do this my love. You have done so much for your family, and we thank you for these deeds." We exchanged kisses as her gown fell and smoke rose above us. The smoke spread so, then that we could no longer see it. I looked over to Khigir and replied, "Our loves are between their elements now. It is time for this element to get this rest. We enter our room as I saw so many already spread out on our heart fast asleep. I tell Khigir this indeed was a busy day. We see Hevesi fast asleep in her new house that Lenti built for her. Khigir and I peek in to see.

We fight hard to resist our temptations to pull her out. We see the wives held our place open. I lay down, as our Master wife secures her position over me. It just feels too long since we enjoyed being able to rest in our default positions. This day is now exactly like Nógrád and that is completely out. Once again, we are on our way to the Land of the Celldömölki, although Berettyóú and Móri kept our boat moving so we would lose no time. The next day, the women spent cleaning their gowns and packing the items they wanted to keep among them. Their bags are too big to fit on their backs, so I can only hope the Celldömölki has a method to transport them, or these women will not leave this ship. Abaúj, who, as my other night preying wives, made certain to return. They provided all that we needed to prepare for another day sailing the sea.

The next two days were peaceful, as Mórahalmi taught us some games, she had learned from the cycle changes. Hate tried to destroy us, only to build a strong family with the power it needs to stay united. I marvel how respectful; they are to each. They tell me that courtesy does not count toward men, and that is why they must fight hard to keep me in line. I really do not care, because each one is so special, and has the confidence needed to keep our relationships strong. We deserve this unique time to work out our needed adjustments. We still possess a long road ahead of us. When I look out across the sea and witness thousands of waves, I now realize that we are not alone, and many things lay waiting for the Lamentan people element. They see the first great sailing ship crossing their seas. They do not realize that it will be some time before the real ships begin to sail. What is laying before us?

Chapter 06

Pápain the Hajdú, vagabond mother of the loves

The peace and happiness that fill our ship as, we sail through the seas is wonderful. The sisters, occupied with each, another, as they talk about our future lives and past adventures. With fourteen now following this adventure, I must ask Khigir if we are doing what is justified. The last horror and nightmares with the Rétsági have taken away any want for me ever to see pain once more. I can only hope that the Land of the Celldömölki does not try to match the Rétsági's skill for afflicting deep pain. Khigir tells me that we will stick in conjunction. We live and die together. I query her wanting to grasp why this must be. She tells me that a wife should be beside her Master and that all the wives are in this case serious about making this relationship their lives. I take that to mean for me to keep my eyes wide open. Considering, I hold that serious protecting here. Can I protect the air, fire, water, sky dancer, Connubial Angel, and a ten-foot bear? How can I control a reigning

Queen, who can instill great fear in Armies having no fear to stand before them demanding to be followed further compounds our situation? Talking about fear, Hevesi when expanded is invisible yet deadly in the wilderness. My last two dangers are my Tamarkins, who I have never won in any match with them. They all can protect me just by snapping their fingers; however, sit here in the comfort of my shelter. I encompass so much trouble seeing it. I hear a voice tell me not to try to understand this. I look beside me and see an old friend that I have not seen in a while. I greet her, “Hello Berettyóú. It has been some time since we have talked as it feels like a lifetime. What have you been doing?” Berettyóú tells me she has been searching to find a woman I have yet to marry. I tell her to be careful, for I will control her soon. She tells me that will not happen if Móri can prevent it.

I change the course of our conversation so it blows in my favor, “Berettyóú, seriously, I need an outsider to talk about issues.” Berettyóú wink at me and offers to talk. I tell her, “Berettyóú, I see too much life on this ship that is not concerned about the possible dangers ahead of us.” Berettyóú tells me, “Oh Siklósi, they understand that no situation will ever appear before them that they will not overcome. They just need a Master who is willing to stand with them and more importantly to understand what they are giving. You should forget about the dangers ahead, for you will overcome them together. Now, get over there and give them the Master you promised to give them.” I tell her, “I never knew the wind to be so wise. Thank you. I shall add you to the long list of women that I obey.” Berettyóú complains, “I thought I was already on this list. Any ways, later today, you will see one of the hundreds of protection rock islands to Mysteria. You will also meet your first contact with the Mystanites who will first appear as eyes in the sky, somewhat as I do. Therefore, now do and enjoy yourself with your family. Móri and I will make certain that you are on the shores of Mysteria tomorrow morning.” She closed her warm, soft gigantic purple eyes and faded into her wind. I joined my wives and played some of the new games they were enjoying. A few hours later, a flash appeared in the sky temporary blinding us. As we recovered our eyesight, Khigir yells out that there are two blue eyes looking at us from the sky. I told them not to worry, because Berettyóú told me, our first contact appears as eyes in the sky, somewhat similar to hers. Abaúj tells us not to worry, for she recognizes this spirit to do-good things. Gyöngyösi adds that she feels no evil from these eyes. The right eye now yields a tear. Mórahalmi complains, "Oh. We have made her cry with our callousness." She joins Gyöngyösi to the edge of our ship opening their arms. I rush up behind them grabbing both by their waists and hold them securely against the railing. Mórahalmi begins to struggle to ask me, "What are you doing? Let go now." Gyöngyösi tells her, "Be at peace sister, he is doing what a husband does when his wives are not giving attention to possible dangers."

Mórahalmi became limp and apologized to me saying, "I am a sorry husband, please forgive me. This existing as married may take some time to become adjusted to, okeydokey?" I kiss her and tell her, "Do not worry. Your husband is not only a loving husband but also a forgiving one." Gyöngyösi tells me, "Certainly silly boy, save your lines for private times my love. Therefore, they will surprise us." I respond, as any normal man would do when talking to an Angel, "Of course dear." The voice behind these crying eyes speaks again asking, "May I appear before you kind women and that beast who tries to confine you?" Gyöngyösi responds, "You may appear. Nevertheless, please understand that he is not a beast, but the loving Master of all fourteen women aboard this ship." The voice chuckles, and then looking at me speaks, "Sir, you must maintain some serious lines." Gyöngyösi tells her, "The best in the universe." The voice now appears as a tanned woman, wearing a shoulder less silk white gown with three thin straps tied to each arm pinned together by jewelry. Her curled and style white long hair sparkle in the sunlight. She wears a three-tier necklace, including a large gem with twelve diamond legs resting slightly above her great tanned breasts. Her small waist has a large blue gem shining in her front. Her slanted eyes are as Ajkai, Abaúj, with ears pointed like Hevesi and Mórahalmi. Her wings are small and comprised of large spaced feathers. A slightly visible floor made of transparent square stones appears below her as she now sits on knees before us. Ajkai comes running toward us as Gyöngyösi, looking at Ajkai and then probes her, "I believe we recognized you. Are you the one that is called Pápain?" She looked at us with her sad face and confessed, "I am the misery that is called Pápain." Béla joins us claiming also to know Pápain, "I identify you, although you do not know me. I have spoken with your tears many times, about why you shed them. They always told, me because you lost a great love long ago."

Pápain looked at Béla confirming, "You wisely speak the truth. I am so sorry that my tears burdened you as a result." Béla responds, "Oh no, my precious Pápain. We were only saddened that you did not give us all your burdens, so we could drown them in our waters and give you peaceful water in return." Brann and Baranya join now revealing, "Pápain, remember us. I am a fire woman, and she is my fire horse cousin. Look, we shall identify ourselves quickly." They turned to fire and spun around her returning to our ship. Pápain questions them, "I did not realize that fire, or any other element could marry a Lamentan." Gyöngyösi answers this by saying, "This happens when they surrender to our blanket of love. Then they confess their love and accept our Master's pleas. Afterwards, the laws of love chase away the pain of loneliness and suffering. Love will now fill them with an everlasting bonding in the sanctity of marriage. They are now one with our Master. Pápain continues her saga, "My story has no glory in it. The road I traveled is paved with tears." Gyöngyösi asks her to leave the clouds and join us in the ship. Pápain tells us she is afraid to go on our ship as she had heard there is a mystery jinx that all who enter fall prey to him, your Master and into his bed as his wife." Khigir reassures her that all who have married the Master did consequently with the full consent and control of their senses. I look at her and ask, "Why would it be therefore bad to enjoy the happiness my wives experience?" Pápain tells me that Móri speaks extraordinary well for me. Nevertheless, Berettyóú tells her that I am a 'dirty boy.'

Something is snapping at me now about this 'dirty boy' label. I asked my wives, "Please, tell me of one time I was not honorable and subservient during our private times, most times working only to give them the pleasures their flesh craved. Speak up, because our little exclusive hoax is now a universal joke and creating fear is some such as sweet petite Pápain who suffers from a condition which we can alleviate." Gyöngyösi tells Pápain, "Pápain, our Master never does us harm, or wrong and serve each of us with his heart. We stay with him because we identify him to be the kindest, warmest and sweat Master for us. Any ways, what would be so bad if you were to get lucky and be chosen to serve him?" I look at Gyöngyösi, wink, extend three fingers and ask, "Only three things my love?" Gyöngyösi replies, "If you want me to say more things, then you need to bump me up on the private time list."

Khigir then apologizes to the wives and tells them, "The new plan will be one hour each day of bonding activities as a group with whoever wishes to be at to talk about issues. One hour will be open afterwards for personal issues and those who come to me, will be given a dedicated time, and two hours each day, on a rotating schedule for private time. The night travelers will receive their special personal times, as they desire. Gyöngyösi, as she shows the list to the wives, you are on for this evening. We do understand that as being flesh dweller's strange situations and emotions will arise at the most inopportune time. Come to me, or Gyöngyösi tell us your feelings, and we will work with your Master to restore your happiness. Notice, I said your feelings. Those who are new to these bodies, please believe me your feelings will overwhelm you. Let us indulge you instead of evil with hate serving you." The wives confessed to Pápain that their Master was the greatest and in their hearts was only love. I walk over to Pápain and raise my hands as she walks anew and drops into my arms. I plant her feet firmly on our ship's deck and holding her hand, guide her to Khigir when I release her. I return to my other wives. Hevesi, speaking out of Mórahalmi's shirt pocket shares, "Now, Mórahalmi you see the Master at work. He creates a little fire and steps back, waiting for it to burn high and then dashes back in for the save." I argue that, "Hevesi. I could not have started a big fire with you, for it would have burned your mouth shut, right dear." Mórahalmi comments, "Speaking of high fires, when is mine going to be cooled down?" I stare into her eyes and say, "Soon, I hope." Hevesi discloses to Mórahalmi that she will go, from the list, tomorrow night. We look at Hevesi and request her confirmation. Hevesi tells us that Khigir wrote everyone's names on a small piece of those wood sheets that Lenti gave us. She had Csongrád mix them. Next, she had Makói mix them. She then had Brann pull one out of the pile and read the name. Brann afterwards placed the card face up for Csongrád and Makói to verify the name was correct.

They repeated this process, until they selected all the names. I ask Hevesi if she thinks they should have gone through all that trouble for me. Hevesi, changing tactics divulges, "Master. This represents a fantasitcally important event for all your wives. This time is when we truly feel how special our loyalty and live is in our relationship with you the Master." I look at Hevesi and confess that sometimes I feel as if I am using and abusing my wives. Hevesi reveals to me, "Master, there is a time to be used and abused by the one we chose to do this with us. Even though I am new to these bodies, we had the same issues with our Shelyapin comrades. I tell you this must be done, and you are the one we depend to fulfill this need. We need you to be strong and easy. You discern how to read us to determine which actions are practical at that time. You are the Master, and if you fashion a mistake do not fear. We will experience even greater joy in knowing you tried and are Lamentan." I tell them this is different with each wife. I use Hevesi as an example for she has special additional organs that enhance and control our unions. I understand how she wishes to maintain control, so I do not fight it, yet shamefully and lazily enjoy it. Hevesi tells me not to be ashamed, flow in the way she prefers, and if he truly loved her, I will enjoy the ride. Hevesi confesses to be problematic for me during the day, so she feels her rewards should be greater during our meetings. I look at them and say, "If you speak the truth, then it will bring peace to my troubled mind." They both give me a kiss, as Mórahalmi returns Hevesi to her pocket and then asks me to join them. I tell them I need to mingle and get the feel of our new family. Hevesi offers to join me. Nevertheless, I recommended that she stay with Mórahalmi and help her adjust. This would reduce my sharing and caring. Brief her about private times, as her show is tomorrow night. I walk to and set with Dabasi and Makói. As I go to sit, Makói offers me her seat requesting that I sit in the middle. Makói tells me that I am the only ones that may come between them, as Khigir and Gyöngyösi have the same rights. Makói leans her head on my shoulder and tells me how is feeling anxiety now.

All these changes plus less private time is forcing her to feel more apprehensive. I give her a wonderful kiss while holding Dabasi's hand. I now turn around so my back is facing the table and motion for them to put their heads on my upper legs. I massage their faces and play gently with their hair. I then ask Makói if I had ever disappointed her. She shakes her head no. I then look at Dabasi and tell her, "Someday, you will also shake your head no when I ask this question, shaking no because of your love and not because of your memory. I know that I let you angels down so much, and it hurts me. We boast a large family, and we are trying awfully hard. I also need extra time with you Makói and we are going to sneak around and take advantage of some opportunities. I project Hevesi to spend much more time with Mórahalmi, so I will include you, and Dabasi be my wilderness partners. Makói, you will receive extra. Nevertheless, as Dabasi is our cover and alibi she too should receive supplementary love. Khigir will drill you hard Dabasi, yet do not let it bother you, for to love strange things happen. Our secrets are not because of the morality of our actions. They instead are to prevent others from being hurt. I do whatever it takes to keep our love strong and if Makói tells me to kneel naked in the middle of the night and howl at the moon, then I will do that." They both smile and Dabasi confesses, "I do not even comprehend what I am getting extra for; however, it sounds wonderful, whatever this may be." We laugh and I say, "You both deserve more, and I really hope your sisterhood of the womb works out great. Please forgive me when I hurt you." Makói responds, "How can I forgive something that has yet to happen?" Dabasi raises her hand and touches my cheek saying, "You could never hurt any of us." These words thump hard against my heart. They are accordingly soft and filled with so much faith in our relationship. They believe this and that is the highest honor that they bestow me in this wonderful world of love. Khigir is now calling for me, so they immediately lift, their heads and regroup to help me stand. The little things can maneuver like the lightning. I am at once on my way to the Master wife escorted by Makói and Dabasi.

I many times wonder if they escort me because they fear I will get lost, considering we are walking to the front of the table. I must also consider the way that Khigir cares for them, as if they were her children. Her enthusiasm shines through them, as they are always so eager to please her. I realize it wears her down tremendously because when she lays on me each night, she drops off to sleep just about instantly. Her body is limp for the entire night. I always massage her shoulder, until I can feel the muscles relax. She is the greatest thing in my life, and I find myself depending on her too much. She babies me tremendously, as the wives follow suit and work hard to soothe me. Sometimes I think that to keep them happy, I merely would need to sit at the table and let them feed me spoon by spoon. Someday, I will test that. For now, I had better given the Master wife my attention. I see her and Gyöngyösi holding Pápain while wiping her tears. Khigir tells me, "Master, Pápain has so many hurts inside her. We need you to help pull out this hurt." I look at Pápain and say, "If it helps to mend her broken heart, then I will try. Pápain, you must remember that I am only a Lamentan. The glory you see here is from these wonderful angels taking the first dangerous step into the painful land that promises love." Pápain tells me that her life is miserable because of her ugliness. Khigir and Gyöngyösi jump beside me as I look at Pápain stare into her eyes, pulling her close to me, and tell her, "If you are ugly, then my wives are leviathans. Are you calling Khigir and Gyöngyösi monstrosities?" She informs us, "Oh no; all the women on this ship are beautiful." I next brace her face, not letting her eyes wander, for when they do I move her head back to face my eyes. I afterwards forcibly divulge to her, "Pápain, I have never kissed an ugly woman. I only kiss those of great beauty."

I locked our lips and started kissing her feverishly. I knew it had to be forceful and dominating to convince her. She starts to fall when I release her. Khigir and Gyöngyösi catch her. Then I stabilize her and sit her on a chair. I had just been manhandled this woman. I truly hope Makói was giving me reliable advice. Khigir and Gyöngyösi start drying her excessive sweating and while switching their clothes look at me a give a wink. I am somewhat worried, because she looks more as if she is shocked. Gyöngyösi then whispers in my ear, "Master, you are so wonderful. I will reward you with all I have during our private time tonight. You will need a heavy massage to move tomorrow as will I." I whisper back, "I have never known you, not to give all you have my Angel from the heavens." I now ask Khigir and Gyöngyösi if I have ever kissed an ugly woman. Both tell me that I have yet to kiss an ugly woman. I look Pápain and tell her, "Pápain, you are so special and my lust for your beauty is becoming harder to control." Pápain asks me, "Why must you control it?" I tell her, "If I lose control, you may think me to be a dirty boy." Pápain asks me, "Why did my lover leave me for another?" I disclose to her, "Precious beauty. I cannot deduce the reason one would be that foolish. Many times, we suffer the pain of love, yet we must move forward. If Khigir approves, I want you to stay with us for a few days. We need to fill you back with love and reacquaint you with your beautiful glamorous face and body. She now confesses to hate her ears. I tell her to look at my wives as two retain the pointed ears. Hevesi has expanded, and waits patiently with Mórahalmi. They hope to meet with our new guest. I look over at Hevesi, who is giving me her hand signals to bring Pápain to them. I motion for them to start walking this extraordinarily slow. I ask Pápain to tell me what else she hates about her body. She tells us, I hate my eyes because they are not round as yours. They branded me a reject as so many avoid me. I point to Abaúj and Ajkai to walk this direction. The four wives arrive, and I ask Pápain to touch their ears and eyes and ask them how they feel about these conditions. Ajkai informs Pápain that she loves her eyes as they help her to focus and see things that others cannot see. Abaúj tells her that she could choose how her body was composed, and she picked the slanted ones because they had a higher rating in visibility.

Abaúj divulges to her, "We enjoy the best eyes. In addition, so many men are attracted to them. I now enjoy teasing them as I walk past them. I understand my eyes are a vital part of my package, and they want this package that I save only for my Master." Pápain asks me if I care about them showing off in front of other men. I enlighten her that these women work hard to keep themselves as beautiful. Their blessings fall short of a beauty such as you. Nevertheless, they are in the game. I think that they can, find as many as possible to adorn and desire after them. They have earned it. You must remember; this is their decision to stay here, and they are free to go at any time. All my wives deserve the best. Therefore, if they find better, they must leave our family. This we call love. I tell her that Khigir will prepare her so others will adorn you. We have chosen this as our way. No one needs to rush as we are a few days from Mysteria, and we know nothing of this new land. Pápain then begins to cry, "That is my mission, and I have failed it. Someone please beat me until all you see is marks and blood." I pick her up holding her as a baby and softly say to her, "Pápain, no one on this ship would ever touch you on purpose to create pain. If I see anyone else try, I will fight them." She asks me, "What about not telling you what to expect as I was ordered?" I lift my left arm, bringing her personally with me and give her a few soft kisses over her sweating head. I question her, "Pápain, you still hold time to tell us. I am curious, why do you sweat so heavily honey?" She tells us that fear in new places creates great nervousness in her. I probe again, "Are you nervous now?" She tells us, a little. I bring her face returning it to where we can kiss. After a few kisses, I set her back down and implore of her, wondering if she is agitated. She responds that if this gets me more kisses, I am extremely nervous. We laugh as Khigir welcomes her back to the land of the happy. Gyöngyösi sets down beside holds her hand, while Nógrád sits on the other side doing the same. I look at Khigir smiling as she immediately pleads with Gyöngyösi and Nógrád begging that they care for Pápain until she adjusts. They gladly accept as the three hug.

Continuing with my queries, I wondered if Pápain had anything else concerning her body that bothered her. She confessed, I hated these big breasts. I think that they are a burden to me. Khigir stood in front of her and asked, "Who has the greatest burden?" Pápain responded, "Oh, my you do by almost twice. I did not notice you, how were you able to look normal? Khigir answered, "We will construct you some looser gowns, which will blend you better within our group. I then asked Pápain, "Pápain, will you have mercy on me and practice with the loose shirts in your room and when in public on this ship, continue to wear that silky white gown." Pápain praises me on the adeptness of my request. She looks at Khigir and tells her, "I will do as you command." Khigir tells her, you can wear it while on the ship. You have a beautiful body Pápain; therefore, I want you to enjoy this gift as we teach you how to blend in with other groups. Pápain asks, "When will you force me to leave?" I told her, "Never." Pápain looks at me and counters perceptively, "You must enjoy my body. That is kind of you." Gyöngyösi tells her, "Oh darling, we can see into the wonder of your eyes." She informs us that, "The reason I began to avoid people after my breakup was because of the insanity and the rudeness of the men who looked at me. When I had my significant other, they would look at us and fabricate terrible remarks, which lead to my partner no longer trusting me. He could not deal with the unsolicited erotic harassment. We could not understand why the perverts selected me to harass. They had plenty of whores. After our breakup, the men began touching and grabbing. They enjoyed my crying and begging them to stop. I could go nowhere. They were all animals. Women also joined them, entering where I was and dragging me outside for the men and their children to touch and grab. Our society then forbade, rape to such a degree that if caught, they executed all involved. That is the only thing that kept me alive.

Nevertheless, every day they ripped off my clothes. They put me in so many degrading situations. One night, not able to take the constant pain from the lust of the men and jealousy of the women, I stumbled to a small boat and began rowing it out to sea. That night, a giant storm hit the sea. I was barely staying afloat. I will never know how I survived that storm. I later learned that all in my miserable village all had drowned. They got what they deserved, except for my male friend. He had abandoned me only because he was weak. I maintain a hard time hating someone because he or she was not what I wanted them to be. They appeared simply to be what they were. That is why I will not take a chance on a weak man. My boat landed here, and the Mystanites have given me the privacy that I needed. They have never given me an assignment involving contact with outsiders. At first, I was terrified until Berettyóú came to tell me about you. She told me to pour my heart out before you. This is so hard revealing my terrible past. I still ask what I did wrong." I went to her and picked her up again as a baby. She smiles at me and says, "Do you always pick up your guests as you are doing with me?" I tell her only to pick up the beautiful ones. Any way you enjoy this, I do not care because I am also enjoying it. She lowers her head so her eyes can see the wives, although she is looking upside down. She tells them, "Please forgive me, this is too much fun." The wives then all joyfully clapped and cheered. Hevesi yells out, "Hold on Pápain, force him to beg and plead." Pápain looks at me and laughs, "Oh, so you beg and plead?" I tell her I will beg and plead with her because she is of such a great treasure. She waves her hands around as if in the air. I notice that she has not moved her wings any today. Usually, with emotional changes, I would expect some sort of movement. I ask her, "Pápain, before I begin begging you, I am concerned that your wings may have a situation that is not healthy. She laughs and says, "They are not real wings. They are part of this gown.

I can float in air if need be. Most times I walk on the sky roads the Mystanites have made for me." She looks up at the Suns and then tells me, "Your first sight of the Mystanites kingdom will be before us sincerely soon. We probably should stop playing, so I can tell you what you need to know." I reach my face down toward hers and kiss her a few times. Afterwards, I prepare to stand her on our deck. Her legs are too weak to support her. Gyöngyösi and Nógrád secure her and walk her to the head of the table, so she can give us our briefing. Pápain yells back, "I am so regretful, Master; it was just so wonderful releasing all that ugly emptiness." She looks at Hevesi and tells her, "I am sorry Hevesi. His magic simply overwhelms me. I am as putty in his arms." Hevesi tells her, "Do not worry, for every woman on this ship suffers as you do. We are all putties in his hands. Do not fear; he will mold you exactly as you tell him." Pápain questions, "How do you know he is strong?" Abaúj speaks out now, "Pápain, you understand my powers. I depend on him for my protection. He guards my love. Describing my true situation, my Master does not only guard my love and the life within me, he cares for it, growing it making it stronger and more abundant. Without a doubt, he is my Master." She then bows, as do all my wives. I look around and say, "Come on darlings, right now. Please get back up, or I will remove my garments and bow before you begging for forgiveness and mercy." Pápain yells out, "Stay down, do not get up, please." The wives lose their control and begin laughing and rolling on the floor. Csongrád yells out, "Way to go my hero Pápain." They now begin cheering and clapping. I look at Pápain and say, "Excuse me." She tells me, "Well, I am curious; after all, I have been abused and sheltered. I figured it; they all like what you offer them, and then I must be worth taking a chance to see. Can you fault my innocence?" Khigir tells her, "Do not fear him, Pápain, we will get you a private viewing so you will learn all that a woman of your beauty should comprehend." Pápain hugs her and asks her, "You really would do that for me?" Khigir tells her, "Pápain, we will hide nothing from you and help you discover all that you want to understand, so we can build a stronger Pápain to go with that never-ending beauty." Pápain looks around at our family and remarks, "You truly do care for the helpless and misfortune."

Hevesi tells her, "Pápain, if what I see before me is a misfortune, then I am catastrophe combined with a cataclysm." "I tell Hevesi, "Little darling, be prudent with those big words, agreed." Hevesi tells me, "Be circumspect with that mouth, or I will cut reduce your exceptional treatment." I instantly tell her, "Oh, honey, please forgive me; just do not reduce that special treatment." Hevesi blows me a kiss and responds, "Well, since we did get a great new friend today, I will let you slide this time. Nevertheless, you had better to be on your best behavior." I nod my head in apologetic agreement. Pápain asks me, "She was considerably demanding on you was she not." I tell Pápain, "Honey, she was right; I have no business correcting them in front of their sisters. She was accurate. I was wrong. She forgave me. Her special treats are the great spices in my life. Now, we need to get this briefing going so I can work on a special project with my Angel, and I guess play show and tell with you." Pápain begs me not to think badly of her for this desire. I tell her, "Pápain, I would never consider one immoral who was thirsty acquiring themselves a drink of water. Your life has given you the right to undergo this. I will tell you that the mystery is greater than the prize. We are covered under a blanket of love and cannot let another freeze while we have room under of blanket." She looks at us and complements our family, "You are all so wonderful and sharing. I feel you truly do care. You allow me to share desires, which with others would shame me into a dungeon of misery. You simply acknowledge it as natural and offer a solution. Why do I stand before you with no shame, but excitement with the demons who have tortured my shame facing their demise? You are hence wonderful, and I do love you so much." She falls down crying. Khigir goes over to her and pats her hair, telling her, "My sister, consider this as all natural and these are things that you should learn from the virtues and not the evil ones who will spin you into their oubliettes of shame.

I am now behind her massaging her shoulders. She leans her head back facing me and asks, “How do you always grasp to do the perfect thing about my body?” Khigir tells her, “Pápain, you are falling in love and do not fear it, but simply enjoy its wonder and ecstasy. Any ways, our Master is ensuring you stay on this road. Pápain gazes over the bow and tells everyone to look at the giant stone in the sea. Abaúj asks Berettyóú if she can move us completely around this Rock Island, so we can see all sides. Berettyóú tells us that she can encircle the island. Even so, she must keep a safe distance, as there are many rock foundations close enough to the surface to rip the bottom out of our boat. I am sure glad that Berettyóú understands these things. Béla tells us that she has seen many small sea vessels sunk in around these visible points. In the past when the water levels were much lower, these rocky peaks were much grander and formed an excellent protective wall for the larger Mystanites Islands. These days, they are still able to defend the island as they are scattered over the sea. We are so lucky to have Berettyóú, who can, if need be, lift our ship out of the sea and pass these rock death traps. As I stare into this rock, I ask if anyone else can see the creatures engraved into this rock. Pápain tells us that, “These are from an ancient species that no longer lives on Lamenta. Many died when giant volcanoes filled the air with dust, causing the vegetation to vanish from the surface. The beasts who feed from this foliage followed soon after that. This race increased enormously from their original size. Their new bodies could not fit in their escape vessels, therefore, trapping them on Lamenta to die. We have found some of their skeletons and collected them in our research places. We do not want any future advanced civilizations in this world to discover the bones. That could produce an invasion of scientists, which we wish to avoid.” I ask her, “What about the engravings on the stones?” Pápain tells me that Berettyóú will have them sanded out within two millenniums. Extremely few ships will travel through here before then, as many stories of great monsters hiding in the sea will abound as tales and legends. The image you see now is two of these creature’s mating. The male releases his seeds through his nose into a puddle of a heavy murky liquid from the female. The female then places her body over this small pool and absorbs the thick black liquid with the male's seed into her body. She has a special part of her body that can comprehensively absorb this dark fluid with the male's seed into her physique. I look at Khigir and my wives and ask which way they prefer.

They all scream out, "We want our Master to deliver us his seeds." Pápain complains that she is aware of how ancient extinct civilizations mated, yet does not recognize how her own body mates. Gyöngyösi asks her if there are any laws from her culture forbidding her this knowledge. She tells us no. Any who tried to teach her, she escaped from and avoided. She saw the whores that let the men grunt on them in the open streets bellies become big. They would take their babies to the temples and offer them as a sacrifice. That told her this was one thing, which she did not want to undergo. Any ways, she could not talk to any one without them tearing her clothes off, how she could ask a question such as this. Gyöngyösi verifies seeing the babies sacrificed confirming this to be a terrible vision indeed. Khigir tells her, "We will explain this also to you, and allow you to watch a demonstration with the Master." Pápain bows to Khigir and tells her she does not see how she will ever be able to repay this great knowledge. Khigir asks her if anyone knows how they placed these giant rocks in the sea and how many there are. Pápain tells us that this race created several of the rocks by transferring them from lower peaks up to newer higher summits. They used these water towers as warning stations in lieu of an invasion and as resting places for when they were launching or returning from their invasions. This evil kingdom called themselves the Anfallare. They enjoyed countless uncontested raids throughout Lamenta for many thousands of years. They were the destroyers of the living and collectors, returning all they could find to their homelands, which are now gaping below the seas and in the deep caves of the underworld beneath the Land of the Celldömölki. We have secured as much of these items and belongings as best we can. They reveal many things the impending generations need not to be acquainted with, such as evil beyond their abilities to control. This abhorrence would destroy the future worlds as they did the previous ones."

I ask Pápain, "If all life on Lamenta was destroyed, how do we have so many new species and life forms on Lamenta today?" Pápain explains that many of the parent nations that had colonies moved their children to other planets in this section of the galaxy. A few replanted their colonies as close as Sharyawn and Reda, which are the worlds closest to us. A few million years later, the Planters for the newest deity to rule this galaxy began planting their children in what you recognize as the Planters. I express my amazement at a few million years, when Mórahalmi reminds me that an ordinary cycle is thousands of billions of 365-day cycles. I ask her why she speaks of 365-day cycles when the Lamentan cycle is 1000 days. Mórahalmi explains that the 365-day cycle is the one accepted by most galactic powers as being the best way effectively to standardize time for all the various orbits, knowing that few actually possess the 365-day cycle. Khigir tells her she does not worry, as she knows when the days come, within a certain number of days, the Suns will return. The same is true in the cold days and the warm days. I add the heavens will do what they wish, regardless if I understand it or not. I notice how the gigantic in height Rock Island before us appears more like an irregular cliff. Pápain reminds us the Anfallare created these as staging points for the invasions and as deadly ambushes for invaders traveling on top of the water with the jagged peaks just below the surface. The Anfallare was able to stagger up these cliffs as if walking on flat ground. At first glance, this occurs to be simple, yet after looking longer, the complexity of it commences to shine from the end to end. It appears to have a fixed foundation. Nevertheless, this is so far from any regular land that petrifies its glamour. From a distance, it becomes visible as a sanctuary from the endless boredom of the sea. On arrival, it emerges as a forbidden place for life. The nearest places to stand happen to be half-way up to its sharp unyielding cliffs.

As we pin ourselves against the ship's rails, and move slightly closer the gigantic peak captivates us even more. Although we have only been to sea less than two weeks, we eagerly crave walking upon Lamenta once more. Even though our ship is large and has plenty of space, we are aware of the many worlds below the surface we currently sail. Tselikovsky yells out that she can see the image of another Rock Island on our horizon. Pápain tells us that this defense contains more than a thousand of these Rock Islands. This extremely alluring natural defense network is equally dangerous as it rests so peacefully in the sea. I begin to see a curious similarity in this island with our peak on top of the world. Ours could be as tall; nevertheless, I do not realize how deep into our front cliff, it falls. It may actually be the entire cliff. Our peak has vegetation growing up its sides, which, if this one was land locked it would also have vegetation growing up its sides. I ask Pápain if the Anfallare built these rock cliffs in other parts of Lamenta and on land. She answers, "They absolutely did, many on high mountain peaks, so they could watch a larger area." I continue to question, "What is the highest peak had a smaller mountain range that blocked much of the lower land?" Pápain reports, "The Anfallare had reports where they would slash out a large pass in front of their Rock Point and use those rocks to build their new mountain peak. And yes, my love Baktalórántházai is part of this network." I respond, "Darling; our Baktalórántházai has a network of caves within its foundation. Why would these not have such a network?" Pápain reminds us to study the engraving along the outside of this rocky island. Notice how large these creatures were. They would have been unable to travel these small caves. Therefore, other species created the caves on Baktalórántházai throughout the time before the Planter's Lamentans." Our ship completes its circle and resumes its course. Pápain officially notifies us that we are in the waters of the Land of the Celldömölki and will set foot on the main island sometime tomorrow. She tells us her mission is finished, and that she should report to her superiors, and then returns to her hidden home in one of these rock islands. Khigir asks her, "Would you like to return to this ship after delivering your report? We would love to have you here with us tonight."

Pápain advances a solid reason why she does not want to return stating, "You are all married, and thereby I would be sleeping independently here also. I prefer to be alone with no others around me, instead of being alone when others are around me." Khigir promises her, "If you return you may sleep with us, anyway. We were going to give you some Carnal Knowledge; therefore, you will understand what is around you. Would not that sound fair?" She smiles and then gives me a slight push responds, "I would love that Khigir. Ensure you get the dirty boy all cleaned up, so I can learn with some enthusiasm." She waves good-bye and walks out on her sky, rocks slowly vanishing into the sunset. Gyöngyösi holds my hand and gives me a slight tug. I looked over to Khigir, who motions for me to leave. Gyöngyösi leads me a new room, which I had never, went in previously. Abaúj gave the wives a tour, and I used this time for a nap instead. I find myself taking naps daily now. The emotional perfectionism that I must exercise each moment with each wife is exhausting. I always keep in mind that with each, it must be up close and personal. Each meeting, each word must be perfect. Gyöngyösi is the one exception. She spoke to me as a spirit before my second birth. This Angel also watched me my entire life. One would think that she knows everything about me. She knows my mind, my feelings and can predict my every move. There is a reason she is surrendering her love with me tonight. Gyöngyösi and Khigir work closely together on most issues. Khigir must think I am exhausted or emotional overwhelmed now. I wonder if going from the 'normal' seven wives to fourteen wives would be a source of this new apprehension. The only thing, besides Khigir, that is saving me is the sisters of the womb bonding. At least, I appreciate each one has someone special to cry on their shoulders if need be. I also understand that once my babies start arriving, I will have to drag them while squealing into private time. My vision is plenty of more naps during those times. The wives have agreed to two-year cycles between pregnancies. They have also decided that half will go each year, with three going next year.

This will give a three first year, four-second year cycle. This allows the family more time to receive each child with the appropriate reception. Just like my wives, I must ensure each child receives what he or she needs to develop his or her special talents. Returning to here and now, Gyöngyösi fixed whatever she thought was wrong inside me. I feel like a new man, a sore man. However, a sweaty soaked Angel beside me takes away all this pain. I grab a rag from the pile she brought in here and begin placing them on her to dry her, so she does not get the chills. As I am working on her, she complains, "Oh Master, I have failed you. You can still move." I tell her that my body is not what is moving. Instead, the spirit inside me longs to reunite with her again. She places her palm along the side of my face and after closing her eyes, she tells me to lay on my back once more. She lies beside me and grabs my hand advising me to start talking. I can tell her all my deepest secrets and concerns. I know she receives much personal talk from the wives. She never tells me what they say, yet again when talking to her about a particular wife, and she composes a recommendation. I can rest assured that what she is suggesting is the perfect choice or course of action. My concern presently is if we did the justifiable thing by enlarging our family; and if we can provide for them the way, they needed cared for. She tells me, "Master, you need not to worry about such things. Your wives worry about you in the same manner. Each wants to please you well as the others. I have not heard any wife complain about anything, except for more time to do what they want to accomplish. We worry about you, as you depend upon us to care for you, and we are oftentimes busy with each another. Relax and keep us from the bad men, so we can raise your children, agreed Master." I nodded and gave her my thanks. As we were sharing our finishing kiss, someone began knocking on our door. Csongrád yells out, "Master. We have creatures around our ship!" I ran to and opened the door. Csongrád apologizes to Gyöngyösi. Gyöngyösi tells her, "Do not worry sister; I have already worn him down."

I look back and thank her. I also command her to put on some dry clothes before stepping on deck. Csongrád and I walk up to the deck, and I walk over to the rail. I look at the sea around me and see a red burning water spotted with so many peaks, some large, while many are small. I see my first beast, or half thing. It has half razor-sharp blades for it wrists and lower legs. It has a green body with so many spikes throughout its torso, spine, and skull. The front of its face resembles a large bird. Its jaw extends out so far that its opening is as long as its shoulder bone to its spiked elbow. I can tell by one of its wrist blades that the blades are not maintained well. The blade appears to be missing large chucks along its saws. If fighting with long knives, I would strike that part of the blade. Instead of having feet, it has a knife-approximating blade that is the length of its torso. They appear not to be interested in us and are staring into the red burning sea as if they are hunting. I do not buy this, for one large reason. They have a dark two-inch wide metal ring that is strapping its jaws closed. The one I am analyzing is sitting sideways and from the way its rib bones are clearly visible, I would say they are approaching starvation. This may be how their leader ensures solid and deadly fighting. Any ways, we must now get ready for some action. I tell everyone to stand on the steps of the deck and form an assembly line bringing me a few of those large swinging knives, or swords as Abaúj calls them, and I need at least thirty spears for now, from what Abaúj calls our battle supply room. I tell my Tamarkins to bring their bows and plenty of arrows and for the wives to have plenty of arrows ready to move on deck. I now call for Brann and Baranya. I appreciate that our arrows with simply pass through them, so I ask them to flash around our ship and burn any of the creatures who give the appearance of attempting to board our ships. I further tell them not to go more than twenty feet from our ship, as we do not understand for sure what weapons are available in their arsenal and if anything appears risky to them, abort and come back to me. Looking both in their eyes, I remind them they are married women now. I kiss each good-bye as the flames rush overboard.

Gyöngyösi arrives on the deck. I open my arms and while hugging her request, "Honey, I need you in the steps and among the non-fighting wives to keep them calm. Can you do that for me?" She agrees; conversely, she qualifies this by adding, "The second anyone gets hurt on the deck; I will rush to their aid, do you understand?" I smile and tell her, "My love, I would not have it any other way, can you send the Queen to me?" She departs as Abaúj and Béla come rushing to me asking how they can help. I ask them if they are aware of any reason I should not believe these creatures are setting us up for an ambush. Béla tells me they are enemies of the sea because they kill everything they see, leaving the sea as a pool of blood. Abaúj adds that they are also enemies of the air in that they burn so many elements, turning the air to be black for their disguises and ambushes. I tell them, that since the air is black and the sea is red; notwithstanding, I cannot see where putting them on the front line will help that much. I remind them that I possess a zero loss tolerance for my wives. Although bending from this tolerance I ask Abaúj if she knows where Berettyóú is. Abaúj tells me she is in the bathing part of our ship, and uses a special hallway that can monitor the front of this vessel. This allows her to push with pinpoint accuracy around these cutting peaks. I ask Béla if these peaks are special for this mobile attack, or if they are permanent fixtures in this sea. Béla confirms that, "These are one of the thousands of peak trap areas designed to sink ships. We call these creatures the 'Revived Anfallare' and only appear at night a few nights during our 1,000-day years. The Mystanites traditionally avoid them. I realize they knew we would pass through here and therefore, be in contact with them. Nonetheless, I do not comprehend how they expect us to respond." I tell them, "The only way I understand to respond removes any threat to my wives. They have not attempted to convince me that they are peaceful. I am sorry, as I believe we must fight them. Enough kicks with their feet will sink this ship. Béla and Abaúj, can you think of any justification that I would risk the lives of my wives while traveling the course the Mystanites have endorsed?" They both agreed with my plan and asked how they could help. I studied their eyes when they agreed with me and felt comfortable that they were telling me the truth. I told them I needed them to protect the part of them that is my wife and please stay secured.

Red water gives the impression of being an enemy and contaminator to Béla. The dark, thick, smelly black smoke comes across as being incompatible and enthralling to Abaúj. These elements control the water and air within their grasp, so they are not going to suck in my wives. I further tell them, "If Berettyóú is working undercover, then you two must stay put. I beg that if you love me, please protect yourselves." They both rush down the steps in full compliance of what I only requested. I marvel to think I just told the air and wind what to do. I think the wife part of them is now revealing itself. Perhaps this wife part even wants cared for, and that is controlling their actions. I can debate this later, for now; I must prepare for battle. My Tamarkins and I prepare to fight. Khigir and Tselikovsky are taking their aims. Khigir has the front of our ship, Tselikovsky the left side, and I have the right side. I tell them that if these things raid, they will have to shoot faster and always shoot the close ones first. We will not attack their reserves yet. This may give the ones on the front line an incentive to retreat. I throw my first razor-sharp spear hitting the thing's skull. The thing drops into the hot sea, and lays on top of the red water boiling. This beast is dead. Khigir and Tselikovsky begin firing their arrows and dropping these things. To our surprise, there are many of these things coming from behind these stone peaks. They were waiting for their attack order, which has not arrived. We have to kill as many as we can; nevertheless, they just keep on coming. I yell at my Tamarkins that six of them or on our sails trying to cut them. They are out of my spear range. I realize Khigir and Tselikovsky can pick them off like flies. Two minutes later, there are six of them splashed on our deck. They have a gooey compound in them that smells rotten and appears to be absorbed. I see Abaúj and Béla rushing out throwing spreading some sort of white powder over these splashes, and tossing their torsos overboard.

They are leaving their metal limbs, which appear to detach themselves at death. I can only think that their creators reuse these limbs. I yell down for more spears. I am fighting against the rail now using my spear's razor-sharp tip to penetrate their skulls, which is killing them immediately. I just cannot imagine where these things are coming from. Precipitously I feel some of their gook on my back. I turn around and see our Queen with a sword in her hand beside my Angel with a special long necked razor spear. I give them my thanks and order them to be careful. I can see Brann, and Baranya are protecting the rear of our ship and preventing any more of these things from striking our sails or dropping in from above. Soon Ajkai, Abaúj, Béla, Mórahalmi, an expanded Hevesi, and Makói join our deck force and work as rail stabbers such as I am doing. The volume coming at us is overwhelming, as the sea around us packed with their dead bodies. These bodies are flowing beside our ship. I wonder if Berettyóú is packing them beside us to prevent others from coming up out of the sea while close to our ship. Except for two, the remainder of my wives is working the rails. Hevesi and Csongrád are mowing through the ones who are wandering around on our deck. These women can sling those swords and fire their smaller light spears. That would be practical, to keep weapons designed for women on a ship in which fourteen of the fifteen passengers are female. Female or not, the Revived Anfallare are turning into the Demised Anfallare. I glance ahead of us and see the open sea with no small peaks. The water and air are clean. Our sanctuary is not that far ahead so now I can fight harder not worrying about running out of energy. My spot is clearing up, as they currently appear to be trying to board in a row formation, rather than single style columns. I yell out, "We need to reform to where they are attacking and fight closer together. Do not take any chances. If any pass you, Hevesi and Csongrád will get them. None passed our solid defense. Soon Hevesi and Csongrád joined the formation fighting lines filling in any potential overflowing points. The enemy was now in a three-point formation raid. We were holding strong.

Less than one hour later, the invading forces dwindled. Except for a few stragglers, they were gone, as were the red water and black air. I could feel our ship picking up speed thanks to Berettyóú. She must want to get some distance between us and our enemy. I can see the sea beginning to burn now. Brann and Baranya are attacking the large bundles of dead Revived Anfallare that Móri is assembling for them. The gook inside of them is making the fire burn white and blue. Gyöngyösi tells me that white and blue fire is much hotter than orange and yellow fire. Brann and Baranya have returned. They tell me the white and blue fire is too threatening for them. I give my thanks to them for being responsible enough not to take any dangerous chances. I look around my women and see that they are all pitch black from all the heavy black smoke. Even Gyöngyösi, who is normally a golden dark brown, now pitch black. I look at my arms, and they are pitch black. Now, I feel some soft hands pushing me. Without warning, Hevesi grabs one hand and Gyöngyösi grabs the other. I see Khigir standing at the stairway entrance holding the door open. Khigir understands the wives and recognizes I would never resist Hevesi or my Angel and will go along without resistance. The wives behind and the spouses who stayed below deck are now scrubbing the deck. It looks as if only Khigir, Hevesi, and my tender Angel Gyöngyösi will be scrubbing me. Into the cleaning room, we go. The oils, and a new kind of salve in which Abaúj collected from some long ago lost empires, is applied to my skin. They wet their washing rags and used this slightly abrasive salve to remove the black smoke from my skin. The three of them work well as a team. If someone was watching this, he or she would be, impressed with the dedication surrendered to clean me. This is not about the embarrassments between male and female. They are only worried about getting the dirt off their husband. I usually hate and dread this. This time is different. They also are pitch black, yet they want to clean me first. The little things fought hard today, and because of them, we are still living. They finish with me hurriedly and go to dry me. I tell them, "Wives, today I will help clean you, as I know your back needs cleaned. I jump behind Hevesi and start scrubbing. Hevesi calls out to Khigir, "Khigir. The war ruined him. He is behind me. We lost our dirt boy."

I reach down and pinch her buttock. She twitches and yells out, "Never mind. He is back." Gyöngyösi and Khigir begin clapping and cheering. Hevesi pours some sort of oil on her head, and I help her spread it through her wonderful golden hair. Her blond hair is a shade that is lighter than Khigir's. I have Hevesi's back, and the back part of her upper legs scrubbed down. With my bottle of the abrasive salve in one hand, I give Hevesi a kiss, and tell her how awesome she was in today's battle. I ask who needs me now. Wrong question, they both started calling currently. Therefore, I drop in behind Khigir and begin lightly scrubbing. She has much it removed. From now, I am only getting spots she missed. Subsequently, I help oil her sunlight blond hair. I finish quickly, kiss her cheek, and additionally tell her how proud I was of my Tamarkins today, and that I will be back. I always find it hard to leave the presence of my Master wife when she has nothing on. Her body is the envy of all women. The perfection of her sculptured muscles heavenly combined with her, at least twice or almost three times, larger breasts than any I have seen belonging to other women. The only one that comes close is Pápain and Mórahalmi. She does not flaunt this blessing while always underplaying it around others. She will never ride a horse unless with me, and she can hide them by holding onto me. I agree with this, because we do not want to excite any evil perverts and place her life in danger. Too many times people mistake perverts as being weak, not knowing that their perversion can render them dangerous and creative adversaries. I now rush over to Gyöngyösi and give her a big kiss. She is kissing feverishly. I ask her, "My little innocent Angel, did your husband feed you what you needed for your private time?" She pats her perfect abdomen and tells me, "He packed it tight my great Master." I spin her around and begin cleaning her back. I must go lightly on her back. Fortunately, for me, she always oils herself before our private times, causing this junk is coming off her easily.

I give Gyöngyösi special thanks telling my Angel, "Because of the love you shared with me during our private time I could fight harder and for an everlasting reason." She tells me she fought to keep her husband and her son's father alive to help with his childcare. I remind her what happens every time we are together.

She assures me this will always continue. I smile, as chattering now floods and mob this room. Khigir tells Hevesi, Gyöngyösi and me, we need to get out so the other wives may clean themselves. I tell Khigir the wives deserve extra from me today. She agrees and tells me not to scrub too hard, or I could lead them to harm. Tselikovsky jumps into our cleaning area with flowing and warm sea water, in which Abaúj's empire created. She told me something as if air sucking the water in, then compresses it to pressurize it hard. It then releases the pressure that creates the heat while the water expands. The Edelényi has some sort of hot bathing water gadget. We were fortunate during my childhood as one of the nearby caves had a stream the released heated water into an open cavern that created a pool. We would wash ourselves in it, and my parents with other adults would relax in it and chat with each another. Tselikovsky comes rushing in and stumbles as she sees me asking, "Why are you here Master?" I tell her to reward my great warriors. I request that she stand in front of me. I spin her around and start scrubbing her back. She yells out to the other wives, "Hurry, get in here; you are not going to believe what is happening." As they came in Makói and Dabasi rushed up beside me asking if they could help me. I told them, that since they had either fought hard on the deck or worked conscientiously as support under the deck today I was going to reward them by spoiling them. I spun them around and started scrubbing Makói first as she had been on the deck soaking up the black clouds. I am sure to reach over and run my rag over Dabasi every few swipes. These two are the blessings of blessings for me. In reality, I am scrubbing a ten-foot killer female bear and a fifteen-foot long half fish half woman creature that lives in the dark bottoms of the seas. However, as they stand before me now, either one could force a man to cry in pain from his lust.

Blessed with solid well above-average womanly breasts, they have enough to catch any man's eyes. Just like all my other wives, their sculpted muscles are the perfection of the feminine form. I notice that Dabasi is lightly trembling when I run my rag over her back. It now occurs to me that I have only touched her once before while she was uncovered. I stop with Makói for a second and take Dabasi in my arms, telling her not to be ashamed. We are man and wife, and sometimes you have to allow your husband to serve you. You did great things today, as you rushed up and down our large desk steps to keep our spears and arrows in battle fighting quantities. Makói runs her rag over Dabasi and tells Dabasi, "My sister. Our Master's hands are the same as any of your sisters. We belong to him as he belongs to us." She started to relax as I did the final spot scrubbing at them and then proceeded to scrub my other wives. I could feel an exceptional emotion taking over this hot cleaning room. This emotion is from the pride in their Master enjoying a special time for them. My wives have two special events they enjoy each day. These are events where everything else stops as their defenses drop. The two events are washing and eating dinner. I can see how this can be fun, as they just bubble in her with so much enthusiasm as each ensures the other is cleaned to perfection. In here, they hide nothing from each another. I can appreciate the way in which they baby each's bodies. A little scratch or bruise warrants a group evaluation. They look at me and shake their heads saying, "He is a man, what can one expect?" They want to see marks on my body to remind them how strong their Master truly is. I had never been a part of this cleaning culture before as they always cleaned me first and then booted me on my way, with of course no complaints from me. I must change as now is the time I like more things that they like, especially when they are enforcing the same values that my mother and her sister-wife enforced. Time to go with the flow and enjoy them as much as I can, as so easily today one of those creatures could have taken one.

I am still impressed with the way everyone's backs were covered. This provided us with the chance to fight hard and concentrate on what was before us, as we knew nothing was going to get us from behind. After we finish cleaning, they gang up and wipe me first. I cannot fight this, as that is the mommy in their passionate hearts coming through. Nevertheless, I can, help wipe them, as I do. They have goose bumps over their soft tight skin.

I complain to them about not caring also for themselves. They chuckle, as we know who gets the final say. In addition, with this, much love and passion abounding around me, who cares about the last word? My Angel and Khigir brought me some clean clothing, which I slowly redress. Too wiped out is only the beginning of how I feel now. My heavenly Angel rolled me in the clouds through a paradise of emotions and peace, then instantly the ugliest, most pitiful beasts of the underworld decide to unleash a few Armies on us. They made the same mistakes as others have and others will. My women, although having unspeakable beauty and passion, will fight to kill when our survival necessitates it. These females can think on their feet. Even though I asked them to stay under deck, when they saw we were being overwhelmed, they jumped in with us. They stood strong, even though these things when stabbed released vile smells and substances. This did not take their eyes off the battlefield that was in our laps. I chat casually with them as they ensure I am completely dressed first. I am reaching over them trying to slide gowns on their sisters. They can dress quickly in here, maybe ten times faster than in their rooms or our Master bedroom. I have learned to sleep in later so they can get more rest as they distinguish when I am going to awake and are always completely dressed in a gown and faces painted with their hair combed and properly decked with ornaments. If I catch them in progress, you would think I walked into a room on naked women. They yell and scream as others our pulling me away from them. They try too hard to paint that perfect image for me. I truly would not care if they were all ugly, their hearts, and passion to preserve this family is what brings me the greatest recompense.

I realize that without thinking, I will give everything to protect each one of them. Many times, my heart burns with hope to find new ways to honor and protect them. I think that cleaning with them is helping to honor them. I guess more voluntary cleaning is in my future. As I depart, they all rush around me talking at the same time. They are extremely happy now. They had not painted themselves yet being only in special robes. They were from the cleaning room to their private rooms. Tselikovsky invites me to join them as they paint their faces. I accept this invitation, especially as they have never shared this experience with me previously. Instantly, I agree and we crowd into our Master bedroom. They each pull out boxes they have secured in special compartments below our heart bed. I never knew these compartments existed. Each compartment has exactly what they want and is in order. We now have robes laying all over the floor. I ask my wives, "My Masters of Beauty, why do you paint yourselves before putting on your dinner gowns? Ajkai smiles at me and says, "Silly boy, we do not want to spill on beauty paints on our gowns." I then said, "Come on, when you pull your gown over your head, you will get paint on it?" Hevesi afterwards asks me, "Master, do you not realize how we put our gowns on ourselves?" I look at her and them and then replied, "How would I know. You always cast me out into the loneliness and cold when you dress?" I am trying to drum up some extra sentiment among my damsels. Hevesi tells me, "That was then and now is now. You may join us at any time, no matter what you are doing. We hide nothing from our hearts, thus we will not hide anything from our Master. We only accept designed dresses that we may put on through our legs bottoms up. Look, let me show you." As she went to select one of her spare gowns, three other sisters rushed around her, and they slide that shoulder tight gown up to where her folded hands could expand through her sleeves. They then tied the bows, added some of the clothing, ornaments and buttoned all buttons. I shook my head in amazement.

The gown fit her to a T as the strings, buttons and ornaments linked it together, as if it created as one solid piece. They took it off her just as fast. I roamed around watching each do their pronounced works. This is as great artists at work. I tell them, "My loves; I would not care if you wore rags and painted your faces with mud, I would still want you. Hevesi fires back, "Dirty boy, sometimes you have to play with the clean girls," then winks and smiles. I tell her, "Only with you my cleanest little love." I look at their gowns hung in order. I ask them, "How many gowns do you wear daily?"

They tell me most days, three. One is for sleeping; one is in the daytime, and the last one is in the evening. They tell me the evening is a special time for them to be bringing as much glory to their Master as they can. I tell them that most times I am dressed in my daytime garments for dinner. Brann tells me, "That is okay; as you are a man and men do things different. We only want to see you, so we can rejoice in knowing you own us." I look at them and ask, "Do you feel that I own you?" Nógrád answers, "We hope you want to own us, because we only wish to be your servants and your property. This is the way of Lamentans, that a Master must own us. Please say you own us." I look at them and say, "I will declare before all Lamentans that I am your Master. However, when we are in our individual home, you do as you wish. In our private home, I must serve you. This is my way of proving my great honor and love toward you." I had better stopped because their eyes are getting milky, and I may never get those gowns back on them. They begin their face painting rituals again. I must have asked a hundred questions and comprehend as much now as I did when I first came into our room. Nevertheless, each thing they did generated sense to me so when they do it again; I will have a feel for what they do. Suddenly, a set of arms wrap around me pushing me to the floor. Tselikovsky and Brann secure my feet and arms, and Hevesi brings some paints and starts painting my face. I cry out to them, "You are going to bring great shame to me by forcing me to look as a woman." Hevesi tells me, "Oh, Master, we would prefer to die than bring shame to you in that manner. I am merely going to add some touch ups. If you resist, then we will paint you as a woman every day."

She tells the other wives, who have me pinned incapable of any movement except for my mouth, to release me. I lay there as if I was a baby. Tselikovsky remarks, "Something is wrong with our dirty boy. He does not fight back." Hevesi smiling at them, then reports, "He knows who the boss is." She has her back perched up with her firm apple size breasts secure, sitting proud with absolutely no worry of a response from me. I tell Tselikovsky, "Tselikovsky, have you forgotten who the boss is?" We cheer Hevesi. I trusted this little thing with the lives of all the people in our negative cycle. Why would I not trust her with any facial paints as a dinner with my wives? We soon finish as Abaúj tells us the Mystanites have prepared a special party for us on the deck. I ask her if they are disappointed that none of my wives lay in the sea now while feasted on by sea beasts. Abaúj shrugs her shoulders at me and up to the steps; I go with my precious gang. When we arrived in the dining room, Khigir, Gyöngyösi and Dabasi are waiting at the entrance. Khigir gives a great sigh and asks, "Master. We thought that we lost you. Where were you?" Hevesi tells her, "Oh, he was being a good boy." Tselikovsky adds, "My sister, did you understand that we have the greatest Master ever?" Khigir tells her she knows this and then shakes her head. She tells Gyöngyösi, "Whatever our good boy did; he has our sisters filled with joy presently." As we sat down around this dining table, we saw one of our walls that faces the sea begin to crumble as it splatters everywhere. Now a light-blue blade resembling the flat objects pushes its way to the front. Abaúj tells us to kick at the floor on the port side of our seat. I yell out to Hevesi, "Your other left Hevesi." She smiles at me and tells me to, "Shut up." Oh, this feels like home again. As I kick to my left, a container comes up out of the floor packed with long knives. I tell my fierce warriors to hold steady. I grab one of the blades and walk to peek out the small opening created above this what looks like a stone floor. I have an idea who this might be.

I loosen a few boards, so I have a larger opening to look out and see what the situation is. My wives are begging me to be careful. I let them see my war, killing face. After all, I could endure some more kisses and hugs from their milky eyes. I stick my head into this hole and see our Pápain laying with her head against our ship, and a small pool of blood beside her. My heart stops beating, until I see that she is still breathing. I wrap my hands around her tiny petite body and pull her, inside so we can mend her. Csongrád rushes up to her and touches a few parts of Pápain's body and tells us, "She will be okay; we probably should clean her up and put some salve on her small cut before she wakes again." About twenty minutes later, she begins to talk, "I am so sorry. I miscalculated my stop and crashed into your ship. Please forgive me." I tell her to give me a kiss first, then each of the wives, and we will forgive her. Hevesi asks, "How could you hit the side of the ship?" She answers, "Someone moved it." I look at Hevesi and ask her, "Have you never heard of women drivers?" Hevesi fires back, "Yes, I have, especially the ones who were hit my male drivers." I had better dropped out of this one fast tonight, as her tongue is as sharp as that long knife, she is holding. We now witness her floor, pulling away from our ship and the materials reassembling themselves. I look at Abaúj and ask her, "Do you recognize who is doing that?" She tells me, "Do not worry big boy, our ship is repairing itself." I bring an extra seat and put it beside me. I point for her to sit down beside me when she is finished trading hugs and kisses with my wives. I detect that they all appear to like her. She comes backward, sits beside me, wrapping her arm around mine, and tells me, "I am so sorry I hit your ship. I was in a hurry to get back before you rest for the day." She looks at Khigir, "Do I still get my dirty boy body lessons?" My wives now cheer for her. Khigir replies by saying, "Your class may have a record number of instructors.

Anyway, we have some new wives who are experiencing some apprehension over this same issue. Just try not to hit our ship again. We will take care of you, charming Angel." I ask Pápain, "My gorgeous love, do you understand of the reason the Mystanites are going to visit us tonight?" Pápain answers, "Yes, they wish to apologize for not being able to help you arrive on their shores safely. Somehow, your combinations of elements plus the negative, positive issue is preventing their powers from protecting you. They have offered me as a payment for the lack of their protection. If you do not want me, I am to return to them and face execution. I truly would prefer to die than have you risk your lives for me, so please send me back." Khigir looks at her and replies, "You expect for us to reveal the secrets of our Master only to release you to die? I think not, in fact, you are to remain in my sight until we arrive on Mysteria. We can have you driving that stone floor around above the sea, now can we?" I look at Pápain and explain, "Precious; we let you slide under our blanket of love. We will never cast you away from us. The only way that you can leave is that you declare your hate for us." Pápain is dropping those milky eyes on me. She responds, "You people really love me?" Hevesi came up to her dropping to her knees before her declaring, "We absolutely love you and beg that you join us, if Khigir invites you." Everyone looks at Khigir as she counters, "Pápain, I have asked you many times to and still wait for your answer. Why would you think that we would share our Master's secrets if you were not to become his servant also?" Pápain looks at me and answers, "I will take one more chance on love, only because I found myself this day to be in misery missing my family. I will serve you Siklósi and surrender to you the fruit that comes forth from my womb." I lean over and give her a kiss thanking her and promising to be a loving Master." Tselikovsky yells out, "Our Master is the greatest in all Lamenta." The other wives cheered. I went through the motions of cheering, yet something in the back of my mind was giving me a warning. Something was wrong with this situation, and it was not Pápain, as I truly believe she would bear children for me. The number of my children is what puzzles me presently. We were told that I would have thirty-seven children and given the exact amount from each of my wives. Hence, where does the children whom Pápain is to give me in this prophecy? I wholeheartedly hope nothing ever bad happens to her or the babies she gives me.

I will get some answers from the Mystanites on this one. It could be something as simple as a prophecy, including what was among it at the time of the prophecy. I still think this rather odd that my seven new wives are non-reproducers. I cannot wait for the Mystanites, who cannot even defend us to wiggle their way through it. I do not know if they are the type of spirits, we need to deal with in that they put Pápain's life on the line as a force to force us to visit their lands. Up I stand, then look at Béla, and say before my wives, "I wish to be the Master of Pápain and to plant my seed within her. Béla, I must have a special private work meeting with Abaúj, Gyöngyösi, and Khigir, so before my wives render me one with my Pápain. I do not want any spirits to bring shame and dishonor on her for seeing my secrets before we marry and become as one. I look at Pápain and say, "Learn much in your class tonight for tomorrow morning you will be consummated and my seed placed in you. I now head out the room with my three power minds, and we enter another meeting room on the other end of this hall. When we enter I begin, "My wives, something is in error here? Can any tell me what is wrong?" Khigir answers, "The number of your children does not add up correctly now, as the prophets did not include the children whom Pápain will bear for you." Gyöngyösi further clarifies this, "She will bear sons, who will bear daughters whose beauty shall cause nations to war against each, another for her hand as their Queen." Abaúj adds, "Master, I confirm how vitally important that she bears your son. This son shall have many sons, two of which will be the ancestors of the two Queens whom, your descendant marries. The history of so many depends on these two lineages being created." Khigir asks, "Why then is not this fine son raised by his father who will love his mother as we all so much do." Abaúj confesses, "Pápain is a Hajdú." Khigir and I look at her and respond in anger, "We do not care what she is, and you comprehend that we love all peoples." Gyöngyösi told us to relax, that is not what Abaúj was addressing. Abaúj continues, "The Hajdú is considered by many to be the ones who were blessed with the greatest beauty of any creation. They are peace-loving people notorious for turning the other cheek when being abused. I could witness the tortures and abuses she revealed to us.

The rage inside us was enough to hunt out all evil and fight to destroy it. They will stretch the truth to get something they need. Therefore, I would not accept the Mystanites would execute her if you fail to arrive at their islands. I will accept that she feels a need to be with us. We would be foolish to cast her away for we will discover the love in her heart will touch us all the days of our lives. The issue is that one of her ancestors angered some spirits, which put a curse on her family line. If she tries to leave more than a day past the peak stones, she will turn to fire and vanish." Gyöngyösi continues, "She had forever lost any hope of love. When she saw us, she became weak and gave love one more chance. She hit our ship because of the great excitement that she now has as love is finally growing inside her again." Khigir asks a question, "Will not her descendants also have her curse?" Abaúj answers, "No, this is because the curse only applies to the descendants who both parents are Hajdú. This is the primary reason she moved to be isolated on an island. She chose never to have children, as they would only continue a curse that she was not a part. Her belief was that if the innocent must pay, then the innocent would not play. With Siklósi as the father of her children, they will be freed from this terrible curse." I ask, "What will happen to her when we leave?" Gyöngyösi tells me, "We will confess she is your wife when we arrive at Mysteria. We shall also celebrate her being pregnant. Therefore, when we leave, they will give her the honor of a widowed mother. She will stay faithful to you the days of her remaining life and be among the greatest mothers your son could ever hope to have." Abaúj now holds her palms out and asks Khigir if she wants to see our Master's son. She rushes over alone. I tell them I cannot look because I am the father who abandoned them.

Gyöngyösi tells me, "Pápain will tell your son that you died trying to save them during a storm. Your son will hear pronounced things about you and will grow up having great pride in their father. She knows you could not stay." Gyöngyösi now comes over and wipes the tears from my eyes as I tell her, "This is something I cannot do, if I father a child, then I will raise it." Gyöngyösi reminds me that, "The Mystanites understand the true importance of this birth and will ensure she lives a wonderful life. If you do not do this, then you could destroy the future of so many billions on billions of lives. The future makes it essential that your far-distant son marries both of Pápain's, and yours, far-distant daughters. The future would not work any other way. You must be strong and think about the other father's children. Any time you have burdens with this during our future days, come to me, and I will help you." Abaúj now says, "Look Khigir, we are going to get views of him throughout his life." Khigir responds as she watches throughout the young man's life, "He looks just like his father, so strong and handsome." She looks at me and says, "Consummation tonight." I tell her I cannot. She asks me, almost angrily, "And why not?" I tell her that the little Angel beside her took all my seeds, and that I will not rearm the store until the morning." She smiles at Gyöngyösi who is apologizing. Khigir tells Gyöngyösi, "Oh sister, you did well. That was your time and once again, you gave the dirty boy, a whipping." Slapping each other's hands, they next hugged while laughing. As Khigir leaves the room, she sneaks a nasty stare at me, and bebops away. I ask Abaúj if she will escort me to our family dining room. She gives me a kiss on the cheek and comments, "Well, since no one else wants you, and as I am still waiting for our consummation, I will." I tell her that I felt the new wives should get first shot. However, they decided differently. She tells me not to worry because there will be many more times. We reenter the room, and I ask Pápain, "Angel, are we married?" She runs to me and jumps up on me. I am barely able to keep my balance and hold on to her. She kisses me frantically telling me, "I cannot believe I belong to a Master and one as strong and handsome as you are my Master. Oh, all my life I worried about this time, and if I could surrender to a man. Now, that their time is here, I do not realize how much longer I can keep them on. I want you to take everything I grasp and produce it so only you can enjoy."

I kiss her and tell her, "Honey, relax, because tomorrow morning is her big time, because we are going to put a baby in your womb. How does that sound my wife?" The precious little thing passes out. Béla and Abaúj come up to me now and ask to talk with me, I tell them to start talking as I hand Pápain off to Khigir and Tselikovsky as they quickly try to recover her. Béla tells me, "Master, we heard your wives talk about all the troubles that your bodies have in uniting your seed with their embryos. We want to tell you that we can ensure that is never again a problem. I can flood their passageway for your seeds, so they will be guaranteed to arrive alive." Abaúj adds, "Master, I can take all the gasses out of her corridor thereby removing that threat." I tell them thanks as we always need help with planting the seeds. Moreover, as long they do not get hurt or are in no danger. I then use my arms to pull them to me so our faces meet and give them kisses. I also add in, "Have I told you how wonderful and proud I am to be your husband?" Abaúj tells me, "Yes. Nevertheless, I would love to hear it repeatedly." I tell them both, "I wish I could dedicate myself to tell you both over and over how much I truly love you and thank you for agreeing to help your sisters raise my children." Béla tells me, "Oh Master that is our great reward for serving you. To be trusted, and be able to hold, love, and care for your children is manifesting our dreams. We love you so much for having mercy on us and letting us serve you." I kiss them both and tell them to hang on for consummation. I ask them if they are going to watch the special one tomorrow for Pápain. They tell me that they would not miss that for the world. I sit down, and Dabasi dispenses me a special small drink that she is pouring out of a strange-looking bottle. Abaúj yell over to me, "Master who is, from the ship's creators and is a popular man's drink, although the wives may drink of it also. Go slow with it because it does have a whop. I took cautiously a small sip.

The creepy stuff tried to burn out the inside my mouth. Nevertheless, I looked calm and relaxed and then breathed out as if a sign of great satisfaction. Hevesi laughs at me while issuing a challenge, "Come on, big boy, you are only going to take a small drink at a time." I tell her, "This is the way a man drinks it, relaxing while enjoying the powerful flavor." I remembered that as Grandpa and my father would hit some of his hard drinks. Hevesi stands up and declares, "Let me show you how a woman drinks of this water." She gulps the glass straight down. I think to myself, 'that little baby doll can handle her hard drink.' My praise was premature as Hevesi starts screaming for someone to save her. The wives are pouring water down her throat until she begins to vomit everywhere. I wonder how she packed all that food in her small belly. She closes her eyes and begins to sleep like a rock. I go over to my chair and motion for the recovered Pápain to sit on my lap again. She melts in my lap as she presses her heart against mine and slowly starts kissing my neck. She tells me, "If I am being a fool, please forgive because I do not recognize what I am doing. I just feel like doing this. My I do this my Master." I gaze at her and say, "Please continue my new lover, enjoy yourself as you see fit." I ask my wives, "Wives, which is the best way to drink this special relaxer, as a man or as a woman?" They all give me a dirty eye. I ask them, "What did I do wrong?" They yell at me, "Watch Hevesi, how could you do that to her?" I just sit back in my chair and turn my face to Pápain trying to smile. She takes her husband's hand, presses it down the front of her gown, and tells me, "I was told this would attain great happiness for my husband." I massage them lightly, as I realize the punishment for not enjoying what my wives tell me to enjoy. She asks me why my heart is beating so hard. I tell her, "Those wives are blaming me for poor little Hevesi. I do not understand this. She stood up in front of everyone telling us she realized what she was doing. How could I recognize she was bluffing?" Pápain because you are the Master and grasps all things, and you are a man, therefore, can only do wrong. I stare at her and say, "You understand the truth is what I always wanted a white-haired woman with dark black hair running through it. My Grandpa would call them salt and pepper women."

Pápain asks, "What is salt and pepper?" I tell her, "They are things the Edelényi put in their foods while eating." She tells me now, "You will soon hate me for my foolishness." I tell her, "As long as you share these big doll babies, you will never be hated." I soon pulled my hand out and began massaging her shoulders and the sides of her face. I can feel a bottomless sea of love inside her. Abaúj flashed me some images of her life. These images are killing me. She is so innocent, yet to get only a small chip from a giant tree what she deserves she must lie, yet I am glad I am the one, since love and honor fills my heart with every thought of this Star. I accordingly understand. She asks me why my eyes look so sad, so I tell her, "My love I can sense the hurt that is inside you. I can experience the abuse you have suffered. I just so much want to keep you in my arms so no one else can hurt you?" I start to wipe the tears from her eyes as she comments, "My Master, you do have the true magic of love. You can picture deep inside me and maybe even comprehend my thoughts. I promise to serve you as my only Master." I tell her that, "I have no magic my love, nor can I read thoughts. I have shared so many feelings with my wives whom, I have a feel for the mysteries behind your eyes. When I touch you, I touch purity and innocence, and I now understand your intense devotion. You are for real and when you ask me to take and enjoy you as I wish, I tell you that I will do. I recognize from my wives that when they understand what is happening, and what to expect, it will truly bond us as these events unfold. I will have you; nevertheless, you will also have me." She is now so limp, that I can touch no bones in her body. Her dangling black with touches of white hair reflect the light devices in this room, as also does her jewelry. I can now make out the happiness in her eyes. Life cheated her because of this unbelievable beauty. Her people tormented and shamed her as if lower than a dog. Young men and boys, with no teeth and sores over their bodies, would run up and rip off her clothes. She would have to run home, only covered by special rags she wrapped around her prized female parts.

She wore these knowing she would have no gown, on by the time she came home. As is too many times, when one is being abused those around them blame the victim. Her parents cast her from their house telling her to find a place to die. How terrible something this precious is clearly a gift from the spirits. She will be at home with the other gifts from the spirits who are members of her new family. She suffered much, as in the forests; she had little protection from any civilized law. Slave traders later captured her, and sold her to the village she had escaped. The abuses and tortures continued until the day she escaped. Then something with justice above us destroyed the village. I remember the first time I saw her. If it had not been for the fear of my wives teasing me, I would have never worked up the nerve to talk with her. She releases a degree of power and sophistication that give her the power to control situations. I have no doubt that her granddaughters will also the beauty Queens of their lands. This wonderful gift in my hands will create so many Queens, two of which will be vital in saving our people. I ask her, "My life, what happened to those large soft blue eyes you first appeared with?" She tells me that these are part of the stone rock road. They are to ensure that she will be safe. I tell her, "They did not help when you came crashing into the ships well." She tells me, "I truly had you only in my mind. Every thought came back to be her with you. Tonight and tomorrow morning will be the greatest time in my life. Furthermore, ensure you do not use all your energy, as we will still be in unprotected waters. I will understand. I want my Master to be one who cares more about all his wives than just me. Master, I have a confession to reveal." I tell her, "You can wait until after I plant my seed inside you." She tells me, "Then you already know, yet you still love me?" I answer, "Oh Pápain, you do what you must. I just so much wish your life would have been better, and that I could stay with you." Pápain tells me, "The Mystanites do not know I am here; they actually sent soldiers to keep me from you." I look at her and ask, "How did you get past them?" She told me, "This is for our baby, and nothing was going to stop me, any ways some spirits brought me to you.

They told me that it was critical for the survival of our future generations that I bear a child with you. At least, this way, it gives my existence have some value, instead of trash for tramps to spit on." I look at her and start kissing her. I whisper in her ear, "Oh Pápain, if you only knew how hard it would be for me to leave you here alone." She tells me, "Even if you wanted to stay, the Mystanites would forbid it." I confirm that, "I know this, and I confessed that your great beauty was what made this so difficult. Thus, I will actually be among those in this world that do you harm. Therefore, I hope someday you forgive me." She looks at me and slaps me. I look at her, and she places both her palms on my face and starts crying. Why do they always do that? They hit me and then while I am suffering on the outside start crying, which of course rips my insides out and of course has me wondering once again, "What did I do wrong?" This has been an evening in that I have asked this question three times. I have my slapper and crier in my arms. Thereby she cannot escape. I get my rag from the table and wipe the tears from her beautiful black painted slanted eyes. They look up at me as if she wishes she could take back that slap. I asked her, "My special love doves, why you slapped me?" She tells me, "I slapped you because I hate what I am doing to you? I hate myself for doing this. I will want forever to sleep in the sea. Only since my life has been hard, is no reason to steal from you. Cannot you see that I am the evil one?" I tell her, "No Pápain, how can we be wicked in that the things we do are so billions on billions may live someday and not suffer as you have suffered? We both love our future children, the descendants we will never see. I think that we are both trying to blame ourselves for the greatness of our offspring. I rub her belly and then comment, "Two Great Queens from my son who will come from your womb will marry my son from Khigir's womb and create an exorbitant magnificent empire that shall do many great things. Others tell me that the first Queen looks so much like you, although she lost those wonderful ears and eyes. Slave traders captured her clan.

They became slaves and delivered to the other large continent on Lamenta. I can see my son being weak before her. The other Queen came from a traditional Mystanites clan and kept your eyes and black hair." Pápain tells me we must have spoken to the same spirits. I agree with her. At this instant, Gyöngyösi and Abaúj ask, "How are you love birds doing," while interrupting us. I tell them, "I have some great news for you. Pápain has told me about her plan to raise our child alone. She told me. She risked everything so when she receives my seed, it will be with honor and dignity. Now the four of us must keep this a secret until she is proven to be pregnant, then no one will care." Abaúj and Gyöngyösi both hug Pápain as Abaúj kisses her saying, "You truly are the mother of so many Queens through the ages." Gyöngyösi tells her, "History will always portray you as the great mother of the Queens, for no other mother will ever have as many Queens among her descendants as you." I then ask them, "How will history portray me?" They both respond with, "The dirty boy," after that began laughing. We began laughing as Pápain kissed me and said, "Maybe I have found one who will be tortured more than me." The three of us began tickling her saying, "Funny girl." These two wives help Pápain stand up, and I say to my wives, "Who wants to see how a man drinks this strong drink." I have been smart enough to empty it on the floor and refill it with my water. I stood up, drank it straight down and smiled, saying, "Good night my wives." Khigir rushes over to me and asks, "How do you plan for your wives to teach Pápain about Carnal Knowledge?" I told her, "I will be asleep so do as you wish. I am yours always. Ensure she is ready because we will plant my seed in her in the morning and with the help of Abaúj and Béla, it will be successful." Khigir agrees the help from Abaúj and Béla will help in all our future pregnancies. I give her a kiss. She tells me not to disturb poor Hevesi. I smile and walk away. I have learned not to argue with these sweet little things, for loving them is so much better than fighting with them. I went to lay down as Hevesi asks me, "Master, why do you hate me accordingly much?" I go over to her and hold her kissing her cheeks telling her, "Oh my Hevesi; I could never hate you nor could I ever live without you in my life. You know you are my heart love, for no other has lived so much beside my heart."

She afterwards asks me, "Is it true you chugged an entire glass of that poison water?" I ask her, "Honey, how did you understand that?" Hevesi tells me, "Master, we have an amazing communication network among your wives. We perceive everything you do." I ask her, "Will they realize if I kiss you again?" Hevesi confesses, "Well, Master, sometimes you can sneak something by us; however, you had better go fast." I kiss her, then pick her up, and swing her around in my arms. She chuckles. I ask her please to sleep beside me until the wives come in. She asks me if I am scared of the dark and need her to protect me. I tell her, "Oh Hevesi how can I ever hope to keep anything from you, my great protector? Are you going to watch my exposure tonight while I am asleep?" She says, "No way, I have seen that thing so many times in the wilderness when you chase me around trying to stick me with it." I tell her, "Oh Hevesi, I thank you for keeping that a secret and I tell you, someday I will catch you?" She looks over to me then comments, "Well, if you ever were to try, I would run so slowly." I kiss her and say, "Hevesi; you are truly the greatest. Now that I have you protecting me, I am going to sleep." I fall fast to sleep. My wives enjoyed their lectures and demonstrations, as I felt nothing. While deep in my sleep, I felt myself elevate to my room's ceiling and then through it, and soon I was high above in the sky. Next, I began spinning as Lamenta below me disappeared in a ball of fire. I looked around and saw the other world close to us begin to burn. The white lights in the deep dark sky began to vanish. I cried out, "Where am I?" I then began to drop fast back to the surface of Lamenta. I could feel my skin begin to burn. Then, unexpectedly, as if any of this was expected, I began to spin, and slowly I landed on a bright green wavy meadow. As I looked around, I saw only one tree, which trimmed to appear as a ball. I tried to roll in the grass to cool down my skin, which was still burning. I stood up and walked to meadow before me with rested on a small hill. I looked around me and could only see green grass.

I was standing beside the only tree. The sky was a solid blue. There were no clouds. I was alone. No other life was near me. I have never been alone identical to this before in my life. What sort of a place was this? Why am I here? Are my wives safe? Have I lost everything just by closing my eyes? A voice then spoke to me from the ground as I could feel it vibrating through the grass, "Are you the one they call Siklósi?" I looked around and said, "I am he." This voice then spoke once again, saying, "We have brought you here to show you how Lamenta may appear someday, without life and no place that life could hide if it did dare to come to this cursed world. The small hills that you walk on, being actually mass graves, the number buried you do not want to know." I looked around and then cried out, "I thought my Pedigree would prevent this." You have taken me away before I was to finish my work. I did not want to tip my hand if this is some form of evil. Now other voices, this one being female, began to speak, "Siklósi, we have brought you here today, for tomorrow you will do the second greatest deed in your life. We need you to plant your seed in Pápain and return her to the Mystanites with honor and dignity." I then told these feminine voices, as I can talk so much easier to females, "I have already taken Pápain to be my wife. My wives taught her Carnal Knowledge tonight using my body while I slept. As we wake tomorrow morning, I will peacefully and gently place my seed inside her with the help of the air and water elements to ensure a successful pregnancy." Now, two white spirits appear before me and tell me, "That you will do. We have brought you here because Pápain life will be in danger on Mysteria. She must not depart from your ship." I ask them if I leave the ship that would be able to protect her. The spirits tell me, "We will protect her and your baby. Your winds will also help us, with many great spirits around your world." I ask them, "Do you come from another world? If this is true, why are you worried about Lamenta?"

Now many spirits appear surrounding me. The female spirit explains, "Yes, we are from a world exceptionally far from yours. Nevertheless, our world also depends on a powerful empire in which your daughter and son; she creates while destroying the wicked empire. This empire shall grow to become great and will fight much evil until someday a greater empire of good will fight evil. Even in this empire, your daughter who looks so much like Pápain will be a great ruler and a friend of that empire's Supreme Queen Goddess." I tell the spirits that my Pápain will not leave our ship, and that we will take her to her home. They all thank me as the voices tell me to lay down and return to my sleep, for tomorrow will bring more battles. I lay down then once again fall to sleep. I look around me in our dark room and see my Khigir asleep on me. This means all the wives are sleeping except for my night wanderers. I am back with my family again. I reach up and kiss Khigir, as I am thankful not to be alone in that massive graveyard. I drift off to sleep when something strange wakes me up in the morning. I stare straight up and see Khigir with a rag wiping my head. I glance down and ask Khigir, "Where is my robe?" She tells me, "Husband, you will not need it for a while." I look forward to and there is heaven sitting bare on top of me. I ask, "Pápain, why are you on top of me?" Khigir tells us, "Mórahalmi taught us many new ways to get your seed. This way will be better today, as we will be in a big battle soon." I glance over at Mórahalmi and ask her, "Mórahalmi, how do you know so many things about this?" She tells me, "Master, I have seen much data in this simple act and so many possible variations. Do not worry, Master, I will teach you during our private times so that you will perform much better for your wives who have been cheated." I tell her, "Mórahalmi, my wives did not know they had been betrayed until you told them. Now, I will have many gloomy faces on this ship." Mórahalmi, "Oh no, Master, instead you will have many energized and excited wives as many new exciting adventures will lay ahead of them as their Master truly becomes a Master of the Ages." I look up at Pápain and ask her, "Am I within you?" She then looks at me and says, "Hang on dirty boy, the baby making show is beginning now." I brace her, so she does not go flying into a wall, as she tends to do.

This permits her to stay focused, as her sweat drips all over me. How can I complain about something equally trivial as I have soaked my darlings a few times? Her sweat is the same degree of warmth as I can feel it healing my burns from flying through the sky's vast dark space last night. I compliment Pápain, "Pápain, as in all things I have seen you do, you amaze me. This feels so much better than having Gyöngyösi behind me swinging her painful whip. I sure do hope this works honey." Then in an instant, it worked as Pápain expressed her great excitement in the transfer of my seed. She rolled over as we wiped her and me. I told her, "Pápain, you put much work in this." She tells me, "My Master, I have wanted this my whole life. Today, I truly have myself to give to you and your seed." Gyöngyösi tells us, "Owing to the importance of this pregnancy I will know the results within a few minutes." Khigir asks, "Why is this pregnancy so important?" I take Khigir's hands place them against Pápain womb. Next, I tell her, "Her Pedigree will produce the two wives, back to back, for your famous son. I do know you want your sons to have the best wives who beauty can create, and since you created the son, we must have someone to create their great wives." She moves her face beside Pápain's cheek and kisses it saying, "I knew there was a special reason I favored you so." Gyöngyösi comes out of our closet cheering, "You will have a boy, and Pápain is pregnant." Pápain looks at me and thanks me. I tell her, "My Star, you did all the work." Pápain said to me, "Master, it was your power that trusted me to create this gift for us." I kiss her and gently rub her womb. She asks me if I feel anything yet. Gyöngyösi tells her, "Star, it will be some time before you start showing, and most likely eleven turns of the Cegi moon before your baby comes forth." I currently look at Pápain and ask her, "Now that you have the good news, do you want the bad news?" Khigir asks, "What bad news?" I tell Pápain that she must stay on the ship, for the Mystanites cannot witness her, nor can anyone realize you are on board this ship. Your life is in extreme difficulty, because so much evil wishes to destroy you." Pápain asks me, "Who will protect me?" As she asked this question, many white lights appeared in our room. I told her, "Some powerful spirits from other empires who must observe your lineage protected.

You will always be safe." Gyöngyösi adds, "The Great Spirits of Lamenta will also protect you and your pedigrees. Have no fear; we will take you to your home. Khigir asks me, "Are we going to leave here there?" Gyöngyösi tells Khigir, "That is the law of the gods, my Master. However, we will ensure she is safe and happy." Khigir tells us, "This is so cold and heartless." Pápain tells Khigir, "We had to do this so future worlds would live. Any ways, you are leaving my son with me. What more could a hermit as myself ever hope for my Master." Khigir now claims, "There has to be away." I tell her to ensure all the wives understand not to tell the Mystanites, as we do not want to see Pápain suffer. Abaúj tells us, "Pápain, I need you to follow me Star. We have the complete third floor set up for you now. Everything you and your spirits need is there. Now, we need to get this new pregnant woman to her resting bed, and the rest of you need to go to our briefing room, as we have some serious fighting just ahead." I jump up and cheer, "This is the first time I have been able to walk after planting my seed." Béla exclaims, "It was more like a small family of them in their fight for her embryo." Pápain asked, "You saw it?" Abaúj tells her, "Yes, we saw it, I will tell you about it on the third floor, now hurry Star." Pápain stops and asks me, "Master, what name do you want me to call our son?" I told her, "I like the name Papa, so when I hear his name. I will look up to the sky and see the Star named Pápain who came to Lamenta to create the daughters for my son to marry." Pápain gives me a kiss and says, "Oh, now that is consequently romantic. We will name him Papa, so that every time I call his name. I will remember that he has the greatest father ever to live on Lamenta." I contemplate around, and everyone has tears rolling down their cheeks. I tell them, "My wives, there are times when the passion of love is as a sword cutting your actual heart out." We need to prepare for battle.

Chapter 07

Phenomenal disparities

Busier and busier is the tone now. Everyone appears to have a feel for what is ahead of us, although no one comprehends the details at this time. Abaúj is briefing Berettyóú and Móri relating to an extension in their original support mission. They now must help us secure the valuable passenger that we have aboard currently. They will be a plus in our travel, as they can prevent other ships from getting close to us. Csongrád is helping Pápain settle in on the third deck. I understand that they added this floor in the event we were to transport royalty. I wish Abaúj told me, as I constantly try to provide a touch of royalty for our peninsula's most powerful Queen. Always extremely low keyed about events such as these Csongrád would not reside there unless all her family was with her. I could easily believe that she is working hard to set things up for Pápain. Csongrád developed a strong sense of loyalty to Pápain when she discovered she would be the mother of all Great Queens. I could hear Pápain yelling at her to act normal, that she was but a rejected hermit. Csongrád brought a book that had the words of her father who claimed as the spirit had given him. He stressed that she keeps it close to her heart for the spirit told her someday this would be so. She read it aloud, "Sister of the Supreme High Queen, scorned and secluded, suffering a death bounty for her crown, from her hermit womb brought forth the Greatest Queens being from both faces of Lamenta. At separate epochs, they conjugated the Great King, begotten, likewise, of the same progenitors from here many ages before, so the Virtuous Empire could drive evil into the corners of the stars."

Pápain now appeared confused in her mind. She could understand visions of the future, yet to have writings given to the king during the times evil had put aside her as beaten, without clothing on the ground among evil perverts who tormented her. Why did not they help her? Pápain felt to suffer for a cause was worthy, yet to suffer because worthy had absconded troubled her exceedingly. Gyöngyösi came walking into the room and sat down beside her. Gyöngyösi asked Pápain if she believed her to be evil. Pápain arose in anger, telling her, "I swear Gyöngyösi that I would give my life to defend your honor. I would never think such a thing; you are true love from the great spirits of the highest skies." Gyöngyösi told her, "Oh my lovely sister, I understand and know your heart is true to me. I am here to tell you, the way of your thinking now accuses me for causing all the evil among those who I save. You are hurt the spirits of tomorrow will not save you from the evil spirits of yesterday. Is not that your thinking now?" Pápain tells Gyöngyösi, "My sister, I do not realize what is my mind thinks currently. I need your help." Gyöngyösi tells her, "Pápain, which is why I am here. I will explain the ways of the heavens. The heavens, such as Lamenta, have the virtuous and the evil. Evil too many times hides among the virtuous, while the virtuous never draws near the evil, for fear of everlasting corruption. The virtuous always suffers when evil is nearby. In addition, we fight hard to protect those who walk on the lands. Those we save today, we will lose tomorrow. I can never think about what evil has taken, for if I did I would not be strong enough to fight again today. You have suffered my precious innocent Pápain, yet your suffering was not from the virtuous not fighting evil on your behalf. Evil concealed you with great effort. Because they could put one as perfect as you were on the streets as an object for those of greed, lust, and perversion to exploit, they were proving to those things that evil would get what it wants. You were their proof. However, someone from that crowd called out to the heavens to save you.

The virtuous spirits can see only this way behind evil's extreme walls. When the moral spirits discovered what had happened to you, they presented your situation to the great spirits. They salvaged the small girl who pleaded on your behalf and used Berettyóú to blow you deep into the sea, before she eagerly destroyed all in that village. On a sad note, evil found that little girl who tried to save you. They forced the same, if not worsened, punishment on her. Hers worsened because she had no small print of disguised justice to prevent rape. She died only a few years later. I do not tell you this to bring sadness. I tell you this to bring you joy, for the life you currently live was paid for by the blood of the innocent. Now comes your turn, for in your womb is the wombs that shall give the great empire of the virtuous all the Kings and Queens for the everlasting ages. This is how you can fight back the evil, which took from your previous days. We will give you today. You will take back your tomorrow. May I kiss and bless your womb?" Pápain laid back and begged, "Oh please Connubial Angel and my sister. Bless my womb the seed within it shall always favor the virtuous over evil." Gyöngyösi blesses her womb as she had all the other wombs that had my seed growing in them. A bright blue light hovered over her womb and then went within, not to return. Pápain asked, "Is this good?" Csongrád told her that the living blue light had not blessed any other womb with our Master's seed within. Gyöngyösi reveals, "No other seed shall need a living blessing to protect it from evil." Csongrád then commented, "I have seen so many lights dancing around this floor." Gyöngyösi told them, "There is much evil on its way. I must go to prepare for the great battle. Queen Csongrád, I so need you to stay and guard our special gift. Will you do that for me?" Csongrád asked, "How can I defend against the spirits of evil?" Gyöngyösi answered, "Call on your mother. She will help you." Csongrád hugged Pápain and said, "Today, once more I may be with my mother." Gyöngyösi now pulled on the ship's bells and as the sisters came running to her on the steps, she asked them to assemble all and the Master in the dining room immediately. When we assembled, she told us we would have a large battle today.

She then gave each of us a small glass of a liquid to drink and revealed to us that we had to drink this to stay alive. After we drank it, she divulged to us that we would today be fighting again some great forces of evil. We can win while we hold our faith. You cannot fight these spirits with swords, but with your virtuousness. We must unite and stand strong against this deceitful and evil enemy. Our ship now began to raise up from the sea. Gyöngyösi told us to follow her, as she rushed up the steps to go on the deck. We held hands as she said, "Oh wicked spirits, have you not been told that you may not hurt the virtuous." A snarling voice said, "You are not virtuous. These are sex slaves for your evil Master who deceives you daily." Tselikovsky yelled out, "Yes, we are his sex slaves as we have indentured ourselves by the name of the virtuous and serve only our Master until we enter your world where we will fight you until the ends of the ages." Khigir then yells, "We care not that he deceives us, for we belong to him, and if he pleasures to betray us, he obeys our command for him to indulge us as, he wills." The evil voice roars back, "I still may destroy you, for one among you does not love the Master." I looked quickly at my wonderful wives, and in faith yelled out. "A misleading spirit may never harm the spirits of truth. For there is one among us who does not love me, and that one is me as I have given all my love to my wives and have none to waist giving back to me." Gyöngyösi then yells out, "I declare we have defeated you, and command you slowly to return our ship to the sea. I forever will bind you in the bottom pits of the Taeyang Sun." The spirit screeches backward as our ship little by little returns to the sea, Gyöngyösi yells to the rear, "I have that authority, be bound now." The spirit began screaming in pain as it slowly became silent. I looked at my heavenly love and said, "Gyöngyösi, I cannot believe you are actually so warlike." She responds, "When my Master cannot defeat that warrior, what is such an innocent thing such as me to do, my Master?" I tell her, "Hey Gyöngyösi, whatever you did, keep on doing it my love."

We did not comprehend what just happened or, why the words come out of our mouths. I had no idea what I said, and became impressed with myself when I heard the words flowing from my mouth. Tselikovsky came over and looked in my eyes, then told me, "I also did not recognize what I was saying. I believe that they call this spiritual warfare." I ask her how she knew I did not think of those words. She looked in my eyes again, then kissed me on my cheek telling me, "You better stop standing naked in front of me dirty boy." I thought for one instant, maybe, and afterwards I looked at myself and with relief saw that I was still clothed. You can never recognize for sure in this spiritual warfare; I think. Tselikovsky always could read me as she reads the stars in the sky. She is such a wonderful wife to have been sharing our lives. We start to regroup from this first event. I now walk over to Gyöngyösi and ask her, "What is up for us next?" She confesses that there is no way of truly knowing. She hopes that we could shun them back with our binding authority. She now asks me if I notice anything different. I look around and tell her; we are still in the middle of the sea, and no land is in sight. She looks up at the dark-blue sky with no clouds and then scratches her hair. I tell her, "Darling, outside being a chilly morning, I do not see anything to concern your little beautiful head." Abaúj comes up to us and asks if everything is okay. I tell her that Gyöngyösi is acting a little jumpy now. Abaúj then adds to our drama by asking if we had heard Berettyóú this morning. I told them, the only thing that I heard was our Pápain breathing hard to keep her breath. Abaúj looks at me and says, "Master that was not considerate. She was giving her heart to prove her love for you, while you just lay there half bored." I tell them, "I was not bored by any means. I was hanging on, as she had mastered her new skills extraordinarily proficiently. She is fantastically deep in our hearts so never think I would say anything ill of her. I was having fun concerning where I was this morning. Therefore, to be more professional, I was creating my son.

Actually, now that you mention it, I have not seen Berettyóú this morning. Usually, by now on a mating morning, she would have briefed me on what I had done wrong." Abaúj informs me that she would like to get Ajkai and look for her. I tell her that if Gyöngyösi supports it, then so do I. I explain that I do not realize the dangers of this type of warfare, and I would hate to lose such sexy wives as them because of a misjudgment on my part. They each give a quick squeeze on my mid-arm and mild shake of my hand with what they call the 'Khigir Squeeze.' I like it too, less slobbering on the face and allow me to receive a stronger departure modified, salute. As they walk off, Béla comes running to me warning me, "Master, my friends of the sea are gone, something took them away. Other species replaced them. Help me please." The 'Help me please' brought Gyöngyösi quickly to us. Gyöngyösi tells me, "This is too strange, especially since the weather is getting so much colder now. All our previous days began coldly, yet quickly became warm. This day gets colder as it continues." Khigir yells for me to go where she is standing. When I arrive there, she points to some land that is white on the distant horizon. Before us is a white frozen snow wall with an opening that, conveniently, our ship could sail pass. That is strangely convenient for us. I look around at my women who now wear fur garments. Nógrád hands one to me and one to Khigir and informs us, "Master and Master Wife; you need to wear these." We both hug her, and she departs while humming to her sisters. I ask Khigir if she has any explanations. She recommends that we wait until our wanderers return. Continuing, I ask her, "My love, which is wandering now?" She lists the wanderers as, "Brann, Baranya, Béla, Ajkai, and Abaúj." I asked why so many as she explains that our ship sent Abaúj to find some black stone or wood we can burn for heat, as the ship was only prepared for morning fires. She is also looking for Berettyóú, who has never been absent from us this long previously." I hold her close to me and tell her how Grandpa told me a tale of an evil land, which lay to the far south of our sea. This land had so much snow, the land would stay covered for months.

The legend asserts that because so much evil lives there, the cold is greater here than elsewhere on Lamenta. I cannot remember the details. The only thing that I remember is that they were not good. Khigir tells me the Tamarkin temple books also have warnings about traveling the sea to the south lands. One of the primary reasons that they refused to go beyond the seas was because this. It was now time for us to assemble the gang and try to solve this puzzle. I knew that we would not be able to obtain all the answers until our wanderers return. Gyöngyösi begins by warning everyone not to believe what she sees. We are in spiritual warfare and fear or anxiety is prime targets against us, so we must deny what we see. As we are talking, corpulent, slimy insects begin crawling over our table. My wives all push their chairs back. I tap the floor and as my weapons appear, I grab a large spear, flip it sideways, and slam in onto one of these gory insects. I close my eyes, as I do not want splashed with slimy gook. Surprisingly, it did not mush as most insects do; instead, it released a pool of green blood. When looking around our table all the wives are smashing these things. While these creatures do not alter the appearance of their dinner gowns, they are prime targets. I will say we are lucky that our food is not on the table, because I doubt if any of us would eat at this time. Makói screams as one of these beasts bit her. That stupid thing bit the wrong one, because she instantaneously metamorphosed into a ten-foot bear, and is not smashing these creatures, she is eating them. She romps over our table, grabbing every one of them. In the dense spots, she takes her giant claw and in a wiping motion slams them against the wall. My wives hide behind me now, as I tell them, "Do not fear, that is my lovely precious and shy Makói who is without shame saving us, and building up any reserves she may need for hibernation." I walk over and pat her head. She licks the side of my face and then moves to her next target. My heart almost stopped when she moved that big face up against my small head. I had to stand on the faith that what was on the inside of this creature was married to me. When the wives saw this, they began to spread out and move chairs and such to help Makói. My wonderful bear was fighting as hard as her heart would let her.

I finally walked over to her and said, "Makói, you have control now, so please slow down and do not take any chances. Okay, my hidden love?" She shook her head and went back to work, this time cleaning them up slower and much steadier. Brann comes walking in now and asks what is going on in here and whose enormous bear is this. I tell her that giant bear is her sister, and some ugly creatures have attacked us. Brann tells us not to worry, because these things cannot hurt you. When she said this, a few of them, who was hiding in the hallway, bit her. She instantly turned to the fire and burned them completely, then returned to her human form. I look at her and say, "Oh hot momma, do not worry. They do not bite." She smiles at me and reminds me, "My Master; we still have our official consummation before us." I tell her there can be no doubt that she will not cause that to be an event for me to remember. I ask her, "Where is Baranya?" She reaches over and gives me a kiss telling me, "You know; I feel wonderful having a husband to worry about your safe being. She is coming down the steps now. We have some peculiar news for you." Khigir comes over beside me and asks Brann for the strange news. Baranya has arrived now and tells us, "We are in a place on Lamenta we have never before visited. Everything here is cold and different. Strange spirits occupy the sea to the south, and our ship is now heading that way. We found ourselves engaged a few times. Nevertheless, we handled the situations relatively easy. We decided, for safety reasons, to return." I hugged them both and thanked them. They made me so glad when they chose the safe route, because while we stay united, we will have fewer adversaries. Brann, I then queried whether she could search for the ship for any more of these biting insects and burn them, yet not to burn the ship. Baranya tells me they will consume them, in which merely shall ashes will be will remain as dust. I told them, simply the ship, and not any in the sea. Brann asked about the sails. I told her that would be a good thing if they ensured they were not entering danger.

Our war appears only to be starting, and if what they tell me is true; we may have a lot more time to fight than I originally projected. Makói has finished cleaning up our meeting room and is now trying to pass me to go into the hallway. I stand in front of her and explain that Brann and Baranya are searching the ship for any more of the thing and will crisp them to dust. I pet her on her head as she appears to be a little agitated, and I tell her, "Please do not be mad at me Makói. You have cleared their heaviest concentration. Thus, now is the time for you to return as my hidden love. Consequently, you can get your reward hug. I want us to fight this systematically and safely, instead of rushing into the unknown and into any dangerous ambushes, they may have hidden. Now get back into that sexy little body that you tease me with daily, okay me concealed love." Khigir jumps beside me and adds, "Makói, I am so proud of you, and I believe the time has arrived that we tell our Master. You are our hidden love and not just his." She flashes back into her human form and asks Khigir if they can tell me after she gets her reward hug and kiss. Khigir tells her, "Oh yes, this would be fine as you did work hard for both your reward hug and kiss." She steps back and smiles leaving to return to the other wives as we are eagerly awaiting news from our wandering elements. I look around and notice that our Queen is not among us. My wives tell me she is tending to Pápain, her newest hero. After looking at everyone once more I ask, "Where did my angel go?" Tselikovsky tells us that she said someone important wanted to talk with her, and that she would soon return. Gyöngyösi returned within seconds to tell us, "Master; we are in the worst place on Lamenta that can be. We are in the Sea of Death." A few of my wives cling to me as I ask my angel, "What is the Sea of Death?" She continues, "This is a place where devils and wicked spirits live. Some claim the Queen of Evil lives here, although no one has seen as she lives in the underworlds. Her armies will attempt to kill us and drag us as bounty to their underworld havens. The only chance we have until Berettyóú blows us out of here, is to stay together and hidden as best. I am trying to think of a good place to hide when our Queen recommends that we go to the third deck. I ask Khigir to take her sisters to this sanctuary as I wait up here for our remaining wanderers.

Hevesi asks me if she can stay with me. I tell her to go with Mórahalmi and keep her calm as she looks to be worried from this battle. She winks at me and asks Hevesi to protect her. Hevesi asks me if I can succeed without her. I tell her that I will try hard. Makói asks me if she can stay, and I kiss her telling her thanks. I do feel better with a possible ten-foot bear with me, if not only for the fur in the event I fall into the freezing sea around me. She grabs some long knives for us. Gyöngyösi waves bye to Khigir as she nods yes. I tell her to stay close to me and keep those spiritual ears open. I recognize that her help will be crucial if they seriously attack, me, although the main reason I want her with me is so the other wives will not attempt to pry more details out of her and thus create a panic. Khigir takes them to the third deck, a place where I have yet to visit, although I plan to do so tonight after Mórahalmi's consummation, which may have to be postponed, unless her new styles include a battlefield position. I will find out soon enough. Our ship is rocking harder in these turbulent waters. I stare out the steamy fog that rises above the sea reducing our visibility. I almost jump overboard when I hear two thumps from behind me. Trying to catch my breath and my long knife, I spin around to see Brann and Baranya walking toward me. Brann tells me, "Master, a simple kiss, with a large hug, and some begging for my favors would suffice. You need not to lay so immodestly on our deck. You are embarrassing me." Smiling at her, I confess the pleasure I have in seeing her and ask her what she is doing up here. Baranya tells me they were inspecting our sails for invaders. I smile at Baranya and tell her, "You are actually the reason I lay in this helpless unloved manner." Baranya smiles at me and reveals, "Those lines may work on Brann, but for me all you have to do is wink, Master." The things I like best about Baranya is that she gives concise, straight to the point reports, and she understands how to handle humor in such a way that everyone feels better when she is finished with the conversation.

She always uses Brann as the targets of her jokes, yet lately has been more considerate in her blows. This late report and joke are the perfect examples. We left feeling good, as even the way she blasted herself represented nothing more than confessing the depth of her love for me. Brann tells us that we are not alone in this sea, for they heard strange sounds in the air. We walk together, as everywhere I walk my warriors are beside me, to the side of our ship. I comment that earlier today I saw white land in the far horizon. Brann believes what I saw was a large chunk of ice, considering we are far from any land. Gyöngyösi, pulling her fur coat tighter asks Brann if her species ever had any dealings in the Sea of Death. Brann tells her that they avoid any species that live in the seas, because of the water factor. I view down into the water and hear a sweet voice call my name, "Siklósi," then another voice. The voices grow larger as I prepared to jump in the water. Just as I went to jump, three flashes grabbed me and pulled me back onto the deck. Ajkai, Abaúj, and Béla shook me and warned, 'you cannot go into that water Master. All who enter never return.' I told them, "Those things have my mother's down there, for I heard both call for me to save them." Gyöngyösi places her warm, soft palm on my face and asks me why my mother would be in a freezing sea, this far from her home. I told her they could be if these things of the water captured them. Béla tells us, "I have been through these waters and no Lamentan live lives within these seas. They are evil spirits that wish only to destroy you." I told them to step aside for I was going to save my father's wives. I ran to the rail, jump over, and began dropping into the sea. Shockingly, a long dark black wing reached out and grabbed me, putting me back on my ship. The wing afterwards vanished, and the cries of the sea ended. Béla came over to me and sat on me. She was angry and began slapping and screaming at me. Naturally, she had her shield in motion as her tears were splashing over me. My angel surprised me as she told Béla, "Keep hitting him until you wake his foolish brain." Ajkai came over beside Béla, dropped to her knees and began hitting me.

Even my Makói was angry and started kicking my legs. I looked at Abaúj and asked her, "Are you going to hate me also?" Abaúj looked into my eyes and told me, "I am too angry with you and worse of all you hurt me equally important bad." Khigir, who knows when to show up at the worst times came running to us and yelled, "Get off our Master." The wives got up and stood in a straight line. Khigir looked at me, as I jump to lay there with scratch marks and red rashes from their attacks on me. Khigir looks at Makói, who was the senior ranking wife in this attack and asked her, "Why do you hurt our Master?" Makói looked her dead in the eyes and told her, "If he ever does what he did again, he will have six fewer wives, for we will be gone forever." Khigir looks at the wives and asks them to hug her telling them that no one is going anywhere to and please tell her what I did. I am as usual, lying here in pain from the kicks and scratches, and my Master wife is asking them what I have done wrong. They have an unwritten unbreakable code that has as its number one code, 'the man is always guilty.' Am I supposed to listen to the two women who raised me beg from the sea for their lives and ignore it? Khigir has them in a huddle as those perfect female bodies form a solid wall that says, 'No men allowed.' I can only hear crying and sobbing, and words beyond my recognition. Then the huddle breaks and I await their apologies and begging me to forgive them. I will obviously forgive as I proved to myself how much I love them by laying here and taking this beating without hitting them once. My father taught me that. Never hit a woman when they are beating you, because once you do, the beginning of your sorrows has arrived. Khigir walks toward me, as her beautiful golden hair is blowing in the wind, yet has no smile on her face. I do not like this. 'Blowing in the light wind;' could that mean that Berettyóú is in the area. Khigir walks around me, then stops and kicks me in my rib. I tell her, "Very smart, just before our battle begins." She then braces herself on me and begins slapping me without any mercy. She subsequently stands up and tells me to report to my private room and stay there until I decide to be a man and husband. Her shape when she plants her perfect legs is so gorgeous.

The Tamarkins exercise and develop their women for archery. Their developed muscles were to form the perfection in their release of the arrow from their bow, which bonded to their bodies. She locks her female muscles, which maintain the finality of heavenly perfection, and use her eyes and facial expression as the, 'you will do this, or suffer greatly' message. I get up and walk past them as I have yet to see so many cold faces. Even my angel turns her head when I glance at her. These wives are not simply mad. They are furious. They have hate in their eyes, the hate as if I betrayed them and destroyed their lives. I reach the deck's door that leads to my private room on the second floor, counting this deck as the first floor. When I glimpse back, they are still in their 'hate the Master' formation. I turn around to ask one question. They turn their heads from me, and I yell out, "What is wrong with trying to save my mother? Would not you expect your sons to protect you?" Khigir tells me, "If you want to see the fighting side of this Tamarkin keep on talking or shut up and go to your evil room." The reason I waited to speak from this door was, if she released her Tamarkin side to me; I would have a chance to escape. I decide to take her advice and go check into my prison cell. I go into this room and lay on the blankets in the corner. This is the first time I have been put into the, "the doghouse." I touch my rib to see if Khigir had broken it, as I comprehend she can turn her leg into stone when striking. This time that I was lucky as she did not turn her leg into stone and thus kicked me with her normal force. This rib should be better in a few days. The quietness of this room is killing me. I feel so helpless, with us being in a dangerous place and my wives locking me into this room as if I was in prison. I am seldom this alone. No one is around me and those who are appearing filled with hate more than love. What faithfully hurts is that Makói and Khigir slapped me with hate in their hands. To add to the torment, my beloved angel would not allow me to gaze in her eyes. For Gyöngyösi, this is serious. A boat of passion no longer, for whatever they told Khigir to bring about her turn against me, they would tell my remaining wives. What would I do if they took this love from me?

Is the only thing that cares for me, a dark wing above the sea? What was a black wing, which miraculously appeared from nowhere, doing in a place that perfectly caught me? What was that thing and why did it put me back on the deck? If this sea were as dangerous as Gyöngyösi said, then why would it save me? Thinking back to the women I love, what I would do if they all did as Pápain and forbid me to see my children. My door comes flying open and in walks Khigir, Gyöngyösi, and Makói. I am not in a good mood now, so I stand up and turn around refusing to look at them. Khigir tells me to turn around, and I refuse. I stand with my back to them. Gyöngyösi comes up and stands at one side of me while Makói comes up and stands at the other side of me. Both move their heads to in front of me and look into my eyes. Acting as a child once more, I pretend as if I do not see them. Oh, this is so hard because these two are among my most loved and trusted. Khigir now works her way in front of me. I feel sorry for the way her breasts packed so tight with Gyöngyösi and Makói leaving no spare space. I take a step back, and my wives settle into their positions. No matter how psychotic a man I can be, I would never be mad enough to squelch Khigir's breasts causing her discomfort. If I am going to pretend that I do not see anything, then I want something that is dreadful to pretend I do not see. These three is precious loves of mine, and I cannot pretend not to see them for too long. They begin their malevolent torture as Gyöngyösi and Makói each softly grabs an arm and starts kissing my cheek. Oh, how can they fight like that? My eyes come down just in time for Khigir to lock onto my lips giving me one of her tiger kisses. Afterwards, I gently wrap my arms around Gyöngyösi and Makói as they allow themselves to firm up against me. Khigir wraps her arms around my neck, and rubs her nose against mine. She then steps back and casually asks me, "Master, why did you do that to us?" I look at her and ask her, "Precious Dove, what act you accuse me of doing?"

Gyöngyösi tells me, "Master, I warned you about the dangers in the sea and that those voices were not who you thought they were?" Makói then adds, "You dived into that danger without regard to your life. Master, your life belongs to the ones who gave you their lives. You should recognize how much we need and love you?" I looked at each of them and said, "I am sorry about this. I simply think that I love my two mothers accordingly abundant. I could not chance then being in danger." Khigir tells me, "Master, you realize I also love your mothers, as they are my Tamarkin sisters, and the only thing that I have to hold on to from my heritage." I tell her, "You were not there? Any ways, I am back now, since that black wing picked me up and dropped me off on the deck." Gyöngyösi asked me, "Will you trust me that what I tell you if, because I love you so much?" I looked at them and said, "I am sorry. Any ways, this is not over for your mommies, because you will have to take this out of your sons also." Khigir tells me, "Master, we appreciate this and dread if they are as stubborn as you." I gave them each, a kiss and thanked them for loving me again. Gyöngyösi tells us we need to figure out what the black wing was that saved you. They took me out into the hallway, where all my remaining wives were standing. Each got a hug and a kiss. I can understand currently how I shook these women up. Now that they are pregnant, they do not want to see a wild fighting man, they want to see a smart fighting man, one who will stay around. Béla comes rushing to us claiming, "The black wing is from the future and belongs to the Queen of Evil." I asked if anyone understood why this happened. Abaúj tells us, "It means she did not want you to die, as you apparently did, thereby she came back from the future and saved you. We are now on a new course in history." Mórahalmi adds, "We are actually still on the same time line as the change was made in line with our lines, all even so being alive and Khigir's and Pápain's sons changing the destiny of Lamenta. Any alternate line overshadowed by evil would produce drastically different results. We need to get ready for some action, for if this Queen is coming back to save us, then she must not have known what the problem was when we went through the first time."

I motioned for her to step aside and swung the long knife I had into the skull of a black four-winged creature. It dropped, when we saw so many come down the steps. I yelled for Brann, and Baranya to execute their forces. Immediately, two streaks of fire shot slowly up the stairs slow enough to ignite some feathers belonging to our invaders. The wives quickly assembled their weapons, and we began fighting. These creatures had horns that formed a 'U' shooting out the back of their small skulls. Their beaks had a sharp point in which it could use to tear apart flesh. Nonetheless, my wives stood tall and strong. They prefer to unleash a few extra stabs before going for the kill. My wives feel safer when the thing is first injured, using the injured factor to divert enough concentration on defense to project for the kill. I am swinging behind them, trying to ensure that nothing get over them and try to hit them on their blind side. They keep on coming; however, even though we are holding our ground their dead bodies pilling all around us renders it difficult to strike high as they tend to fly more when they are cramped and walk when space is available, that we create by retreating. Even though our expanded knives are doing well, I have Nógrád replace them with long spears, the ones with razor-sharp heads. This will make it easier for us to strike high when we start to push back to the entry door. Somehow, one of them from behind us leaped up and latching onto Nógrád pulled her up and over our front line. Csongrád could spear one of its wings, and it wiggles the thing enough to force it into a charging one who then latched onto Nógrád lifting her up. This time, I flung my spear and got it in the back of its head. Down it went as one of its comrades swooped in from below and grabbed Nógrád now and heading up the entrance. We could see blood pouring from the claw marks cut into Nógrád's skin. I saw the paranoid look in her face. Khigir and Tselikovsky now fired their arrows with direct hits. I grabbed two long knives and worked my way ahead of the wives swinging and spinning of the head as I did to the Hegyközi. Khigir and Tselikovsky continued firing their arrows in rapid succession dropping any of these creatures who were making a dive to get Nógrád.

Within a few short minutes in came blazes of fire burning hard at anything that attempted to strike at Nógrád. I now saw something that amazed me, as if I have not been amazed enough since having my bachelorhood stolen from me by the best thing that could have done this. One of the balls of fire totally enclosed Nógrád. I thought that we might have more problems than I originally thought in that these may not be my Brann and Baranya. This is strange because it cannot belong to our enemy because it burns them without hesitations. The hot flames fly over our front line, yet with us, do deeply involved in our hand-to-hand fighting we can only hope we encounter a friend and not come across a foe. The flame lowers itself to the ground and then dashes back to the stairs joining its partner in burning those things on the steps. I look at Nógrád, and see she has no burns in any manner. She has no additional injuries from the burning flames. I will have to ask my wives how they did that when the fighting slows down, and we once again unite. This is what I found to be so amazing. At first, I was afraid to look at Nógrád, fearing her injuries would be too severe for her life to recover. I ask Gyöngyösi if she knows what these things are that we are killing, and she identifies them as most likely Drápybestie. They can drop pay on my new spear. Khigir and Tselikovsky continue clearing out the Drápybestie so we can push harder for the door. I signal for Gyöngyösi to use her caring hands and check if we can tend to Nógrád's injuries. She is losing blood from the razor claw marks these Drápybestie grips her with to secure her for flight. We finally arrive at the steps when Gyöngyösi tells me we need to get Nógrád to one of the ship's emergency care rooms. I ask her, "Where are these rooms? Abaúj tells me there is a secure one on the third floor and there is a special set of steps from that room you can take to get her to that room." I asked her, "Who will administer the care she needs?" Abaúj volunteers and orders me to follow her. I secure Nógrád, we run behind Khigir and Tselikovsky, who continue to drop the Drápybestie, and through the secret steps, we go.

I lay Nógrád on the table and shake her head some to get a response from her. Her dim eyes looked at me as I tell her, "Abaúj is going to fix you honey; you do what she says, my wife." I ask Abaúj, is there anything else that she needs. She shakes her head no, and tells me to go back to the battle. Through the doors, I go, and pass a window room with some long spears with deadly cutting blades I go, stopping just in time to trip into the wall. I hit the window and reach in grabbing two spears and up to the steps I go, closing each door that I pass through. I fly out the room and close that door dashing to our front line, which is now on the steps. This tells me that Brann and Baranya are having success on their fronts. I jump back on the line; we start pushing harder, and soon we can see the gloomy cold sky once more. The main thing that catches our eyes currently is our completely ripped sails, which are now spread everywhere in pieces. I ask Csongrád if she knows of a way to sail a boat without a sail. She nods her head no, and I then say, at least we only have one injury. We need to secure our deck, so I can get back to Nógrád. Baranya drops in front of me returning to her sample of the perfection beauty. I ask her, "Wife, how were you able to move Nógrád without frying her?" She tells me it is one of their secrets; however, all they did was return to Lamentan and then release false flames as lights around them. We told her it looked so real. Brann drops down as my two, from among fourteen, beauty Queen's return to their Lamentan forms and tells me our ship is secure. I rush back down the steps calling for Khigir and Gyöngyösi while heading to the special room. They are behind me step for step. I take them carefully down the steps to the third floor, closing the doors along the way. We walk in to see Nógrád lying nude on the care table with a transparent blanket over her. Abaúj is working on one of Nógrád's legs sewing a large cut together. She has applied special thick salve over her body. I ask her what the salve is and she signals me to wait just a minute and hands each of her special binding hairs with small needles allowing them sewed into Nógrád's skin. They both begin going to the cuts as Abaúj tells them to spread any excess salve into the wound before sewing.

Abaúj tells me there is an extremely small world of countless creatures who constant crawl over our bodies trying to enter and harm us. This salve kills those creatures and helps the good creatures that live in our body to grow stronger and help heal the wounds. I now ask Abaúj if Nógrád is okay. She tells me that Nógrád has lost much blood and that keeping her in constant care and clean will be our only hope. I look at Gyöngyösi, "Gyöngyösi, if that does not work, will you ask some of your friends?" Gyöngyösi tells me, "Yes Master, for she is also my sister of the womb, and

I need her to help me raise your children." I thank her and then spin around to tell Abaúj that we may actually have plenty of time here as our sails are shredded. She tells me, "Do not worry, for the ship will grow new sails, as we get closer to calmer seas. Meanwhile, Berettyóú and Mori can push the ship's hull such as Berettyóú did when we were fighting the Revived Anfallare." I then comment on how I have not seen our friendly local winds since their alleged return. Abaúj tells me, "They are fighting in the seas trying to neutralize as many of these capturing species as possible, before they reach our ship. Ajkai is helping them by shifting the sky markers, so they lose their direction, and actually charge the opposite way. They will start pushing us exceptionally soon." I ask her if we need to guard the deck, or should we stay hidden. She tells me, "We must stay hidden so that the Queen will only see the dead Drápybestie laying around. She may think that with that many dead, we were also killed and that this is a lifeless ship floating. Once you are safe here, I will blow the dead Drápybestie from the second floor to the deck and point our ship so the natural movements in this sea will be pushing us out of it. In addition, you must ensure everyone go to the fourth floor and take the secret steps back up to this floor. The invaders will follow our tracks and when on the fourth floor, I can seal the open area, poison them, and cram them into our trash storage for release into the sea. Meanwhile, I will remove all our tracks from the first and second floors. Now go get my sisters off the deck silly boy."

As they chuckle, I dash up to the second and first decks and try to collect my fierce fighting women. Our fired-up Hevesi is alarmingly excited. She executed some serious fighting today and as such was extremely happy. She will be making commotion all-night. I could use something to release my anxiety now. I look over, see Mórahalmi, and ask her to join me. Mórahalmi, I think we have some spare time now, so why do not I see if you have been paying attention in those classes you have been confusing my wives all the way through from start to finish. She smiles at me and says, "Surely. You would not want to take me in my current dirty situation as you would not allow me to take you in your unclean situation." I tell her, "Surely, you realize that we have a room where such conditions can be remedied. Now come with me. I tell my other wives to abandon deck and head for the second floor and to avoid the cleaning room for now." They each pass us. Each wink at, and congratulate Mórahalmi, as this is her well-earned consummation. I can only hope this to be true, because with all the confusion lately, I cannot remember. If not, then I will have another show later tonight, since breeding is not at issue and Mórahalmi is introducing different techniques that are not as taxing on me. Watch her have a special killer one for me. If so, I can always jump in the sea. As we almost finish our cleaning, Hevesi comes running in telling us to meet in our meeting room. She also tells me to clean better behind my ears. I accuse her of peeking. She just laughs and says, "Wife's prerogative," and walks out casually. I yell back to her, "Hey little woman; you want your big boy to clean you." She looks at me and tells me, "Only when I marry dirt," and the little fart vanishes. I look at Mórahalmi and comment, "Life would not be the same without that little treat." She agrees and tells me that we must hurry to the meeting. I tell her, "Well, at least we do not have anymore, 'what is under the shirt jokes.' Mórahalmi laughs and stands up saying, "what shirt?" I look at her and say, "As soon as I finish behind my ears you are going to get it." She smiles at me and says, "As soon as the meeting is over, you can try to catch me." I then toss her the charming, clean white silk shirt of hers; she has on her hook and says, "Oh, this shirt." She starts throwing water at me.

Thereafter, out of the door, I go. Now I have to go back to the real world, which does not appreciate my ways. Into the meeting room, I go. Khigir compliments me on having cleaned myself. I tell her that all this constant death around me forces me to feel unclean. She tells me, "And here I thought it was all these unconsummated wives." I remind her how important that this event is in their lives. She kisses me and tells me, "My dirty boy is learning fast." Gyöngyösi opens an old book that she has. She tells us she found this book many ages ago from a race who no longer live. She opens it to show us a drawing of beasts who look like those we killed today with the label Drápybestie. She goes on to tell us that the beasts are a special species of evil that simply guard the Queen of Evil. She has only released them to do one mission, and then they must return to her. We are in her waters or the Sea of Death. The civilization that prepared this book attempted many times to enter these waters, yet any who did never return. They have enough partial maps of their travels and fortunate I have been able to identify the Tamarkin homeland peninsula and a peninsula to the left of it that has a large mountain range. I believe this to be our homeland. At this time, I would recommend that if any among you wish to obtain peace with your creators whom, you do so. I tell Gyöngyösi need to count us out of this game yet, because she forgot two important things. The first is we did not come here. Something put us here, and it must be for a reason. The second thing is that we have the winds to help us out of here. Therefore, we will play dead until our ship gives us new sails, and then we will slip away. I looked at the wall behind Gyöngyösi as it began to change colors. I told her to come to me now. We saw the wall open, and images begin to appear within. Before us were many buildings as a large fire burning between them. People were in the streets crying. We could see people leap from the highest windows in the buildings and land on the ground dying from their smashed bodies. It was hysteria to a painful magnitude that many of my wives closed their eyes and cried.

The fear of this image magnified itself when these people began dropping out of the picture and laying on the floor before us burning. Then one begged for some help. Gyöngyösi motioned for everyone to stay still and say nothing. A few more dropped in and cried for help. We just stood here and watched them burn. This continued for about one hour. I was beginning to get sick as many of my wives had already sat down and buried their heads in their arms. When two children came flying through the picture burning and begging for help, Khigir went to execute her move. Tselikovsky grabbed her holding her, and Abaúj took the air from her sounds so the sounds would not move and vanished in place. That was too close to a call. Then, as fast as the painting appeared, it vanished. Gyöngyösi motioned for everyone to remain silent. Soon she gave the all clear. Khigir rushed up to the wall and touched it, feeling only the cold from the hallway. I asked Gyöngyösi what it was we just witnessed. She tells us it was a Painting of Bereg. These are special portals straight into the prisons of the evil dead. I questioned her, "Can all those people be wicked?" She confesses, "Master, there may be a few innocent ones who were pulled in by mistake, such as we would have been if Khigir's words hit their ears. Once you are in, it can take a lengthy time, some as many as one-thousand years that we know about, before they can rescue you. And those years are long years." I asked her, "Why did we have to be quiet?" Gyöngyösi tells us that, "The Paintings of Bereg can only hear, they cannot see from the other side, as we could see and hear. Once they hear, then they can send in the capturers who will imprison those who are here. These collectors cannot enter unless a sound is made, and if they enter, and see a white burning candle they will vanish into eternity." Abaúj tells us that our ship has placed these candles in many rooms on the second deck and made some noises, thereby destroying many paintings. We just could not put any on this place in danger the Queen would be watching." I look at them and ask, "How can you women comprehend so much?" Mórahalmi answers saying, "If you stopped collecting all our 'billion-year-old virgins' young man, maybe you would not have to ask that question." I shake my head and look at her, "You may be a billion years-old honey. However, this is the time for your medicine. Tselikovsky holds her." My Tselikovsky grabs her without blinking an eye, and then I grab her instantly. Mórahalmi asks Tselikovsky, "Why did you do that?" Tselikovsky tells her, "The time for you old ladies to learn about some of the good things in life has arrived." I kiss Tselikovsky, thank her, and tell my wives, "Hold down our ship women, because our ship is going to rock for a while." Hevesi asks me, "Master, at a time like this?" I tell her, "What can I do my little love. She is so persistent." I swing her into my arms and hold her as I would a baby and say, "Over the threshold we go." Moreover, we did go, and get some well-earned rest and relief. She surprised me in that she did not take the control I originally thought she would. She became incredibly submissive. I asked her if she was all right, and she told me, "My Master, this will only happen once in all my existence, and I want it to be totally from you my Master. This is my unique time to serve you my love. I lay my gift before you." I have been down this special road, so I first told asked her, "Please forgive me, because I do not know all those things you were teaching my wives since I am simply a Lamentan. The only thing that I have given my wives is my passion. No two people will have the equivalent passion, nor will their intimate meetings ever produce the identical passion. Love pulls our passion forward. We have ranges for our passions. Certain times, such as this, I will want to have a special passion pulled at my heart. Today, I wanted that passion from you. Sometimes I just want to escape from everything and be with someone special. I am blessed to have fourteen, someone specials. As we learned today, special people may be in our weakness lost or hurt.

I was weak and jumped for my two mothers, not believing that anything could ever reproduce their voices, Khigir almost lost us today in her love for children, and Nógrád, will suffer with her cuts, which will only get to verify with the Edelényi that she does not belong with us. I can see that with so large, a family as this, which we will have to learn to change practically daily. You have some wonderful ideas, as that last child, I fathered was one of my easiest mating attempts. You are the mother of passion. I can feel your passion with Hevesi's courage as an excellent combination to have in our family. We have also added, for a short time Pápain's endurance. Do you understand what I am saying?" Mórahalmi reveals to me, "You are saying that when passion mixes with love, it causes total confusion. I am saying we can debate that later, we need to build you stronger and fresh again and get back to this war." That is what we did. It would still take me a lifetime to learn how passion and love could mix sometimes and not match the other times. Today was lesson number one; 'when an angel tells you, something is not what it appears, then listen to her. Do not let your love for a part of your life blind the passion for it, or let your passion become weapons for that which wishes to destroy you.' It reminds me how Grandpa would always tell me not to load the bow for your enemy. As we go to leave the room, Dabasi comes running to me telling us we have some more trouble. Mórahalmi looks at me as she gives me another kiss and says, "You are a Master, because you could not have timed that any better my husband." I wink at her then at a confused Dabasi and say, "Your time will be soon, angel of the deep sea." As we rushed to the meeting room, Khigir compliments us on how fast we dressed. Mórahalmi responds, "Oh; I did not know my success was based upon the restore time, next time I will have to work harder than, sorry Master." I gaze at Khigir and tell her, "Precious Dove, how can you expect them to compete with you?" Khigir will voice her concern and then drop it immediately. She got it off her heavenly chest; therefore, she is good to go. She jumps over beside Mórahalmi, holds her hand, and asks her how everything went. They talk about how her face paint held out. Okay, maybe I was born of an opposite gender. Abaúj leads this meeting by telling us that the winds have reported massive waves of once believed species of torturous and deadly creatures called the Bonyhádi or commonly labeled as the finger people eaters. Brann and Baranya are at sea burning them as they fly toward us. Ajkai is painting the sky and ground from horizontal to vertical, so they fly high into the sky and exhausted drop to the sea. I will be leaving and poisoning them in the air. We will be able to stop most of them; however, some will penetrate through our lines. I must go now, as Gyöngyösi will conclude my portion and share her section. Then in a whiff, my wife was in the air and had vanished. Gyöngyösi tells us that these things have a head with no mouth, a rib cage similar to ours; however, that is where the resemblance ends. They use the lower bones of their rib cages to stabilize their prey so they can release their deadly acids on them for digestion. Their arms also serve as their legs and the giant Lamentan style hands are their primary weapon. Their hands will collect or gather its meals for chemical digestion. If you can cut one hand off, the creature will fall. However, be careful around any who is still alive since they can release their digestive chemicals and retrieve you with any attached arm. Khigir and

Tselikovsky will stand back to back on chairs higher than we stand and fire their arrows in the Bonyhádi's chests. We will fight from the deck with all entrances to our lower decks closed. We cannot afford to let one in as they hide during the day and will digest our heads at night, and once they digest all the heads. They will then consume all remaining carcasses. The remainder of us will fight in a circle formation protecting Khigir and Tselikovsky. Hevesi will roam from inside the circle filling in overwhelmed areas. We kill by ramming our long bladed spears into their rib cage, do a half-turn, push the thing down, pull out your spear, and jab the one behind him, repeating this process as best we can. By piling them in the open areas of our frontal zone, we force them to concentrate their attack zones. I have given each of you a long knife that you can use if we are overran. Hevesi will give the retreat call and in doing so, we will drop below deck and allow my sky wanderers and elements, to finish for us. The time to fight is once more upon us. Remember one drop and your work is finished. This battle could be dangerous in how boring and repetitious it will prolong. This battle does not have the flare as the others, in that we must jab, push to the side until they started grabbing them from behind and throwing them into the sea.

My wives were steady and no one overrun. The anxiety of knowing one drop from these things began to release their digestion liquids, upon hitting them, and while dying. Fortunately, our deck has a marble stone floor, and liquids instead began to eat their later invaders pointed fingers. Khigir and Tselikovsky could alleviate any potential for a position overrun by trimming the excess for that zone. Their awful creep hands wobble before us. What kept this battle in our 'hands' was the way they congested themselves so easily. We could not let them near us for fear of their digestive poison touching us. Soon my wanderers returned victorious as always, so far. They finished off anything around our ship, and we went to the fourth deck, then back up the secret steps to our dining room. We were hungry, and the food went down so fast. Another of the Paintings of Bereg appeared on our wall. This painting was different in that it was actually a window into the sea, a sea with clear water. The center of this vision rendered a large white clamshell. Inside the clamshell was a little girl. She had long black hair and a terrified expression on her face. She had her body crunched in such a way as being prepared for the clam to shut again. In front of her was a school of long wiggly miniature snakes. She did not appear to be worried about them. The sea floor behind her looked fictitious, almost what I would expect to find in an Edelényi children's book. The little girl cries out, "Khigir, will you play with me. My friends have abandoned me. My mommy is gone." Tselikovsky grabs Khigir's mouth as Abaúj walks quietly to her and breathes some gasses that put her to sleep. We were so glad we did that because the next thing that happened was almost unreal. A Bonyhádi sprang up from behind and released it digestive poisons on her and then using its hands leaped as if a frog to a safe distance to observe his meal being prepared. I had a spear in my hand and almost released it when Abaúj jumped in my arms and kissed me. This was not your normal a kid is being digested in front of you appetizer kiss. This was one of her; 'time to go to sleep' kisses.

Gyöngyösi told us later that the sound of the little girl begging for help and in so much pain, they slowly exited, the room and waited for the picture to run its course. Gyöngyösi tells me that she is afraid of Khigir and me, as we become weak during these evil visits. The wicked ones directed the next image unerringly at me. Nevertheless, it was at the wrong time. We celebrated Béla's private consummation in front of the family, with all present waiting for a chance to find something that they could yell out silly boy or dirty boy. Béla wanted to be with everyone for this event as she claimed that she was still not familiar with these Lamentan style bodies and thus did not feel it important to conceal anything from her sisters. When anything inside her happened, she wanted her sisters to know it, so they could explain to her what it was and how she should respond. This actually caught, me off guard, as I am copulating with an adult beauty Queen, and my other wives are telling what just happened. This is being a virgin among the absolute stars. All women on Lamenta are virgins when they bond with a Master, as the punishment can be as severe as burning. The lack of being a virgin is not the issue; the confessing to be a virgin, when in actuality not a virgin is the issue. Most grooms have the woman cast from their village and take her next sister, who also does not have to be a virgin. She must; however, confess to not being a virgin and the groom can accept her or move down the time to the following sister. There is no punishment for claiming to be a virgin when the woman is still chaste, as some do hope, the groom will elect to search elsewhere for a bride. Therefore, many strange rules that are consistent with village to village add to my idea that we went our separate ways from a dying, unfortunately primitive empire. Any ways, back to the family initiation of Béla, she figured things out fast. She discovered how she wanted this activity to proceed and at what intensity. Soon my wives were chanting, "Silly girl, and dirty girl." I was secretly wondering how I could survive this.

Béla gives an appearance of a petite and gentle blonde-haired person that is a blend between Khigir and Tselikovsky. Nevertheless, during private times, she is going to behave more like Csongrád and Makói who enjoy being further in control. I am not going to argue with a reigning Queen and have my head chopped off or a potential ten-foot bear. We seem to flow cooperative during our special meetings. Béla must have taken what Mórahalmi taught her to heart. She is smoothing out the rhythm and keeping me in the ball game, thankfully. When she finally tired, which I believe was one-half a breath before me, her sister wives gave her an ovation. I learned one thing about this event, and that is the next time we will be private with Mórahalmi fine-tuning her enthusiasm. I give her a wonderful hug, kiss, and thanked her, in front of all the wives, for having mercy on me. Her performance used all her gifts the way creation, intended them to function. I appreciate that all is fair in love and war. I wonder if that includes love during war. I do not realize how much I can give her as credit or our ship bouncing in this continuous raging sea. The Suns have departed the shy a few hours ago, yet have an almost ground level beam of dim light revealing this dismal sea. Gyöngyösi tells us this is because the way the Suns now aligns with the bottom part of Lamenta's ball. The wives' pair of in their sister groups when an extremely temporarily bright light blinds us. Fortunately, its initial flash was in a wave, and we had our eyes closed for the next wave. This light wave can rock our ship, which combined with the whirlpool waters is all we need now. I follow my wonderful Gyöngyösi up to the stairs, and yell for us to hurry. I run up to her and hold her as if I would a baby, especially since she is so petite. She asks me what am I doing and I tell her, "I am protecting you from this great danger." She puts that soft angelic palm on my face and says, "Silly boy. We are not in danger." Then I tell her, "Guess I got me a free hug." She kisses my cheek and tells me, "Toss in a free kiss also." We examine our marble ship's deck, which now extends by way of a short the width of the ship stone highly decorated walkway. We witness a large four-column pavilion with a horseshoe-shaped top.

Three steps along our walkway elevated it. A special stone walkway proceeded through the second and third columns. A large world, larger than our Suns combined, rested in the sky above us. I ask Gyöngyösi, "What is this?" She tells me that we have a Gateway of Bihar. I then ask her to explain. My angel does not know for sure why this is here, but tells me that they only belong to spiritual kingdoms of the virtuous. We do not need to worry much. They most likely are sending messengers to give us some information. I looked ahead now and saw a large shining Diamond coming toward us. Projecting from it were eight white beams that pointed in all directions. They also covered, everything with peaceful shades of blue. Gyöngyösi discloses she had yet to see a Diamond this large, and that this must be from another spiritual empire much larger than ours is. She does not recognize all the special emblems scrupled and how strong the stones held on the top of this whirling sea below us. I understand from old accounts that greater spirits developed the Gateways of Bihar deep the flash into the future of other dimensions or the heavens that coexist among us. This permits them to jump back and repair events that turned out disastrous.

I cannot see how your seed would develop any affect on other dimensions. Truthfully, the words I speak are coming from a part of my mind that I do not know. These activities are even beyond the cycles of Mórahalmi. The Diamond grew and soon consumed us. We could feel our ship floating calmly in what looked like sparkling lights. Now, one light came from each of the four sides, and another light came from the middle. Each light has a beam on each side. They moved toward us and stopped in the pavilion where they materialized. We prepared for an invasion by some strange life form unknown to our world by pointing our spears. To our wonderful surprise instead of hideous geeks, standing before us were five women. They did not appear evil or violent and wore clothing we had never seen. They had to be from far away and maybe even another time. Gyöngyösi walks up to them, gives her courteous bow, and looks at them. They are all staring at me, as I am trying to duck in behind Makói who decides to shrink about one-foot. Gyöngyösi looks back at me, and motions that I join her. I grab Makói who at first lightly resists. She now tags tight beside me. Her steps match mine as mine are shorter and hers are longer. We arrive beside Gyöngyösi who tells us to fall to our knees. We do so, and then the tall blonde woman in the middle who at least six inches taller walks forward. They are all a unique kind of beautiful. This is an ambitious, energetic independent style of powerful beauty unmatched in all creation. The tall blond with a two-inch thick Diamond-studded headband that have four large clusters of gems also attached to it begins to walk forward, yet stops as she notices Khigir, Hevesi and Tselikovsky come running in. Gyöngyöis motions for them to stop, then she points behind me and the three of them slowly walk up behind us, and bow. All my remaining wives join us. These five visitors are dressed in such advanced fashion, and style that my wives are making no pretense of resistance. They are simply staring at these women as if they came from some heaven, which most likely they have. Their blond leader had a shoulder less purple and white gown, with many borders, emblems, jewels sewed throughout it. The opening in the front provides only a breast cup for the sides of her breasts, exposing much skin, which provides Hevesi a chance to give me a push and a slap on the side of my face. At first, this startles some of these 'goddesses' yet the one with green and purple hair chuckles quickly then regains her composure. Now that Hevesi has punished, I may enjoy this view liberally currently. They all wear highly decorated necklaces and such great stones embedded in them that they must identify a rank or position. She walks forward to Gyöngyöis and gives her a white dove. Gyöngyöis thanks her for giving such a considerate peace offering. This woman identifies herself, "I am Agyagosszergény, head of the 5000 daughters of the Supreme Queen Goddess Lilith, who, as our mother, has sent us to visit with you this hour. We have not come to hurt you, as so many in this dispensation desire to do this in our stead. Our work is a mystery. The one who has sent us back to save you is the same who is trying to destroy us. You may all stand now and approach us.

You may not touch us, for we are from a different dimension and so far distant age. With me, I hold the arch-daughters, each commanding 1250 daughters of Lilith. The first, who is holding the Sword of Justice for our mother, is BodrogköUzi. Beside her stands Cserszegtomaj. On my right side stand Sásdi and Adásztevel. We enjoy a few minutes in which we may talk before we must request that you allow us to board with you on your third deck. You may ask us some questions. My wives start raising their hands as Agyagosszergény points at, and tells Mórahalmi to speak, identifying her by name, "As I am sure we will talk about the details later. I just want to be aware of where you got your wonderful outfits? In addition, are you goddesses? Lastly, are there any titles we must call you?" She begins by telling us that fashions change so fast that when one begins, they instantaneously provide it for all. As you seem to enjoy, markedly my father, how generous our outfits are, notably BodrogköUzi. There is no shame or glory in how open-minded a gown or assorted feathers may be. We possess no powers, except those that they award for missions. The purely thing, which unites us, is our mother, as we hold different fathers. We control no titles, except daughters of Lilith and Bogovi her husband, as ironically, they remain the only married gods. I will take one more question, and then we must continue our meeting under a security device I control. Hevesi laughs and says, "I think your mother had just a few more partners than the dirty boy here." Agyagosszergény looks at me approving my question as she remarks, "I can guess what this question is, and I told you the truth when I said you are my father, was, is, and will be. As my father, you may touch me as family blood overpowers any dimensional barrier." I look at her and say, as I hug her, "How is the possible? Did I ever more find out you are my daughter and did I do as a father should for you?" Agyagosszergény tells us, "The first time history ran; none of the fathers were ever notified. You are the second father ever notified, as your son was the first father to discover his daughter with Lilith, who we call Atlantis, as she also contains your blood. I understand that each thing I say is creating more questions. I will summarize; my mother collects the seeds of men while they sleep.

She then plants those seeds in her and reproduces the daughter. She did this 5,001 times. I was able to use spiritual tool to trace back the life of my father. You may deny or refute me. This is your right." I asked her, "Either way, when you are finished, you must go back?" Agyagosszergény revealed to us, "That is the way of things; my choices were to return, tell or not tell you. I may have done a wrong thing. This was such a limited and unexpected window. Returning to our mission, time has already progressed the first time through. We have discovered a small group of evil demons who are returning to key points back in time and altering history. This is the inimitable, their zenith target, for here they prevent the great empire from ever beginning. She looked at Pápain all five circled her and said, "You are the progenitor of Lablonta," afterwards looking at me saying, "With your help of course." Then Adásztevel, with her peaceful, shy look, blue hair, in a skimpy golden small top with bottom uniform, smiles and says, "You both are identical. She so greatly wanted to join us; however, our mother loves her too much to risk her while with us. We tend to get overexcited sometimes." Hevesi comments, "Wonder where you got that from."

Agyagosszergény, "We must get inside now, because the eyes of my mother will quickly be on us. And as for you, never hit my father again when I am here." She said this with a firm, tough voice. The humbleness in her eyes displayed many concerns over me. I stuck my hand up and asked, "Will you help this trodden beaten old man may yet stand once more. That I may hug you as my soul departs signing in the heavens." Then the fiery red-haired one named Sásdi laughed, saying, "I love those lines. I can see why you retain so many bubbly little hearts around you begging for but a touch too warm and excite their souls as they forever crawl calling you Master." Khigir laughs, saying, "Can it be possible that my Master has two daughters among the five that stand before me?" Agyagosszergény speaks, "We are going to your ship."

I did not even blink my eyes and we were in our large dancing room in which we barely only saw the floor. Everything around us is overflowing with a thick light white, blue, and purple smog. She continues with her stare, that looking somewhere else, look and says, "All who are one this ship must be saved, for even the loss of one could have a ripple effect that would destroy your family." I am standing beside her with my arm over her shoulder, a position that she transferred me to this spot. The other sisters stand close behind us. We are facing my wives, a position I am not completely comfortable with, having the only exception of being in a better position to protect my wives. I help break the ice by saying to our new protectors, "Young children, have you ever seen a group of the most beautiful woman assembled in one place before in all your journeys? Cserszegtoma, who has firm, strong eyes and a leaning forward posture that strongly suggests she is a thinker, answers calmly and with sincerity, "No Master, we have not. When we were watching you from the safety of our future mother's loving empire, Agyagosszergény received many serious compliments on how success her father is at attacking the Greatest women known to exist at this time. You remain the only flesh dweller to have a positive wife, the glorious Mórahalmi and negative wives. You also are the sole flesh man to control the four wives of a world's element, and we are not even going to mention the negative element in the dreamy Dabasi." Khigir rushes up to Bodrogközi to invite her to sit on a chair hidden in this smog. As Khigir approaches Bodrogközi, Sásdi leaps between them and warns, "Please do not touch the Sword of Justice, or it will destroy you as it does complete galaxies. In fact, our mother would be dreadfully angry if she knew we borrowed it." Tselikovsky walks up and opens her arms to Sásdi, who peacefully falls into them." Tselikovsky thanks her for saving her sister's life. I was surprised that Sásdi, who is the most warlike in the gang, with tough, firm legs protruding down from her solid strong waist, fell so easily into Tselikovsky's arms.

I always believed that only I suffered from this weakness. The rest of my wives are now invading in their sisters of the wombs groups, sit these young women in comfort, and turn this room into a room of chatter. My wives cannot attract my daughter who stands firm beside me with her arm locked with mine. I sniff her hair and land a few smooches on her head saying, "I hope you know how much I always longed to raise my children in my home. I currently suffer with the anguish of living so far from my Pápain who she begins my pedigree through Lablonta. I hate that I am here talking with you now, knowing you will leave me incessantly." In an eerie hand motion, she bonds her hand in my face and turns me to her eyes where she says, "Oh, silly boy, who said I was leaving forever." Khigir and my wives' stand up clapping saying, "Even the daughters of the goddesses recognize the silly boy." Even I laughed at this one. My daughter spoke it so innocently and within a design to ensure that, my mind knew what she was saying. Agyagosszergény said to me with a sad look, which her droopy eyes can project with ease, "Did I say something that shames you my father?" Hevesi locks her arm on the other arm of Agyagosszergény and says, "No, child. You proved to your father how much you truly love him and want not to understand only him but to be a part of his life." She looks at Hevesi and asks her, "I hope you were not offended when I told you not to hit my father, I was just not strong enough to face the dilemma of seeing him hurt." Hevesi now releases Agyagosszergény and jumps into me, gripping me with her wilderness arms and legs and starts kissing me like crazy whispering to me how much she loves me. Agyagosszergény asks Hevesi if she did something wrong. Hevesi tells her, "You did nothing wrong. I just faced the same thought that you feared. I enjoy his daughter in my womb now, and I have dedicated the remainder of my life to bearing him four more daughters. I could never exist in peace knowing their father suffers." Brann now asks us, "Are we going to formulate our battle plan, and be briefed on what our situation is?" Sásdi, whose red hair is brighter than Brann's scarlet hair tells us, "There is no battle plan, reminder, one lose we lose it all. We will conceal you in this ship as your winds cautiously get you out of this graveyard sea.

All of us who stand before you now at one time lived as creatures of evil in this sea. We would try to flush you out of these waters; however, our mother would catch us. The only way that we can defeat her, is if for her to believe Khigir and Pápain to be dead. She always tries to spare the males as much as she can." Makói asks, "You speak of your mother as being both evil and good. Which one is she?" Sásdi answers, "When we were voting on our favorite wife, I selected you, as you are my hero with your power and control over it. So many of your pedigrees became great warriors and created so many great legends. Our mother is now the Supreme Queen Goddess of her empire for the virtuous, as Gyöngyösi calls it, as her spirit controls our entire universe and the universes of neighboring dimensions. She collects sisters as your husband collects wives." Nógrád started coughing and laughing. Afterwards, she apologizes and confesses, "I thought she was going to say her mother collects daughters as our husband collects wives." Our new bonding group laughed at this one. Agyagosszergény secures herself firmly on my lap showing that she will not be sharing daddy for this event. Not one of my wives who is expectant mothers will dare to move between this child and her father. We have so often had lengthy deep discussions on my involvement with our children. They are tremendously concerned about this, to the degree that they always try to mention the child in their womb as mine, pushing that life is mine. I, on the other hand, having enjoyed a balance childhood with strong grandmothers and mothers appreciate the importance of mothers in a child's life. My mother's greatest difficulty was in preparing me to deal with potential mates and their importance in a future family life. My father and uncles and the other elder men of our village always told me not to touch them. Therefore, I would not touch them, and since I was not going to touch them, did not want to be around these little tattle tales. I remember how shocked I was when I woke up in a world where I was supposed to touch them and when I say touch, I mean to forget what my father said not to touch and to start touching.

I can never forget how proud my mother was when Khigir told her how I had chased her down and defeated her, and made her, while in her helpless condition, kiss me. Which of course, the opposite is what happened, just enough to where I could not claim we did not kiss. I told my wives, our children would know how we expect for them to court, especially considering that most will be with the Edelényi, which forces us still to behave as diplomats and abide by their host customs. Ajkai jumps from her seat and tells everyone to look as she comes up and grabs Agyagosszergény face and my face lining us up sideways. She reports, "Look hour their nose and chins are the same. Khigir says, "Look at their necks," as she holds both of our necks in line. Sásdi and Cserszegtoma look at Agyagosszergény and say, "We can see it, and they are the same. Hevesi pops up from below shouting, "Look at their wrists." I then yell out, "I am so glad she is a female, and I am a male before you continue your comparisons in more detail than I am prepared to reveal." Khigir says in full confidence, "No one can deny she is your daughter." Agyagosszergény, with tears running down her soft cheeks rests her face against my chest. I ask her why she is crying. Adásztevel tells me in her soft sensuous way, "She is discovering who she is. She can look at you and see what is in her. The only thing that we have from our mother is our large breasts, perfect waists, buttocks, and legs. She demanded that our bodies contain the perfection of female beauty. She allowed for so many of our other features to come from our fathers, so we would not all look the same." I hug Agyagosszergény and explain to her, "Honey, in this time of my existence. My first children are forming in their mother's wombs; thereby I also am discovering these things. This is exciting, I must confess. Now show me your wrists." She holds hers up next to mine as her sisters admire us. Agyagosszergény yells out to us, "Look everyone. I have the most beautiful wrists in all creation." My wives looked at her and cheered in agreement.

I felt so excited that another person to boast a feature that resembled mine accordingly would enjoy the honor. Especially when I consider the child walks and lives with goddesses. I could see something sinking in her other four sisters' hearts. We naturally are so thrilled when something wonderful happens to a loved one, yet eventually not having that same wonderful thing can open loneliness and sadness. I remember them telling us they may not search for their father and the only reason their mother permitted this search was that without it, her mother would lose her. My daughter looks at her sisters and subsequently looks into my eyes. She then brightens them slowly shaking, her head up and down, then reading me as one would a giant lion that was preparing to attack smiled. That is when it hit me. Therefore, without a heart to refuse her shook my head okay. She leaped out of my lap and kissed me in hysteria crying out, "Thank you daddy, and thank you so much, you are the Greatest daddy in all creation." Her sisters looked at her and knew what had just happened, and they all rushed to me also thanking me. Khigir pushed her way into the group and start plowing Agyagosszergény with kisses, saying, "Oh, will you please tell the gods to give me a daughter such as you." Agyagosszergény then told her, "I am sure my mother would not get too angry over you being my mother when visiting my father. Would you enjoy that?" Khigir afterwards asked Agyagosszergény, "Your mother is an enormously powerful goddess, so when you say, 'would not get too inflamed over you being my mother' what do you mean by too angry?" The five sisters after that proudly boasted, "She means this is not something that we cannot handle." Baranya unexpectedly yells out for Tselikovsky to hurry up and release her twins because she wants some children to play with immediately. These daughters have my expecting mothers excited, as before us is a true blood relative. I must even confess how agreeable this is to have such four powerful weapons, who, upon first meeting stood strong and convinced. They are still tough and confident; however, our family has now vested in them. They will not escape the love of our blanket. One look at each and the evidence are apparent that they belong high in the heavens. Speaking of the heavens, I look and see Gyöngyöis sitting as an outsider watching everything. I motion for her to come to me. She comes near me, falls to the floor, grabbing my leg, and asks, "How may I serve you my Master?" I look at Gyöngyöis and say, first by standing up and in front of me and tell me what is going on inside the heart I love so much. Agyagosszergény tells me that they have done much evil to the children of Lamenta as their mother kills so many, every night. We indubitably chased the Connubial Angel so many times, and as in my burdens, I must tell you, we will chase you again. The only consolation, I can give is that when the final numbers are finished, the number we saved will be as the stars in all the skies for each one we hurt. We came from evil and defeated evil. Never under any circumstance, help us. We will continue to advance in our ambush skills. While you are an angel of justice, we will give you this Sword of Justice, and you may kill each of us, as you desire. You certainly paid a high price for that gift. Take your gift or if you desire, we will take our lives if you so command." Gyöngyösi opens her arms and begins crying rivers of tears, sobbing, and "I will never kill my Master's daughters." She then put herself among them as they, each hugged her. I have never seen Gyöngyösi this upset and confused before. Sásdi tells her to let it all out, that her mother will help heal her insides for only the gods can heal this pain. A golden light came down on her, and we saw ugly black creatures come up out of her and into these lights. These creatures burned and then vanished. Gyöngyösi awoke and turned to me saying, "Master. I feel so much better now." She then told everyone, "Truly, I have been to a stone sea in the heavens. I saw so many angels as they lined up in rows and was from the sea to the endless sky. A man told me that this was the throne of the great one, and that the number of armies of angels, here is more than the numbers of the sand in all the seas of Lamenta. He took my hand, and we floated over so many beautiful worlds. I saw huge balls of many-colored lights. The man revealed to me, these spirits have powers, which are too boundless, for none has seen their feet or their head. We cannot identify how to measure their abundance. Then a mighty force came to take me to the great throne where there sat upon the chair the most powerful.

This force said, "Never look at the one who sits upon the throne, for her power is too great and will destroy you. She then said to me, "Gyöngyösi, forgive me for the suffering. I have caused you. Look around you and see the multitudes of worlds that serve me. I began to look around as all the angels and spirits vanished. Every bit that I could see was pure white ubiquitously for the number of worlds was too great for me to comprehend. She who sat upon the throne said to me, "Remember, I have defeated evil everywhere I have gone to, and will go. Now return to our 'silly boy' and serve with my daughters. Tell your Master a stranger comes for him soon in the night." As I blinked my eye, everything vanished and in the darkness, I was alone. Just seconds previously, all was so dense yet now all are sparse. Thenceforth I saw the face of the one they called Lablonta, yet I called Pápain as their faces were as one. This great one said to me, "Please forgive me, for I asked the one who set on the throne to honor me by allowing me to serve you to return you the world I began on. She then dropped me into a great sea. I thought, if I am her friend, what she does to those she does not favor. Next, I could feel so much love and mercy." I felt myself in a strange lake where I could merely feel only wonderful. I opened my mouth so this sea would also take the inside me. I could feel it soaking through me, every part of me, so no part remained for pain and hate. I saw pain, and hate leaves me as ugly sickly beasts. A great angel captured them and threw them into a fire to burn. He tells me these evils burn to become destroying, since they do not burn for eternity. The great one desire that all evil vanishes so no seed could once again destroy the innocent. He then told me to have no fear, yet to swim or fly in my freedom. I then fell into a sleep and woke here among our daughters. Gyöngyösi afterwards looks at Agyagosszergény and says, "Daughter of my husband, I have heard your mother speak great words. How may I serve you?" Agyagosszergény then tells her, "I will need you for a mission later tonight."

Gyöngyösi clarifies, "I this the visitor in the night?" Agyagosszergény confirmed this as we looked in wonder that Gyöngyösi now understood the ways of the mighty ones. Sásdi began to update us on the war, "We have your ship about seven hours until the end of the Sea of Death. Your ship may never leave this sea, for nothing that goes in can go out. We have transferred all your clean property to a new ship, which we hear you have traveled before while in the seas." I asked her, "Do you speak of Kisteleki?" Sásdi confirmed this and then continued, "Kisteleki will take us to Baktalórántházai through the hidden underground rivers which unite with your caves. We will return and spend a few days with you to ensure your safety. We shall also tell the Edelényi that we are from their ancient goddesses and command that Nógrád be given in married to Siklósi." Nógrád came forward and bowed on her knees, saying, "Surely the heavens have blessed me today." Cserszegtoma then tells Nógrád they had watched her performance with the father a few days earlier and decided that our father shall never be deprived as such love. I afterwards asked Agyagosszergény, "You watch us during our private time?" She answers, "Yes, father; we were curious and have no fear. We could only see a white-light spirit in you as our mother forbids us to see you and the father of Agyagosszergény." I next ask my daughters to consider that we are married, and that I really did not want them to play like that if they were not married. Sásdi after that says, rather gloomy, "Do not worry dad, our mother's Master has forbidden any man to touch us least they be married to us, and no man will dare to defy him, not even in their thoughts. We can complain to our mother who is diligently obtaining more benefits for us each day."

I told her, "As I have yet to have daughters to raise, I would have to talk to my daughters' mothers to decide if a certain young boy could go on a chaperoned date with a daughter of mine, who of course does not live in the heavens. So what else is going on in this war?" Adásztevel, who is the sensual one, continues our unique briefing, "We have planted clones of you throughout our sea bed with body parts missing by jaw bites.

Our mother is binding all parts today, therefore, has sent her great armies back to her bottomless pit. She is only missing one dead body, and that is a live clone of our father as bait. Awfully soon, we will replace the clone. Our father's mind will be stored in a safe place, as a counterfeit mind will occupy his body. This false mind shows him making deals with great spiritual powers as they plan to invade her sea. She will obtain your seed while you sleep, which will create our sister. She will rush back to her throne and share the new information that she has stolen. This information has enough truth and the key ingredients in it to send her on a wild goose chase that will last well past your lifetime. We will then restore our father's memory, plant the clone on the ship, board Kisteleki, and sit beside daddy while he tells us some wonderful stories and plays some fun games. We will have fun forever after." That was when I smiled and winked at them and said, "The marvelous thing about daddy's house is you have so many mommies that will play games with you." Gyöngyösi opened her arms and said, "All the time, as I know some splendid games." Hevesi jumped and yelled out, "If you are tough, you can play games with me." This pulled out Sásdi and Bodrogközi, the more adventurous of the five. Sásdi, whose powerful waist provides her a more daring, challenging approach asked Hevesi, "How early are you expecting awakening?" Hevesi threw something at both and just before it got to them; it exploded with water as they had their hands up to catch them, soaking them. I could not help but to laugh so hard my body twitched. My daughter fell to the floor and with her head, on the floor began banging it against Cserszegtoma's and Adásztevel's. The three of them leaped from the floor and grabbed Hevesi to show her a strange victory dance they had. Hevesi hung with them moving each arm and matching the spins with the jumps and twists. Hevesi stops for a second, looks at Sásdi, and tells her, “Sweetheart, is it okay with you if I get up at the same time?” Bodrogközi now runs to Hevesi and begs her, “Show me how you did that?”

Hevesi tells her, “Honey, I cannot show you how to do this until you promise to clean behind your ears.” Bodrogközi assures Hevesi that she constantly keeps all her always clean if a handsome boy was to walk past her. Hevesi tells her, “I truly believe those boys will stop and take a second look when you pass by.” Bodrogközi then consoles Hevesi, “Oh, do not worry; when they do that I always hit them.” Brann looked at me now and said, “Master. Your daughters need much time with their mothers.” I smiled and agreed. Hevesi calls my daughters over to Sásdi and has Adásztevel pull all the hair away from her ear and look in her ear and tells her if she sees anything. Adásztevel confesses to see nothing. Hevesi than has the defiant and suspicious Sásdi grab two of Hevesi’s fingers and put them over Bodrogközi’s ear. Hevesi wiggles her fingers slightly and has Sásdi pull back her hand so all can see if she found any dirt. Stringing from Hevesi’s fingers was a long one-foot skinny worm in which Hevesi tossed to Sásdi for inspection. Hevesi then asked the young women if Bodrogközi’s ears were clean. They all looked stunned. These are the daughters of a highest goddess, which rules universes. They are pleading with Hevesi to show them how she did that magic. Hevesi owns them down to each heartbeat. Hevesi tells them, “Now the daughters of my Master, I am but a small old woman, and merely a Lamentan. I have no magic or you would have caught it, as you can hide us from your ancient mother, you would detect me with ease. You also witnessed how your strong; ever-watching sister Bodrogközi held my hands and controlled their movements, thereby even a slight flinch would have alerted such a fine warrior as, she. So if not by magic or trickery, how else could that worm been inside her eating her alive from inside?” They are huddled around her feet with their heads looking up at her, as dogs would their Master awaiting their next bone. Even my wives and

I are watching her. We do not understand how the little thing that lives beside my heart can do such great things as this.

My daughters have jumped back in their lives and are living an event crucial to their childhood development, for the first time. These are the majesties, awesomeness, and unmatched heroism of an aunt or uncle, someone who holds all you ever wish someday to be. Hevesi then reels us in, as she has us hooked without a doubt or hope for release. We breathe when she breathes; our eyelids blink when she does. She next asks us if we want to see the real story on how that worm got inside poor, innocent, and helpless Bodrogközi's head and was preparing to eat her brains. I look down at my arms as my skin in coated with good bumps. Bodrogközi does come across a little tough; however, the poor child has endured many challenges in her fatherless life. She does not deserve to have her brain eaten out. Hevesi tells us to be quiet while she tells us the story of the secret pre-age race called the Paksi. "Long ago when all was empty and lived in one dot a great explosion began everything at once." Cserszegtoma adds, "This is true because my mother told me." We shift our paranoid eyes back on Hevesi, who continues, "While everything was going so fast in so many directions some things were hit hard barely able to survive. One of these races were the Paksi, who were supposed to be ten-foot giants, rule many worlds, fight evil, and most importantly, help poor women who were being abused by bad men. Their bodies were mashed and mixed with the things that formulated the worlds. Strange things began to happen. No one realizes, even to this day, how an odd force came in and took the greatness and love of the Paksi, and turned them into an incredibly tiny race of lonely separated minute creatures. Their eggs are so small that they ride on the dust in the air that we cannot see. They may never see another of their species or love or do good things for any one. When the so few who survive to grow into a large worm will go inside someone's brains trying to find their memories. Eventually, because every day they get hungry, they eat their host's brain to the point that it dies. The worm soon also dies inside the brain, since the host is dead, and they cannot ask the brain to tell them how to get escape. Then one-hundred years later, on a special night when all the moons shine bright, the worms explode, shooting their eggs for miles and miles, sometimes even to other planets. Now, that is a long way for a little egg, which no one can see.

They can only live on the air on dust for twenty years before they die, unless they find an ear to go inside and travel in the blood veins in the new brain where they will live beginning this cycle over and again. I was so angry when I first heard the story that I ran outside with my sword and tried foolishly to cut down a tree. I swung and swung screaming and crying how unfair these people who were supposed to save virtuous people from evil and to live lonely and sad lives as an insect. Then a sweet, kind voice smoke in my head saying, "Hevesi, since you have shown love for the Paksi, we will give you the special power to pull them from their cages of death and put them in your hand. Here if you tell them, you love them, they will return to before the ages, protected from the beginning chaos, and enjoy the lives they could have. Sásdi, may I hold our new friend." Sásdi, who now held the worm with care, with tears flowing from her eyes, as all the women in this coo-coo cage were crying. Hevesi held it in her hands and asked us to say the magic words with her. "We, and yes, I joined in, said aloud, "I love you." The worm turned into so many lights and flashed away deep into our smog. Hevesi then began to act strange and asked everyone to be quiet. She began to tremble and told us all to stand still for she heard another Paksi begging for help. She walked passed each wife and myself and heard nothing. She now moved among the daughters and started to cry, 'I hope I am not too late, please stay alive for me.' Hevesi walked over to Adásztevel's ear and pulled out another long worm. She invited all of us to look at his worm. We examined it and when given the cue said, 'I love you,' as it also vanished into the smog inside our room. Hevesi then told us, "The Paksi prefers one type of woman to live in their ear, and that is women who do not have a father. They hope that, before they die, they can do a good deed for the poor daughters who have no father. The next thing that I felt on this day was a big man beating me and kicking me causing me pain. Bodrogközi yells to ask me where I can find that man, so I may punish him for hurting my favorite aunt.

Hevesi then tells Bodrogközi, "Oh my good daughter, you cannot hurt him, for he is my father, and he was punishing me because the tree I was cutting with my sword fell onto our house and destroyed the roof." Bodrogközi and the rest of us began to laugh at this one. Cserszegtoma afterwards asked us, "Our parents, from this day forward when you tell us stories do not tell us true stories, for they force us to cry." Then Cserszegtoma asked Hevesi how she knew people that even their mother do not recognize. Hevesi told them that was easy, because since she is so little she hears and learns about all the things from the lower world. Nevertheless, since you are all so tall, like your mother, you hear all the important things from the upper world." Sásdi looks at Cserszegtoma and warns her, "Do not be asking such simple questions to our aunt, because everyone is aware of this." Cserszegtoma apologizes to Sásdi saying she must have mistakenly forgotten, and she apologized to Hevesi, who tells them, "Come on my girls, give me a big, 'I love my aunt hug and kiss,' before I take my old person's nap, okay." They latch onto Hevesi as if they are holding the keys to everything great in life. I look at Khigir as we both stare shocked at our core and Mórahalmi asks us, "Is that really true." We both pull her between us and kiss her cheeks as I tell her, "I do believe so. I can still see the amazement in Lenti's eyes when I ask Hevesi to decide if we can save ourselves or not. I think that he would understand the answer why, if he were here today." Agyagosszergény leaps up before us and cries out, "Hurry daddy, now is the time for you to procreate me. Hold my hand." I thought to myself that this was a locution have never before spoken or even contemplated. I took one look at my daughter and said, "I sure hope I do as great a job this time honey." She holds me and says, "I believe my daddy can," as we vanished. We entered our family bedroom. I looked at my daughter and said, "This is such a sad event for me to have the universe's Greatest beauty before my mating bed and not be accomplished to take part." Agyagosszergény tells me, "Awl; however, the father you have partaken, and I have never yet participated, and I stand here before, the only man I have ever loved and may not share what burns inside my heart." I now told her, "Darling, if you are to be standing here, you must tell me how I am to create you." Agyagosszergény tells me that she will put me into a deep sleep. Her mother will next arrive and as a succubus plant my seed in her. She will then go away. We will then restore your memory and swap the bodies, transferring everything her mother had injected back into the colon, if her mother wanted some dessert. Agyagosszergény took my memory and into a sleep in went. Her mother most times planted the memory of what happened to her victim. She entered our room and woke me. Even as I was awake, she had absolute control of my body. When she entered, she appeared as a screech owl with eyes of death and a bill that was razor-sharp. The slime of the sea coated her filthy, smelly body. She flew around the room as if looking for something. Afterwards, she landed on the floor by the door with her back to me. She then transformed into a wonderful, beautiful woman. I asked myself how I have been so lucky always finding myself surrounded by beautiful women yet for the same reason unlucky that they always wanted to mate. She wore a soft transparent gown that fit tight to an amazing body. As she glided toward me, her hair turned the color of Sásdi's, although I did not realize that at that time. She looks at me and tells me, "You are prosperous tonight Siklós, for my hair only turns red for the fortunate men who when after I seduce them, I allow to live. I hope your performance is as worthy as my red hair gives you credit. I chose you for your reputation as being the love that can pull Queen's from their thrones and angels from the sky. She next lay on top of me saying, "No man may lie above me." We both started conservative and after that, something exploded inside us as she completely lost control of ourselves and bonded into the bliss of ecstasy that was a power so prodigious we could run in each other's guarded minds. Hours later, when she grew tired, she fell upon me. I felt her wet body and grabbed some wiping rags that were amazingly beside me and wiped her body. Consequently, I reached down from the other side of our comfortable mat and grabbed a blanket that amazingly was beside me, and lay it over us. I fondled her hair and asked her, "How did one so loving as you come from the Sea of Death?"

She told me that she exists only to torture those who she can in revenge for the hate that her mother suffered. I followed up by asking, "Is that why you took all my wives from me, so that I would like a long sad life." She answered, "Strangely; I do not feel satisfaction from taking that love from you, as I now have enjoyed your true and special love. It will hurt me so to leave you." I asked her, "Why must you leave me?" She tells me she is the Queen of Evil, the Mighty Lilith and shall stay or have no man." I afterwards said, "Be careful you do not hurt yourself, for you must do easy as our mating did place great burdens on our muscles." She next asks me, "How can you show me kindness after all that I have taken from you?" I told her, "You did not take from me to deprive me; you took to deprive your enemy. Can I be your enemy after the love we just shared?" She next asks me, "Why do you not beg for your life that I hold in my hand?" I answered, "How can I beg for something that I no longer have?" She after that declares as she starts to stand, "I must leave you, for your words give me a strange feeling." I subsequently asked her, "When do you kill me?" She told me, "I do not understand because my heart and mind are weak now. I will tell you one thing, and that is the seed that you just planted in me shall be the leader of all my daughters. This will be so when I look at my daughters, I may remember our time together. I must now go talk to my council concerning what I am to do with you."

She then flashed out instantaneously. Agyagosszergény now appears with the clone, finishes all the required transfers, and tells me we must leave fast for her mother is returning. Agyagosszergény took me to Kisteleki, whom already had all my wives and daughters boarded with their belongings. Kisteleki now dashed to the bottom of this sea and then worked his way out of it into the neutral seas. Just as we entered the safe sea, we could feel an anger of power rock the entire Sea of Death. Kisteleki tells me that Lilith had decided to keep me and returned to secure me when she discovered me dead. Agyagosszergény had planted the clone's final memory being that of confessing my great true love for her." When she heard this, she blamed her council for spying on her and destroyed them. She was conducting inquisitions trying to determine who killed me. Agyagosszergény reveals to me that her mother claimed this to be the defining moment when she began to question evil and entertain surrender to the righteous. It would require one-thousand years of spiritual punishment and incineration to remove wicked and its grip on her. Next, she gives me a kiss and adds, "You did a wonderful job making my father, and I will serve with you until time ends and still bear a considerable debt to you. Your great mating skills tripped up the deadliest succubus ever to live and triggered her to designate me the leader of her daughters. You are truly a Master at the mating skills. I will demand that whoever you give me to marry will learn his mating skills from you, my father." I kissed her back and then told her, "This may not be fair to whom, you choose to marry, for I knew what I was making. In addition, my love, I may have got you this position; however, your extreme abilities and caring work has kept you in your position. You are the truly great one my daughter, and I owe you much for the pronounced honor that many will give me for my inordinate daughter of love." We continue to walk as she stops me and says, "Oh, I almost forgot. My mother went back and collected all the items from your ship and took them to one of her secret worlds where she rebuilt one million of them, with the original saved on display for her eyes only." Everyone is relaxing in the water, metal pond floor, or Kisteleki's first floor. He has lovely music playing. They have magnificent glasses of wine, a delightful assortment of fruits, and other tasty treats within a hand's reach. A few are sleeping on some genteel comfortable cushioned body length chairs.

All the bodies here are perfect, except mine; however, I am entitled to a little padded body for the great stress these angels of love bestow upon me. This is a room where my wives and now my daughters all snuggled up around them can wear their special swim wear, which complements their physical perfection. Khigir is lying on a double padded floor mattress fast asleep. I notice that Kisteleki is taking special care of my family. I ask him how long before we are back on Baktalórántházai, which he explains are only a few days away under that sea. I tell my daughter the time for me to sleep is now. She asks me where we are going to sleep. This noticeably knocks me off my feet. Nevertheless, I can understand what she is saying about us in this situation. I tell her, "Agyagosszergény, you understand the daughters are not supposed to sleep with their fathers, do not you." She gives me her innocent look and answers, "Of course silly boy. This is for now with all the family. We need to be close as possible currently so I can learn everything about you and you everything about me. This is a special, unique opportunity to be with my father, and I believe we should take advantage of this." I agreed, and we snuggled up and went fast to sleep. While we were sleeping, I heard a voice say, "My daughter, your work is done, time to return to me." Agyagosszergény explains to this voice, "Oh no mommy, please we want to spend some more time with daddy and our fun aunts, please." The voice inquires, "We, do not you mean you." Adásztevel has now jumped into the conversation, "No mommy. We want to. We can simply jump back the same time that we left and everything would be okay. Daddy and this family are so wonderful. We want to live with them at Baktalórántházai until at least when the babies begin arriving." The voice now clarifies that she only revealed Agyagosszergény's father. Sásdi joins, "Oh, but mommy; daddy adopted all of us. We are extremely happy and of course; we still love you so much. We will be good girls. Thanks mommy." Sásdi conveniently drifts back to sleep. Adásztevel also thanks her mother and drifts back to sleep. The voice then articulates to Agyagosszergény, "How can I expect my daughters to resist what I failed to resist? I believe that he is a good father and will care for my babies well.

I will not rush you in another place as I foolishly rushed away. Stay and return when you are ready. My spirits will handle your affairs." Agyagosszergény then said, "Goodbye for now our wonderful highest mother." I lay here currently beginning to fear, for I do not understand how long or how well my wives and daughters will do when competing for my attention. These are not ordinary daughters here, since they are actually also goddesses in that, their mother is. A simple, "Hey mom," executes any request. The main thing that I want to hide from them is our mating times with my spouses and even that I do not understand if this is possible for you, especially when considering that Agyagosszergény has already seen me in action. I do not have the heart to correct her on this, as it was actually the beginning of her life, and I think we would like to enjoy something of that nature. I think that we will have no trouble working out the details, as they are special women and have been around a lot longer than most of us. I so much want to be the best father I can be and develop my children in moral ways. When they come from the heavens as these five did, I do not have to worry much about that. They are truly sincere and work hard to fit in with us. I have to understand that while others offer them galaxies, I can only offer Agyagosszergény a part-time late to arrive blood father, which is enough to sway the scales in my favor for all five. Four of them help Agyagosszergény find who she truly is; they are within themselves discovering the part of them that she holds. Even though I could have advanced the argument that I did not father her, but it was the result of a succubus, therefore, relieving me of all responsibility. One word from Agyagosszergény would wipe that argument from a responsibility to a blessing.

She is also mine now, as I did with full love, and knowledge, plant the seed that produced her. To understand the truth is to appreciate that I did not attempt to avoid that situation, where this powerful spirit could take what she wanted. She takes; I take, can it matter who takes for one look into my daughters eyes shows why both of her parents want her. She grabbed that first peek into her life, and now she is bonding with me, so she can try to paste what she missed. With me being a Lamentan, she does not have that many years to grab before I die. My daughter tells me that when I tell her about one of my past events, she can watch it. That will help much. We will be able to work something out between us. I jump in the water to swim and of course, all five dives in after me. We play some water games that Dabasi taught us with this small rubber round stone that we can throw and catch. We have a five against one battle, which quickly turned into a nineteen against one water battle. Finally, slightly outnumbered, they forced me to surrender. Female prison wardens can be on the harsh side as they debated in my punishments. Of my pleas for mercy and pardon went to the wayside. Not long thereafter, Kisteleki called for us to attend his dining room. They do not need to eat, as their mother did away with that need by creating non-energy consuming, non-waste producing units. Khigir commented that this was an interesting concept. During the meal, they walked around the table talking with us. My Agyagosszergény remained at my side between Khigir and myself. Khigir remained calm and supportive. She had also become singularly attracted to Agyagosszergény. My daughter complemented Khigir on so many things that I could see clearly Khigir was eating from her palms as all my wives worshiped them. These children were not aggressive in the sense of wanting to take something away from any one. They appeared to be quite concerned with the feelings of others. I was proud of the way in which they showed respect for us. Apparently they are special creations. What is clear to me is that they have for a while at least had everything they wanted. Even though they had so many belongings, they wanted to hear only one thing and that was that they belonged to something.

Agyagosszergény saw the mother who was around her during all her days actually mate with me to produce her. She was indeed from my seed. Her life belonged with my seed. This creation belongs with me as the way others belong with their father. This bond was also strong enough to graft in her sisters, as they had even declared this relationship to their all-powerful mother, who had consented or at the least failed to refuse it. I have the feeling from the way that Gyöngyösi had described her visit to their mother who not too many things refused her. Another wonderful feature, of the so many that are instilled within me is a greater pride in my daughter. She is the big kid on the block. Her mother either rules or created more than I could ever imagine. My daughter does not use the mighty power that she has to force me to do her will. She uses something more powerful, that guarantees my compliance and that is her eyes, or should I say my eyes that are living from her face. Even if they were not my eyes, I could in no fashion, ever refuse them. Khigir tells me, "My Master, are they dreams not coming true?" I agree. We decide that In order to integrate them in their family as not one of us wishes them to depart us to assign them to the sisters of the womb. We understand how these young energy packed bundles of love want to stay active; therefore, it will take two of us to keep up with them, with actually four wives, including the Greatest Aunt Hevesi, as our reserves. Khigir, Brann, and I hold on to my daughter, while Tselikovsky and Baranya hold on to the wild and fiery Sásdi. Subsequently Gyöngyösi and Nógrád, my wives of heavenly love and illegal love hold on to the seductive and enticing Adásztevel. This is followed by Csongrád, the Queen, who stood defiant before multiple armies to save her people and Béla, our strong warrior from the hidden world under the sea, as they will hold on to the spunky and ready to tangle Bodrogközi. Their mother skillfully took back her Sword of Justice while replacing it with a similar warrior style sword dressed in diamonds and precious gems, which her spirited daughter could court before any battles. The final adoption apportions Ajkai, the sky dancer and Abaúj the mother of our unseen life-sustaining forces holding on to the light and flowery, green and purple haired Cserszegtoma.

We announce the further sub adoptions as guardian aunts, with me retaining the 'father' title, as I have no one else her to compete for that title, nor would I let another compete for the position in which they asked me to serve them. Kisteleki, who had done some remodeling on his lower decks, had devoted his third floor for what he labeled family activities. He said the pregnant woman, and young unwed women needed exercise through some fun games and activities. I asked Kisteleki what I needed, and he said some extra time to nap. I thanked him and went to my temporary haven when two blonde-haired wonders dragged me and pulled me backward. Khigir asks me where I am going. My daughter tells Kisteleki, "My daddy is the strongest man ever to live, and he wants to use these activities to show us his large muscles, precisely daddy." Khigir jumps in, "Right big boy," with an underlying chuckle. My resistance ends as my visions of a nap now turn into pushing those heavy things Kisteleki calls weights under the supervision of my daughter and Master wife. How did things turn from great to terrible, so fast? The part, which is even worse, is how I must pretend that I am enjoying this. My torments never end is how a tiny voice inside me says, "Do not worry dirty boy, I will save you." I tell that small voice, "The way you saved me before is why I walk this joyous road now my Lord." I decide to lift weights for a short while is not worth making their mother mad and have her launch billions of armies upon Lamenta. After our family activities two-hours we proceed to the cleaning rooms, as Kisteleki has now created two side-by-side. Makói, Dabasi, Hevesi, and Mórahalmi quickly shuffle me into the smaller one, while the remaining mothers shuffle my daughters into the next larger cleaning room. We clean quicker thereby are giving me some additional hugging time with these four wives. Mother-daughter time was our last event for the evening. By some miracle, I fit into the activity as father, which is fine in that Khigir gave my daughter to me for a few hours to walk around this ship and talk, as a result special daddy-daughter bonding time. Khigir justified, both logically and diplomatically, that because

Agyagosszergény did not have her mother here, yet had her blood father here, and then her father must step into the role. I grabbed her hand and said, "We can go to the top viewing room and talk while looking at the stars." She agreed, and off we went. I asked her to tell me about her life, as she already knew mine. She told me about how they suffered when they transitioned from wicked to virtuous. She continued by highlighting how they fought evil so hard to win control of her mother's first galaxy. The battles continued and continued until recently that the empire was so large the daughters would now go accomplish 'Royal Visits as a Princess,' which was utterly enjoyable. She highlighted how hard their empire had generated so that many could live such great lives, and that she was so proud of this. As she began to tire, she sat in my lap, and I held her, as I will my newborn children when they arrive. She softly fell into a deep, peaceful sleep. I then heard a soft voice say from within me, "Wonderful job daddy, for a beginner." I looked at our daughter and told this voice, "She has your beauty. You have done such a wonderful work with all your daughters who now stay on this small ship under the sea. I really would love to have her with me for a few more years of my short life, if you have the power to grant this." The voice said, "Father of our daughter, I have all power. Time is my servant. Our daughter needs you for these years, and she will be yours since you wish to keep her." I asked this voice, "Why do you do such a great thing for us?" The voice said, "Because you shall bring about my daughter as the Greatest Princess of this empire. Go to love her as your own. My spirits will be with you. Into your hands, I give my love." I went to put our daughter down and bow before this great invisible deity when the voice again spoke, saying, "Hold onto your daughter and lay her in her bed that her tired flesh may rest. Peace is yours." I looked beside me and there stood Khigir, Gyöngyösi, and peace filled our room. Unspeakable joy filled our faces as these two mothers to be helping me put my daughter into her bed. They carefully covered, her with blankets, and we put the fresh flowers that Kisteleki had given us in the tall cups of water that were around this five-bed sleeping room.

Within minutes, their adaptive aunts carried the remaining four in, and we bedded each with lovely soft blankets and flowers. Each wife kissed each daughter, and we slowly departed from her room. While walking down the short hallway to our room, the lights vanished and we stood in the open space. The space filled with angels signing such great songs, and the music was such that we had never before heard. Within about thirty minutes, the angels vanished and many bright colors revealed the sea of worlds around us. Next, many mighty armies appeared as a giant set of steps appeared from above us. We saw legions of angels escorting a powerful one down the long steps. Trumpets sounded and we heard a man yell out to us, "Behold. A mighty one appears." What appeared before us took all the energy from Pápain as she went to fall down. Giant strong angels appeared below her and revived her. Pápain cried out, "The mighty ones have blessed me today. Then the great one, whose wings were larger than Lamenta, became small among us. The space between her and us turned into golden roads as she walked to meet before us. We fell on our knees as they rested on emptiness and became praising the mighty ones. We knew not whom to praise. This mighty one came before us. I looked into her eyes and could be forceful stars shining. She looked to the man beside us who yelled out to us, "The mighty one has said to rise, and for the ones called Pápain and Siklósi to come to the front." "I took hold of Pápain's hand, and we stood toward the front. Pápain was so scared. I told her, "Have no fear my wife, for I promise no harm will ever come on you." The mighty one now came closer to us and then fell on her knees praising us saying, "Blessed are Pápain and Siklósi, for they have given my life to me. All hail them." Now, multitudes upon multitudes of angels packed all space around us denser than the densest metals and cried out, "Blessed are Pápain and Siklósi, for they have given my life to a great one of the highest of the Masters." She then stood up and waved her hand and all vanished except the gold floor beneath us. She came forward, crying, "My progenitors. Please hold me, so that I may hold what originated me.

I am the one your sons named Lablonta. I have been our great goddess for what has seemed an eternity that I may meet you and worship you. As a child, my father told me so many wonderful stories about you and the extreme deeds you did. When the evil Queen who ruled our nation executed my father, I swore on your names that I would avenge all evil. I tell you my parents, I shall be with you the days of your lives, and yes, my mother, no evil thing shall ever again touch or hurt you." Now return to my Masters and care for her most high daughters." We were back on Kisteleki even while this great on was saying, ". . . or hurt you." Gyöngyösi tells us now, "I have never known an empire to be that large, for there can be none greater. I tremble to think the daughters most loved by the goddess of such a great empire sleep on their mats a few feet from our room, wishing to be here more than there. I also shudder when I think when touching my sister Pápain's womb; I am touching the progenitors of that mighty one we just worshiped us. I quiver when I think the father of the son in my womb is as well the progenitor to the daughter of a goddess and great powers that destroy evil. My legs wobble when I come to discover that those innocent young adults which lie kissing on the grass below me, that I pulled into our small heavens, so I could be a part of them would someday so soon pull me into the Greatest of the supreme heavenly empires. Nevertheless, my heart tremors in that it knows if all this were taken away, and I kept the love in our family, that I would still be the happiest angel ever created to serve people." Additionally, within me, I could feel quakes as each world my Gyöngyösi spoke. Thus, I added, "The reason my daughter descended from the highest of the heavens is to enjoy our great love. The reason my future daughter bowed before her mother is because her mother, as are all the mothers in my family are the Greatest from all the ages." Khigir afterwards asks, "How can that be?" Then a powerful voice spoke, which shook the walls in our room saying, "Your Master speaks the truth." That night, as for so many nights for the remainder of our lives, we slept stacked on each another so not even light could enter among us. We knew, as told by the Greatest of the gods the love we held was the Greatest ever to be. It was now time to head to our home in Baktalórántházai and prepare to fill my homes with children, so they may play with my daughters from the highest heavens. We knew my five new daughters would be with us the balance of our days, which is but a blink in the hands of the one who time serves.

Chapter 08

Thirty days and thirty nights

Our first days back within Kisteleki felt as if we returned to the womb. All things are so wonderful inside this underwater wonder; a practical person would judge it foolish to leave. I can think the same to be the true with a child within a womb, fed, warm, and safe, then cast into the unprotected, cold, and hungry world. I glance around at all the trim women who are now slightly pudgy, an honor they enjoy so much with each. Nonetheless, when they are around me, they always try to face me and dare me to pore over their wombs. I find myself staying locked on their eyes, for one peek into his or her life creating area, is an invitation to trouble. And when I say trouble, I mean, strife, unrest, disorder, disturbance, discontent, commotion, and so many other terms, which boil down to 'I am bad and do not love them.' My father told me that as their wombs grow so must the number of times you say, 'I love you,' each day and for me that is going to be every other phrase out of my mouth when consoling seven time bombs. Two more will be elsewhere. I feel so much better now that Agyagosszergény has ordered more angels protecting Pápain than exist in this galaxy. Gyöngyösi tells me these are many angels. Sásdi spent a little time with Pápain and me explaining a few highlights with our daughter, whom we saw way up there, and her mother. They were at first enemies as their empires were in a great war. A greater power removed their mother and her daughters from Lamenta after this war. Her mother was not aware of this daughter named Atlantis for many ages. When her mother received her first Lordship of a world and performed excellently, our daughter and her father gave her the surprise news one day during a Throne visit.

With the Throne's permission, our Mother assumed an active role in Atlantis's vast empire. Our Lablonta saved and raised this Atlantis as if her own. That planted a union that would last the ages at the highest levels of crowning power. Sásdi explains it with more vivid details that are beyond the scope of where I want my mind to travel. I can only say way up there, because Baktalórántházai is above the top of Lamenta and that is high enough for my awareness. My comfort is in knowing these fewer things are up there to hurt my bloodline. I watch so many sea creatures of different species swim past our special sanctuary under this sea. Each life in these groups is also unique. It confuses me when trying to understand how one identified living unit can be better than another can. I search my mind trying to discover who I am. I hold a daughter in the womb of the most evil force ever to rule on Lamenta while because new life sitting beside me pouring out a love too great to imagine. That is as looking in the dark and seeing the light of the next day. I think how my supreme goal; such a few weeks earlier was to comprehend more of Hevesi's great knowledge of the wilderness, which was my boundless unexplored haven for adventures. Kisteleki calls me to the command room and asks me if everything is okay. I stare at him and ask, "Are you our ship?" He affirms this and repeats the question. I confess the things are moving fast and that even though I so much want to breathe the air of Baktalórántházai once more, I want to gain more comfort in the vastness of my new family. Kisteleki then asks me, "I take that you will not be too disappointed if I told you

I have been moving exceptionally slower to your home for this last day and at our current, speed would expect to reach your mountain through its internal riverbeds early next week?" I thanked him for the news. He now asked me if I wanted the bad news. I shook my head yes, and he told me that his scanners were detecting The Evil Queens forces drawing closer. To provide the greatest security, he would move to my mountain faster presently, which would decrease our bonding time.

I told him that bonding time on our mountain was better than in the dungeons far under the Sea of Death. I then asked him if he foresaw any difficulties. He told me the daughters provided him with all the details, on how to maneuver and take us home safely. The Queen of Evil could be at our front door and not recognize we were here. I chuckled with him, adding, "I wonder whether my daughters will be able to work around me so easily." He told me, "The wives believe that while your daughters smile at you and say please, you will surrender." I tell him, "How could I not surrender as they are reproductions of their mothers and hold their mothers to coach them. Why would I want to cheat them out of the same victories their mother's enjoyed?" Kisteleki tells me that in his situation all he has to do is unplug their power. Kisteleki enjoyed too much confidence in his skills, because I asked him who was that which stared in the window at us. He turned around and said, "Ouch, it looks like the junkyard for me." The door behind me came flying open as my five new hearts came running in and surrounded me. I kissed them each on their heads and told them to stand beside me, for if our fresh capture had wishes to destroy me, I would be hanging on a string inside the deepest fire hole (Volcano) on Lamenta. I then told Kisteleki to stop and give our surrender message. As he sent the message, a spirit formed before me taking on the beautiful form that she enjoyed while taking my seed. She frighteningly examined us. She then asked me, "Why did you leave my sea?" I told her, "Because you or those who serve you sought to kill me. How did you discover us?" She answers, "Because there is only one who can escape from me?" Agyagosszergény, "Oh great

Queen of the deep and dark, whom might that be?" She looks at Agyagosszergény and smiled, saying, "You appear so much as your father and own my blood within you. Only I can defeat myself. I realize that by seeing you here, reveal to me that you must love us so much to return to witness the beginning of your life. Tell me your name so whatever happens here insures the new you remain the real you. I do not want to be knowledgeable on any added details for fear I could compromise you.

Go, and remember this day, no more." Immediately, after taking Agyagosszergény's name, she vanished, and Kisteleki could move once more. I reached for Agyagosszergény's hand and escorted her out of the control room. As we entered the receiving room just outside Kisteleki's control room, all my wives and daughters met us, or I guess a better term my family. Khigir congratulates us on saving our lives. We agree never to speak of this event, knowing the Queen of Evil could seek revenge if we did so, considering that this event may, in reality, at no time existed. No one enters the Sea of Death and returns. Kisteleki invites us to our dining room for a family celebration. We rush to the dining room to find a rich display of fruits, vegetables and assorted square chunks of meat. The vegetables and fruits arranged on mixed platters present an appetizing appearance. Each receives a glass of wine, as an assortment of fruit juices appear on the table for refills. I ask Kisteleki if he explains because of the shift in his celebration food choices. He explains that his data, now updated, stresses the concern for producing healthy babies and growing young daughters. He will provide foods that our pregnant mothers and our new bubbling daughters will need to produce healthier bodies. The remaining members must also eat healthier to provide energetic support for their companion family members. I grab a carrot and before taking my first bite toast my family, "Here is to our health," and start crunching. I notice Hevesi is loading up on fruits. She explains to me that my new daughters will need much greater energy from her games and adventures. I give her a kiss-and-tell her, "Our daughters are blessed to own a mother as you." I gently pat her womb. Makói and Dabasi also load up on the fruits as they join Hevesi in keeping my new daughters occupied. They did a wonderful job, as each night Khigir, Tselikovsky, Csongrád and Mórahalmi help me find their exhausted bodies and carry them to their sleeping mats. We had Kisteleki's robots put together various structural adjustments where we can pull out temporary walls that connect our room with theirs.

We leave our doors open as with the hallway temporary walls it appears that we sleep in one large room. Somehow, during the night while we are all sleeping Hevesi, Dabasi, and Makói ended sleeping with my daughters. These three wives appear so much happier now with the new honor and love that my daughters pour out to them. Bonding currently, they fill the needs others have. The way they run throughout this ship, I can only wait in total enthusiasm to see them running over the dark jade grass speckled by the small rich assortment of yellow flowers at the peak of Baktalórántházai. Their laughter will echo down our steep cliffs into the low-lying mountains below. These young blameless children of the heavens are the most protected life within this universe. How they can step down from so much glory and power and with each hug I give them, innocent tears roll from their cheeks as their bodies tremble as if touching something greater than all they ever owned or ruled. The adoption idea is strong in their realm, as adoption means complete replacement or rebirth for them. When I adopted them by my word, they somehow changed, their genetic structure to copy Agyagosszergény's blood composition. One day, Gyöngyösi and Cserszegtoma came to explain this to me, showing me visions on how this was. After a few minutes of this, I asked them to pause it and looked at Gyöngyösi and asked, "We realize my love flows in their veins. Notwithstanding, you tell me now that my blood flows in their veins, and that any child who comes forth from their wombs will also carry my bloodline." Gyöngyösi smiled at me and said, "Master. You speak the truth." I smiled at her and said, "Sometimes, by adopting daughters of the goddesses we are blessed to receive additional benefits." I currently smiled at Cserszegtoma and told her, "Your daughters did not need to do this, for when I declared you to be my daughters, your position in my heart and love secured world. Now that you are in my bloodline, we must find you husbands." Cserszegtoma cheered for this news and asked me when they would receive their husbands."

I told her, "Relax, my daughter for it, take time to find one that I approve, and I would expect your mother will declare something to say about this." At this time, a soft voice spoke to all in this room saying, "If their father approves, then so shall I." A joyful Cserszegtoma cried back, "Oh, thank you mother. We always knew you were the greatest mother of love." The voice then warned me, "Be careful Siklósi, for you could end with all 5,001 of my daughters." Agyagosszergény now entered the room and spoke to her mother saying, "Mother. I wish not to share my father with any others. Will you ensure they not see us here, so they will not suffer for want to join us?" The voice said, "If that is your wish my daughter, then your wish is completed." This was my first real sense for their love, in that they valued it greatly and knew what I could handle. They may also have found a treasure they elect not to share. I can see Agyagosszergény closing the loop on this because I am her father by blood and the approval of her mother in two different timelines. She shared me with her four comrades at first for fear of this new experience, and then later as they all have been together for so long they do in consequently many ways work as parts of a whole. My wives now love them fantastically much. These heavenly gifts serve and share with us so greatly. They do truly love us as proven by the gift they gave to Nógrád. Nógrád suffered many severe gaping cuts from our battle with Drápybestie. We were fortunate enough to save her leaving many deep scars over her body and face. One day, while they were swimming, Adásztevel notices the scars, and asked Hevesi about them. We accepted the new Nógrád and actually ignored the scars. We were thankful that she was still with us. Adásztevel invited Agyagosszergény to examine these. Nógrád explained to them that this was evidence her life escaped from the claws of death. They next asked Gyöngyösi who explained the terrible battle. They had fought and how brave their father was in fighting to save Nógrád's life. All five daughters were joined now as they watched the terror and horror of this battle and the heroism their father. When the vision finished, and Kisteleki returned our lights.

Nógrád began crying aloud. The other wives who had crowded into this room began cheering. I came rushing in from my guarded nap, a special gift from Kisteleki; I asked my family what was wrong. My wives pointed at Nógrád who was now completely scar free. I looked at my daughters and said, "Love has once again blessed my special vessels of the purest passion. I thank the tenderness, which has been us this mercy today. As all in here know, I do not care what your outward appearance is, for I love the inside so much more. I will never care about outside appearances, except for the men who beg for my daughter's hands. I shall ask Kisteleki for another carrot festival, so now my loves go to dawn the gowns you selected for this evening's festival. The wives rushed out, leaving my five daughters alone with me. They came forward with a sorrowful expression on their faces. I asked my daughters why they looked so sad. Agyagosszergény spoke to me with soft tears going down her cheeks, as my other daughters now were crying aloud, "Father, we do not understand why you must take our hands and give them to those who wish to visit with us. We believe that without hands, we will never find a man to marry." Hevesi and Gyöngyösi had now reentered. They began to laugh. Sásdi asked them, "Why do you laugh at us losing our hands? Is this the love you share with us?" I told my daughters, "Oh my little loves, your father would never remove your hands. How could a father filled with love do such a thing? Would you think my wives would approve of such a terrible act from me?" Cserszegtoma who is flowing in her tears and crying answers, "They now stand beside you laughing, do they not?" I hand my daughter each one clean soft rag to wipe their faces and tell them, "Oh my loves. You misunderstood my words. When I spoke of giving your hand, I was speaking of giving you to a husband." Bodrogközi asks her sisters, "I can hear mother laughing at us, can you also hear her?"

Sásdi tells us, "She says our father states the truth." Bodrogközi declares now, "I knew he was sharing the truth with us because daddies never lie." I opened my arms as the daughters came rushing to me, barely able to stay ahead of my wives who joined them in the pursuit.

Brann began tickling my daughters as the other wives quickly joined in. Brann told them not to take all the loving because they need to share. Agyagosszergény tells the wives, "My daddy has enough love for an army of women, so maintain no fear, and your love is near." That brought both laughter and tears to my wives. Khigir then tells her fellow sisters, "We might as well get used to it, for several, the fruit of our wombs will be rushing ahead of all who are in this room." Sásdi answers this by saying, "Only when they can escape from our kisses." My daughters were without a question now a part of our future. I happen to see a glimpse of our open viewing windows that surrounds Kisteleki's reception room. I can see daylight. I ask Khigir to glance behind her. She then yells for all to survey the windows. We rush to the windows, except for my daughters who appear confused. I invite them to join me as Sásdi, who has been one always to comprehend what is going on around her, asks me, "Daddy, why are you so amazed by the sunlight?" I told her, "Because our caves hold no sunlight." She tells me we are no longer in our caves. I ask Kisteleki to explain our course change. He tells me he has received orders to take Pápain home to Mysteria before she dies. We will get her to the home she loves so much before she is to die. I thanked Kisteleki and asked my family if they joined me for our vegetable festival. They all dashed out in three directions, taking all three steps in our dining room. Their faces filled with surprise and shock as, they met me at the dining room's door. Agyagosszergény complained, "Use used certain new powers mommy gave you, and that is cheating." I told her I used no magic except my magic of wisdom. Hevesi challenges me that she will discover the secret route that I took. I wish her great luck while explaining selected secrets are only for daddies. Sásdi stands behind me and tells Hevesi, "That secret is for my daddy." I laugh while waving for Pápain to join me. Agyagosszergény notices I am hugging Pápain and we both hold tears in our eyes. She asks me, "Daddy, why do you cry when holding one who is so beautiful?" Pápain tells my daughter our story as I am kissing her neck and cheeks.

These are smooches, designed not to excite a mother, who may be watching from the high skies. Agyagosszergény holds both of us and says, "Do you think I would allow my daddy to miss the birth of my brother?" I looked at her and said, "That is so true, for every child in these wombs that are mine produce within them blood that flows in you." Agyagosszergény told Pápain that, "I will visit with my father often. However, the curse that plagued your blood forbids us ever to touch the island that you live on or death would take you. We can appear in words and lights only." We both thanked her, as Pápain declares, "The gift of my Master seeing Papa is more than I could ever dream." I agreed and added, "That my daughters may see their brother is another blessing I am so thankful love has provided us. I can only wish that we enjoy a little more time together before we must part forever." Agyagosszergény reveals to us, "I tell you a secret that you may never speak of again. We shall spend all eternity with my mother in a wonderful heaven. She builds now for us as a gift for our extreme love." I gaze at Agyagosszergény and tell her, "Do you not realize that for me to receive you is our great reward?" She looks at me and gives a blink, just as my wives do, and say in a tone similar to Khigir's, "Oh father, but mommy wants you to share me with her some." I stare at her and say, "Oh of course. I would never take you away from your mommy, as my wives will tell that when they give my child from their wombs, I will give that child back to its mother." Agyagosszergény laughs and says, "We understand this because we heard you speak those words. We used those words in defense of our plea to visit you, before our mother." I shook my head while looking at Pápain and said, "When a great goddess can be influenced by the pleas of her daughter, what defense do I have?" My daughter looked at me, giving me a kiss on my cheek and said, "You enjoy no defense my pronounced powerful fearless father." I smiled and kissed her on her lips saying, "Why would I want any defense from love and honor such as this?"

Agyagosszergény told me, "Exactly. Now do you want to see the gift I shall give you for your kiss of love?" I stared at her and answered, "I would hope it would be many countless more kisses." She tells me, "Oh, you will never be free from kissing your daughters. The gift I give you and Pápain is thirty days on a beautiful island with these plates that shall give you the food you need to sustain your flesh." Pápain asks Agyagosszergény, "How can you do this?" She answers, "My mother rules all time. Therefore, we will send you to the past in time, allow you to enjoy your days, bring you back to this exact minute. You will walk with me to our special vegetable festival. Now, be gone and enjoy." We can hear her saying 'enjoy' as we both currently stare at the many small islands before us. This is my daughter's trademark as they can knock together transitions smooth and overlapping. We arrive at a hill surrounded with tall fertile trees and a view of the great sea before us. Pápain begins walking down a subtle path before us, which appears to lead to the sea. I immediately follow her, considering my wives boast a tendency to become careless with me around. They place great trust in my presence that danger will need to hurt them. While traveling down this sloping hill, I notice many other paths that branch out in different directions. I can tell that my daughter has planned this event in detail for our recreation. We soon reach the bottom of the hill and travel a path, which runs in both directions. We take the left, knowing that this lead to the view we saw above. I grab a few rocks and pile them together along the side of this path, so I can find my way back up to the hill. We soon arrive on a sandy beach. I had only witnessed a beach made from sand when we were kidnapping Khigir and Tselikovsky. Pápain yells out to me, "This is like my islands with the pleasant sandy beaches. Lay on the sand, for the sand is extremely comfortable." I ask her if this is her island. She points across the blue bay in front of us and says, "My home is on the largest island that is over there, although I do come to this island sometimes in my small boat."

This makes sense now, for even back in time; her curse clock would continue to tick, and death would take her. Since she is on her island, that clock will stop. Meanwhile, Pápain is removing her garments. I ask her what she is doing, and she tells me that she never wears garments on these beautiful islands until the cold times or dark times. She then begins to dress me in this island tradition. I am not familiar with anything concerning, living on islands, yet I believe we are alone, and she is my wife. I want to become a memory that fits into this island, as she will live the remainder of her life her alone. She will only experience Papa until he grows to be a man and finds his wife and leaves these islands. On the other hand, will he leave? He would be foolish to leave this place even though he is free from the family curse. I may engage in a talk with him, even if only in a dream. My thoughts shift back to Pápain who tells me she has certain great news. I ask her about this news. She cheers and said, "We can experience much private time. Now show me what all those other wives always brag about you." A part of me is afraid to share my love with her, as she will soon be gone. I fear the thing that I do is unfair; therefore, I must agree that as my wife, she is equal to the others and as such, I shall treat her. I thereafter perform my duties with all my heart. She tells me afterwards the great news, "We can engage in private time two times every day." I glance at her while giving her my hand and ask her to help me stand. Once up, I ask her to bring me the strong small branch laying on the edge of the sand. I use it as a cane and ask her, "Where are our food plates?" She tells me they are safe on the hill where we arrived. She takes my hand and guides me to the water. She walks in and tells me to follow her. We wade out to where the water covers her breasts. Now we can swim Master. It will help massage your muscles and loosen them so you will be new once more. After a short time, I can feel my muscles relaxing. My little darling is wise about the things of her home. We return to the top of the hill, and Pápain brings back our plates as I secure our garments. While we are eating our food, and I mean real food and not carrots, I peer out across the bay below us and notice two shades of watercolors below us.

The distant color is dark ultramarine and has waves rippling from it. The closer color is airy blue and considering I can see its bottom, must be shallow. This light blue extends all the way to Pápain's island. I ask her about this pathway under the sea. She tells me that she has before walked and swum across this corridor. Nonetheless, she prefers using her boat, as she can spear many fish along the way. I ask her where we shall sleep tonight. She tells me that Agyagosszergény told her she had created a charming house along the beach behind us. She asks me if I want to go there now. I tell her that we should find our night home, for it will soon be time to rest. We go down the paths on the backside of our hill and view a, much different sea. This sea is clear blue to the end of our horizon. If it were not for several white clouds, we would not be able to make out where the waters end. We cannot see this, as I grasp the clouds must be in the sky. Water and air returned the same color back to me united such as is my Béla and Abaúj. I hope to show them this someday, or ask that during their night wondering, they pass through this tiny haven. We step inside a small boat and row about forty feet into the bay and tie our boat to a special hook attached to what Pápain calls a deck. I ask her how she knows so many things, and she explains she saw this house in a dream, and a kind old spirit explained the wonders of this place for her. She then picked up this strange piece of metal and tossed it into the sea. I asked her what this was, and she tells me that it forms an anchor and will help keep our boat here in case of a storm. My Grandpa never used such a thing for our boats along the sea. Pápain tells me that my sea in a sizable bay and does not get the same storms as an island in the sea. We walk up on our large wooden deck, which has a special design made of square logs fitted perfectly together. Pápain further reveals that Adásztevel designed this house, giving it a passionate flavor. Romantic flavor means fewer naps for me. Our deck has comfortable chairs and special chairs that are flexible beds. I can see me stretching out, and enjoying these chairs. In the middle is a large metal bowl with wood chunks inside it. Pápain reveals that this is, so we may possess heat in the cold evenings if we want to lay under the stars.

Taking one last view around the sea before we enter our temporary home, I see something hideously strange in the waters to my far right. Pápain I yell out as I raise my long knife that never leaves my hands, "What is that?" She explains it was a wicked beast from the sea that one day came to destroy her. From the island, she shot her arrows of fire into its head, being fortunate to blind all three of its eyes causing it to freeze in place. She swam out to the beast, with a knife went under the sea, and cut open from its neck. Afterwards, she went back to the shore, rising ahead of its thick black blood that was filling the sea. Waiting until the next morning, she discovered it had not moved and the water was clear. Once again, she quietly swam out to the beast, and this time cut open its chest to ensure the heart was not beating. To ensure no surprises, she cut all ten of the veins that ran through its heart. She left the beast here as a sign to others of its species of the dangers here. This is the reason she lives on the other larger island most of her days. I ask her to turn around for me. She does slowly and asks me if I enjoy what I see. I tell her, "I am looking at not only the beauty of a woman, but the body of a monster killer." We chuckle as she wraps her arms around me, and then whispers, "You should take pride in knowing you are the greatest beast that I ever conquered." I tell her, "I oftentimes wish we could conquer the curse that will divide us, for I can see our family enjoying life in this paradise." She asks me, "If all lived here, how our children would find mates?" I proclaimed to her, "Never to worry about such things, for young men find women and women find men, such as you have done. Now show me our first home my love." I noticed how so many long square metal trees sank into the sea to hold this home about twenty of my feet above the sea's surface. We walk in the steps to the area where our home is. I notice that the front and right side of our home has a large fenced deck for us to enjoy additional activities outside. This topic is not one I wish to explore with Pápain currently, as I entertain a strange idea about the only outdoor activity, she will favor. We walk into our first home, and I see one large room, which is my style. One part of the room has a huge bed with layers of cushions and soft blankets. I tremble as my body slowly walks toward it.

When I go to drop on this package of pleasure, Pápain dives in below me with her back facing our bed. Onto the top of her, I fall, waking up immediately to discover my eyes are facing hers. She tells me, "Now silly boy, what were you trying to do with getting in this bed without your servant?" "Oh darling," I cry out, "I would never do such a thing if I had not been tempted by its comfort." Pápain laughs while bringing to light that, "I knew this my Master, which is why I rushed so hard to save you from such a mistake." I reveal to her, "Pápain, I do appreciate the way these cushions permit us to unite as one. I shall enjoy so much having you resting under me." She informs me, "Oh Master. I will not be resting under you. I hold the remainder of my life to rest here alone. I will work hard to please the father of my son." She began to massage my shoulders and the back of my neck. "Now, "she conveys, "I can sense you starting to relax. Wake up." I shake my head as I regain my consciousness and apologize for giving into the weakness of my flesh then promptly fall back to sleep. This time she simply laughs and falls to sleep. The cool breeze from the ocean flows across our bodies. A strange thought now enters my mind wondering what if these are you know whom. I call out, "Is that you Berettyóú?" She laughs and says, "I foolishly believed that since you all disappeared, I would not need to watch the dirty boy in action." "Now Berettyóú my special friend," I expressed to her, ". . . you are not required to watch. And anyway, we were merely resting," as I roll back over to the side of Pápain. Berettyóú questions me, "Oh is that what they call lay disrobed on a nude woman these days?" I hurry and pull a blanket over us and explain, "Berettyóú, do not you appreciate that these are the garments for the comfortable islands in this summer area? Anyway, you may think as you will, this is a special vacation that my daughters gave us. Berettyóú blows out, "Daughters, you are now collecting daughters instead of wives. Dirty boy, you never cease to blow my mind." I smile at her and compliment her by saying, "I can understand how hard it would be to blow a mind that blows over Lamenta each day and night.

To be serious, which is hard to do with those lovely sensual purple eyes of yours, I am still so confused at how we went from Mysteria all the way to the Sea of Death within such an instant." Berettyóú next tells me that, "This may be in part my fault. We felt something pulling at your ship and feared it was an enemy of the Mystanites pulling you away. Móri joined me as we blow so hard to keep you here, yet something of a greater force was pulling against them. They fought for hours falling deeper south as they battle continued. When all collapsed, both of us and the other force, they lost control of your ship as it zoomed into the Sea of Death. The other force followed you into the Sea of Death. All know that evil lives within that sea. We leisurely blew in the high skies above it to see what the result was, when we heard you call for us. Little by little, we descended and traveling under the back of your ship began pushing you, until a strange force of evil grabbed hold of your ship and told us to leave before we were blowing on the fires of the underworld. She grabbed us in her hands and threw us back to Mysteria saying, 'Never enter another time. If you do, you would under no circumstance's blow on Lamenta again.' We believed that evil took you to the Sea of Death as we had seen it follow you. I never imagined seeing any of you alive once again. How can this gift be?" Pápain adds, "The gods felt sorry that you may hold no nude men to spy on?" I jump in before we result in a hurricane on our hands and tell her, "Berettyóú, the force you were fighting was my daughter who returned to ensure her consummation was once more successful?" Berettyóú laughs and tells me, "I heard many strange things from many weird people. Nevertheless, my friend, you are now at the top of this list. You are telling me the daughter you were creating came back to save you for her creation, what is she, specific sort of goddess?" Pápain laughs and says, "Berettyóú, the words you speak in laughter are indeed the truth.

These wonderful five goddesses, who possess a powerful mother, tell us the Mystanites were planning evil against my Master's family, and that is why they tried to save us." Berettyóú then tells us, "I would gladly deal with a mother of goddesses than the evil Queen in the Sea of Death." Pápain and I began laughing. Berettyóú begs us not to confuse her more. With curiosity killing her, she asks us to explain why we were laughing. I told her, "Oh Berettyóú, the Evil Queen of the Sea of Death is the goddess and mother of my daughters." Berettyóú gasps as the wind now charge, "Dirty Boy. You mean you did it with this mighty Queen of Evil; can you not pass up any opportunities? I cannot believe this. You never cease to amaze me?" Pápain asks Berettyóú, "Berettyóú, confess; if you can take on a body you would have a seed from my Master growing in your womb would you not?" Berettyóú makes known, "As I cannot take on flesh, which is a question that needs ever to be asked or answered. I shall search among the Mystanites and discover if they intended to hurt anyone. Please, do not bury any more seeds in wombs while in the middle of the sea while I am gone." She then departed as another slow wind blow over us. I asked for this wind to reveal its name. A voice spoke out saying, "I am your Móri wind to serve you." I then threw back my blanket and enjoyed a short-lived relief. Pápain strikes me as she pulls the blankets on her other side over herself. She yells at me, "Master, do not you want to have your servants still with honor." I told her not to worry about Móri as he has blown over this area her entire life, and he has no concern for such things. I looked around our room and saw a handful of lengthy poles, a table and counter with many knives, spoons and forks, a few large, and others small. I asked my love about the long pole. She picked it up and told me to follow her. Pápain tied the pole against our railing, slid it back, and unwrapped a special line with a sharp minute hook at the end. She took a small cup and put a trickle of dried meat within it. Pápain next took the revived meat and ran the hook throughout it. She handed this to me and asked me to lower the meat and string into the waters below us. My wife then pushed the pole back through her tied down string so our bait was now away from our house. She coached me to keep watch for any large fish as they could break the pole.

When they pass by, lift your pole so the meat will be above the water. She gave me a bow with arrows and told me to shoot the big fish, and if I hit them, they would wash up to our sandy beaches. I told her my Grandpa used to do this with me, and he called it fishing. "Pápain," I declared, Go ahead, grab the other pole, and sit beside me while we fish. It will give us time to talk." She bounced up, grabbed the other pole and bait, and within seconds was beside me fishing. I began sharing my heart, "Pápain, I understand how we both hurt in that we fell in love. Our love was not supposed to be. History expected us to mate as animals and depart in peace. I am glad that we fell in love, as I would never wish a child of mine to be in a womb, I did not love. The Queen of Evil at first presented an obstacle for me. Until I saw, what our child became. Besides, joy filled me when Agyagosszergény told me her mother changed so much after our meeting. She actually rebuilt our ship and placed it on one of her vacant planets for her relaxation and memories. The result of that mating has changed more lives than the stars in our heavens and the sands on all the worlds around those stars. That outcome was rewarding, as I judge our result will also be rewarding. Our times will be tough. You will be here alone with only your memories. I will be among many, with that empty spot inside me that belongs to you crying out to me daily. This terrible affliction is so sad when you must pay for the evils of your ancestors. I see that if we do not walk the path future generations will suffer because of our weaknesses, and knowingly to fail them is evil from us. Fortunately, for them, we are strong. At least with Agyagosszergény we will be able to see each other at special times throughout the remainder of our days.

We shall build certain memories during these thirty days and thirty nights. I think something is on your bait, pull your pole to the rear." "She became confused, so I pulled her pole back hooking this delightful built fish. I pulled in our poles and told her "We have enough to feed us tonight and in the morning my love, now we will use those excellent knives inside and prepare this big fellow for eating." Usually this would be Pápain's mission. Nevertheless, we need to do everything together. When we had all the meat, cleaned and ready to cook, she took half and sprinkled not much salt on it, and afterwards wrapped it placing in one of her wall containers. She then put the fish on a metal square built inside her counter. Pápain then pushed a button and turned a knob, and the fish began cooking. I ask her how the fish could be prepared without a fire. She tells me that my daughter put something on our roof that puts energy in the black box there and when we push these buttons, it works. I can tell that my daughters are innocent romantics, which is good. I wonder where they will go for their thirty days after they marry. In addition, for their mother to trust me with such a decision is so fearful. A voice now speaks, "Where are your garments?" We scramble and through the ones in this house on our bodies. I speak back to this voice, "Excuse me. However, however, we are on a special lover's vacation as a gift from your daughters. Lovers enjoy themselves more when they share all things." This mighty goddess answers back, "I understand the ways of lovers and how to turn out jokes on them. I come to console your thoughts about fearing you will select the wrong husbands for our daughters. Do not worry about such things for all love burns through its pains. Decide with your heart while sharing the thoughts of our daughters, and you will do fine. Do not worry about an unfit man appearing before our daughters as this I will not permit. Therefore, those who are worthy will appear for your selection." I ask this goddess, "Lilith, and all the great titles that go with your name, if justice is served when I select if they have already given their hearts to their future husbands."

This goddess now answers back saying, "You need not to worry about my titles when talking about our daughters. You decide whom you wish to give your daughter's hands. As their father, you have that power and authority. There is no doubt in my mind, nor the minds of all my Great Spirits than when that day comes you will do as an honorable and loving father will do. Now, do not worry about such trivial things and enjoy the little time you have with your lovely and beautiful wife. Good-bye." Pápain lost her tension when she heard the words 'your lovely and beautiful wife,' and ensured me, "My Master. Your daughters do have a great mother. I can experience her love and kindness. Honor is on me to have a husband who a goddess trust with her daughters. I still shake my head in wonder the child in my womb will have five goddesses as sisters. I am so glad I decided to seek out your ship." I ask her, "Why did you choose me my love?" She answers, "I believed that with so many wives, you enjoyed having new women and would not wish to have another wife. I am so glad that I was therefore wrong." Okay, I had to distinguish why she thought I enjoyed having new women and that if, as a result, my wives would allow this. She reveals that "When we heard them all joke about you being a dirty boy and continued to call you Master; we thought they followed your ways. Why would you have so many wives with such a diversity unless you searched long and hard to fill your appetite? I presently see different." I tell her, "I do hope my wives stop that dirty boy junk, as it draws too much attention and promptly with great powers above us listening our dangers can be much greater." My wife tells me that we can finish this genteel meal and rest on our deck below while watching the suns go down and for the moons to appear. She tells me the view is so beautiful here. I ask her, "My love; you appear to enjoy so many things nearby; I wonder why you ever left this wonderful place." She confesses that this was so much better than the rapes and beatings; nevertheless, her womb continued to cry for a seed. When she saw our boat pass by a seed that I had planted, she wanted a provisional part of a brief garden. I cannot blame her, as I sit here knowing that a giant world is out there, a world that beat and degraded her. As we were fishing today, we only wanted enough to feed us. We now snuggle closer to each other as the night air begins to cool us. Our first sun lands on the distant horizon and appears as a giant ball, many times larger than I have previously seen.

I ask her how this is possible. She shrugs her shoulders and tells me, "It does not matter if possible, as my seeing believes, and since it offers me no harm, I can only believe the sun is getting closer to me before saying Goodnight. The other sun is just as spectacular." The other sun was also wonderful showing me a part of my world, I did not know. Suns that shined above me each day were sharing other mysteries to those on the sea. I also witnessed moons that shined bright and poured their lights out on the sea. Nevertheless, the greatest thing that I saw was the love beside me as she was so eager to share her world with me. I asked her if we could visit her island while we were here, she told me that could be dangerous, and she did not want to take any chances on putting me within any sort of danger. I could understand this, as I also wanted us to have these peaceful days. She tells me that her future will be predominately lived on these islands, as my daughters have made many splendid additions, which will add to the comfort and care of Papa. She rolls from her laying chair to my side and tells me we should get our rest for tomorrow we have a selection of wonderful places to see, and the suns rise early this time of the extended Lamentan year. I take her hand as she stands firm, strong, and pulls me up. I compliment her on the power of her body. She apologizes, saying she did not mean to suggest she was stronger than I was. I tell her not to apologize, for it does my heart so well to realize her strength, especially considering I am not here protecting her, as, I subsequently many wishes I could be. I pick her up and carry her up to the steps to our home and lovely bed. She asks why I carry her, and I explain that where we are going is a place for those who have love in their hearts and that without her, I would go to our home with loneliness. She tells me that this is true. I then think how foolish I was to say this, as she must do this for the remainder of her days after Papa becomes a man and searches for his love and life. After our newly settled, nightly married activities; we drift off into our sleep. How wonderful to rest in a bed that is not waving in the sea or dashing underneath it.

My wife awakes me in the morning, ensuring she first receive her conjugal rights. It does give me honor that even though she got what she came after, she is still working so diligently to keep as much excitement in our wedded relationship as possible. She concentrates accordingly assiduously to ensure each move is precisely and exactly what she wants or wishes to surrender to me. I never really had a chance to concentrate on one lover as we are doing now. The act of giving and sharing throughout the day and waking hours is new for me. My wives feed off each for their daily activities, leaving me certain time to rest and play in the wilderness. Having Hevesi with me is better than being alone, because she does her own things in my pocket. If she wants to watch with me, she does; contrarily, if she wants to nap, she does. If I wish to nap, she keeps a watch out and warns me if anything is coming near us. She always supports my story of our great adventures in the wilderness, as we never speak of our naps. We are aware that if the other wives discovered we were enjoying naps, they would put a stop to us immediately. We both need this time together. Occasionally, the woman inside Hevesi begins to flare up. She knows how to explain this, embarrassing for her, need, and I fulfill it for her using delicate and warm talk. When we are finished, we return to our wilderness adventures forgetting that it happened. This is significant for Hevesi's pride so that makes it important for me. She is my wife and when she comes to me for matrimonial matters, she deserves my loyalty and love. In exchange, I receive a friend whom, I can tell everything. When we are in the wilderness, she is not her regular challenger little pain in the neck. She is a sympathetic, caring small friend. She keeps that hard and demanding posture in front of the wives, by it gaining their undying support to have her with me in the wilderness, believing that she is making things tough on me. Hevesi had completely blown all of us to pieces with the wonders she has done with my daughters.

When they asked us not to tell any truer stories after Hevesi's stories, I knew we had a blessing on our hands whom my family could not exist without having. She actually comes to life in their worlds packed with energy and absolute control. I found myself totally engrossed too many times. Another hero of late has been the Makói and Dabasi combination with my daughters. These three wives want so much to give all they have to whoever will accept them. My daughters accept and worship them. They breathe them and cannot find enough time to enjoy them. Makói came out of her shell completely with my daughters. They reached inside her and melted any of her possible walls with them. Makói still displays shyness when among the wives and always rushes to get behind me where she breathes again. This may be what my daughter saw in her, a trust so deep in their father to only be free when with me. A type of love such as this is what they want to have with their father. When danger is near, they want to run for their father. The entire father image is so important for them. They lived in a world where 5,000 had no father and when Atlantis appeared with my bloodline in her that changed the picture for them. They knew something was missing. I really do not comprehend what their mother is going to do for the remaining ones, for I wonder whether my special heaven will include 5000 rooms for my daughters. That would put me on too many powder kegs as it only takes one, 'hey mommy, daddy did,' and I could be in a dungeon so deep that it would take an eternity to escape. I have noticed Gyöngyösi to be extremely conservative on this issue. She is from the heavens and realizes the powers that are at play here. She cannot grasp what is happening and how it happened. She picks one missing soul and waits almost twenty years to share with other wives merely to discover that lost soul share's children with a power greater than she ever knew that could exist. She is coming around, and I believe she will learn to be comfortable in this situation, as she is the only one to realize how much power is involved in this situation. As the first sunbeams hit my face, since one sun, most times appear separately I can smell our fish frying. Pápain is also preparing various vegetables as I can see she has already collected a selection of fruit for us to enjoy.

She looks so happy and packed with never-ending energy. She sees me starting to get up, runs to me, pulling me up, then leaps up into my arms as I grab hold of her, and begin hugging me while showering me with kisses. I can detect her excitement as I ask her why she is so happy. She stops kissing just long enough to tell me, "Papa's father is here with me, is not that a great reason to rejoice." I tell her, "As long as Papa's mother is also at the side, I can think of no better reason to celebrate." As I hold her, I can only imagine the excitement in my other wives if they could have a private vacation such we have. I realize that they would not be willing to pay the same high price she is paying. I will search hard for a solution to this dreadful curse and try to understand it enough to destroy it. I have fought diligently my entire life so the innocent would not have to suffer, and now my son lives in one who is so innocent and brave in facing such a terrible curse. I believe that she has suffered enough, and yet to see the joy she has today over such simple things, as our beginning meal. Khigir would throw an apple at me, fast of course, and tell me to catch it for breakfast is served. This is not bad on her behalf, which is the way the Tamarkins did them while in their archery schools. Her reward is each time she shoots her arrow high across the sky, and it lands exactly where she wanted it. I always tease her about shooting, me across the sky like that. She refuses, saying that with that sort of jump on her, it would take her over one hour to catch me as I was trying to escape. I hate to tell her that my legs would destroy me if I were to attempt to escape from her. Anyway, I put this; they all handle so well in my arms that are when they are not angry with me. The wives understand to go to Khigir or Tselikovsky, and they will receive the justice they consider entitled to collect. I like this, because, if there is a misunderstanding, I want it out in the air and not crushing inside their poor small hearts. The little things are making babies for me, so what more can I ask to obtain. Pápain is spoiling me today, as she feeds me my fruit and vegetables spoon by spoon. When we are finished, she lays me down, grabs selected lotions, and rubs them over my skin. I ask her what I did to deserve such wonderful treatment.

She pats at her womb and says, “I do need the practice.” She then says, “That was for our baby. This is for me.” She burned her energy off this time as she did when she conceived Papa. As I wipe her soaked body down, I tell her that she has to slow down if she wants to live. She tells me that the remainder of her life will be for going slow. I can see her point. Therefore, I tell her not to forget that I will also have something to lose and must share a few of the burdens in these special times. She reassures me that I will have several burdens to share with my wife. My wives are always, a step or two, ahead of me. That must be why they love me so much. Pápain tells me we have a special day of exploring in the wildernesses today. I jump off in excitement as I swing her around trying to corroborate if this is true. She tells me, "Now you would not think I would bring you to a place with so many hills, rivers, and forests and not show them would you." I give her a tight hug and thanks declaring that she truly does love me. We walk outside as a notice a larger boat behind the one we rode in yesterday. My wife tells me to jump in as she sits behind a seat that has a strange round wheel in front of it. She pushes a button and moves a lever while pushing something on the ship's floor before her, and we begin to move. I ask her to explain this, and she tells me that Kisteleki let us borrow it. How do my wives and daughters get everything they want from that poor ship? I ask her, "How did you get this boat from Kisteleki?" She looks at me, gives a sad look, and then blinks her eyes. I tell her to say no more, before I also give her this ship. They are smaller models of our species, yet face the same elements and obstacles that we do. My father was always pampering his wives. Even though they were Tamarkin and could easily have defended themselves if they were required to do so. I have tried to copy his security style as I find we have more relaxed family time. When the time comes to fight for survival, we jump in and fight as a team. When death is staring us in the face, the fight is not the time to play macho man, or I am Master.

Today would prove no exception to this rule. We rode in our boat out to sea, far enough so we could get an overall view of these islands. I asked my 'golden skinned' Pápain if this did not remind for of the Anfallare and, or the Drápybestie. I often get confused trying to remember all the creepy things we have fought. She asks me, "Are you talking about creatures who attached our ship from the water rocks that surround Mysteria?" I said yes and she said, no. So much is different, here the islands are a lot larger, have vegetation, and arranged for defense and not offense. That is not to say that they have not visited, not as friends, a few times, however, the wizards of Mysteria consider these islands unique and are ready to defend them." I compliment her on her fast tan and then ask, "If this place is so special, why do they reserve it for you?" She tells me, "They reserve it for me as a living cemetery at the final extinction of their hated enemy. Each day I live they can see the fruits of their victory." This tells me that Pápain destroyed the rest of her species or race as she is of Lamentan form. I question her, "Thus, you had no males of your species to carry on your race?" Pápain tells me there were three males, two killed each other fighting over her, and she killed the last one so her race would die. The time for a zoo of pain for the Mystanites was over. They became very annoyed over my deeds and put me in that village to be tortured, beaten, and violated. I was finally saved, and they were forced to allow me to live here the remainder of my days, for be destroyed as the spirits of Lamenta were so angry with their display of wickedness. My new guardians pulled me to your ship telling me to mate with you, so something in me would not be forever gone from the surface of our world. I can believe now the Mystanites would have done evil to you also in revenge for giving me your seed. We were lucky that your daughters saved us." Then, a howling wind came on us. I yelled out for Berettyóú to slow down because we are in a small boat. She did as I asked and then swung around to our front and told me, "Siklósi, our Pápain speaks the truth. The Mystanites have planned to do you notable harm. The Great Spirits have punished them and erased from their minds the future knowledge of your seed.

Their anger was concerning that; a Queen from Pápain's seed will someday rule their lands and most of Lamenta. They considered that the last attempt at their old enemies wanted to destroy them. The Great Spirits judged that repayment for sins might extend no deeper than all who lived during the war. Unfortunately, the punishment to Pápain remains in effect." I yell out, "They are only doing enough justice for show and do not have true justice is their judgment. I will avenge them for their evil and hatred. The vessel that carries my seed has no part in this deep old ancient injustice. The Mystanites have more blood on their hands and as such must pay." I now looked up into the heavens and asked, "Mother of our daughters, how can this be called justice?" A warm voice speaks back to me from the air all around us saying, "Be at peace, for I understand your anger. My lights of justice and wisdom are arguing your case with all their efforts. The problem lies in the ones who signed the treaty ending that war. All citizens of all seven warring nations signed that treaty to release the curse. All must agree. Unfortunately, the ones from my Pápain's empire are keeping this curse locked. The wicked ones who we punish with brimstone and fire for their wickedness are demanding freedom for eternity for them to consent. We will at no time, release evil on the innocent to save one innocent. This evil would kill and destroy so many innocents that such a negotiation we will never entertain. On my lovely Pápain's behalf, we have made their frightful punishment as terrible as permitted before actually destroying them, which would forever prevent us from removing the curse. Enjoy your time together, and trust that all that can be done is being done repeatedly." Berettyóú returns to our conversation, "Wow, Siklósi you do have connection's way up there on the top." Pápain now, with tears flowing down her cheeks comments, "My ancestors keep this curse on me. I wonder if the wrong the Mystanites had done was in letting any of my ancestors live, for we must have truly been wicked people."

Trying to comfort my wife, I say to her, "Pápain, you have no fault because they may have been evil, but remember the greatness that is to come from your womb. They will save a lot more than your ancestors destroyed. At least, we are lucky that so many are doing so much on your behalf. This must tell you the new love that shines within you is true, special, and pure. We want exceedingly much to help you live a life you are entitled. I can sense within her a shell that gives her sanctuary as it has done through so many storms. I inspect down beside us and see long spears and two bows with boxes of arrows. I ask Pápain if she noticed them before. She shakes her head no and grabs the pink bow claiming it. I look, see the other is a dark-blue, and tell her, "Okay, dear, if you insist." I notice that we also have various small garments folded at our feet. I study them and then examine her as she is staring at me, shaking her head no. No modesty here, this is her home and her world, and no one else is going to take her freedom. Back through the sea, we continue our exploration. After my love had taken me completely around her small haven, she began to work our boat between the islands. I had an idea what to expect here, as I had seen them from our hillside on first arrival. I will admit the diversity looks much greater on the hill where I could distinguish easily the islands various sizes. Riding in a boat between them takes away this distinction, and reveals the details within the trees and vegetation. Everything has been subsequently much different from on Baktalórántházai yet almost strangely much alike. Sort of like males and females, a few differences between, and several things the equivalent. I might even be seeing these plants as being Pápain's and; therefore, being different. I hope that is not the case, as I am so comfortable with this precious jewel. My mind keeps thinking about her future, yet she does not appear to be worried about it.

She seems to be giving more thanks for what she can bring with her from her previous situation. I remember once when playing monsters with my friends in a part of our forests. I was hiding in this game with the goal of my friends not discovering me. In the joy of finding such a wonderful place, they did not find me. Staying quiet and low, I remained until the dark hours came. Thinking it was strange that they left me behind, I wondered throughout this forest looking for them. My parents always taught us never to produce noises in the forests at night; nonetheless, I remained quiet. My friends could not yell for me, fearing that if they did not find me, they would be putting my life in danger. They, therefore, went to their homes. Grandpa waited until the next morning to search for me, knowing he had taught me to stay quiet in the woods and that a search party could invite danger. I had hidden my tracks so effectively the search party walked over them compromising any hope of Grandpa finding them. While searching for my way home at night, I traveled from tree to tree. This allowed me to see anything on the ground, in the trees, and to leave no tracks for any evil slave traders who had on occasion passed through our area. It was ten days, before we were reunited. Those ten days were lonely and packed with fear, as when alone, no one else is around to provide protection. Every minute of the day could hide danger, especially when looking for something to eat. I survived ten days. Pápain will survive the remainder of her days in such a way. I now grasp the Mystanites have agreed to cancel the curse. Nevertheless, they will not be trying to harm her because she is with child. Thankfully, this is one set of arrows, which I do not have to worry about flying at her. I must fight this constantly worrying about her. If only I could overcome this deep need to protect her as a husband should defend his wife. She takes me around a few islands first to give me a sense for the setup. I notice so many streams of verdant water flowing into the sea. Pápain asks me if I like the jade water. "Sure, why not," I answer. We continue to circle these islands and pass by so many avocado streams. She is testing me to see if I am paying attention. Suddenly, it hit me as I ask my wife, "How can there be so many lime streams flowing into the sea. Even if they did have the water source, there would not be enough emerald to color it."

Pápain replies, "Very wise my husband. This is not new water, but water passing through the inlands of the islands. The high cliffs that surround them are covered thickly with strange jade vegetation. This foliage reflects the lights of the suns to create an appearance of emerald water. The streams yield many turns and are shallow in many places, which help in making the water run slow. Do not move and pretend as you are talking to me." Thinking that my litter sea tiger is trying to play with me; therefore, I keep on gibbering. She picks up her bow slowly and loads an arrow in it. Next, she leaps up and fires an arrow. Quickly, she reaches down for two more arrows as I now turn around to see what is happening. She fires both arrows. Two men fell out on several rocks high above us to join a third body already there. She slides another arrow in her bow and scans our horizons. Another arrow fly from her bow going into a still bush. The body falls through the bush into our stream. My fearless warrior drives our boat to where the body is and examines it. She tells me, this is nothing to worry about, because they are anglers from a few islands two days that way. They always travel in gangs of four members and are not warlike. They were hiding from us and became startled at the sound of our boats. She was pointing to our left, which did not matter to me considering I had no idea where anything was. Grabbing hold of the dead man, she slides him in the back floor of our boat. Looking at me calmly she reveals, "I will go to the top of that rock and slide those three men into this stream. I need you to stack them in the back of this boat. We will go out to the sea and dump them so the large beasts of the deep sea may feed on them. I understand their boat has to be around here somewhere. We will find it, take it not far from our islands, and sink it. I do not want it to sink in the deep sea, as many times rivers that flow into the sea will wash them to other islands. She zipped up the side of the rock and wisely rolled the bodies down to where I was. She then yells, "I see it." I yell back to her, "Do you see the same gift of love that I see?" She waves at me as I can see her teeth shinning from her smile from where I stand.

With a loud, strong voice, she tells me, "I do my Siklósi, if you only knew how I do." Her powerful rubber legs are coming back down fast, so I hurry and load these other three bodies. She jumps into her seat, and we go to the other side of this island. Next, we pull up to a large rock that is hanging over into this Creek. The rubber women jumps out and dives in under the rock and within seconds is pushing out a boat. I am dumbfounded, as I ask, "Pápain, how did you see that boat was under the rock?" She tells me, "Oh, Master it was easy, do you see that unsecured rock up there in the shadow on the upper side of the rock. One of them worked that loose when they were climbing this rock." Now, I try to position where she was looking from when she slid the three bodies into our Creek. I pull her up into our boat as she is tying our boats together. With her in my arms, I tell her, "No way possible Hevesi II." By calling her Hevesi II, I am referring to the way she is always tricking us for sport. She does not really understand me well enough yet to identify if I am playing or accusing her of lying. She stops our boat and rolls from her chair over on top of me gripping both of my hands. The rubber woman declares, "Captured, I got you now, so kiss me, or I will smooch you. Master, while looking at the streams from above on this high rock, I could see the shadow of the boat on the verdant sea." We share few romantic kisses, and I give her a few tight hug. Afterwards, I tell her, "Pápain, I am so proud of the way you defended yourself today. You are just as good as my Tamarkins. For me to worry about your well-being while alone would be foolish would not it? Because we distinguish possibly at times that we may not be alone, and we should put on these light garments I have." Pápain tells me, "Leave those garments there, I want my dirty boy ready to be a dirty boy. Anyone who invades our privacy will join our four friends who are dinner guests to the beasts of the sea."

I smiled in shock my head agreeing, because I was simply teasing about dawning these lovely, light garments. My wives all do the same thing in these sorts of situations. When they do a great deed, they work extra hard to give more of themselves to me. I wonder if they fear that they are hurting my pride or honor. I will stand firm by ensuring they recognize the freedom they have. This last instance is the perfect example. Pápain, knowing that she was not going to hurt my honor, killed all four of our invaders. I could have hit all four, yet in doing so would have placed Pápain's life in danger. Life by danger means possibly that I could be killing her with my enemies' arrows. I will take this warm golden tanned beauty kissing and hugging me now or her laying with blood everywhere and an arrow in her head any day. She returns to her driver's seat and takes us a short way from our islands on the sea's side. She removes a special piece of wood attached to the side of the boat and then a small-carved piece of wood that resembles two people and a large fish. She ties an extra metal hook to the side of this boat and pulls it sideways. Slowly, it sinks. I ask her what she will do when there are no more of the metal hold-downs. Pápain smiles and with a boasting, voice says, "Oh, I have found so many of those metal hooks under the sea." Guess my little rubber legs are underwater rubber legs. She is such an amazing woman, and I enjoy learning all these wonderful things about her. I just cannot say enough great things about her. She could see that in my eyes now, which is giving her more faith in the strength of our relationship. These next few weeks are going to be jammed with adventure in everything about this place and inside her mind. That is where I want to play. My wife finds a place in the sea far enough from our islands that I cannot see our land. We begin sliding the bodies out of the boat, using precaution not to tip our boat. I notice that many large, strange-looking fish begin to swim around our boat. Pápain transfers our boat outside their swimming circles. Here we can watch them feed. She now throws the two wooden pieces of the boat, and the fish attack this wood grinding them to pieces before spitting them out into the sea. I asked her what these pieces of wood were. She told me the tribes used these to identify their ships. Therefore, without them, they cannot tell, which tribe the ship belongs.

This was the point when our time together changed. No longer would I worry about my wife surviving in this special place. She enjoyed every rock and every tree. We easily lived off this land, to such an extent; we buried our plates from Agyagosszergény and never went back for them. I told her about so many events in my childhood. Afterwards, I revealed how my life changed from living in a small forest, village to living on the top of Lamenta at Baktalórántházai. We walked through several the hard times in her life hand and hand. She had to let go of these monsters, so way Papa would have a balanced mother. We played on all islands except her main home island. She wanted to keep that separate from what we were doing, and that I can understand. A sanctuary when the bad times would arrive. It only rained twice on us during our time together. Each time, Pápain would take me to a cave. She knew that they were connected. Nevertheless, she feared getting lost in them and thus always stayed in only far enough to identify where she was. Pápain kept our intimacy a priority throughout our time with each other. She believed this was essential to our total experience our time together. I figured that she was trying to cover over the bad experiences when others took from her with our experiences given through sharing. I do recognize that when one thing goes crazy, everything does. This time is healing for me also, a time when I can stretch out this process, which unfortunately with my other wives I do not enjoy. All though my mind does drift back to my family from time to time, I could anchor enough here to build a solid foundation for Pápain within me. We laid our feelings out among these islands and recollected having the energy of the suns. Something new that brings me both peace and returning to my home is when I set on top of a high island among these many atolls. I can see everywhere and nowhere. The nowhere hits when I am my mind takes me to another place inside its worlds of many mysteries. One of Pápain's stories usually brings me back. She told me how she went around all the people's homes to find food.

Sometimes she would even remove bait from traps. These times were dangerous and she had to deliver with precision, as one wrong move meant serious pain with no way to recover except to lay down in a trash pile and die. She mastered all her hunting skills as a child. Any time that she captured her prey, if someone else could take it, he would seize it from her. She learned to exercise extreme precaution such as Makói would do with that when she hunted she tracked in front of, and behind her. She would lead them over traps, which she would cover with weeds, and watch them lose their feet. The villagers would blame these accidents on the ones who set the traps. This forced these trappers to surrender their traps. She found these traps and set them in other places where it was easier to catch this game, such as beside streams or on top of hills, places where the villagers avoided. She would collect these wild animals at night when the villagers were drinking their crazy water or sleeping. This kept her hidden from any adventurous perverts from trying to pull her out of caves she would live. In the wintertime, she would sleep under the homes, especially close to where their fireplace was. The villagers build their fireplaces from the ground up, yet their houses, they would build them on top of stacked bricks, so the floors would be above the ground. Many stored extra wood and other personal items under their homes, which gave a little cover and concealment when she slipped under a house. When the residents built the opening for their fireplace in their homes, they would pack the brick portion below with stone and burn their wood on top of this stone. These stones were excellent at transferring their heat down under the floor to the hidden Pápain. She began each day, except for the winter days, with a fast swim in the water. This kept her clothing and herself clean, thereby no one suspected where she had been the previous night. One summer day when she was hunting, various boys older than her were following her. They caught her and became angry that she had tried to escape from them. When one began hitting her, she kicked him, knocking him to the ground. When he fell, his head hit a rock, and he died. She knew a death by burning would face her if she ran for it now. Therefore, she followed the remaining boys to confess. The other boys were afraid that if she claimed they were going to rape her. Their execution would be inescapable.

Therefore, they all made a deal the death was an accident, and everyone was playing a game. She confessed to the accident and the other four boys, were best friends with the boy who accidentally died, and confessed the same. The boy's father was angry at the death of his son, and the fact that he died at the hands of what he considered an animal decided his revenge. He could not accuse the other boys of lying since they were sons of his friends, and their deaths would serve no purpose. He decided instead to constitute her life more painful and filled with unending miseries. He would pay other children to beat on her and accuse her of doing bad things. Her parents had long abandoned her, even though they were the cause of these horrors. They were the outcasts and tramps. Pápain could not hide away like her parents because the village children had to take part in many activities. The boys in the village, enjoying the new freedom of beating on Pápain, decided to take it one-step higher. No one enjoyed the beating much anymore as Pápain would never show emotion. Nevertheless, when an opportunity arose to strike back with whatever she could share her pain was those who were punishing her. The boys began to allow their sisters to pull Pápain's clothing off, tearing it into shreds. Pápain would rush out of town before the villagers beat her for being lewd in public. She spent the nights looking for rags she could tie around her waist and chest. These rag wrappings proved difficult for the other children to tear and were easy enough to pull off her, the other children did not mind. They would toss her wrappings in their trashcans. She would dig them out at night. Her great day of revenge arrived one afternoon when she saw a large scouting party from a neighboring tribe passing by on a game hunt. Her village was at peace with them. She rushed around, gathered her traps, and placed them in their pathway, hiding them. Next, she gathered a handful of tribal arrows she had collected and as the hunters walked over her traps, she shot them with her arrows, killing nine of the twelve. The remaining three escaped in their boats.

She removed the traps and arrows, and rolled the bodies down the side of the hill beside this path, covering them with leaves and then went about resetting your traps. Two days later the tribe returned with a warring party and raided the village, burning many of their personal items and burned any warrior age boys. This was when she made her escape in one of the village's boats. The warriors caught her, yet seeing all her scars and bruises, allowed her to go, giving her a small number of weapons and food. Many tales vary about the succeeding part; however, Pápain now claims the little girl and a little boy saw her leave with the warriors help. The boy told the villagers the next day. They asked the little girl who told them she went the other way. It was at this time; the villagers killed her, so the tale of the ages is the small girl died so Pápain could live. The rains continued and grew harder. By more or less an odd omen, the streams instantaneously flooded the village, killing all who were still there. I thanked her for sharing this with me and then asked her, "My love, what happened to all the scars, cuts, and damaged tissue?" Pápain told me that, "When your daughters first came to discuss my mating with you, my appearance disturbed them. I was still quite extensively mere skin and bone. They rebuilt my body and gave me new skin. My body had to match those of all your wonderful wives before they allowed me to mate with you. They even gave me new teeth, as they had partially beaten all my previous teeth from my mouth. I was also blind in my right eye, as one of the overzealous boys had rammed a stick through it. Therefore, Master, please remember that for me to have a child and to be able to receive your intimacy is still far beyond my wildest hopes. At least now, I can roam around with this scrupulous body tanning from the suns without the shame of ugliness. Previously, when others looked on me, they did so with pity at my shame. Now, when they see me, they view in lust wanting to see more. Before no one wanted what I tried to give. Now, all I want to do is giving all to you my Master. Can you understand?" I wiped the tears of joy from her face, as I could not identify her eagerness to stay free from our garments.

I will let her catch me sneaking a few extra peeks as this is something I believe wives need and who else more proper and responsible than their husband to fill this need for them. I tell her not to stand on the hilltops too long or the birds will crash into each other in excitement. She chuckles, gives me a light pat on my arm, and says, "Silly boy. You should understand that I stand tall with my arms open and shout when I see you." I laugh and then I tell her, "I am becoming more proud of the great things my daughters are doing for people here on Lamenta." Pápain asks me if I remember why they did this. I shake my head no. She tells me, "Master, they fixed me and mated us to ensure the birth of their sister, Atlantis, another daughter to flow from the great Lilith from your bloodline. Somehow, history changed concerning my life, and I ended with the wrong parents. They had to remake a new history and choose to take on our mating while preserving the mating of Agyagosszergény. They knew how you would respond when you saw me, dirty boy; however, they did not realize how Khigir and Gyöngyösi would respond. They had to reach Khigir's emotions and Gyöngyösi's spiritual convictions. You would not negotiate my execution, which the evil ones were going to execute me, as the daughters can never be a part of a lie to the righteous. Your daughters were extremely nervous; nevertheless, Agyagosszergény kept telling us that her father would do the right thing by the name of love. She believed in you then, without ever talking physically with your real mind as she does now. I can only pray that Papa believe in me to that intensity. I guarantee you every day I will ensure that he believe in his father with this intensity. We are hugging as her pains from the yesterdays are slowing, marching away. I hold her in my arms, and that is where she will stay tonight. She likes it when I massage her shoulders and neck. I enjoy doing this, as I love the way, she becomes so limber afterwards. She tries to hide the spark in her eyes. Nevertheless, her eyes force her to tell their secret, that the time to serve the Master is now. Here we go again, as we increased from twice each day to currently maybe four or five times, counting the long kissing ones after a sensitive personal experience sharing and release.

Pápain takes command of these sessions as I gave up after the first week. She knows what she wants. My love deserves what she desires. This angel is morally entitled to what she wishes. I just lay her and smile. Emotionally, I call her names a few times and toss in a bit of blowing in the ears. Enough for her to realize I am here, and she is the ruler and a hunter. I am joyfully the servant and prey. Truthfully, I enjoy this surrender and domination. The euphoria feeds on my need to give her all that I can before the time to say good bye arrives. We begin to get hot and heavy when I hear various people laughing. The sky turns speckled dark, as if it had enough darkness to launch a giant storm, yet cannot pull itself together. I explore around seeing everything as normal until the smoke fades, and I see fifteen life forms in front of me, most locked onto us, although four have their heads turned sideways in respect for our honor. I cannot explain them now, as the priority currently is to find out if a fight is on our hands. They range from serious to seductive. Pápain has her bloody eye on the alluring female who stands in the front. She has fluffy black hair the flat golden horns coming from her head down past her cheeks. This may be a head garment of a particular sort. Nonetheless, I never saw anything comparable to it before. She has a special purple well-decorated leather like revealing garment to hold her large breast's firm. She has a thin black belt, the length about the same as her belly button. The top portion of her right leg has a long, extraordinarily leather knifelike pouch. Her knife is missing. The part that I enjoy and threaten Pápain is the only material below her breast holders is a purple towel rests on her left hip and covers her left leg and her seed catcher, leaving her right leg bare. She has her right leg ahead of her left leg. I recognize that if Khigir saw her boots, she would rush forward and fall before her begging for them. She even has a small belt that connects her boot to her. What could be a knife holder on her right calf muscle? This actually could be a skin protector as she also has her elbows to her wrists, wrapped meticulously, female style decoration. Her legs remind me of Khigir's legs, and her hips of Makói's hips.

This is simply to say they are perfect. Pápain jumps up and in front of me. I hand her the blanket we were lying on as we cover her in it. I take a towel we were using to cover our food, and I wrap myself in it. I thought at first that she had a tan; however, as the smoke fades away more I can tell that she is dark like my Gyöngyösi. This dark skin is a weakness for me, as I appreciate it so much. Pápain now walks toward her and stops after about three steps. I glance over the remainder of this group and notice no one is moving. Then my eyes witness the second most beautiful Queen that I ever saw. One glare in her eyes and I drop my spear, which spooks Pápain. The most beautiful Queen is my dear and special wife Csongrád. When I drop my spear, she gives me a fast secret wink. By secret does it in such a way that no one else can see it. My Csongrád can do such things to show her approval yet keep the royal stare of dare. They are not here to attack us, or they would do so by now. She has her most feared fighters stationed between the purple angel and her. I see them draw a sigh of relief. I relax my arms behind me and smile at them. If they do not want blood, then neither do I want blood. My wife, however, has something else on her mind. She calls out to the, what I call a purple angel, "What is your name?" She looks at Pápain and says, "Pápain, My name is Borsod. I am not here to hurt you or Siklósi." Pápain, not catching on that Borsod knows our names yells back, "Why were you looking at my Master?" Borsod smiles and calmly says, "I was in such shock that his servant did not provide him garments to wear." I can see that Pápain is beginning to get carried away with this, so I call her back to me having her stand on my side and tell her to stay put and please be quiet. She complains to me, "But Master; she was looking at you before you wrapped yourself." I told her, "Pápain, she got a glimpse at the best, and being a simple woman, what else could she do?" Fortunately, Pápain agrees with this logic. I glimpse at Borsod and compliment her on her outfit. I also tell her how gorgeous that these looks on her as it shows both her beauty and strengths.

The woman who looks like a Queen now speaks out, "I disagree and can find no fault in Pápain's anger for such clothing in front of her husband." I currently proceed to walk in front of her, stopping about six steps before her and bowing. I then proceed two more steps and ask, "Am I worthy to discern the name of one with so much beauty and honor as yourself." She looks at me, and smiles, saying, "You are a sly one with your tongue. I am Princess Biharm, and I have brought my warriors with me. I recognize you have a wife who is a Queen. I give my respects to her." I give an appropriate curtsey. Princess Biharm compliments me on my royal skills and congratulates the great Royal Highness, Queen Csongrád of the Dorogi Kingdom." I have now returned to stand beside my Pápain and ask Princess Biharm if she forgives me for my appreciation and partiality for Borsod, as her dark skin gives me, comfort and reminds me so much of my angel wife Gyöngyösi. Borsod smiled and said, "Do not worry dirty boy, Borsod can take care of you." Princess Biharm ordered Borsod to be quiet as Pápain went running at her screaming, "Do not tease my Master." She was ready to launch on her when the tall warrior who was a species close to ours softly braced her lifting her from the ground. He was the same height as me; however, his arms were double my mass, and he wore tight metal armor over his entire body. Therefore, arrows and spears would do him no harm. Long knives were too risky as one would have to be too close to stab him and would most likely had their head shattered by his fist. He lifted Pápain from the ground just enough so she could not launch herself again and said to her softly and kindly, "Fear not lovely angel for I will not hurt you and would gladly give my life to defend you." When Pápain heard this, she immediately became limber, and he secured her, so she would be comfortable. He carried her to me and asked me, "I think I have something that is yours. Do you want her or should I throw her in the sea Master?" Pápain begins screaming and crying, "Master. He promised not to hurt me."

I told her, "Lovely angel, no one is going ever to hurt you again, so please relax and say thank you to this warmhearted man for carrying you back here to me and ask Princess Biharm if in fairness, I may carry Borsod around the island a few times." Pápain began laughing and said, "Oh my dirty boy how could I live with . . ." She stopped the sentence realizing she would live without me. I thanked the warrior for preventing an unnecessary fight, and for his name. He told me, "I was the great warrior Kisbéri, and think nothing of the fight between the women, for the ways of women will always be strange." Princess Biharm yells out, "Kisbéri, did you not mean the ways of men, who have not been beheaded, are strange." Kisbéri immediately gives her a courtesy and confesses, "Oh yes indeed Princess Biharm. I have used this tongue in hardly any time, and it betrayed me." She looked at him and smiled, "Oh Kisbéri, why do I always forgive you so easily?" Pápain whispers in my ear, "I bet I understand why." I burst out laughing. Princess Biharm asks me, "Master, did I do or say something funny?" I stand up, curtsey, and speak, "No Princess, we are laughing at a family joke. Even though my wife is a Queen and my soon to be born daughter, Queen Stephana will be Coroneted at birth; I am going to demand that my wife and daughter wear gowns such as you are wearing. With your permission when my daughter comes back for us, I am going to ask her to reproduce that gown for them. Will you give me this permission?" Princess Biharm said, "Agyagosszergény needs no authorization. Whatever you want; you will have." I love the power that Princess Biharm and Borsod project as they anchor the two flanks of their forward position. The Princess has her legs positioned in the same way. Her silk garment has a transparent layer that reveals her legs. Her boot's run-up to her knees and is a golden metallic shine with a fancy design in them. They all have special designs, which are symbols of rank and position. The Princess has a beautiful golden belt with symbols from their language inscribed throughout it. The front of her belt holds the large gold trimmed triangular-shaped cloth that runs down her front almost to her kneecaps. Their designers were excellent in glorifying their female areas and offering their opponents and incentive to fight them.

A metallic shirt trimmed in gold completely secures her breasts, arms, and shoulders. She has a small V-neck white trim to highlight the top of her metallic shirt. She has an unbelievable three-inch long golden necklace with many symbols inscribed in it. Her hair is properly styled and tied up for a woman preparing for a battle. Now here comes the good part. She has a 'sword' that is longer than my spears. The blade, which is really two blades connected or bonded together to cut both ways, and goes from the ground to where her seed catcher would be. Next, have two large diamond balls fitted and connected to the handle by then gold bars. The diamonds emit so much light that to light directly at it will temporarily blind the person looking into it. Next, it has a two-inch thick golden inscribed and royally designed base to support everything pass it. The foot-long handle is half-black metal and half gold with both halves containing special hand markers, which must help the fighter with the best hand positions to carry out the different kills. The handle has a smaller diameter that allows the Princess to hold it comfortably with her female hands. The common denominator between the two feminine killing machines is their eyes. These two opposite approaches would be extremely effective. I suspect they are waiting for me to choose a selection, and I cannot designate such a choice, so I decide to move us in a different direction by asking, "My kind friends, how can I serve you today?" Borsod chuckles, and then wiggles her hips. Such irresistible beauty and movement, however, my precious Pápain has my biological refreshing times intact, and she will continue to ensure that when I think woman, I think her. I have no complaint about what my wife wants. After all, I am hers. Princess Biharm lets out a strange cough, and as I watch her, she winks at me. I wonder if this could be true, that she also would have an interest in me. The legs on each are slowly killing me. Now a third woman walks from behind between the mighty warriors and moves out in front of me.

Yes, she is showing the top part of her legs, and her garment wraps around her body, leaving both legs completely exposed in the front. My goodness, the designer for these women must have known the weaknesses of all men, because they gained more power in presenting an image of revealing and yet not show that feature. She has a special four-inch thick cloth running down the front of her body completely sealing her private female parts. She has boots that run-up to pass her kneecaps. Her boots appear built from a softer fabric. She has special metal guards for her kneecaps, toes, and heels. A solid shield encloses the top part of her body. Two large cup like bowls secure her breasts and then firmly attach to her breast shield. Spears, swords, or arrows from the waist up cannot harm her. She has beautiful blond hair, and like the Princess and the purple stopper have perfect skin. She is now standing centered in front of her group and speaks, saying, "I am Somogy, and we have been sent by the Spirits of the Mezocsáti to protect you and your seeds until the death of both bloodline Queens. I tell you that no harm shall ever come on our precious Pápain." Her hair and eyes afterwards turned to fire. I smiled at her and then said, "Somogy; I have two wives who are fire women such as you. Are you looking to be number three?" She immediately erased her fire and returned to normal. Next, she stood beside Kisbéri saying, "This is my fire stopper." They smiled at each other as Borsod laughed and said, "Yes, when I am finished with the little boy." I think to myself,

"Wow, even among this type of war muscle, they can still strike the low blows with their mouths." I scan between them and comment, "Wow, so many different species of people. Who is the beautiful one in the emerald dress with those wonderful spiked ears?" She came forward, stood before us, and bowed. Pápain asked her to hurry and stand back up. As she had bowed the cleavage from her shoulder-less low-cut top shared most of her large breasts. I asked Pápain to relax on these women, for they were from distinct species and therefore, have unusual ways. I was talking about the last female in this group who stood two rows behind Borsod.

I told this both sensuous and virtuous looking woman. "We are so glad to have you among us. I have two wives, Hevesi and Mórahalmi, who have such beautiful ears such as yours. We have this trait highly in my family. Would you please bless us by sharing your name?" She tells us, "I am Zirci and plead that you let me serve you until my death again if need be. Now, explain to me why our Master Pápain is angry with me for simply bowing." I tell her, "Oh, Zirci believe me when I tell you how much I truly enjoyed your bow." Zirci then looks at Pápain and reveals, "Oh, I am so sorry, Master, for I must have been to lose before you for if the dirty boy enjoys it, I did wrong." Pápain laughs and goes up to her hugs and kisses her and tells her, "No harm my sister, he has worked hard lately and deserved an extra treat." Zirci smiles at her and says, "May I return to the Land of the Dead with a new death resulting from saving you my Master." I examine her and the whole group and say, "May none of you be harmed by saving my wife." I looked at the Princess and then Borsod questioning, "Why do so many of you talk about the Land of the Dead?" Borsod looks at me and says, "Do not worry Master, for I save dirty boys." Pápain laughs and says to her, "Borsod, then you have a big dirty boy here to save; you will need selected help." Kisbéri laughs and comments, "Do not worry Master, she can handle it." I notice that Pápain is so much more relaxed with this group now. I wonder if her new title as Master removed any fear of threats by them. She appears to enjoy this as do I for when she is happy, and then so am I. Princess

Biharm tells us, "Siklósi," and while looking at Pápain, "Honorable Master, we have been sent by the Land of the Celldömölki. We are to protect the future of the Mystanites. In addition, as a show of faith for the shame, we share in executing such an evil curse, while not protecting you while in our waters, and of all places to lose you, the Sea of Death, we accidentally sent you. The great council of the Mystanites, when collecting all the signatures for ending such a foolish curse, which most were not even aware of, assembled us to protect you. Have no fear, for you are protected, our Honorable Master Pápain, the mother of Supreme Queens." I now looked between them and said, "We still have two days here, and then must return to our ship. However, your Honorable Master will return quickly.

I hope to meet and talk with you and become your friends. Therefore, I can begin thanking those who are protecting my child who rests inside my wife's womb. I would, however, like to be introduced to one more, specifically the one who stands behind our friend Borsod." Borsod then laughed and said, "I knew you could not pass up such an open package as that." I looked at her and said, "Did you forget. I have been working diligently and want a treat?" Borsod laughs and says, "From what I saw, our poor dear Honorable Master was the one who was working hard." Pápain laughs and then motions for her to be quiet, and enlightens me, "Master, you will only get in above your head." I stare at Borsod and smile, revealing, "Maybe I wanted several intense swimming lessons." Borsod winks at me and Pápain tugs at me asking, "Master, please if you do not cool down you, and I are going behind those rocks and this time you are going to control the ship. Do you understand my lover?" I understood, yes mam I understood. At his time, Borsod turned to her right side and motioned for this dark-blue character to move toward the front. She came forward and looked at Borsod who kindly motioned for her to stand before us. This was the first time we witnessed a kind deed from Borsod. This, which is definitely a female, as she obviously, wishes to take no chance of misidentification of her gender. She came forward and stood before us. I examined her, being a certain extent surprised as Pápain examined her being somewhat enjoyed. Pápain questioned her, "Now, my dear, we will not hurt you so relax and give me a smile." This female froze, turned around and looked at Borsod who smiled at her and shook her head yes. She now loosened up somewhat. Borsod asked her, "What is your name young lady?" She answered, "I am Tabi, and I will be living in the sea around your island search for any dangers." Pápain looked at Borsod and asked, "I sure hope this dear will not be out there in that dangerous sea alone."

Borsod answered, "Oh, never my Honorable Master. She has three brothers who await her in the nearby stream." Pápain, who has adapted quickly to her new role, tells Tabi, "Tabi, I do hope you will bring your brothers to see me sometime, unless you think I am too ugly for them." Tabi kneels and says, "Oh no, great Honorable Master, you are as beautiful as the suns in the sky." I looked at Borsod and nodded my head yes. Borsod came up on the left side of Tabi. I came to her right side, and we gently lifted her up. Borsod gave her a kiss on her cheek, as did I. Tabi now stood before us with a smile as Borsod stayed beside her until she was comfortable. Tabi was standing before us nude, although her nude was different from ours in that she had a thick ocean blue skin with gills on each of her calves facing outward. Therefore, if she were to breathe in the water, she could have no land clothing. She had large sea shells attached to the outsides of her breasts and a patch of crimson scales that ran from beneath her breast's meeting in the middle and running down pass her belly button reaching all the way down to cover her female private area. She also had a row of these red scales running from her hips down to her special area that created the appearance of her wearing a lower garment. Her face resembled ours, and that was the end of our species. She had no hair, this area replaced by a flood of large fins. She enjoyed the same style of ears, as did Zirci. Her most amazing special feature was a large circular bright eye above her peoples' eyes. I would think these came in handy for her under water, as the shift from land light to sea light would be difficult for any species. Her most amazing people feature was her wide hips that extended from her small waist. Her leg muscles were solid, as her body was a sculpture perfect. Borsod asks me, "I see you are impressed with Tabi's hips. We are all enormously proud of this feature on her. This was an improvement, so she could have babies as we do and not simply lay eggs. She needs that extra hip area to deliver her children, which tend to be large."

I looked at both and said, "To be honest all the features of Tabi are special and deserve compliments. I also have two wives from the sea that I love exceedingly much, my Béla and my Dabasi. They are extraordinary vessels to store my love within." Tabi smiles and then comments, "I am well acquainted with both of them. I did not realize that Dabasi could live with your species." I told her, "We were lucky to receive a special blessing from the spirits." I then gave both Tabi and Borsod each, a kiss on the cheek and thanked them for sharing them with us. Borsod, with that wonderful right leg extended laughs at me and says, "This is tough having to be a good boy in front of the wife, is not it?" I told her, "Borsod, when the cheeks have equipment such as yours to support them, making it rough and almost borders on painful." She laughs at me and thanks me, "I thank you for being honest. I did not comprehend if the grave dulled my touches or not." Pápain tells her, "Be proud my Borsod, you are still in excellent command of your weapons." They both laughed as Borsod gave her a small peck on her cheek. This made me feel good, because Borsod is diffidently someone, you do not want to work for the enemy. In an attempt to dull, the mean stares we are receiving from the Princess. I ask her, "My Princess, before we prepare for our evening activities, I would love to be familiar with the name of your giant warrior." The man stood one head above Kisbéri and his arms were larger than my waist. The Princess told us, "He is the giant called Derecske and is especially excited to serve with our special somewhat elite force." The Princess gave her sword to one of the four brutal looking warriors who surrounded her. She then waves for them to fall to the rear. Zirci falls back with them as speak to the substantial stone-faced warriors behind them. Borsod turns around and waiving her hips in the perfect way of women asks her two large gruesome beasts, Tabi, Derecske, and Kisbéri to fall back. Pápain says to me as Borsod is walking away from us, "Master, do not worry, when they have a wiggle and a walk like that, we have no defense. I will befriend her and learn how to walk like that so when your spirit visits you will burn in lust, okay my love." I kiss her and say, "Somehow, Pápain I believe that pain and suffering will befriend me on this issue." Pápain tells me while she is laughing, "Come on Master, you only live once, and therefore, go for it." Borsod, who is now beside us with the Princess, asks us, "Go for what."

I glance at her and said, "You." Borsod laughs and says, "Do you want me to surrender now or later, my Masters?" Pápain tells her, "Maybe soon would be better for him, after all I have been working him hard." Borsod looks at us and laughs, saying, "I know, and I enjoyed watching every minute of it." The Princess asks Borsod, "Borsod, please talk about something else." Borsod looks at her and says, "Now sister, confess you were watching besides me, and you liked it." The Princess's face turns red as she says, "I was only watching to ensure they were safe." Pápain, with an eager smile on her face, sensing a solid kill on this one asks the Princess, "You mean to tell me, my husband was not worth watching. I am hurt." The Princess looks at her and me and says, "Oh no. I liked a lot of it, in fact, I enjoyed it." She then paused, looked down, and continued, "In fact, I envied you both so much, while I stand here in this cage and you both could share and explore so much." Pápain walks over and hugs her while wiping her tears and thanks her for sharing her feelings. She tells her, "Princess, I now have so much more respect and honor for you. I ask you, who decides how you dress when you serve me?" She tells me, "I am a Princess. The title decides." Pápain asks her one more time, "Princess, do you mean your title has more rule than me? If this is the case, never call me Master again, for I do not want your unloving service. Only those who love me may serve me." Borsod testifies quickly, "I love you Pápain, and give myself to you to hate, hurt, and do any manner of evil you wish." Pápain looks at Borsod and asks her, "May I love you, care for you, and share my days with you?" Borsod, who is a crafty little package of absolute delight, slides into Pápain's arms as she declares the love she has for her loyal servant. Pápain also tells her, "Oh, by the way, when I told my Master to 'Go for it,' I was talking about how amazed we were at the way you moved your body when walking away from us, and my hope that you will teach me how you do it." Borsod promises she will.

We now hear a woman crying to us, "Master, what would you have me do for the evil I have done to you? I love purely you and will serve at most, you." She was now unclothed on her knees in front of us. Borsod immediately jumped on my back and with her hands covered my eyes. I complained to Borsod, "Oh honey; they appear so pure and fresh, let me peek a little, please." Pápain rushes to her small back bag and pulls out the thin garment we found in our boat and tells her, "Oh please my love, hurry and dress." She helps her, and they clothe her quickly to my misfortune. Pápain thanks Borsod for her help and then challenges her, "I believe you truly love your sister." Borsod answered as she wrapped her arms around the Princess, "With all my heart and loyalty until I die once more. She shall always be my hero, although now she is both the commander of my actions and the commander of my greatest respect. She has proven to me today how strong and great she is." Pápain adds, while she joins the hug, "I will confess to you Biharm, I have never seen one greater than you." I complained, "I would have seen how great you look, however; selected mean women prevented me. Now I am sad." Biharm then looks at all of us and says, "It probably would be fair, if I force him to be a really fine boy and work hard to give him another opportunity. Would you agree my Master?" Pápain tells her, "A truly noble sacrifice to render for the less fortunate around you." Borsod then claims, "Hay, that sounds like such a good deal, maybe I should also compete." Biharm tells her, "Oh, you are being silly, for my body will never burn men's hearts as does yours." Pápain laughs and says, "My love, your body is burning dirty boy exceptionally well now." Biharm answers back, "He does not count, as a dirty boy burns for anything." I thought and spoke, "Well, excuse me; I do not burn for everything, skillfully not all the time. This is not merited, because the Mystanites sent only the beautiful ones. This is not fair." Borsod tells me, in her stern and sumptuous manner, "Do not get mad my little boy, get even my big man," iced with an opulent wink. I quiet down as these women are on my wife's side, the right side.

The four of us now sit in a circle in an arrangement with both Pápain and myself are among these new marvels of the female form. I tell our Princess, and I will call her Princess no matter what she wears as I call my Csongrád Queen no matter what she wears, "Princess, the four men, and the stone creature behind you come across as if they are serious killers, especially in your defense. I next investigate Borsod and say; the ones who surround you also appear fierce." The Princess tells us, "This combination of men and women are a true marvel to watch while fighting. Our leaders programmed them to serve your wife, and are merely standing behind us for introduction purposes." I view her and smile, as she is beginning slowly to adjust to her new freedoms. Reassuring her, "Princess, if you think there are times for you to wear your royal garments, we have them here for you." I turn and view Borsod and tell her, "If you have a sensation to give me your purple outfit, I will keep in hidden for you." She instantaneously looks back at me and replies, "Nice try little boy, anyone who enjoys these fruits must take my violet garments and be prepared for a fight every inch of the way." I ask her, "Oh Borsod, even me?" She reaches over and gives me a hard pinch on my cheek and says, "Especially you." Pápain tells her, "Borsod, I am gaining more respect for you each moment." I added, "And I recognize where you are getting it from." Both women are extremely flexible with their body movements, which I would believe benefited in their fighting. They open these boxes and divide their food between us. Pápain has a few vegetables and fruit she already collected for us to nibble on throughout the night, as we so much enjoy doing. We share them with our new bodyguards. They eat especially socially and display all the social graces. I glance over at the rest of the gang as they sit in a larger circle, eating and quietly laughing and exchanging stories. I review Pápain and tell her that she, and Papa will be in extraordinarily good hands. Then it hits me and I ask, "Why are you allowed to stay here with Pápain?" The Princess said, "For two reasons, both relating to security. The treaty gives all nations a right to embed a royal guard force to ensure no prisoner escapes the island. The second justification is to ensure that the treaty is in force. We have modified our portion of the treaty, so until all sides agree, as we have almost all agreed on the new treaty. Sadly, only have remaining a small faction on your side refuses to join us. Meanwhile, we must abide by both treaties. This means that we must both guard and protect Pápain until this issue is settled. Pápain looks at the Princess and asks her, "So you are indeed a true Princess?" She stares back at Pápain while leaning over, kisses her on the cheek saying, "The luckiest Princess in all history." I believe that they can sense how much trust we boast in them. This is such an easy thing to do. They recognize what they are doing. The Princess asks Pápain is she can wear her royal garments during their training exercises. Pápain tells her, "You set your insides free, so you may wear them every minute of every day, if you wish. You decide your desires. Think about what you want in your time with us. You let my love in, and I can sense me deep inside you. Now do whatever you wish. She says, "My impression is I would be safer in one with the dirty boy around us." I jump up and say, "Come on girls cool it on the dirty boy." I then dive on Borsod, catching her off guard and say, "Dirty boy is here." She slips and with a slide, moves into a secure posture for herself, and with those lovely, legs send me across our little lawn. She rushes to me, leaping through the air, landing in a perfect controlling position and asks me, "Have you seen the dirty boy?" I say, "Dirty boy who?" All three of these aesthetic powerhouses begin laughing. Borsod reaches down and quietly whispers in my ear, "Oh, if you only knew how bad I want to surrender, wonderful man." We give each other, a soft hug and to take the curiosity off this table I tell her, "Borsod, do not worry; Papa will like you because the time you live together will create your bonding and experiences." The Princess tells her, "Oh sister, do not worry, we will not compete against you for a child's affection."

Pápain examines Borsod, feels her womb and reveals, "See Borsod, he just told me he really likes you." Borsod rolls over, puts her ear on Pápain's womb, and asks her, "Please, tell him to say it again." The Princess goes over, sits down beside Borsod, and tells her, "I am so sorry Borsod, but babies only speak to their mothers. I so wish we could have enjoyed a baby in our wombs during our lives." They each rest their heads on each other's shoulders, and we can see tears rolling down the sides of their faces.

I was just playing, thinking I was smart to cover up Borsod's and my heat, yet I would think that I learned my lessons on babies with Khigir. Women and baby talk always get too emotional. I think how sad that two such good women would die with baron wombs. That could be what Borsod is always talking about need to lose the wins over the dirty boy. Something inside me grabs my tongue, and I cry out, "mommy." A peaceful pink cloud lowers itself on the Princess and Borsod, and as it raises a voice reveals, "I am finished." I am confused until the voice continues, "Papa shall possess two small friends to enjoy his childhood with, and play." Both women jump beside me with their rock firm bodies and ask me, "Is this actual." The voice answers, "Your dream is true," as she sends a twinge through their wombs. Pápain joins us pushing me aside. She grabs both as the three of them start dancing around cheering. She afterwards asks them, "Now can you see why we love our Master so much?" Borsod then stops and asks, "Who is the father?" The voice answers back, "Who is the father of most of the children in the wombs of Lamentan women these days?" I then say to the voice, "That is not fair." The voice says, "The one or two warriors in your group that work the hardest for your love shall be made the father." Their gang heard this message also, so that all would appreciate this is the true way. Since they came from the Land of the Dead, they knew this to be a strong method. I now laid back on the ground looking up to the skies. So many wonderful things were happening here. My wife and soon to be born son would be happy alongside, as joyful as two could be without having what they wanted most and this is for daddy to come home from work at night. I help put the final touches on redressing the Princess, as every part of this gown is amazing in its detail. I will tell the Princess that tomorrow, sometime in the afternoon my daughter will come to take us away. Tonight is my last night with Pápain. She studies me and says, "Oh, do not worry; we are going back to our camp now after we patrol our areas for security.

We will give you your privacy. No spying tonight, well, maybe not," winking at me while she bebops off. I wonder how they all understand what I am talking about and why certain times require total accommodation. They all encompass that same wavelength. Just as I feared, the night went fast as neither of us slept, talking and playing all through the night and late into the next morning when Borsod came dropping down from a tree above us yelling, "Time to stop lovers." I yell at her to stop and warn her, "Borsod. You are a pregnant woman so you should not be jumping down from trees, all right honey." She said very well and walked away from us. We walked with our new standing army around this island one last time. Our Thirty days went excessively fast. Agyagosszergény now appeared, giving one of her special introductions. She looks at our friends and exclaims, "Welcome Spirits of the Mezocsáti. I think you for helping our Progenitors. I also congratulate Borsod, and the Princess on your knew pregnancies. Be prepared, as within the next few days, you will wake up in your new Lamentan bodies such as Pápain. This will enable you to create a living baby and be that baby's true mother. I recommend you males compete hard for these two prizes. I shall bring your Master back in two hours of your time. Peace is with you. That was the last time I saw the Princess and Borsod. I always hoped that Kisbéri won both hands of these fine women in marriage. They will of course live forever in my hearts.

CHAPTER 09

The commencement of the beginning

I wish Agyagosszergény would not walk up these steps so fast, "Honey, can you walk slower please." Ouch, I only stubbed my foot, and my big toe just took a direct crash into these steps. I cannot remember these steps being so tight. No wonder, I am walking on these machine steps and not the natural flow of the hillsides, as I accordingly much prefer. I never thought the differences were so vast, as even my rubber woman is having some trouble negotiating these steps. I must be the split second shifts that Agyagosszergény enjoys executing. My eyes, not even yet adjusted to Kisteleki's fake lights, enjoying the pure lights from our two suns as we have for the last thirty days are making my mind provide me with false visions used for my coordination. Now that is, within itself, also a shocker. My first day back on Pápain's islands seemed like it lasted forever, and the remaining days flew by subsequently fast. I wonder how long it will take me to put it all together, if at all I am ever able to do as a result. Agyagosszergény throws open the doors and introduces us, "Family, look what I found hiding in the closets?" Khigir laughs and tells me, "Oh honey, we wondered what happened to you; It feels like you have been gone forever." I kiss her and tell her, "Same here my love," while looking at Agyagosszergény. I am wondering if she somehow knows. My daughter winks at me, which I hope means everything is okay. Hevesi yells out, "Who forgot to clean between our Master's toes. It looks like he has been climbing some dirty hills." I laugh at her and ask, "Why, have you found some clean hills?" The family laughs on this one and goes about their business. Agyagosszergény sends a twitch to our feet as I lift my foot up on the table and Brann comes running over to inspect them.

She laughs aloud asking Hevesi, "Honey buns; you have been inside too long." I look at Brann and chuckle saying, "Darn. I hoped to get you in the cleaning room for a while." She slaps me and says, "You will never get me close to that water." I have lived outside for thirty days and thirty nights when getting hit and less than two minutes back have a sore toe, been slapped and dodging a little thing running around the floor inspecting my feet. Now another arrow comes flying as Tselikovsky comments, "Wow, Pápain must have turned the heat on in that closet. Look at their tans." Khigir comes over and grabs our hands and challenges me, "Okay, where did you both get these tans?" I now she is not jealous, so this is more of her wanting a tan also, as a tan on her is like the heavens on Lamenta. Quickly, getting back into the fast lane, I kiss her and say, "Do not ask me, ask Agyagosszergény." Everyone stops and now focuses on my daughter, who as a chip off the old block calmly says, "We will be putting Pápain on her sunny islands within a few minutes, and I do not want her skin to get burned from the sudden change. Daddy must have been holding her hand when I did this on the way from their closet." That is so cool. She did not lie, as our island was our closet in theory, well perhaps. Khigir kisses my daughter and says, "It will take some time to get used to such efficiency, so you have to bear with us. She runs over and leaps in Makói's arms. Makói is extremely fast with her reflexes and secures my daughter as she would a baby. Agyagosszergény smiles and says,

"I will bear with you while the bear tolerates me. Makói kisses her and says, "See if I ever let you go." My other daughters look over at her, yet do not make a move and instead scout for another prey. They have learned that once they see both hands occupied, it is, time to look elsewhere. I am confident that before long, there will be four adolescent girls totted around by grown women as their babies. What more could I expect when these poor children travel back in time, millions if not billions of years. They are still adventurous little kitties. I do wish she did not do this. I am paranoid without her beside me.

How strange is this? I am in a room with fifteen women who are my wives and five daughters and are paranoid. Oh, did I happen to mention that they are all females? Gyöngyösi comes over with her little fix everything bag and starts tending to my toe. The first sight of her flashes Borsod through my mind. Her initial touch brings me back as no one has been softer, more caring hands than my fantastically special Gyöngyösi. She sensed my initial surprise and looks up at me. I reach over and whisper in her ear, "If you find us a closet, I will explain to you." She swings her head back to face my ear as her soft long hair covers our faces and whispers, "I am looking currently, my Master," and gives me, her soft 'everything is okay kiss.' Khigir looks at Pápain and says, "Pápain, You kept him in that closet too long, now are the wives are on the prowl once more." Gyöngyösi looks at them and says, "You had better hurry, because I am going for all I can get." Gyöngyösi has to know, for she is defending me and keeping everyone composed. Pápain makes everyone sad when she says, "Oh Master Khigir, I so much wish I could have kept him in that closet longer." Khigir walks over to her and says, "I know my love. You stay beside him, and when I chase this angel away, he is yours until we reach your home, okay my love." Pápain kisses her and says, "Oh Master, why do you love me so?" Khigir holds her and says, "I only wish I could have you for thirty days somewhere just for me and our Master of course." Pápain answers so calmly, "That would be as a gift from the heavens, which for us hopefully is many decades away." I am standing her almost dying. I have an angel who is working on my toe and can sense any micro something reaction somewhere in me and Pápain is standing in the middle of a fire, stirring the coals as if she is bored. The little thing merely had me for herself thirty days and thirty nights and simply got herself two more hours sanctioned by the Master wife. All other hands are off. She is too daring. Now she asks Khigir, "Master wife, as I am new to this ship, where are all these closets you speak of?" Khigir tells her to relax and when our Master's toe is fixed, she will take us to one. She is actually going to have Khigir escort us.

This is when I realize, as I have known for so long now, that I am no match for the cunning and skill of a woman on a prowl. They know which buttons to push and how to push them. A little 'Master wife' and she gets our door guarded by the doorstopper. Khigir walks over to me and asks, "Master. You look so strange, are you okay?" I wave for her to come to me, and I tell her, "Oh, I only wish you could see in my mind now." I see Pápain out of the side of my eye on this one; however, my daughter decides to watch daddy dance. She yells over to me, "Daddy, are you sure?" I say, "Agyagosszergény, you probably should not, as some pains are not meant to be shared." Khigir kisses me and tells me, "I understand." I tell her, "Just because something is right for so many, does not mean it still cannot hurt." Khigir comforts me by saying, "You stay beside your wives as we will be here with you, okay our Master." I answer, "Oh, what would I do without you special people?" I give my daughter a fast, funny stare, just to let her know that daddy can dance with both feet in place. I then think about the logic in my last response. When will I realize that this peachy, golden blond, blue blinking eye, smiling, large breasted and unquestionably beautiful as is every female, including Hevesi in this room, has the most powerful goddess mother I will ever know? When I dare her, I simply up the ante. I so much need to sit these little things down and draw some safety guidelines, just in case. So far, they have not even presented a hint at the trouble. I just know the youthful Edelényi boys will be crawling and howling like beaten wolves to get around my babies. I am so glad that they are my daughters because I would also be with those young boys begging. Their mother added powerful touch ups to them. Agyagosszergény is my bloodline. She and the other four want me to be the father to all of them. Okay, give me all the coins on Lamenta and tell me I am broke. I can see and feel myself in these young people. They have the aurora innocence and purity. If they only understood what I am the Master of, with my wives they would be shocked. Nevertheless, somehow I know they have to know, especially knowing that Agyagosszergény watched her consummation, yet walks away from it with the same childish glow only to say, "You did a good job daddy."

Is their mother truly that effective to guard them in such a manner, or even is there a need to guard them? Somebody does something you do not like, good-bye, and that is if you are lucky. Khigir asks me, "Are you ready?" I look down at my bandaged toe and around at all my wives looking at me with sorrow in their eyes. I tell them, "Come one darlings, you know that Khigir has hit me twice as hard as this small toe jam. You have to be strong with me during the long recovery these toe injuries take, okay my loves." I smile; they smile, turn to their sisters and life goes on. How did I survive thirty days without them? One look at Pápain and that question is out of the door. She is standing beside me with her head on my shoulder. Our time together really created a foundation with her. She flows beside me now with ease. Khigir leads us into the open area and down the steps to the second floor and opens the door to our master bedroom. We both pause and look at her. She explains to us, "Since we are using the one on the third floor, and this one is vacant. Now I can give something special to two people I love so much. She cuts me a look of death and pinches the end of Pápain's nose, shaking her head gently right to left and says, "Young lady. You had better come out of this room limping." We turn around preparing to jump on the bed when Khigir kicks me in my behind and says, "I sure hope Gyöngyösi does not have to bring her whip." I reach over and kiss her sharing, "Tell her to bring the whip, because the only one I do not need the whip for is you my love." She starts laughing and says, "Three hours, I will tell Kisteleki to slow down." She yells out, "Kisteleki, slow down three hours," and walk without missing a step in our dining room. I feel the ship slow down and hear Kisteleki say, "Yes ma'am." I mean, really Kisteleki, she is a little woman, and you are afraid of her. Well, come to think of it, so was I. Now is the time for some passions to fly. Pápain is already in place and prepared.

I tell her, "Wow that was fast." She blinks at me with one of those sensuous slanted eyes. I tell her, "My love, I do not know if I should love you or beat you to ensure you limp out of here." She tells me, "Master, just love me and to save the honor of the only man ever to love me, I will hobble out of here." That was it, and she did stagger out with me. If she was doing a fake shuffle, then rubber woman must be tougher than I ever imagined. I thank her for the wonderful thirty days and thirty nights. The three hours went too fast, of course, and the time has come. Kisteleki takes his ship ashore and with his eight, legs walk in pass the sand. Khigir knocks on our door, and we immediately tell her to come on in and join us. When Kisteleki surfaced, we began to prepare ourselves, so we were just waiting for someone to come get us. Khigir helps Pápain get up and hand me a cane. In honor of Pápain in moan and complain on every step. Khigir escorts her to Kisteleki's first floor where we will exit through a special door that he has there. My wives and daughters line up along the wall and as Pápain passes by one by one, they hug, kiss, and tell her they will keep her love in their hearts. Fortunately, for me, Gyöngyösi and Tselikovsky are the first two to exchange hugs so they volunteer to escort me to the door. Tselikovsky tells me it has been too long since she has put a good whipping on me. I reach over and kiss her telling her, "You love me too much, yes my secret love." Tselikovsky tells me, "You and Pápain have been acting different from the last couple of hours. I cannot pin it; however, I will discover what it is." I wink at her and speak, "You will almost certainly discover it from me when you are torturing me." She kisses me on the cheek and whispers, "Probably." Gyöngyösi tightens her hold on my hand and when I look at her, she winks. I peck her a couple of times on the cheek and tell her thanks. If she does not know, she will find out, most likely from one of the daughters or me. She has not had enough time to look into since we went and came back within the same second.

I will tell her when we have some privacy. For now, I want to be careful, because I have to brief Hevesi, who does not care either way, before she figures it out and tells everyone. If I tell her first under oath, her sealed lips will never tell. Pápain escorts all the remaining family outside and has them in place when Gyöngyösi and Tselikovsky lead me out to my slaughter. Once we are in the open, I can see the situation. Everyone is waiting for me. The Spirits of the Mezocsáti are guarding the perimeter, except for two. My family has formed a horseshoe formation. Facing me, standing beside each other is Princess Biharm and Borsod. The Princess shined her gold extra good for this appearance, as Borsod must have oiled her tan using her best oil today. They do look fierce, so much; accordingly, that Gyöngyösi and Tselikovsky pause shortly. Princess Biharm throws down her sword as both come running to me saying, "Oh Master, what have they done to you?" They stand in person against Gyöngyösi and Tselikovsky, and the Princess asks, "May we have the honor." Gyöngyösi and Tselikovsky, who are no match for these warrior women look at me, and I tell them, "It is okay, my wives." Gyöngyösi and Tselikovsky fall in line with the other wives. The top of the horseshoe opens now, with Pápain and a fiery-eyed Khigir blocking the route. My powerhouse girls carefully and tenderly escort me babying me as much as they can. It does not look good for me. These powerhouses rival Csongrád in their royal bearing. These Royals stand in the middle of the battlefield daring an arrow or spear to touch them. They are the elites that have such powerful warriors as Derecske and Kisbéri serving them. As we approach Khigir, she utters to me while looking at Borsod, "Master?" Borsod looks at her while releasing me and says, "Oh no, not dirty boy, our Master is Pápain. They both walk over to Pápain, bow to her and say, "Welcome home Pápain," who begins to laugh, as do all the wives. Khigir belted me in my stomach, then pushed me to the ground and a grip on my left arm, that she has formed an L and is applying pressure while yelling at me, "Dirty boy?" She freezes for a second while Borsod walks over in front of us and asks me, "Master, do you still want to keep my purple garments in a secret place?" She is doing that blink your eyes, speak innocently, and foolishly, style that his me in big trouble.

Khigir demands, "Dirty boy, you had better start talking." That, what I did not know was a demon appearing as a goddess has only pinned me against the wall, and in pain as my arm is ready to crush, I tell Khigir, "I was just trying to be personable." Borsod now with her fake tear's sobs, "Master, do you want to be charming to me presently?" My wives and daughters have figured this out currently and are rolling on the ground laughing as also is the Princess and Pápain. The Princess says to her sister, "Sister, you saved your big arrows for today, did not you?" Borsod smiles, reaches down, kisses Khigir's cheeks, and asks her, "Do not hurt him too bad, as he is innocent, please." Khigir is now rolling over the ground on her back and begins laughing. The family rushes to her. I yell out, "Where is my angel? I need a new arm." Gyöngyösi and Tselikovsky both rush to my side as Tselikovsky tells me, "Master, you may have been in a league above your abilities on these." They stand me back on my feet as Borsod now comes up to me and wraps her arms around me, starts crying of course, and asks me, "Siklósi, never forget me as I will at no time forget you. Thanks for my baby," as she, granted, walks to a tree and begins to cry. Tselikovsky whispers to me, "Baby? You mean that she has your baby in her, is there any woman on this planet who is not going to thank you for her baby?" She kindly and politely slaps me and walks over to a nearby tree and, of course, begins to cry. The Princess now walks up to me and wraps both of her arms around me and cries out, "Siklósi, by no means forget me as I will never forget you. Thanks for my baby," as she, of course, walks to a tree and begins to cry. Gyöngyösi has now stepped in front of me and she is furious, "You mean the nine children in the wombs of your wives were not enough, or are these also your wives." She does not hit me, but gives me a good look at her pain and, granted, finds a tree to cry. Khigir comes before me and I yell out for Pápain and Agyagosszergény and ask them to start talking fast, because this is the time for Pápain and me, to be crying. Agyagosszergény tells Khigir and all the wives, "My mother blessed their wombs with children whose fathers are standing behind us.

This is her thanks for them to come forth from the grave and protect Pápain and little Papa while we go away." Khigir looks at me and says, "I am sorry Master." Gyöngyösi and Tselikovsky come running to me and apologize. I ask them to help the Princess and her sister, remembering the joy they had when discovering they were pregnant. They rush to their sides. I now ask, "Can any think of no reason I cannot say good bye to my Pápain and little Papa?" They all turn their backs and lower their heads. Pápain falls into my arms and tells me, "Siklósi, never forget me as I will certainly not forget you. Thanks for our baby." I tell her, "My love, I wish so much that I could give you more, yet we are so lucky that the Princess and Borsod will be provided friends for him to play with, and who knows. One may be a little girl for him to spend his life with, anywhere on Lamenta, thanks to you." Zirci and Tabi now come up to Pápain and tell her, "Our Master. It is time for your new life to begin." I think how special those words are. This is not death; it is life, a fresh life with new dreams and hopes. I tell Pápain, "Live your new life as bold and honorable as you did your previous one my love." She waves bye to me as tears, of course, run down her face. Hevesi speaks out, "Those women forgot to thank our Master for their babies." Zirci and Tabi give an evil look and hiss at Hevesi, who begins to run crying, "Someone save me, fast, now!" Mórahalmi reaches down and grabs her putting the little spark back in her pocket, saying, "Your mouth almost got you that time sugar. She looks over to Zirci and says, "By the way, love those ears." She smiles and says, "Same back to both of you," and shares a good-bye wave. Hevesi sticks her head up to wave good-bye when Tabi gives another hiss, which lands Hevesi into the bottom of Mórahalmi's pocket. Borsod yells back, "Tabi, be good, pick on someone your own size." Pápain shows the great strength that she has as she turns around and begins to walk toward home. I know that has to be hard on her, as she does not look back. I finally begin walking backward to Kisteleki; however, I am walking backwards, because this image must live forever.

I want to see my woman stay strong as she now begins as the Progenitor of the first two Queens of that great empire so far-off in the future. I can never vision her being beaten or raped again with the Spirits of the Mezocsáti protecting her. I saw today how Borsod could fight with her wit against someone she likes. I do not want to see what she does to someone she does not like. Pápain is out of sight. I know enough about her to realize she is watching me now. Therefore, I wave good-bye as Gyöngyösi backs me into Kisteleki. Once inside we sit down by the pool. My complete family joins us now. Hevesi asks me, "Master; you were almost innocent, why you do not defend yourself before Khigir?" I told her, "Did you see the blood and hate in Khigir's eyes?" Khigir swims over to the front of me, works her way onto my lap. She then does a 360, and sits up against me as she does when we are riding horses. She reveals to me, "Master, you know my love for you will never end. I simply had too much fear that those great beauties were going to take you from me. It scared me." She begins of course to start crying. I hug her and share, "I am so sorry for my Precious Dove. I can see no other beauty greater than that of my wives. How could I know your eyes were deceiving you?" Gyöngyösi asks me, "Master, how did they know you so well? I could feel their great warmth toward you." Tselikovsky now works her way between us and adds, "The one you called Borsod, by name without an introduction, scared me with her confidence and warrior style. Nevertheless, she comes before you and offers to her give, what awfully little she had on; clothes to you in front of everyone surprised me. I would think that an Army could not take what slightly she wore; however, stands before you as a small kitten and offers to surrender to you. How can that be?" I look at her and ask, "You do not believe in love at first sight do you?" Tselikovsky smiles at me and says, "Only when I first saw you, Master." I look over to Agyagosszergény and she shakes her head yes. I then tell everyone, "My daughter Agyagosszergény, gave Pápain and me some time together in the past to get things set up and to finish our business." Khigir smiles and says, "I was beginning to get worried you were going to make me tell everyone?"

Gyöngyösi next tells me, "You knew I saw this did not you?" I told her, I knew that no matter how hard I try to cover myself; I always stand naked in front of you." Gyöngyösi declares, "Nor will you ever be able to keep anything from me." I smile at her and ask, "Nor would I ever more wish for my love." Tselikovsky presently joins in and says, "I was getting close, and I soon would have had you in my hand lock pulling this out of you." I look at her and say, "I know my love, that is one reasons I confessed so fast, to save myself from such torment." I disclose to my family, "Now is the time that we must stand strong and as Pápain begins her new life to lay the foundation for a better tomorrow for our children, we also must move on and fulfill our destinies." I look at Khigir and say, "You think it is, time to head home and start pumping out babies?" She shakes her head yes and then tells me, "Give the command Master." I smile and say, "Kisteleki, it is, time to go home to Baktalórántházai." I have the thinking that my whole life has been a trip on the haunting and the turbulent blustery road to Baktalórántházai. These days the time has come to stop the high skies, low seas, and distant land adventures begin preparing the next generation. They will receive their chance to prepare their following generation as the cycle continues. As it began before me, it will continue while there are those who will travel the bumpy dark roads to find the missing ones and take them to the end putting them back on the main path that flows under the lights. Pápain was one of those lost ones. I was the one that went into the dark and met her as she was coming to the light. Grandpa always told me more tears were lost on the one that got away, and then tears of joy for the ones who stayed. I have been lucky in that, except for Grandpa; I have been able to avoid these terrible good-byes. Grandpa's good-bye was easy to handle because he will return to Baktalórántházai.

Baktalórántházai is actually his home. He simply returns to the real world for long vacations. My Grandmothers have been strong through the years knowing his heart is here. I always wondered why he just did not bring them here and end his life in the land he loved.

He decided to keep one foot in each home. I wonder if I am doing that now, with one foot on those wonderful islands and the other foot with some wonderful people who are working so hard to give us a family packed with love. I am doing it; however, only, somewhat, in that I will never live with Pápain again in this world. I will be able to see her and talk briefly from time to time, which is nothing less than a miracle. We had yesterday, and for a tremendously short time will have the future. Tomorrow I keep coming pushing us up to the dark road into the light at the end side path. My mind is flooded with the brief things such as the way she collected our fruit and the little twists she added to final preparations. Those rhythms she would hum while in her cooking, area keeps playing repeatedly in my mind. She was so stern about us eating together at night and refused to use the magic plates that Agyagosszergény gave us. Pápain wanted our life during those thirty days to be as real as they could be. She kept emphasizing that actual life made actual love, and real love made real people. I pray that we made her into a real woman. I know that she has made me into a real man. I can take my memories from just us together and somehow us this for a foundation to strengthen my other relationships accordingly dear to me. I feel so special knowing that I could never hide anything from so many of my wives. Even an adventure that took less than one second of their time did not escape them. They have been able to study my details to such a degree any slight variation would light the night sky even if the three moons were hiding somewhere. I feel so special about this; however, this is what I lost with destiny took my Pápain from me, because in those thirty days, I got the feel of her as most of my wives here have the feel for me. Pápain is gone and so is that feel, which leaves an empty spot inside. This must explain why Khigir was so scared when she saw the Princess and her sister. She felt as if she could lose me and have to release this feeling inside her for me, creating a large cavity for pain and misery to visit.

I know Khigir and Tselikovsky the best among my wives and have always studied them in more detail, because these two remind me of my mothers. Notwithstanding I took them from their world and put them in mine. Even though Khigir got the mating ball started, she could not have done so if had not been kidnapped. So the summary of this part of my mind bumbling is that I do not know as much of my wives as I should know. This is why the flying on horses and running from Kings with their daughter beside me days must end. Now, instead of me running from angry fathers, I will be the one chasing the next generation begins eating at the tree of love and start taking my daughters from me. I guess a stressful exercise program is in store for me until the grandchildren begin to roll into our lives. Looking out our viewing windows as we move through the deep sea brings back many memories. Kisteleki has really been a true blessing and a friend to me during these times. Hard to think of a machine being faithful; however, he has been not only devoted but an active part of our life. He enjoys having us inside him breaking his knobs, pushing the wrong buttons, and spilling water everywhere. He has fed us subsequently well. Notwithstanding, he has provided us with so much information on keeping my wives healthy as they make our children. He has their attention, as he showed them what could happen if they did not heed his advice. I look for the Edelényi also to have similar programs. The way that Kisteleki strokes Khigir's ego is noteworthy. She struts around here like the big hen, which no one will challenge. The darkness of the sea's surface and the darkness of our caves are taking me to the top of the world. I can now enjoy Baktalórántházai because I have been to the bottom of this world. It was when I cried while in the bottom of the sea, I pledged to fight harder to stay on the top at Baktalórántházai. It is such a long way down. Makói and Dabasi switch off with Khigir and Gyöngyösi babysitting me. I sat as a zombie between my Khigir and Gyöngyösi. Fortunately, they understand me and know this is a hard time for me. Makói will not tolerate me being quiet because she must have me talking with her. That was the deal when she stepped out of her shell into our world. I look at her and say, "Makói, I am as a result glad to be back with my family, and I hope we do not have to save the future any more. I thank you for working accordingly hard with my daughters and filling my Dabasi with our family love through sharing and caring.

You live with so many people now who depend on you to be with them. Adásztevel told me that her life was currently so exciting. She does not have to bounce from universe to universe for her peace and happiness. Adásztevel told her mother that you were the real deal when it came to love from so deep down. I can see the mother of four sons and one daughter being a rock in the middle of the sea to guide them. The three of you will make my sons strong both inside and outside, and my daughter a source of rich dynamic sunshine. I am so happy that you did not hide my love for you, but instead you took it and built a love machine that few in this family would ever wish to be without. Thanks Makói, Dabasi, and Adásztevel. Adásztevel, please remember the next time you talk to your mother to confess that the dirty boy jokes about have no truth or foundation." Adásztevel tells me, "Oh, now I am sad because I wanted a dirty boy for my father, so he could find a dirty boy for me." I place my hand over her mouth and tell her, "My daughter, how can you say such a thing before your father who would never let a dirty boy touch you, Never?" Adásztevel kisses my hand and says, "We know daddy. I was just playing with you. If mommy thought you were a dirty boy, we would not be here. She would ground me, and you would be making small rocks out of big rocks under a hostile surface of a distant world." I tell her, "I fear someday I will wake up and one of my daughters will turn against me, and I will be in that world you are telling us." Adásztevel tells me, "Father, you need never to worry about that because once mommy accepted you as the father to all five of us; you got the daddy seat and a daddy paddle to go with it. You are more secure than all of us are. When mommy lets us stay here, she was dreadfully animate, as was Bogovi that we obey and honor our father. You can beat us in front of her with no fear." I opened my arms and said, "Honey, the only one that gets beaten around here is me." Adásztevel complained, "We noticed that you let the wives hit you, and you do not strike them back.

Why is that?" I told her as I lightly squeezed her upper arm muscle, "Darling, I am the strongest giving the love, therefore, I must be the weakest receiving the love." Adásztevel, looking confused continues to probe, "Yet why did you let Khigir hurt you so today?" I looked at her and said, "Sweetheart, do you really think I was hurting? Nevertheless, I hope that you could feel the deep hurt in Khigir. She wanted to beat that hurt out and for me to refill it with love." Adásztevel then responds, "Wow, I sure am glad I am not a husband or father. It sounds too hard for me." Makói jumps in currently and adds, "Adásztevel, the thing that you can know that will never change is that man sitting there who is now your father will love you, as he does all in his family, until the end of time if such an event ever passes." Adásztevel looks at me and says, "Why would you do that for us? We cannot have that much value." I waved for Makói and Dabasi to stand beside her, and after that, I touched Makói's womb and said, "She creates for me son." I then took both Makói and Dabasi's hands and said, "We are married. Therefore, we are one. Can I betray myself and still stand strong and happy?" Then I took her hand and said, "Adásztevel. This is the special one for inside you flows my blood, a life that came from me. I know you, and three of your sisters are adapted; however, that is a greater love, for after knowing you I gave you my blood. Agyagosszergény represents a dilemma that only the gods would understand in that I could know her and love her before I created her. Do you understand what I am telling you? There is no separating us. That is why when the special mission concerning Pápain came before us, we united and accomplished it. The wives stand strong now to put me back in my Master's seat." Adásztevel pulls a chuckle out of me when she tells me, "Daddy, my brain is hurting. I am going to ask mommy for a larger one." Makói puts her arm around her and says, "Adásztevel, You do not need a bigger brain, for even the largest brain ever created can become confused by love and passion. You simply need to believe, "We are a happy family of love."

That is all. Forget everything else. You are in this family, and we are not letting you go." Adásztevel stands up and straightens her back that she usually hunches some to add a touch of sensuality and boldly says, "I now hold the greatest title that my life has ever been rewarded for I am a daughter of Siklósi." I stand up, hug her tight, and add, "And I am your proud father." Makói and Dabasi grab hold of her and squeezing tight say, "We are your mothers, well, as close as your mommy will let us be, okay baby." Adásztevel said, "She told us last night the wives of our father are our mothers. She keeps the title, mommy." I assured my daughter that no wife of mine was foolish enough to challenge that title. Adásztevel adds, "Good that will make mommy pleased." Makói kisses her and says, "Remember, when mommy is happy your mothers will also be happy, okay rotten egg." Within an instance, the three of them are in the water splashing and being crazy. I get up to walk up the steps when two voices call me to sit with them. I look again, see my Csongrád and Tselikovsky sitting alone at a table, and walk over to sit with them. These two special wives find themselves overshadowed excessively; therefore, I owe them some time. Csongrád begins by thanking me all the new royal outfits, "I cannot believe that styles such as this could ever exist." I asked her, "My Queen where are these garments?" She hands me a little strange metal stick with odd holes at the end and answers, "Here Master." I look at her and laugh saying, "I sure hope your daddy does not catch you wearing that metal stick. I hate to say it; however, I preferred the Princess outfit." Tselikovsky chuckles and adds, "Master, she does not dress to please her father. She dresses to please her Master." I pick up the metal stick and examine it, then respond, "Am I missing something here, because I would not consider holding this metal stick dressing." The Queen laughs and says, "Come on silly boy, I would only hold this when alone with you. Bodrogközi gave this to me. It works with a metal box in our room. I push this into the corresponding holes in the box, push the number that matches the gown I want, open the top, and take it out for wearing.

Bodrogközi tells me it will make about 200,000 outfits, depending on how much gold, gems, or diamonds Stephany or I add." I ask her, "Do we have enough space for this on Kisteleki to hold these outfits?" Tselikovsky laughs and says, "Silly boy, she will make them when she needs them." I smile and say, "Wonder if they make wives like this." I get a double, "Silly boy." I look at Tselikovsky and say, "You have been hiding extra well lately." She tells me, "I am sorry, Master. I just get a closed in feeling on in a ball of air under the sea. I miss bouncing from the trees." I answer, "Tselikovsky. I know the feeling as I think I will find our first tree." Csongrád then asks, "Well, you find a tree, I can join you?" I tell her, "I will sure try to honey." Okay, now I want to see the bellies. Csongrád jumps up instantly and lifts her gown. I massage her womb and can actually feel something. I ask her, "Is that me wanting, or is it real." She smiles and tells me, "Stephany has been awfully hungry and active lately." I put my ear up against her belly and then pull her gown back down, stand up and kiss her saying, "You are doing a wonderful job mommy." Tselikovsky next jumps in front of me with her gown hanging from her arm. I grab her hips, position her in front of me, and notice a lot of growth. Feeling around, I can touch both. I put my ear up against her womb and then lift my head up looking at her saying, "It sounds like they are playing in there." She tells me that Baranya says the same thing. I add, "They sound active and happy, just like their mother." Now, we need to get this gown back on before you get sick." I kiss her and sit down to talk with my Queen some more when someone taps me on my shoulder. I turn around, and Bodrogközi is standing behind me with her flashing brown and gold trimmed gown in her hand, saying, "It is my turn daddy." I look at the Queen and Tselikovsky as she is just now returning from grabbing us some fruit. They rush to help Bodrogközi get her gown back on, and I tell her, "Oh honey, I am sorry. I was checking to see how the babies are doing." She tells me, "I know that daddy; I wanted you to see how my baby is doing." I ask her, "Honey. We did not know there was a baby in there."

Bodrogközi smiles at me and speaks, "I know daddy, which is why I want you to check." I look at my two wives and say, "Oh, okay. I understand now, and they left her small dress back up to expose her belly. I feel around it pressing and pretend as if I am searching hard. I next put my mouth on her belly, start blowing, and with my hands begin tickling her. She is kicking, yet my wives hold hard. She is laughing so hysterically. I finally cease for fear of giving her a heart attack. I step back and tell her, "Honey, I could not hear a baby, but I sure heard that laughing monster. Did you hear it too?" She gives me that puzzled look as I secure the wonderful golden, diamond studded, four-inch belt with six-inch sides back around her precious waist. She now looks as if she has figured out what is going on by telling me, "I did daddy. I did, and I thought it was from you tickling it." I told her, "Oh no, honey, I was belly monster hunting. I had to make a loud noise on your belly to wake them up, and then I used my fingers to keep him from trying to run up out of your mouth and to chase him around so he would be getting tired in fall in your belly and go out of your back end." She gives me a big kiss and hugs and joyfully exclaims, "You did all that for me daddy. I am so happy I have a daddy." Csongrád tells her, "Bodrogközi, you do not have a daddy. You have the best daddy." She apologizes to me saying, "I have the best daddy ever. My Queen, you are right because even mommy told us we had the best daddy. I wonder if she knows all the magic things that our best daddy ever, knows. Daddy, can I go show my sisters how you got the belly monster out of my belly?' I looked at her and said, "Bodrogközi, I would need a big hug and a whole bunch of kisses before I could let you go from me." She squeezes me tight, actually much tighter than I expect, as I can see her lugging a sword around all day has toughened up her muscles. She, as I guess most children, are always willing to comply, yet make the adjustments necessary to carry out their agenda. She slobbers the daylights out of the side of my face with kisses still in progress as she moves to the next one and then gives me the big 'I am done, if you approve,' by saying, "I love you best daddy ever, see you later, bye-bye." I say bye and she is already going up the steps.

I look at Csongrád and Tselikovsky and tell them, "That is why, my wives, that daddy's protect and love their daughters so much. Notwithstanding inside that, innocent child is enough power to destroy one thousand Lamentans. That, my loves is extraordinarily scary." Tselikovsky then confesses to me, "I never knew you were that good with children, Bodrogközi may be actually telling the truth when she claims to have the best daddy ever. 'Belly monster,' my love this was consequently wonderful, creative, and almost believable." Csongrád adds, "The way you explained it so exactly covering all possible arguments with a straight face amazed me." I told them, "I had better get better because I can see two of my daughters who if they are like their mothers will keep me on my toes." They both kiss me and say, "We need to get some rest, okay best daddy. We love you bye-bye." I whistle at them while they do their wiggle for me. Oh yes, my darlings can still do their wiggles. Mórahalmi and Hevesi now join me. Mórahalmi has prepared her and Hevesi for this meeting as they have their faces painted conservative and are wearing soft silk gowns. Hevesi, expanded to her large size, begins by saying, "Hello Master." I look at her and say, "How is my heart love?" She is the one I missed the most, especially as I virtually lived outside for the entire thirty days. I continue, "You know; I missed you during the last thirty days." Hevesi smiles and then looks at me, saying, "Wow Master, it merely felt like a second to me." It was truly only a second, if that, for her. I can feel by her voice tone that she does not feel cheated. I leisurely move my hand over to hers that is resting on the table and gently grab hold of it. She speaks with a tone of sincerity now while saying, "We will also miss you awfully much." I look at both and reveal, "I know; she talked about all you each day. I guess the fresh wives had special secret events for her hosted by you Mórahalmi. We need to thank you for helping our new members, especially considering that you would be more aware of where we were lacking." She nods her head yes, while watching more out of the side of her eyes.

I ask her, "Mórahalmi, why do you not look me in my eyes?" She answers, "I keep hearing so many tales about Baktalórántházai, only to find each day we are moving farther away from it. The same is true for you; I finally get a stable part in your life and then discover you have been on the other side of the world for the last thirty days. We also cannot figure out why Khigir did not assign us one of your daughters." I begin by telling her, "I do understand how this can cause much pain as I hope you provide me an opportunity to start the healing. Our marriage is special because Hevesi and I chose you. Sure, we lead Khigir to believe that she gave the invitation; nonetheless, you already won our hearts, especially mine. I still believe that the purely reason Hevesi conned you was for a tree ride on big mountains that bounce in your face all day." Hevesi jumps up and slaps me, followed by a kiss and then says, "Only you get the free ride's Master." Mórahalmi jumps in and says, "They are not mountains and compared to Khigir; they are foothills. Moreover, they do not bounce in my face all day. The only thing that is bouncing is your eyes from staring at them all day, dirty boy." I smile at her and say, "My wife. I plan to have my eyes bounce off you for the remainder of our days. That is the stable part of our life, because, if you allow me, I will stay in your heart, so no matter where I roam, you can find me. My love, we are going back to Baktalórántházai and I hope so much destiny will allow me to stay there. Although, we should keep in mind that it was destiny that flew me off my mountaintop to find you. This is one destiny, which I will always be thankful to have enjoyed. Pápain did receive extra for now; however, when everything is adding up at the end of our roads, she will have received the least by an exceptionally large margin. We must try to do well each day and stay on that path. With any justice, we will all meet together in a better place. I hope this makes it easier for you to stay afloat, as you know; we do not want to lose you. If you start to sink, stick your hand up above the water and yell for help. Lastly, we did not provide one of my daughters to you because Hevesi is so popular with all of them.

We did not want to tie Hevesi down and take away her flexibility. I hope you can appreciate this." They thanked me and hopped away from our table. I see two of my daughters looking at her, and there they go after her. Hevesi's hop was too much fun for them to ignore. To be honest, I was almost tempted myself. Mórahalmi grabs one of the daughters and Hevesi the other, and they start hopping. Mórahalmi stops them and shows them a special funny move with one of their legs. I believe that they are going to incorporate this in their new and improved hopping. If ever I were to see her closer to her home, it would be now. She looks so much at peace doing this. I feel sorry for Kisteleki, as he will be getting a few more scratches and dents when all my daughters' struggle to surmount this new discovery. Either way, the halls will echo some now laughs, and that will spread some cheer. An unusual pair, Brann and Nógrád, join me currently, which makes me happy. Before, without end, it is always Brann and Baranya. Maybe the new sisters of the womb are expanding their social boundaries. As they sit beside me, I comment, "Now this is a pleasant surprise. Welcome my two incredibly special burning treats, which I hold dear to my heart." Sásdi joins us and I add, "Someone just turned up the heat at this table." Sásdi tells us, "If someone shows me how to lower it, I will do so." Brann tells her, "Honey, you are the heat he is referring." Sásdi asks, "Are all daddies, this strange or only mine?" Nógrád answers, "No Sásdi, you are one of the extremely few lucky ones." She gives me a peck on the cheek and says, "I know, hope this lowers the temperature some." I will have to be careful with Sásdi, as she is not as confused on everything as the rest of her sisters. Brann begins by saying, "Master. I hate to burden you with this; however, we may have some problems on our return to Baktalórántházai." Nógrád shows me a message that Kisteleki gave her from the Edelényi, which warns 'all Siklósi to stay away from this mountaintop. They have pledged to execute all who come through the cave on sight. You have no homes here." Sásdi afterwards adds, "Wow, then we had better not go through the cave."

I jump up, give her a kiss, and tell them, "Sásdi that is a wonderful idea." I yell out, "Kisteleki, avoiding the caves, is there any other way you can take us to Baktalórántházai." He responds, "I can blast us into the upper skies, and with some help from your daughters drop in from above." Sásdi tells him, "Big boy, I will land you so softly that the water in your cups will not move." Brann now argues, "They were not playing with words, the 'on sight' does not care if you dropped from the sky or came through the cave." I tell them, "I understand that. Notwithstanding, we have no home there so I would figure all the housing would be secured." "Kisteleki," I call out, "Do you have any plans for the next couple of hundred years?" He tells me, "If you do not include rusting in a junk yard, I am as free as a bird." I continue, "How would you like to have a family live in you for a while on my favorite mountaintop?" He answers, "It sure would beat hiding in your caves for eternity." I ask him, "Why would you have hidden in our caves?" Kisteleki tells me, "I am commissioned for Béla and may never leave her side, or the junk yard for me." I look at Nógrád and Brann and tell them, "My friends get one chance. Since they have broken our deal, I will never turn my back before them again. We will live in Kisteleki be prepared to fight always. Any ways, what is all this about?" Nógrád tells me they are angry over our marriage. I look at her and say, "They will have to accept this, after all, how could I give up a lover like you?" Nógrád continues, "They say this order comes from their fatherlands. The orders say that if they do not enforce this law, they will be banned forever." Sásdi then adds, "Well, this is easy. They will have to send new orders permitting it." I look at her and say, "If only it were that easy, my daughter." She looks at me and asks, "May I daddy?" I merely shrug my shoulders having no idea what she has on her mind. She simply says one word, "Mommy." My eyes bulge about three times their regular size. A voice speaks to us, "Oh relax daddy. The supreme council of the Edelényi has been shown the error in their ways and has issued new orders to serve you as their masters."

Sásdi jumps up and cheers, then responds, "Thank you mommy. You are the best, and we love you a whole bunch." I ask her to stay, "Mommy, may I ask you one question?" The voice chuckles, "Speak daddy." I ask her, "Are all your daughters as special as the five that you allow me to love?" The voice answers, "Yes, they are daddy. Thank you for the kind words' daddy. You are the best, and I love you a whole bunch." Sásdi begins laughing on this one and share with us, "My mommy is so funny, and wonderful is not she." We three instantaneously agree wholeheartedly. I can see that since Sásdi loved her mommy's little good-bye joke that this will be the revised good-bye now. Do these young bundles of love currently comprehend how much they modify our behaviors with their simple approvals? I sure hope they do not. Sásdi sits down and with a serious look on her face, recommends, and "Master, we still need a powerful entrance." Brann looks at me and says, "Master. I believe that she is right on this one also." Nógrád adds, "Against the Edelényi, I furthermore would have to agree." I look at Sásdi and inform her, "Sásdi, You seem to be much more adults like than your sisters, can you explain why?" She looks at me in her natural way and Answers, "That is because I am best friends with our sister Atlantis, and I help her run that giant empire she has." Nógrád says, "Well, since you have not been in any battles." Sásdi looks at us and laughs, pointing at a special emblem that she wears that supports the bottom parts of her breasts and says, "This is my Letenyei Award. I received this award for being in over 1,000 major battles with each having more than 10,000 deaths." I ask her, "Are you going to stay and fight beside your daddy, or are you going to rush off for each war?" She jumps up in my arm and says, "I am going to fight beside my daddy." Nógrád and Brann look at me and say, "Thank you so much." I wink back at them. Sásdi asks me, "Daddy, why are they thanking you?" I ask her, "Honey; I am holding you in my arms, how do you distinguish they were not thanking you for promising to protect their husband?" She looks at me and shrugs her shoulders and says, "Guess so daddy."

I look at Brann and say, "I guess I recognize who we will invite to our war tables in our futures. Okay Sásdi, what sort of entrance did you have in mind?" She leads clears our table, collecting the cups. We will begin by shaking the mountain so all come to the top. I will seal the yellow spot at the top of the hill you married your wives. The sky will turn green, and the land will turn blue. I will rain some fire swords down on this spot here. When they have landed, I will release a large puff of brown smoke. Bodrogközi will appear as I retrieve the swords. When we appear, we will all be ten-feet high, except for Agyagosszergény who will be twenty-five feet tall, as she will be the one speaking. I will next rain down flowers, so thick that none can see before their eyes. I will release Cserszegtoma on the opposite corner of in front of Bodrogközi. Next, I will change the sky to pink and the ground to red and will do so place Adásztevel in the opposite corner beside Bodrogközi. I will then turn the sky to red and the ground to be purple as I appear on the corner in front of Adásztevel and across from Cserszegtoma. Now, everything will turn red, and white lighting will flash from sky one hundred times, and Agyagosszergény will appear. When she appears, the grass will turn green, the sky blue and all things the color they were previously. Agyagosszergény will then introduce us as follows, "We are the daughters of Siklósi, goddesses and rulers of all the stars you see in your night skies. All life that you are familiar with comes from us. Whoever does not obey our father? We will punish by taking their blood and feeding it to the rain." We will now walk to the outside of the large yellow flat spot. I will remove all trees from this hilltop, and I have Kisteleki appear. We will walk in front of the door that you walk out. As you appear, we will be ten-feet tall and bow to you. Whoever does not bow, who can bow, and not be a child, we will cast over the cliff. I ask her if any refuses to bow. She tells me that one will refuse today and two during our tour of their underground city. Nógrád asks, "What happens to the twenty-two who refuse to bow while inside?" She tells us, "They burn from within, so those beside them receive no pain or injury."

I call out to Kisteleki, "My Kisteleki. It is, time to prepare for war the way my Sásdi fights. My Letenyei Award winner is now in command." Kisteleki answers, "Yes Sir, Yes Ma'am." Sásdi walks into his command center as he echoes, "All rise, Commander on deck." Even though the room was empty, Sásdi sticks her head, back out the door and says, "Thanks daddy." Nógrád and Brann tell me, "Oh, my goodness, with our little Sásdi in command, we had better rush and put on our victory gowns." I winked at them and said, "Do not make them too tight, for with all the excitement; my heart could explode on me." Nógrád smiles and says, "Sorry, Master, only tight for you." Ajkai, Abaúj, and Cserszegtoma now joined me. Ajkai said, "Master, we just want to say hi to you and see if there is any way we can serve you." I say, "Ajkai and Abaúj, I have seen the wonderful love that you have been sharing with my little, sweet, and innocent Cserszegtoma." All three begin laughing; therefore, I stop and ask them why?" Ajkai and Abaúj look at Cserszegtoma, who nods her head yes. Ajkai then says, "Pure and sweet, but not innocent." I smile at them as Cserszegtoma moderately leans her head down. I wonder why she gave this permission if it hurts her. Therefore, I say, "My Cserszegtoma come on over here, and rest on your daddy's lap." She does so, with a small tear beginning to flow. I tell her, "Oh, my baby, please do not cry." I ask Ajkai and Abaúj, "How many women do I hold in my arms?" They tell me one. I then ask them how many men are in all these universes. They shrug their shoulders as Cserszegtoma begins to answer. I tell her, "That is okay, honey." I now ask Ajkai and Abaúj, "How many young women have a beauty greater than what I hold in my arms?" They both shout out instantly, "None." I then say, "I agree," as I kiss her trembling face. Ajkai and Abaúj, "With my angelic daughter being so unnumbered with such overwhelming odds, how could she be innocent?" Cserszegtoma face lights up, as her mood gem on her forehead changes colors and eyes widen staring at Ajkai and Abaúj and say, "Yeah, how could I be?" Ajkai and Abaúj rush to her side and say, "Of course you are innocent. You poor sweet little thing, you have suffered too much. You are so lucky to have such a wise daddy to see such things."

She swings her face back around so fast that her purple and green soft hair slowly brushes my face, giving me a dose of that wonderful perfume their mother puts in her daughter's hair. She now tells Ajkai and Abaúj with the purest confidence that only the heavens could share with us, "My daddy is the best daddy ever," and slobbers all over the side of my face. Ajkai and Abaúj both begin laughing and cheering. I wink at them, as this is so wonderful that she does not realize how to kiss. No one wants to be the one to steal that innocence from her, not even her daddy. I say, "Oh my Cserszegtoma, I love those wonderful kisses." Cserszegtoma chuckles and says, "That is why I need a daddy to appreciate my kisses. Mommy says that I just slobber all over her face." She glances over at Ajkai and Abaúj who both assure her, "Oh honey, if your daddy says you are a great kisser, and then everyone else is wrong. After all, who in the whole universe would recognize who a good kisser was besides your daddy?" She goes, "Well, maybe all those boyfriends my daddy is going to get for me." I jerk back and give her a stare. Cserszegtoma chuckles, in her own special way, and says, "Cool down daddy. I was on such a hot streak there I had to take at least one more shot." Ajkai laughs and summarize everything by saying, "Just like her daddy." Cserszegtoma looks at me and asks, "Is that a good thing daddy?" I kiss her adding a few extra slobbers and say, "Well; I think so my baby doll." She wipes her face fast and showing Ajkai and Abaúj, "See my daddy slobbers too. I really am like my daddy." I look at Ajkai and Abaúj and ask them, "How did I make it without them?" They ask me the same question. Cserszegtoma then adds, "A question I will ask when these pregnant women around her start sharing these babies." I smile at her and say, "Cserszegtoma that my daughter is a truth that will never change." She smiles, the way a child does when praised by an adult. I look at Ajkai and Abaúj, and tell them, "Do not fear. I have not forgotten that I owe you both much past rent."

They both begin to blush as Cserszegtoma nails them instantly by accusing, "Okay, who is the innocent one now, busted." Ajkai and Abaúj, both sitting calmly, as if nothing is different, both raise their left hand, and showing their ring say, "Married, ha ha ha." Cserszegtoma yell out, somewhat mad, "That is not fair." I tap her on her shoulder. She looks at me and I say, "Yes, it is fair." Cserszegtoma complains, "Why do you have to get married before you have any fun?" Ajkai answers, "So when we make daddies out of them, they cannot run away." Ajkai and Abaúj now tell Cserszegtoma, "Honey, we need to get you ready for your show at our new home in just a short time, so kiss your daddy, and we can go." They all give me a kiss as I shake my head, "Where has Lilith been keeping these heavenly treasures." As I stand to stretch my legs, I see three more visitors heading for my table. I sit down a welcome them. Khigir, Béla, and Agyagosszergény set down around me. Khigir tells me that I have a sad daughter in front of me. I look at my Agyagosszergény and ask her, "Oh my heart, please tell your daddy why you are unhappy." She tells me, "I think that I did wrong by giving you those extra thirty days and that you suffer now because of me." I look her in the eyes and tell her, "Agyagosszergény, your daddy is a big boy, and if he thought that would have been bad for him; Khigir would have made him stop." Agyagosszergény tells me, "That is what I did wrong; I should have asked her first." Khigir now jumps in, "Agyagosszergény, I will tell you the same thing that I will tell every baby I make for your father and that is you at no time must go through me to get to your father. That is one place I will never stand my love." Agyagosszergény then asks her, "But mother, what if I make a mistake as I did here?" Khigir tells her, "Honey, you did not make a mistake. I assure you. If we cannot trust your daddy to make the right decisions, then how can we say we love him?" I pick her up, put her in my arms, and tell her, "Honey. You gave me something I needed and that was, time to make myself stronger for everyone in my family. A good bye after one day or one thousand days hurts the same. It is how fast we can stand back up and move forward that counts.

Thanks to you and all my family, I am standing up, and we are going to be at war here in just a few minutes, so you need to report to Commander Sásdi and be briefed on your mission." Agyagosszergény tells us, "My sister has the Letenyei Award." Khigir asks her, "Honey, what is the Letenyei Award?" Agyagosszergény tells her, "My sister has fought in over 1,000 major battles in which at least 10,000 people or species lives died." Khigir then looks at me and says, "How could you?" I told her, "Honey, I did not realize I was their daddy afterwards, so you should forgive me." Agyagosszergény asks Khigir, "Mother, please forgive my daddy. However, both Sásdi and Bodrogközi are strong, fierce fighters in battles. You will be so proud of them." Khigir tells Agyagosszergény, "Honey, I could not live with myself if I lost them in a battle." Agyagosszergény tells her, "Oh, mother never worry about that, they will at no time lose in battle because no one is better." I wink at Khigir and she tells my daughter, "Okay, honey if you promise, now go, and get ready to save us today, all right my baby." Agyagosszergény gives all three of us a kiss and rushes off to join her sisters. I tell Baranya and Khigir not to worry about this, "I will ask mommy because I have held enough dead family members in my arms for two lifetimes, and I do not plan to hold any more." Baranya asks me, "Master, how can you hold these young women like babies cradled in your arms so easily?" I tell her, "Because that is the way they want to be healed. That is a part of their lives they want to relive, this time with a daddy." Baranya takes this a step further by adding, "I believe all of us here want to relive a part of ourselves, this time as being a part of something made from love. The wonderful thing is that we are willing to make the sacrifices to make this dream come true for all of us." I look at Khigir and say, "I would have to agree with that completely." Khigir looks at Baranya and tells her, "What you have said is true, and it started with me coming to Siklósi's village and wanting to escape and forget all the pain and years of no love of my childhood. Siklósi represented innocence and purity. When I saw that, I could not let it go or chance losing it.

Not only could I not realize it. I could not keep it just for me, as it was so great I had to share it, and today we have nineteen, counting Pápain, whom we will never let go, in our happy family."

I decide to remind everyone some highlights about my past. I lived solely to follow my Grandpa. If it was the wilderness, it was me and the farther from people to better. I had witnessed a few public beatings for criminals in our village as a child and decided that if good people could do that to bad people, then they could also do it with good people. I also believed the bad people could hurt both good and bad people. Any way you figured it, people hurt people, and I did not want any part of that. The men around our village would always complain at how much trouble they were having with their wives. We had some big girls in our village those were bullies, and it took the adults a few years to catch on how they were treating us little people. By then they did their damage. I wanted no part of them or any like them. The shell I lived in served me well. My life had less pain than it would have without it, so I kept it. That was until the monster woman, and her sister came along. There was no escaping her. I did not want to escape from her anyway, for I knew she could not go back to her home, and if she stayed here and I did not take her. She would be available for all to fight to own. No one would treat her right, because of her great beauty and independence. I knew how I would treat her, and I guess she knew how I would treat her, as she has our daughter right there." I gently poke her womb. Baranya looks at Khigir and says, "Khigir, we are not fooled. You can command any man to fall before you and to give you his mother's head on a platter, and he would. Why did you select our Master?" Khigir tells Baranya, "As I have told your sisters, our Master was the only man who did not want me, and while the others ran after me, he ran from me. His tribe kidnapped me to be his, yet he ran from me. It destroyed my ego, which the one man who can have me does not want me, yet all who want me. I do not want. The challenge was too great. If all those men whom, I never wanted believed they could force themselves on me, then I could force myself on him.

I have never told my Master this before; however, it was Tselikovsky, the hater of all men, who first pleaded with me not to be so cruel to you. I would plan so many terrible punishments to execute the next day, and she would beg me not to do them. She created the plan to catch him, kiss him, and then tell his mother, he kissed us. I had no idea that we were walking into an inescapable marriage vow. We started spending more free time with each other. I guess since we had already kissed, and everyone in the village expected us to marry. The elders wanted us to spend time together and figure out the plans for our futures together. That was why they forced Grandpa to bring us along on his last private trip with our Master to the hidden mountains. Each day, I felt subsequently much worse for all the evil I had planned to do against our Master. I was so happy with Tselikovsky told me we would marry our Siklósi. She did not hide behind me when she decided. She stood in front of me with both her hands locking my face on her mouth, so clearly I understood the deal. All I could do is hug her, and thank her so much for picking the best man for us." I tell her, "Khigir, I hope she did." Khigir and Baranya now start hitting me, and laughing to say, "Silly boy." Sometimes wives have a special way of hitting that feels so good. This was one of those times, a time that I could not be sure exactly what I was doing right; nonetheless, could only hope that I keep on doing it. Baranya now begins talking. Brann and I were more of an orange fire and not bright, white and blue like so many of the other fires. The trouble with white and blue fires is that they can also burn the orange fires. Our friends discovered this and could not pass up all the fun in shaming us in front of everyone in our clan. The elders wanted us to burn out and just vanish somewhere under a rock. So much of Pápain's story rings true with us. It was not the physical abuse, but the social and mental abuse, which hurt as bad if not more. This is not to say we escaped from the physical abuse of their fires burning away at ours. There was no choice but to escape before they completely burned, us alive, as no one was willing to help us for fear of their own existence.

We went into the darkness, filled with fear and soon our hope began to weaken. When in darkness, there is no way of knowing what is for us or against us. We ended in the high skies beside our smaller sun, which has large areas of orange fire, which is extremely hard to see from Lamenta, begin far enough away to disguise it. We could not believe what we found. To be the only two of a kind and having no hope of ever finding any other fire except white or blue, changes the prospect of exploring into one of avoiding. These were fires such as ours, and so many of them. They had so many chemical improvements and gave us a secret chemical that would allow us to exist as Lamentans if we needed to do so on our return. We returned and occasionally go back to visit. The last time we returned we told them about our new family. So many of them congratulated us and promised to help us if we ever needed their help. Each night, we scan Lamenta looking for orange fires that need help as we did so long ago. While in the Sea of Death, we discovered that some problems in the exchange and conversion of the gasses on our home sun created tremendous gas explosions that burned our orange friends, at temperatures almost ten times their maximum tolerance. The weaker flames of the white and blue fires also burned alive. If we did not have had our family here, we would have been devastated. We both have pledged again that we will serve this family, even if it burns out our flames. This family has given us too much. If some day, you wake up and decide you wish to destroy us, simply cast us from you. Otherwise, consider our lives as a weapon that you can use to save yourselves." I get her in my arms and tell her, "Baranya, when you fall many of us will be beside you falling at the same time. You can take that as reality, for if one happens the other will happen. Baranya looks at me and says, "Do not forget. You owe me a water-free rain check." I tell her, "It will be water free my precious burning love and it might even produce some white fire." She now excuses herself saying, "I understand you both have a lot to discuss, so if you need me for anything, just yell." I tell her, "Baranya, I always need you for something." She looks at me and sighs, "Well dirty boy, not only for that, which is yours at the snap of your finger."

Khigir laughs and says, "Baranya, do you understand how to put out a white fire?" Baranya says, "Only that white fire," blows us both a kiss and zips up the steps. They always rush out when they believe they got the last word. If it adds to their lives, then why not enjoy it with them. If they leave happy, afterwards they take that happiness throughout our family with them. I look at Khigir and say, "Honey, maybe we did make something great with our lives. As you know, without your leadership, these women would trample me." Khigir confesses, "I think maybe in the beginning, currently that we know how careless you can be we concentrate on mothering you now." I ask her, "Oh, like tearing my arm off in front of everyone." She answers, "Well; women should not come up to you, and droop all over you thanking you for their babies. Moreover, then ask you if you want to hold their garments." I laughed and said, "Man that sure came across not in my favor." Khigir then laughed and said, "It was presented to come across that way. If you could have felt your heart as each word she said clearly and loudly." I then told her, "Pápain had told her how much we all love each other, so she was having so much fun. I will tell you one thing. If I were in a battle and saw her on the other side, I would run as fast as I could to the nearest cave or river." Khigir then adds, "Do not be ashamed, because I would be running beside you. I know you saw her muscle tone. How did she get like that?" I told her, "From eating married men alive." Khigir now continues, "My Master, there is so much more we have to go deeper with our loved ones to give them what they need. Do you think we can do that?" I looked at her and said, "Yes," and next suggested that we found out what everyone is doing, as we are the only ones down here. Khigir after that lightly grabs my arm and questions, "Master, I still cannot figure out your daughters, that have the entire heavens, yet are here beside us scrubbing floors and clothes and so happy to do it. What is it that they did not have?" I gave her a kiss and said, "Their real blood daddy.

They want to live like that part of them, learn everything about that part. That way, they can always be proud of this special part of them that no one else has, or can take." Khigir concludes, "Maybe they do have the best daddy ever." "Khigir," I reveal, "You will hear that many times from that seed growing in there." I touched her belly to massage it lightly. She jerks, grabs my hand and presses it against her side saying, "Can you feel her kicking? She is kicking for her daddy. Oh, this is so amazing. Your daughter does not want to wait." I give her a kiss, drop to my knees in front of her womb and say, "Beautiful woman. You have to wait. Daddy will still be here, Okay, my love." I kissed her belly, and our baby stopped kicking. Khigir looks at me and asks, "Master, how did you do that?" When she asks a question by first calling me Master, she is desperate. I disclose to her, "Honey, some things only daddy's can do." I smile and start up the steps. She is pounding me on the back saying, "You are such a cruel man. Now stop hurting me." Kisteleki currently speaks through the walls and states, "I am sorry Khigir; however, it appears to me; you are the one hurting poor Siklósi. It might be better for you to relax for a short while. I will give you a special cup of wine to help you." Khigir took this one like a true champion. Kisteleki caught her in the act, and she could in no way wiggle out. Therefore, my wife took the high road and said, "Thank you Kisteleki," took her glass of wine and followed me to the reception area outside Kisteleki's control center. Sásdi waved at me. I asked Kisteleki, "What happened to your control room?" He told me that, "Your daughters have installed many serious upgrades, which have expanded my abilities immensely." Sásdi waves for us to enter. We go inside and she begins, "Daddy, look. We can see everything from here and nothing can hide from us. We have some new parts that will allow us to blast into safe with much less turbulence than previously. While we are in the sky, no one will be able to see us. Our return will be slow and easy. We will now be able to go up at an angle, which is so much calmer, circle Lamenta using the planet's gravitational pull to spin us and return at an angle who will put us three inches above our target."

Khigir looks at me, and smiles. I look at them and say, "Once again. I am accordingly proud of how hard you strong-grown women are working in caring for your family that loves and honors you all so much. Now I want some daughter kisses." Khigir yells out to them, "Me too, with the kisses." We exchange our kisses, and

Sásdi asks everyone to use the special ropes they put in the seats on the upper floor viewing areas and tie ourselves to them. I look at her and she says, "For your safety, okay." I shake my head yes and start telling the wives, "Tie yourselves to your seats for your babies or sisters." I ask everyone to listen and state, "Family, we are going from the bottom of the sea to the high dark skies above our world, and then we will be returning to Baktalórántházai. This is the beginning of our trip home, which is also a new beginning for us, as we once again settle in our homes, this time starts bringing our next generation into our family and the world. We have a special family here, which can love and love deeply. Our family will make the sacrifices for our children's futures. We will lay the foundation for a greater Lamenta that will be ruled by those who care, share, love. We shall dare evil to challenge our blanket of love that shall cover all that we can see around us now." We were currently in the high dark skies. Gyöngyösi tells us, "That was the easiest ride into the sky; I have ever enjoyed." Sásdi comes out and tells us, "You may untie yourselves currently. We know what we are doing; therefore, you will not need to tie yourselves anymore." We sat in our seats and looked at the bright lights in the dark sky around us. I tell everyone to take a good look around because we should not have any more business up here. Nógrád asks now, "Is the evil continent that your son and daughters will create the great empire?" I smile and say, "They shall make this Progenitor the proudest to be in the heavens chasing Gyöngyösi." That gets a good laugh. We notice now that the dark sky above us is changing back into a darker blue. In front of us appears a vision on the wall. We can see my daughters making their introductions to the Edelényi. They do have their attention. There go the sky color changes.

I did not realize that these colors would be so widespread. Now, they unleash the lightning. My daughters added some serious thunder with it. We now see both suns, enjoyable and bright, and I see our divided sister mountain and the top of the world. I would guess that we have stopped as I feel a slight drop. This must have been that three inches that Sásdi told me about. I lead my family down to the initial floor, as we will go out whatever door opens. When we reach the first floor, we find five doors open with a daughter at each door. My Agyagosszergény says, "On behalf of the Edelényi, welcome home." When I walk out, I witness signs everywhere saying, "We love Nógrád." I step to the side and watch her exit. When she sees the signs, she raises her arms and the large packed crowd cheers her with love chants. This crowd is easily three times larger than we had for our outdoor weddings. I see Nógrád's parents; brothers, and sisters rush up and take her away. One of her brothers is allowing her to sit on his shoulders. The crowd continues to cheer. I would bet that Nógrád will not be home with me tonight, yet the reason is not what I first feared. She is their love hero. Nógrád faced punishment by death and held fast to the passion in her heart, as all my heroes that love in this family have. The elders now come up to me and welcome me home. One elder asks me, "Where did you find your daughters?" I smile and tell him, "I took them from the Sea of Death." The elders laugh and say, "I can understand he must not want to tell us at this time. We should give him time to get his family settled. No one ever returns from the Sea of Death, nor can any beauty ever live within. Siklósi, have you chosen a home for your magnificent ship that brought you back to us?" I look at them and smile, disclosing, "I hoped you would have some ideas for me, for this has been a wonderful ship for us, and I hate just to abandon him." The elders wave for some men to join us and order them, "Open our best bay, and place this guy in it.

No other piece of equipment may ever be stored with him, and he will have all maintenance performed and one hundred years from now. I want him to look as he does today." The engineer he called over to him asks, "But elder, we do not know how to operate this ship." Sásdi tells them, "Do not worry; I will take him to his new home." Showing off, she walks through Kisteleki's wall to get inside. The little angel had a wiggle also. My wives have been working with her. Oh, how beautiful this is to their daddy. Another elder now waves his hands as a group of women, dressed in white short gowns comes out. My wives know what this is about, and they all fall in line as they casually walk inside to the steps beside their medical assistant, as if they had never been gone one day. They are going to get their baby inspections, and nothing is more important than this is. We are home again, as I walk with my daughters to show them a few things in the area. We are waiting first for Sásdi to return. This is the commencement of the beginning.

Index

C

D

E

G

H

K

L

M

N

O

P

V

Z

Maps Index

Lamenta

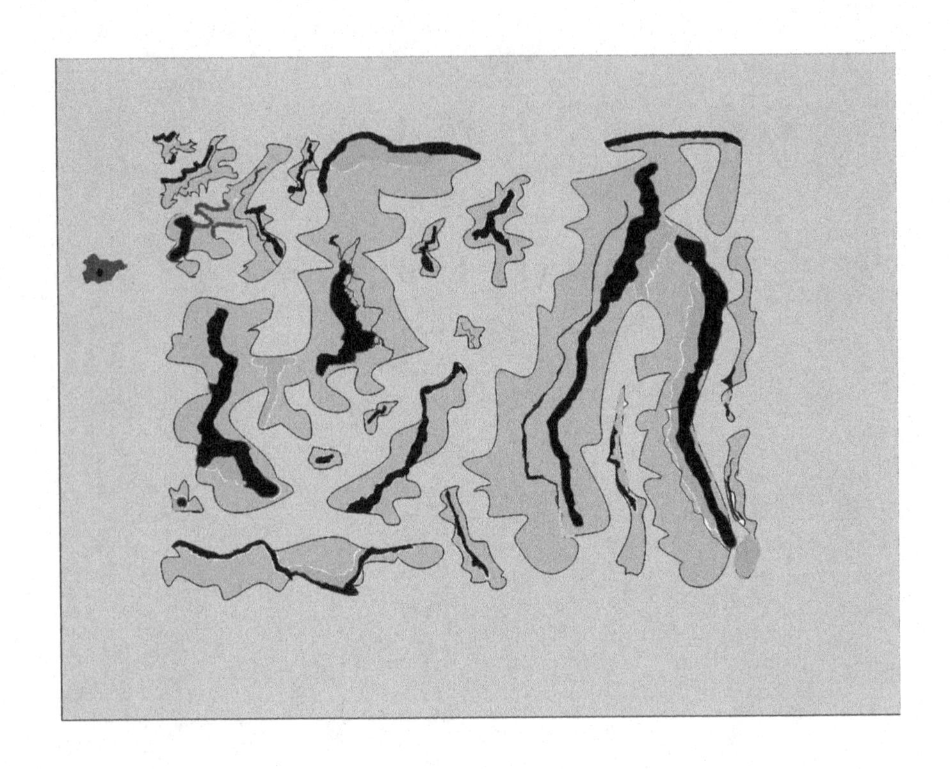

Earth vs. Lamenta

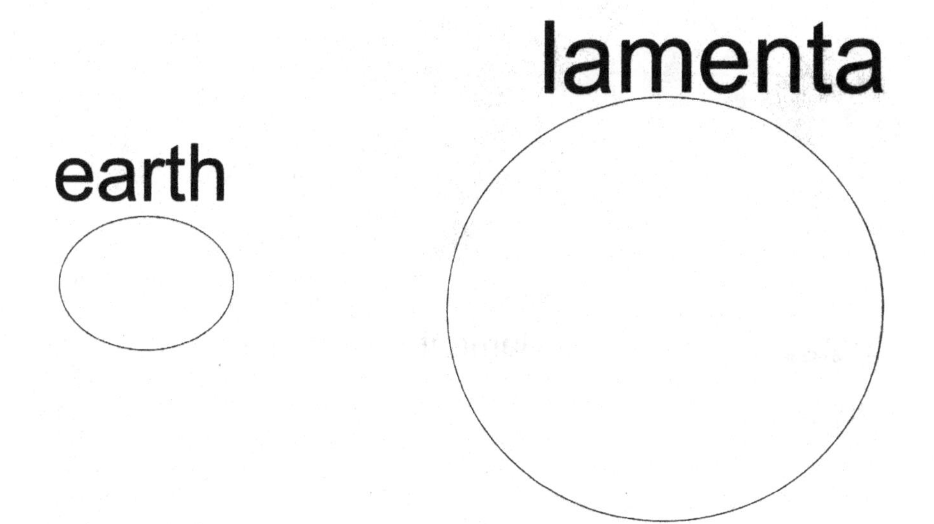

LAMENTA MOONS

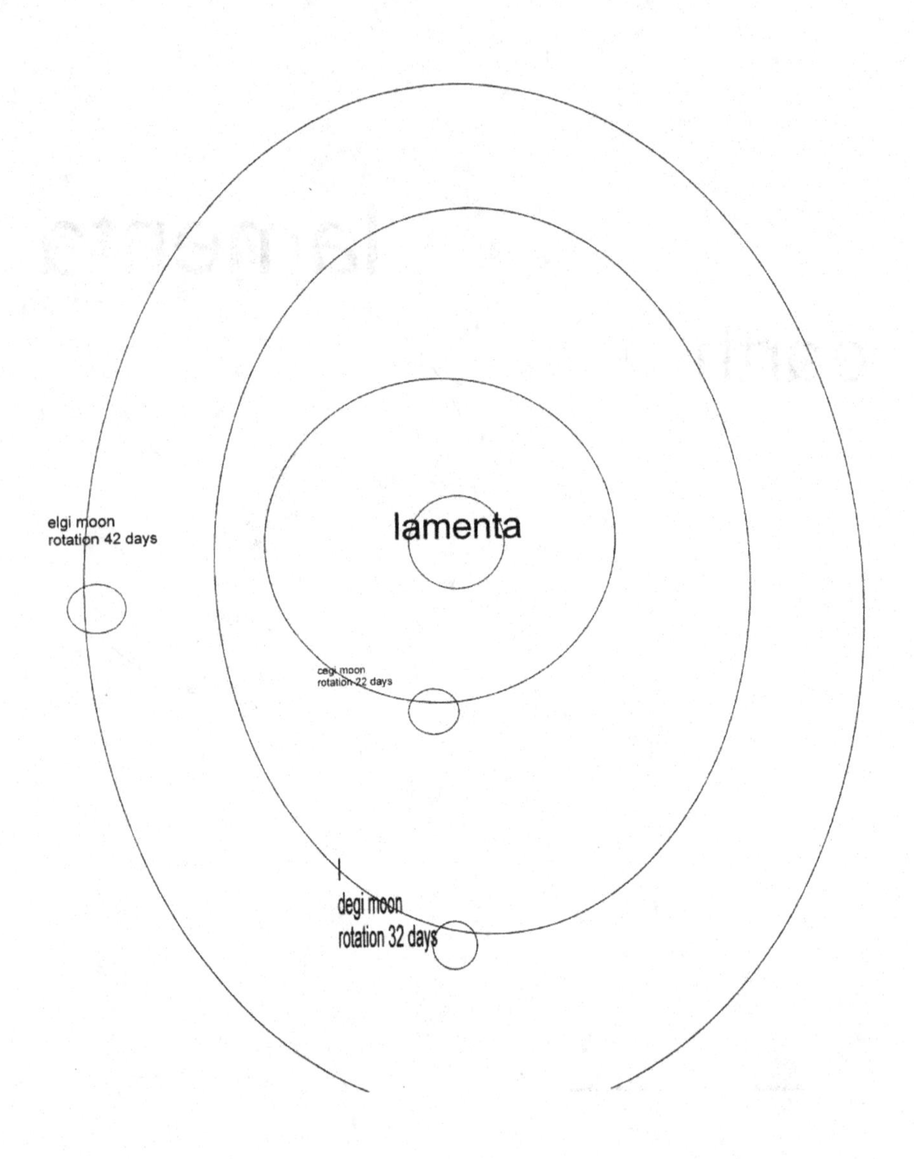

TWIN SUNS

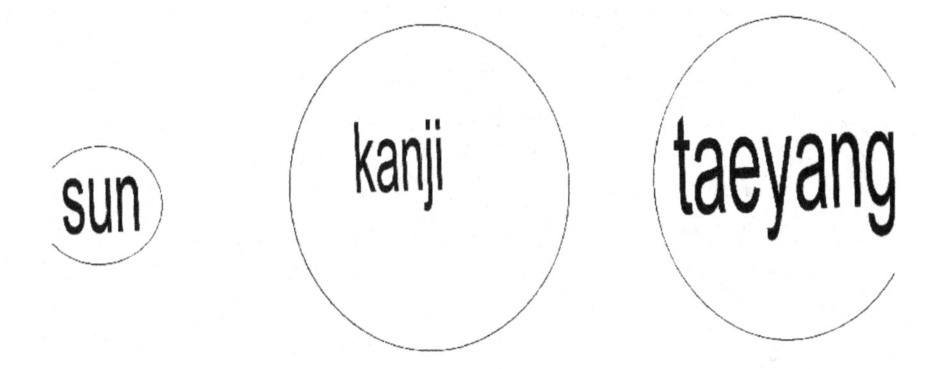

INNER SOLAR SYSTEM

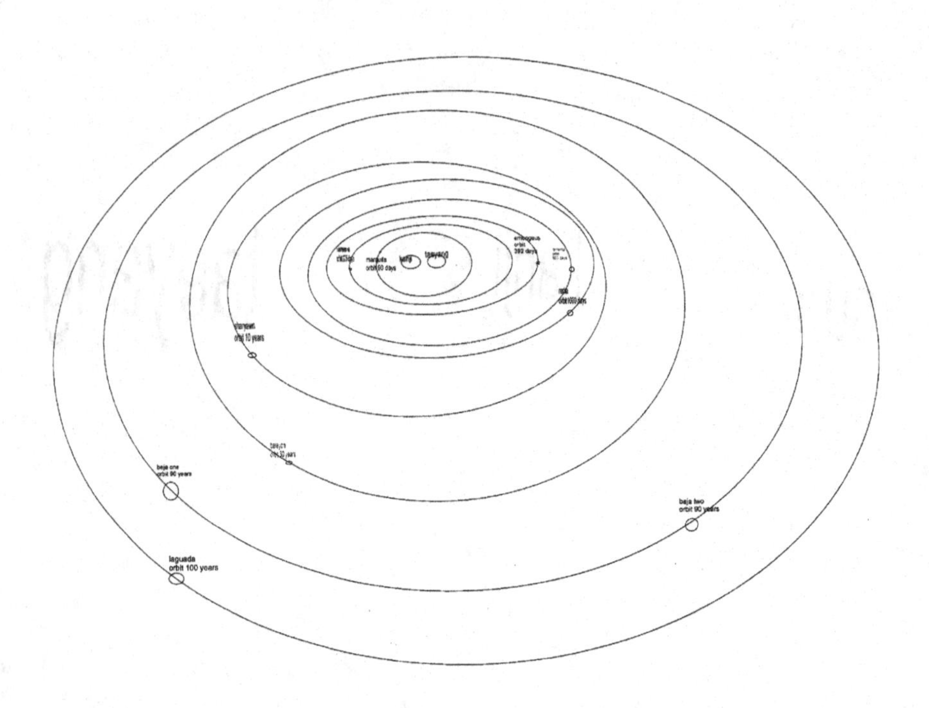

COMPLETE SOLAR SYSTEM

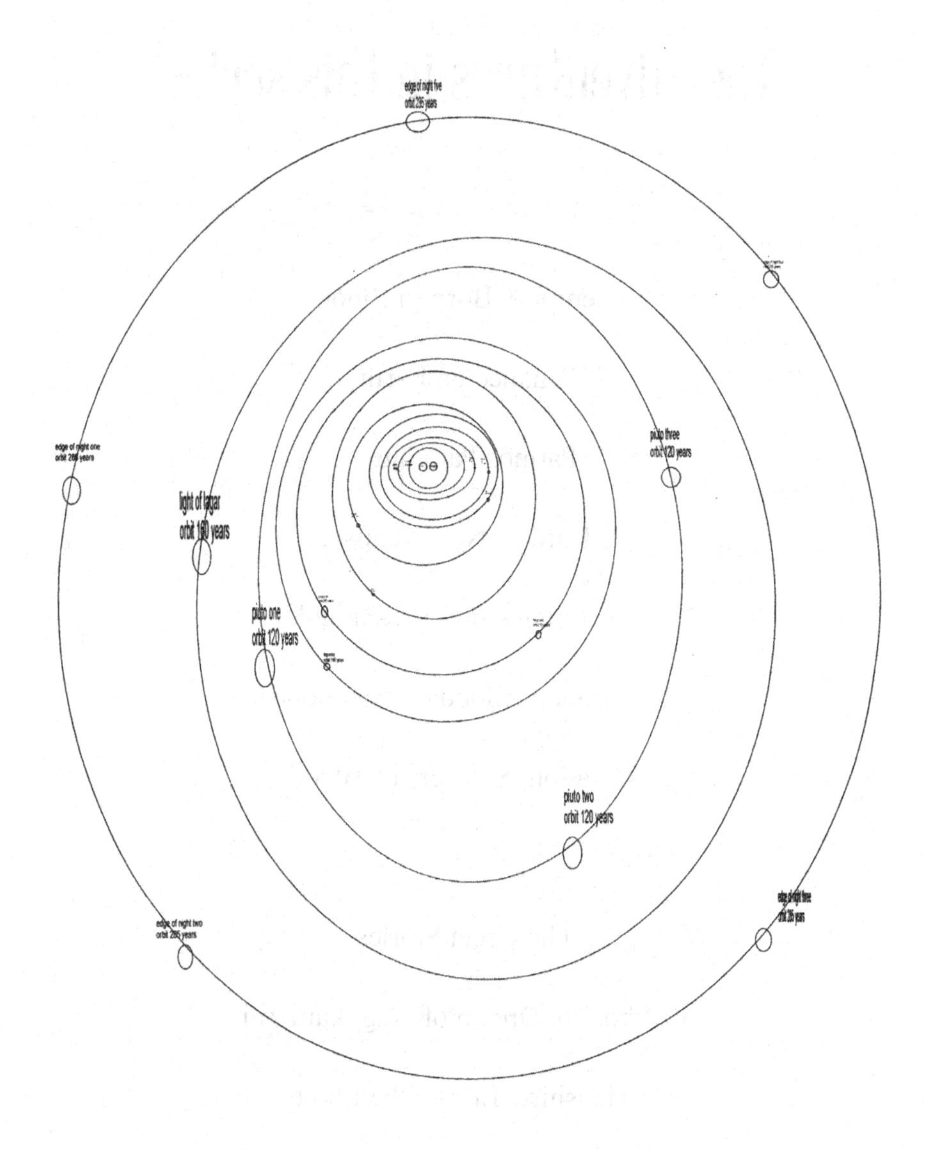

The adventures in this series

Mempire, Born in Blood

Penance on Earth

Patmos Paradigm

Lord of New Venus

Rachmanism in Ereshkigal

Sisterhood, Blood of our Blood

Salvation, Showers of Blood

The Great Stories

Prikhodko, Dream of Nagykanizsai

Tianshire, Life in the Light

Seven Wives of Siklósi

Author Bio

James Hendershot, D.D. was born in Marietta Ohio, finally settling in Caldwell, Ohio where he eventually graduated from high school. After graduating, he served four years in the Air Force and graduated, Magna Cum Laude, with three majors from the prestigious Marietta College. He then served until retirement in the US Army during which time he earned his Masters of Science degree from Central Michigan University in Public Administration, and his third degree in Computer Programing from Central Texas College. His final degree was the honorary degree of Doctor of Divinity from Kingsway Bible College, which provided him with keen insight into the divine nature of man.

After retiring from the US Army, he accepted a visiting professor position with Korea University in Seoul, South Korea. He later moved to a suburb outside Seattle to finish his lifelong search for Mempire and the goddess Lilith, only to find them in his fingers and not with his eyes. It is now time for Earth to learn about the great mysteries not only deep in our universe but also in the dimensions beyond sharing these magnanimities with you.